His For
Christmas

CAROLE MORTIMER

NIKKI LOGAN

AMY ANDREWS

MILLS & BOON®

CONTENTS

His Christmas Virgin

Carole Mortimer

CAROLE MORTIMER is one of Harlequin's most popular and prolific authors. Since her first novel was published in 1979, this British writer has shown no signs of slowing her pace. In fact, she has published more than 135 novels!

Her strong, traditional romances, with their distinct style, brilliantly developed characters and romantic plot twists, have earned her an enthusiastic audience worldwide.

Carole was born in an English village that she claims was so small that "if you blinked as you drove through it you could miss seeing it completely!" She adds that her parents still live in the house where she first came into the world, and her two brothers live very close by.

Carole's early ambition to become a nurse came to an abrupt end after only one year of training, due to a weakness in her back, suffered as the aftermath of a fall. Instead she went on to work in the computer department of a well-known stationery company.

During her time there, Carole made her first attempt at writing a novel for Harlequin Books. "The manuscript was far too short and the plotline not up to standard, so I naturally received a rejection slip," she says. "Not taking rejection well, I went off in a sulk for two years before deciding to have another go." Her second manuscript was accepted, beginning a long and fruitful career. She says she has enjoyed every moment of it.

Carole lives "in a most beautiful part of Britain" with her husband and children.

"I really do enjoy writing, and have every intention of continuing to do so for another twenty years!"

CHAPTER ONE

MAC CAME TO an abrupt and wary halt halfway down the metal steps leading from the second floor of her warehouse-conversion home. She'd suddenly become aware of a large figure standing in the dark and shadowed alleyway beneath her.

A very large figure indeed, she noted with a frown as a man stepped out from those shadows to stand in the soft glow of light given out by the lamp shining behind her at the top of the staircase.

The man looked enormous from where Mac stood, his wide shoulders beneath the dark woollen overcoat that reached almost to his ankles adding to that impression. He had overlong dark hair brushed back from a hard and powerful face that at any other time Mac would have ached to put on canvas, light and piercing eyes—were they grey or blue?—and high cheekbones beside a long slash of a nose. He also possessed a perfectly sculptured mouth, the fuller bottom lip hinting at a depth of sensuality, and a firm and determined chin.

None of which was of the least importance—except

maybe to the police, Mac wryly acknowledged to herself, if the man's reasons for being here turned out to be less than honest!

She repressed a shiver as the chill of the cold wind of an early December evening began to seep into her bones. 'Can I help you?' she prompted sharply as she finished pulling on her cardigan, using both her hands to free the long length of her midnight-black hair from the collar. All the time wondering if she was going to have to use the ju-jitsu skills she had learnt during her years at university!

The man shrugged broad shoulders. 'Perhaps. If you can tell me whether or not Mary McGuire is at home?'

He knew her name!

Not that any of her friends ever called her Mary. But then, as Mac had never set eyes on this man before, he was hardly a friend, was he?

She glanced at the brightly lit studio behind and above her before turning to eye the man again guardedly. 'Who wants to know?'

'Look, I understand your wariness—'

'Do you?' she challenged.

'Of course,' he confirmed. 'I've obviously startled you, and I'm sorry for that, but I assure you my reasons for being here are perfectly legitimate. I simply wish to speak to Miss McGuire.'

'But does Miss McGuire wish to speak to you?'

The man gave a hard, humourless smile. 'I would hope so. Look, we could go back and forth like this all night.'

'I don't think so.' Mac shook her head, deciding that perhaps she wouldn't need to use those self-defence lessons on this man, after all. 'The Patels shut up shop in precisely ten minutes and I intend to be there before that.'

Dark brows rose over those light-coloured eyes. 'The Patels?'

Mac elaborated. 'They own the corner shop two streets away.'

'The significance of that being…?'

'I need to get some groceries before they close. That being the case, would you mind stepping aside so that I can get by?' She stepped down two more of the stairs so that they now stood at eye level.

Blue. His eyes were blue. A piercing electric blue.

Mac's breath caught in her throat as she stared into those mesmerising blue eyes, at the same time screamingly aware of the subtle and spicy smell of his aftershave or cologne. Of the leashed power he exuded. Even so, Mac was pretty sure she could take him; it was skill that mattered when it came to ju-jitsu, not size, and she was very skilled indeed.

The man looked at her beneath hooded lids. 'The fact that you're obviously leaving her home would seem to imply that you're a friend of Miss McGuire's.'

'Would it?'

Jonas deeply regretted the impulse of his decision to call and talk to Mary McGuire this evening. It would have been far more suitable, he now realised—and far less disturbing for one of the woman's friends—if he had simply telephoned first and made an appointment that was convenient to both of them. During the daylight hours, and hopefully at a time when one of her arty friends wasn't also visiting!

The fact that the thin little waif standing on the stairs had long, straight black hair that reached almost to her waist, and almond-shaped eyes of smoky-grey in a delicately beautiful face, took nothing away from the fact that she had obviously taken to heart the persona of the 'artist starving in a garret'!

As also evidenced by the overlarge dungarees she wore over a white T-shirt, both articles of clothing covered by a baggy pink cardigan that looked as if it would wrap about the slenderness of her body twice. Her hands were tiny and thin, the skin almost translucent. The ratty blue canvas trainers on her feet were hardly suitable for the wet and icy early December weather, either.

Jonas had spent the last week in Australia on business. Successfully so, he acknowledged with inner satisfaction. Except he now felt the effects of this cold and damp English December right down to his bones, after the heat in Australia, despite wearing a thick cashmere overcoat over his suit.

This delicate-looking little waif must be even colder with only that thin cardigan as an outer garment. 'I apologise once again if I alarmed you just now.' He grimaced as he moved aside and allowed her to step down onto the pavement beside him.

The top of her head reached just under Jonas's chin as she looked up at him with obvious mockery. 'You didn't,' she came back glibly before wrapping her cardigan more tightly about her and hurrying off into the night.

Jonas was still watching her through narrowed lids as she stopped beneath the lamp at the corner of the street to glance back at him, her face a pale oval, that almost-waist-length hair gleaming briefly blue-black before she turned and disappeared around the corner.

He gave a rueful shake of his head before turning to ascend the metal steps that led up to Mary McGuire's studio; hopefully she wasn't going to be as unhelpful as her waif-like friend. Although he wouldn't count on it!

Mac lingered to chat with the Patels for a few minutes after she had bought her groceries. She liked the young couple who had opened this convenient mini-market two years ago, and Inda was expecting their first baby in a couple of months' time.

Mac's steps slowed as she saw the man who had spoken to her earlier sitting on the bottom step of the metal stair-case waiting for her when she returned carrying her bag of groceries, those electric-blue eyes narrowing on her coldly as she walked towards him. 'I take it Miss McGuire wasn't in?' she asked lightly as she stopped in front of him.

It had been fifteen minutes since Jonas had reached the top of the metal staircase to ring the doorbell and receive no response. To knock on the door and get the same result. The blaze of lights in the studio told him that someone had to be home.

Or had very recently been so?

Leaving Jonas to pose the question as to whether or not the young woman in the dungarees and baggy pink cardi-gan, who had hurried off to the Patels' store to get grocer-ies before they closed, was in fact Mary McGuire, rather than the visiting friend he had assumed her to be.

Something he found almost too incredible to believe!

This young woman looked half starved, and her clothes were more suited to someone living on the streets rather than the successful artist she now was; Mary McGuire had become an artist of some repute the last three years, her paintings becoming extremely valuable as serious collec-tors and experts alike waxed lyrical about the uniqueness of her style and use of colour.

Her reputation as an artist aside, the woman had also be-come the proverbial thorn in Jonas's side the last six months.

This woman?

He stood up slowly to look down at her critically as he

took an educated guess on that being the case. 'Wouldn't it have just been easier to tell me that *you're* Mary McGuire?'

She gave a dismissive shrug of those thin and narrow shoulders. 'But not half as much fun.'

The hardening of Jonas's mouth revealed that he didn't appreciate being anyone's reason for having 'fun'. 'Now that we've established who you are, perhaps we could go upstairs and have a serious conversation?' he rasped coldly.

Smoky-grey eyes returned his gaze unblinkingly. 'No.'

He raised dark brows. 'What do you mean, *no*?'

'I mean no,' she repeated patiently. 'You may now know who I am but I still have no idea who you are.'

Jonas scowled darkly. 'I'm the man you've been jerking around for the past six months!'

Mac frowned up at him searchingly, only to become more positive than ever that she had never met this man before. At well over six feet tall, with those dark and dangerous good looks, he simply wasn't the sort of man that any woman, of any age, was ever likely to forget.

'Sorry.' She gave a firm shake of her head. 'I have absolutely no idea what you're talking about.'

That sculptured, sensual mouth twisted in derision. 'Does Buchanan Construction ring any bells with you?'

Alarm bells, maybe, Mac conceded as her gaze sharpened warily on the hard and powerful face above hers. A ruthless face, she now recognised warily. 'I take it Mr Buchanan has decided to send in one of his henchmen now that all attempts at polite persuasion have failed?'

Those blue eyes widened incredulously. 'You think I'm some sort of heavy sent to intimidate you?'

'Well, aren't you?' Mac bit out scathingly. 'So far I've had visits from Mr Buchanan's lawyer, his personal assistant, and his builder, so why not one of his henchmen?'

'Possibly because I don't employ any henchmen!' Jonas bit out icily, a nerve pulsing in his tightly clenched jaw as he glared down at her.

He had decided to come here personally this evening in the hope that he would be able to talk some sense into the reputed and respected—and mulishly stubborn—artist Mary McGuire, and instead he found himself being insulted by a five-foot-nothing scrap of a woman who had the dress sense of a bag-lady!

Those deep grey eyes had opened wide. '*You're* Jonas Buchanan?'

At last he had succeeded in shaking that mocking self-confidence a little. 'Surprised?' he taunted softly.

Surprised was definitely understating how Mac felt at that moment; stunned better described it.

She had known of Buchanan Construction—impossible not to, when for years there had been boards up on building sites all over London with that name emblazoned across them—when she was approached by the company's legal representative with an offer to buy her warehouse-conversion home.

Yes, Mac had certainly known the name Jonas Buchanan, and, if she had thought about it at all, she had always assumed that the owner of the worldwide construction company would be a man in his fifties or sixties, who probably enjoyed the occasional cigar with his brandy after no doubt indulging in a seven-course dinner.

The man now claiming to be Jonas Buchanan could only be in his mid-thirties at most, the healthy glow of his tanned face indicating that he didn't smoke even the occasional cigar, and the muscled and hard fitness of his body told her that he didn't indulge in seven-course dinners, either.

Mac looked up at him shrewdly. 'Do you have a driver's licence or something to prove that claim?'

Jonas scowled as his irritation deepened. He had travelled all over the world on business for years now, and never once during that time had anyone ever questioned that he was who he said he was. Until Mary McGuire, that was! 'Will a credit card do?' he snapped as he reached into the breast pocket of his overcoat for his wallet.

'I'm afraid not.'

Jonas's hand stilled. 'Why not?'

She shrugged in that ridiculously baggy pink cardigan. 'I need something with a photograph. Anyone could have a credit card with the name Jonas Buchanan printed on it.'

'You think I forged a credit card with Jonas Buchanan's name on it?' Jonas was incredulous.

'Or stole it.' She nodded. 'I would much rather see a passport or a driver's licence with a photograph on,' she stubbornly stuck to her guns.

Jonas's mouth compressed. 'On the basis, one supposes, that I haven't had either one of those forged in the name of Jonas Buchanan, too?'

She frowned. 'Hmm, I hadn't thought of that...'

No, he definitely shouldn't have given into impulse and come here this evening, Jonas acknowledged with ever-growing frustration as he pulled out the passport that he hadn't yet had the chance to remove from his pocket following his flight back from Sydney yesterday. He had stupidly allowed his success in Australia to convince him, after months of getting nowhere with the woman, that talking personally to Miss McGuire was the right way to handle this delicate situation!

'Here.' He thrust the passport at her.

Mac carefully avoided her fingers coming into contact with his as she took the passport and turned to the laminated photo page. Unlike her own passport photo, where she looked about sixteen and as if she ought to have a prisoner number printed beneath, this man's photograph showed him as exactly the lethally attractive and powerful man that he appeared in the flesh.

She quickly checked the details beside that photograph. Jonas Edward Buchanan. British citizen. His date of birth telling Mac that he had recently turned thirty-five.

She thought quickly as she slowly closed the passport before handing it back to him, knowing she could continue this game, and so annoy the hell out of this man, or… 'What can I do for you, Mr Buchanan?' she asked politely.

'Better,' he rasped impatiently as he stashed the passport back in his breast pocket. 'Obviously you and I need to talk, Miss McGuire—'

'I don't see why.' Mac brushed past him and began to ascend the stairs back up to her home, seeing no reason for her to linger out here in the cold now that she knew—or, at least, assumed—that this man wasn't about to mug her, after all. 'I'll be turning the light out at the top of the stairs in a minute or so; before I do, you might want to get back to the main streets where it's more brightly lit,' she advised without turning as she took the key from the pocket of her dungarees to unlock the door.

Jonas continued to look up at her in seething annoyance for a mere fraction of a second before following her, taking the stairs two at a time until he stood directly behind her. 'You and I need to talk,' he bit out between gritted teeth.

'Write me a letter,' she advised as she unlocked the door before stepping inside and turning to face him, her expression one of open challenge.

Jonas placed his hands on either side of the doorframe. 'I've already written you half a dozen letters. Letters you haven't bothered to reply to.'

She grimaced. 'There's always the possibility that I'll reply to the seventh.'

'I doubt that somehow,' Jonas accepted grimly. 'I don't think so!' He put his booted foot between the door and the frame as she would have closed that door in his face.

She opened it again to glare at him, those smoky grey eyes glittering darkly, bright colour in her normally pale cheeks. 'Remove your foot, Mr Buchanan, or you'll leave me with no choice but to call the police and have you forcibly removed from the premises!'

It was all too easy for Jonas to see that she was more angry than alarmed by his persistence. 'I only want the two of us to sit down and have a sensible conversation—'

'I'm busy.'

'I'm asking for two minutes of your time, damn it!' Jonas exclaimed.

Mac really wasn't being difficult when she said she was busy; she had a major exhibition at a gallery on Saturday, only two days away, and she had one more painting to finish before then. Besides, no amount of talking to Jonas Buchanan was going to make her change her mind about selling the warehouse she had so lovingly worked on to make into her home.

Her grandfather had left this property to Mac when he

died five years ago. It had been one of many warehouses by the river that had fallen into disuse as the trade into the London dock had fallen foul of other, more convenient transportation. Three floors high, it had been the perfect place for Mac to make into her home as well as her working studio. From the outside it still looked like an old warehouse, but inside the ground floor consisted of a garage and utility room, the second floor was her living quarters, and the third floor made a spacious studio.

Unfortunately, the area where the warehouse stood had recently become very attractive to property developers such as Jonas Buchanan, as they bought up the run-down riverside properties to put up blocks of luxurious apartments that had the added allure of a magnificent and uninterrupted view of the river.

It was this man's bad luck that Mac's own warehouse home stood on one of those sites.

She sighed. 'I've already given my answer to your lawyer, your personal assistant, and your builder,' she reminded him pointedly. 'I don't want to sell. Not now. Not in the future. Not ever. Is that clear enough for you?'

Jonas Buchanan's expression was one of pure exasperation as he gave an impatient shake of his head. 'You must realise that the area around you is going to become a noisy building site over the winter months?'

She shrugged. 'You've fenced off this area for that purpose.'

He frowned. 'That isn't going to lessen the noise of lorries arriving with supplies. Workmen constantly hammering and banging as the buildings start to go up, followed by huge cranes being erected on site. Exactly how do you expect to still be able to work with all that going on?'

Mac's eyes narrowed. 'The same way I've continued to work the last few months as you've systematically pulled down all the buildings around this one.'

Jonas's mouth firmed at the implied criticism. 'I offered several times to relocate you—'

'I have no wish to be "relocated", Mr Buchanan,' Mary McGuire growled out between clenched teeth. 'This is my *home*. It will remain my home still, even once you've built and sold your luxurious apartments.'

And, as Jonas was only too aware, be a complete eyesore to the people who lived in those exclusive multimillion-pound apartments! 'In my experience, everyone has a price, Mary—'

'Mac.'

He frowned. 'Sorry?'

'Everyone who actually knows me calls me Mac, not Mary,' she explained. 'And maybe the people you're acquainted with have "a price", Mr Buchanan,' she said scathingly, smoky-grey eyes glittering with contempt. 'I happen to believe that my own family and friends have more integrity than that. As do I!'

Jonas now fully understood the frustration his employees had previously encountered when trying to talk to Mary 'Mac' McGuire; he had never before met a more stubborn, pigheaded and unreasonable individual than this particular woman!

His mouth thinned. 'You know where to reach me when you change your mind.'

'*If* I change my mind,' she corrected firmly. 'Which I won't. Now, if you will excuse me, Mr Buchanan?' She raised ebony brows. 'I really am very busy.'

And Jonas wasn't? With millions of pounds invested in

one building project or another all over the world, Jonas's own time was, and always had been, at a premium. He certainly didn't have any more of it to waste tonight on this woman.

He stepped back. 'As I said, you know where to reach me when you've had enough.'

'Goodnight, Mr Buchanan,' she shot back with saccharin—and pointed—sweetness, before quietly closing the door in his face.

Jonas continued to scowl at that closed door for several minutes after she had carried out her threat to turn off the outside light and left him in darkness apart from the lights visible inside the warehouse itself.

He had already invested too much time and money in the building project due to begin on this site in the New Year to allow one stubborn individual to ruin it for him, or Buchanan Construction.

Obviously the money he had so far offered for this property wasn't enough of a reason for Miss McGuire to agree to move. Which meant Jonas was going to have to come up with a more convincing reason for her to want to leave.

CHAPTER TWO

'CHEER UP, MAC,' Jeremy Lyndhurst teased as the first of the guests invited to this evening's viewing began to come through the gallery. The fifty-something co-owner of the prestigious Lyndwood Gallery continued, 'A few hours of looking good and being socially polite this evening, and tomorrow you can go back to being reclusive and dressing like a tramp!'

Mac chuckled huskily—as she knew she was meant to—at this reminder of the affront it was to Jeremy's own impeccable dress sense whenever she turned up at his gallery in her paint-smeared working clothes. Which she had done a lot the last few weeks as she came to deliver the individual paintings due to be exhibited at this evening's 'invitation only' showing of her work.

Jeremy's partner—in more ways than one—Magnus Laywood, a tall, blond giant in his forties, was at the door to 'meet and greet' as more of those guests began to arrive; mainly art critics and serious collectors, but also some other individuals who were just seriously rich.

There were twenty of Mac's paintings on show this evening, and all of them expertly displayed by Jeremy and Magnus, on walls of muted cream with their own individual lighting so that they showed to their best advantage.

It was the first individual exhibition of its kind that Mac had ever agreed to do—and now that the evening had finally arrived she was so nervous her knees were knocking together!

'Here, drink this.' Jeremy picked up a glass of champagne from one of the waiters who were starting to circulate amongst the guests in the rapidly filling room, and handed it to her. 'Your face just went green!' he explained with a chuckle.

Mac took a restorative sip of the bubbly alcohol. 'I've never been so nervous in my entire life.'

'Oh, to be twenty-seven again,' Jeremy murmured mournfully.

Mac took another sip of the delicious champagne. 'What if they don't like my work?' she wailed.

'They can't all be idiots, darling,' Jeremy drawled. 'It's going to be a wonderful evening, Mac,' he reassured her seriously as she still looked unconvinced. 'I know how hard this is for you, love, but just try to enjoy it, hmm?'

The problem was that Mac had never been particularly fond of exhibiting her work. Selling it, yes. Showing it to other people, and being 'socially polite' to those people, no. Unfortunately, as Mac was well aware, she couldn't make a living from her paintings if she didn't sell them.

'I'll try— Oh. My. God!' she gasped weakly as she saw, and easily recognised, the man now standing beside the door engaged in conversation with Magnus.

Jonas Buchanan!

He was as tall as Magnus, and dark and dangerous where

the other man was blond and amiable, there was no mistaking that overlong dark hair and those hard and chiselled features dominated by piercing blue eyes that now swept coldly over the other guests.

Mac's heart hammered loudly in her chest as she took in the rest of his appearance. Dressed like every other man in the room, in a tailored black evening suit and snowy white shirt with a perfectly arranged black bow-tie at his throat, Jonas nevertheless somehow managed to look so much more compellingly handsome than any other man in the room.

'What is it?' Jeremy followed her line of vision. 'Who is that?' he murmured appreciatively, his longstanding relationship with Magnus not rendering him immune to the attractions of other men.

Mac dragged her gaze away from Jonas to look accusingly at the co-owner of the Lyndwood Gallery. 'You should know—you invited him!'

'I don't think so.' Jeremy's eyes were narrowed as he continued to look across at Jonas. 'Who is he?'

Mac swallowed hard before answering. 'Jonas Buchanan.'

Jeremy looked impressed. '*The* Jonas Buchanan?'

As far as Mac was aware there was only one Jonas Buchanan, yes!

'Ah, I understand now.' Jeremy nodded his satisfaction as a puzzle was obviously solved. 'He's with Amy Walters.'

Mac turned back in time to see Jonas Buchanan placing a proprietary hand beneath the elbow of a tall and beautiful redhead, the two of them talking softly together as they crossed the room to join a group of guests, Jonas easily standing several inches taller than the other men. Mac turned away abruptly.

'Amy's the art critic for *The Individual*,' Jeremy supplied dryly as he saw the blankness of Mac's expression.

A completely unnecessary explanation as far as Mac was concerned; she knew exactly who Amy Walters was. It was the fact that the other woman had brought Jonas with her this evening, a man Mac was predisposed to dislike, that made things more than a little awkward; Mac was only too aware that she would have to be polite to the beautiful art critic if the two of them were introduced. Something that might be a little difficult for her to do with the arrogantly self-assured Jonas Buchanan standing at Amy's side!

The reason for that current self-assurance was obvious; invitations to this exhibition had been sent out weeks ago to ensure maximum attendance. Meaning that Jonas Buchanan had to have known, when they had met and spoken so briefly together two evenings ago, that he was going to be at her exhibition at the Lyndwood Gallery this evening.

Rat!

If he thought he could intimidate her by practically gate-crashing her exhibition, then he could—

'How nice to see you again so soon, Mac.'

Mac stiffened, her earlier nervousness completely evaporating and being replaced by indignation as she recognised Jonas Buchanan's silkily sarcastic tone as he spoke softly behind her.

Double rat!

Jonas kept his expression deliberately neutral as Mary 'Mac' McGuire slowly turned to face him.

To say that he had been surprised by her appearance this evening would be a complete understatement! In fact, if Amy hadn't teasingly assured him that the delicately lovely woman with her ebony hair secured on top of her head to reveal the slender loveliness of her neck, and wearing a red Chinese-style knee-length silk dress with matching red high-heeled sandals that showed off her shapely legs to perfection, was indeed the artist herself, then Jonas wasn't sure he would have even recognised her!

She looked totally different with her hair up, older, more sophisticated, those mysterious smoky-grey eyes surrounded by long and thick dark lashes, the paleness of her cheeks highlighted with blusher, those full and sensuous lips outlined with a lip gloss the same vibrant red as that figure-hugging red silk gown and three-inch sandals.

In a word, she looked exquisite!

Whoever would have thought it? Jonas mused ruefully. From bag-lady to femme fatale with the donning of a red silk dress.

Although the challenging glitter in those smoky grey eyes as she glared up at him was certainly familiar enough. 'Mr Buchanan,' she greeted dryly. 'Jeremy, this is Jonas Buchanan. Jonas, one of the gallery owners, Jeremy Lynd-hurst.'

Mac watched through narrowed lashes as the two men shook hands, finding Jonas's appearance even more disturb-ing tonight than she had two evenings ago. He was one of the few men she had met who wore the elegance of a black evening suit rather than the clothes wearing him, the power of his personality such that it was definitely the man one no-ticed rather than the superb tailoring of the clothing he wore.

'Have you managed to lose Miss Walters already?' Mac asked sweetly as she saw that the other woman was talking animatedly to another man across the room.

Those electric-blue eyes darkened with sudden humour.

'Amy pretty much does her own thing,' Jonas Buchanan replied with a singular lack of concern.

'How…understanding, of you,' Mac taunted. Really, she was nervous enough about this evening already, without having to suffer this particular man's presence!

'Not at all,' Jonas drawled with deepening amusement.

'I do hope you will both excuse me…?' Jeremy cut in apologetically. 'Someone has just arrived that I absolutely have to go and talk to.'

'Of course,' Jonas Buchanan accepted smoothly. 'I assure you, I'm only too happy to stay and keep Mac company,' he added as he took a deliberate step closer to her.

A close proximity that Mac instantly took exception to!

One or other of this man's associates had been hounding her for months now in an effort to buy her home—but only so that it could be knocked down to become part of the area of ground landscaped as a garden for the new luxury apartment complex. The fact that Jonas Buchanan himself had now decided to get in on the act did not impress Mac in the slightest.

'You're looking very beautiful this evening—'

'Don't let appearances deceive you, Mr Buchanan,' she interrupted sharply. 'I'll be back to wearing my dungarees tomorrow.' Mac had made the mistake of dating a prestigious and arrogant art critic when she was still at university, and she wasn't about to ever let another man treat her as nothing but a beautiful trophy to exhibit on his arm. 'Exactly what are you doing here, Mr Buchanan?' she asked him directly.

Jonas studied her through narrowed lids. Two evenings ago he had thought this woman looked like a starving waif with absolutely no dress sense, but her exquisite appearance tonight in the red silk dress—which Jonas realised almost every other man in the room was also aware of—indicated to him that she must actually dress in those other baggy and unflattering clothes because she wanted to.

He shrugged. 'Amy asked me to be her escort this evening.'

Those red-glossed lips curled with distaste. 'How flattering to have a woman ask you out.'

Jonas's gaze hardened. 'I'm always happy to spend the evening with my cousin.'

Those smoky-grey eyes widened. 'Amy Walters is your cousin?'

He arched a mocking brow at her obvious incredulity. 'Is that so hard to believe?'

Well, no, of course it wasn't hard to believe, Mac accepted uncomfortably. But it did mean that Jonas wasn't here this evening on a date with another woman, as Mac had assumed that he was...

And why should that matter to her? She had no personal interest in this man. Did she...?

Lord, she hoped not!

The fact that he was one of the most compellingly attractive men Mac had ever met was surely nullified by the fact that he was also the man trying to force her out of her own home, by the sheer act of making it too uncomfortable for her to stay?

She steadily returned Jonas's piercing gaze as she shrugged. 'I don't see any family resemblance.'

He smiled wickedly. 'Maybe that's because Amy is a woman and I'm a man?'

Mac was well aware that Jonas was a man. Much too aware for her own comfort, as it happened. At five feet two inches tall, and weighing only a hundred pounds, in stark contrast to Jonas Buchanan's considerable height and powerful build, she was made totally aware of her own femininity by this man. And, uncomfortably, her vulnerability...

Her mouth firmed. 'I really should go and circulate amongst the other guests,' she told him as she placed her empty champagne glass down on a side table with the intention of leaving.

'Maybe I'll come with you.' Jonas Buchanan reached out to lightly grasp Mac by the elbow as she would have turned away.

His touch instantly sent a quiver of shocking awareness along the length of her arm and down into her breasts, causing them to swell inside her bra and the nipples to engorge to a pleasurable ache against the lacy material.

It was a completely unfamiliar—and unwelcome—feeling to Mac. After that one brief disaster of a relationship while at university, she had spent the following six years concentrating solely on her painting career, with little or no time to even think about relationships. She wasn't thinking of one now, either. Jonas Buchanan was the last man—positively *the* last man!—that Mac should be feeling physically attracted to.

Her body wasn't listening to her, unfortunately, as the warmth of Jonas's hand on her arm began to infiltrate the rest of her body, culminating uncomfortably at the apex of her thighs as she felt herself moisten there, in such a burst of heat that she gasped softly in awareness of that arousal.

She raised startled eyes to that hard and compellingly handsome face above hers, Jonas standing so close to her now she was able to see the individual pores in his skin. To recognise the lighter blue ring that surrounded the iris of his eyes, which gave them that piercing appearance. To gaze hypnotically at those slightly parted lips as they slowly lowered towards hers—

Mac jerked herself quickly out of his grasp. 'What are you doing?'

Yes, what *was* he doing? Jonas wondered frowningly. For a brief moment he had forgotten that they were surrounded by noisily chatting art critics and collectors. Had felt as if he and the exquisitely beautiful Mac McGuire were the only two people in the room, surrounded only by an expectant awareness and the heady seduction of her perfume.

Damn it, Jonas had been so unaware of those other people in the room that he had been about to kiss her in front of them all!

Her appearance this evening was an illusion, he reminded himself. Tonight she was the artist, deliberately dressed to beguile and seduce art critics and art collectors alike into approving of or buying her paintings. The fact that she had almost succeeded in seducing him into forgetting exactly who and what she was only increased Jonas's feelings of self-disgust.

His mouth thinned as he stepped away to look down at her through hooded lids. 'I really shouldn't keep you from your other guests any longer.'

Mac trembled slightly at the contempt she could hear in Jonas's tone. As she wondered what she had done to incur that contempt; he had been the one about to kiss her and not the other way around!

Her gaze returned to those sensually sculptured lips as she wondered what it would have felt like to have them part and claim her own lips. Jonas's mouth looked hard and uncompromising now, but seconds ago those firm lips had been soft and inviting as they lowered to hers—

Get a grip, Mac, she instructed herself firmly as she straightened decisively. The fact that he looked wonderful in a black evening suit, and was one of the most gorgeous men she had ever set eyes on, did not detract from the fact that he was also the enemy!

She eyed him mockingly. 'I would be polite and say that it's been nice seeing you again, Mr Buchanan, but we both know I would be lying...' She trailed off pointedly.

He gave a humourless smile in recognition of that mockery.

'I doubt very much that you've seen the last of me, Mac.'

She raised dark brows. 'I sincerely hope that you're wrong about that.'

His smile deepened. 'I rarely am when it comes to matters of business.'

'Modest too,' Mac scorned. 'Is there no end to your list of talents?' She snorted delicately. 'If you'll excuse me, Mr Buchanan.' She didn't wait for his reply to her statement but moved to cross the room to where she realised Magnus had discreetly been trying to attract her attention for the past few minutes.

Jonas stood unmoving as he watched her progress slowly across the room, stopping occasionally to greet people she knew. Unlike her behaviour towards him, the smiles Mac bestowed on the other guests were warm and relaxed, the huskiness of her laugh a soft caress to the senses, and revealing small, even white teeth against those full and red-glossed lips.

The tight-fitting silk dress emphasised the rounded curve of her bottom as she moved, and the slit up the side of

the gown revealed the shapely length of her thigh. Jonas
scowled his disapproval as he saw that most of the men in
the room were also watching her, with one persistent man
even grasping her wrist and trying to engage her in conversation before she laughingly managed to extricate herself
and walked away to join Magnus Laywood.

'So what did you make of our little artist...?'

Jonas turned to look at Amy, compressing his mouth in
irritation as he realised he had been so engrossed in watching Mac that he hadn't noticed his cousin's approach. A
tall and beautiful redhead, with a temper to match, Jonas's
maternal cousin wasn't a woman men usually overlooked!

'What did I think of Mary McGuire?' Jonas played for
time as he was still too surprised at his reaction to the artist's change in appearance to be able to formulate a satisfac-
tory answer to Amy's archly voiced question. 'She seems...a
little young, to have engendered all this interest,' he drawled
with bored lack of interest as he took two glasses of champagne from the tray of a passing waiter and handed one of
them to his cousin.

'Young but brilliant,' Amy assured him unreservedly as
she sipped the chilled wine.

'High praise indeed,' Jonas mused; his cousin wasn't
known for her effusiveness when it came to her job as art
critic for *The Individual*.

Amy linked her arm with his encouragingly. 'Come and
look at some of her paintings.'

Mac continued to chat lightly with a collector who had
expressed a serious interest in buying one of the paintings
on display, at the same time completely aware of Jonas Buchanan and his cousin as they moved slowly through the
two-roomed gallery to view her work.

It was impossible to tell from Jonas's expression what he thought of her paintings, those blue eyes hooded as he studied each canvas, his mouth unsmiling as he murmured in soft reply to Amy Walters's comments.

He probably hated them, Mac accepted heavily as she politely tried to refer the flirtatious collector to Jeremy for the more serious discussion over price. No doubt Jonas preferred modern art as opposed to her more ethereal style and bright but slightly muted use of colour. No doubt he had only agreed to accompany his cousin this evening in the first place because he had known that by doing so he would undermine Mac's confidence.

He needn't have bothered—Mac already hated all of this! She disliked the artificiality. Found the inane chatter tiresome. And she found herself especially irritated by the opportunistic collector she now realised was unobtrusively trying to place his hand on her bottom...

Mac moved sharply away from him, her eyes snapping with indignation at the uninvited familiarity. 'I'm sure that you'll find Jeremy will be only too happy to help with any further questions you might have.'

The middle-aged man chuckled meaningfully as he moved closer. 'He isn't my type!'

Mac frowned her discomfort, at a complete loss as to how to deal with this situation without causing a scene. Something she knew was out of the question with a dozen or so reporters also present in the room.

In their own individual ways Jeremy and Magnus had worked as hard on producing this exhibition this evening as Mac had. If she were to slap this obnoxious man's face, as she was so tempted to do, then the headlines in some of tomorrow's newspapers would read 'Artist slaps buyer's face!' instead of any praise or constructive criticism on her actual work.

She gave a shake of her head. 'I really don't think—'

'Sorry to have been gone so long, darling,' Jonas Buchanan interrupted smoothly as his arm moved firmly about Mac's waist to pull her securely against his side. He gave the other man a challenging smile, those compelling blue eyes as hard as the sapphires they resembled. 'It's rather crowded in here, isn't it?'

'I—yes.' The older and shorter man looked disconcerted by this unmistakable show of possessiveness. 'I—If you will both excuse me? I'll take your advice, Mac, and go and discuss the details with Jeremy.' He turned to hurriedly disappear into the crowd.

Mac found that she was trembling in reaction—and was totally at a loss to know if it was caused by the unpleasantness of the last minute or so, or because Jonas still held her so firmly against him that she was totally aware of the hard warmth of his powerful body…

Jonas took one look down at Mac's white face before his arm tightened about her waist and he turned her towards the entrance to the gallery. 'Let's get some air,' he suggested as he all but lifted her off the floor to carry her across the room and out of the door into the icy cold night. Something he instantly realised was a mistake as he could see by the street-lamp how Mac had begun to shiver in the thin silk dress. 'Here.' He slipped off his jacket to place it about her shoulders, his thumbs brushing lightly against the warm swell of her breasts as he stood in front of her to pull the lapels together.

Her eyes were huge as she looked up at him. 'Now you're going to be cold.'

She looked like a little girl playing dress-up with the shoulders of Jonas's jacket drooping down at the sides and the bulky garment reaching almost down to her knees. Except there was nothing childlike about the sudden awareness that darkened those smoky-grey eyes, or the temptation of those parted red-glossed lips as she breathed shallowly.

'How old are you really?' Jonas rasped harshly.

She blinked. 'I— What does that have to do with anything?'

He gave an impatient shrug of his shoulders. 'When I met you the other night you looked like someone's little sister. Tonight you look—well, tonight you look more like most men wished their best friend's little sister looked!'

She tilted that long elegant neck as she looked up at him. 'And how is that?' she prompted huskily.

This is a bad idea, Buchanan, Jonas cautioned himself. A very, very bad idea, he warned firmly even as his fascinated gaze remained fixed on those moist and parted lips.

A taste. He just wanted a taste of those sexy red lips—

Hell, no!

He was trying to transact a business deal with this woman, and he made a point of never mixing business with pleasure. And Jonas had no doubts it would have been very pleasurable to touch and taste those full and pouting lips with his own...

His expression was deliberately taunting as he looked down at her. 'In that dress you look like a woman who's ready for hot and wild sex.'

Mac's eyes widened as she gasped at the insult. 'I'll wear what I damn well please!'

That blue gaze moved deliberately down to the split in

the side of her dress that revealed the long, bare length of her silky thigh. 'Obviously.'

'You're no better than the idiot whose attentions you just appeared to save me from,' she accused furiously as she pulled his jacket from about her shoulders and almost threw it back at him before turning on her heel and marching back into the gallery without so much as a second glance.

Rude. Obnoxious. Insulting. Rat!

CHAPTER THREE

'I DON'T GIVE a damn whether Mr Buchanan is busy or not,' an angry voice—that unfortunately Jonas recognised only too well!—snapped in the outer office of his London head-quarters at nine-thirty on Monday morning. 'No, I have no intention of making an appointment. I want to talk to him *now*!' The door between the two rooms was flung open as Mac burst into Jonas's office.

Jonas barely had time to register her appearance, in a fitted black jumper and faded hipster blue denims, her hair a silken ebony curtain over her shoulders and down the length of her spine, before she marched over to stand in front of his desk, her cheeks flushed and eyes fever bright as she glared across at him.

She looked like a feral cat—and just as ready to spit and claw!

Jonas tilted his head sideways in order to look over at his secretary as she stood hesitantly in the doorway. 'There's no need to call Security, Mandy,' he drawled. 'I'm sure Miss McGuire won't be staying long…' He looked up enquiringly at Mac as he added that last statement.

Her eyes narrowed menacingly and she seemed to literally breathe fire at him. 'Long enough to tell you exactly what I think of you and your strong-arm tactics, at least!' she snarled.

'Thanks, Mandy,' Jonas dismissed his secretary, waiting until she had quietly left the room before looking back at Mac. 'You appear to be a little…distraught, this morning?'

'Distraught!' she echoed incredulously. 'I'm *furious*!'

Jonas could clearly see that. He just had no idea why that was.

Thankfully Amy had been ready to leave the gallery on Saturday evening when Jonas returned, allowing no opportunity for him and Mac to engage in any more arguments. Or to tempt Jonas into wanting to kiss her…

In the thirty-six hours since Jonas had last seen Mac, he had managed to convince himself that temptation had been an aberration on his part, a purely male reaction to the fact that she had looked as sexy as hell in that red silk dress.

Except that he now found himself facing the same temptation!

Mac wasn't wearing any make-up today, and her hair was windblown, her clothes casual in the extreme—and yet he still found his gaze drawn again and again to the fullness of her tempting lips.

Jonas's fingers tightened about the pen he was holding. 'Perhaps you would care to tell me why you're so furious?' he asked harshly. 'And what it has to do with me,' he added.

'Oh, don't worry, I'm going to tell you exactly why,' Mac promised. 'And you know damn well what it has to do with you!' she said accusingly.

Jonas raised his palms. 'I really am very busy this morning, Mac—'

'Do you have someone else you need to go and intimidate?' she scorned. 'Oh, I forgot—you usually leave that sort of thing to your underlings!' She snorted disgustedly. 'Well, let me assure you that I don't scare that easily—'

'Would you just calm down and tell me what the hell you're talking about?' he cut in coldly, those blue eyes glacial.

Mac was breathing hard, too upset still to heed the warning she could see in that chilling gaze. 'You know *exactly* what I'm talking about—'

'If I did, I would hardly be asking you to explain, now, would I?' Jonas retorted.

Mac's gaze narrowed. 'You knew I wouldn't be at home on Saturday evening because of the exhibition, and you shamelessly took advantage of that fact. You—'

He threw his pen down on the desktop before standing up impatiently. 'Mac, if you don't stop throwing out accusations, and just explain yourself, I'm afraid I'm going to have to ask you to leave.'

The anger Mac was feeling had been brewing, growing, since she'd returned home on Saturday evening. Having no idea where Jonas Buchanan actually lived, she'd had to spend all of Sunday brooding too, with only the promise of being able to visit Jonas at his office first thing on Monday morning to sustain her. Having his secretary try to stonewall her had done nothing to improve Mac's mood.

She drew in a controlling breath. 'My studio was broken into on Saturday evening. But, then, you already knew that, didn't you?' she said pointedly. 'You—'

'Stop right there!' Jonas thundered as he stepped out from behind his desk.

Mac instinctively took a step backwards as he towered

over her, appearing very dark and threatening in a charcoal-grey suit, pale grey shirt and grey silk tie, with that overlong dark hair styled back from the chiselled perfection of his face.

Those sculptured lips firmed to a livid thin line. 'You're telling me that your studio was broken into while you were out at the exhibition on Saturday evening?'

'You know that it was—'

'Mac, if you're going to continue to accuse me like this then I would seriously suggest that you have the evidence to back it up!' he warned harshly. 'Do you have that evidence?' he pressed.

She shook her head. 'The police didn't find anything that would directly implicate you, no,' she admitted grudgingly. 'But then, they wouldn't have done, would they?' she rallied. 'You're much more clever—'

'*Mac!*'

She blinked at the steely coldness Jonas managed to project into just that one word. Shivered slightly at the icy warning she could read in his expression.

But she didn't care how cold and steely Jonas was, the break-in had to have been carried out by someone who worked for him. Who else would have bothered, would have a reason to break into a building that, from the outside, appeared almost derelict?

Jonas was hanging onto his own temper by a thread. Angered as much by the thought of someone having broken into Mac's home at all, as at the accusations she was making about him being responsible for that break-in. She could so easily have been at home on Saturday evening. Could have been seriously hurt if she had disturbed the intruder.

He frowned. 'Did they take anything?'

'Not that I can see, no. But—'

'Let's just stick to the facts, shall we, Mac?' Jonas bit out, a nerve pulsing in his tightly clenched jaw.

She eyed him warily. 'The facts are that I arrived home late on Saturday evening to find my studio completely wrecked. The only consolation—if it can be called that!— is that at least all of my most recent work was at the gallery that evening.'

Jonas nodded. 'So there was no real damage done?'

Mac's eyes widened indignantly. 'My home, my privacy, was invaded!'

And he could understand how upsetting that must have been for her. Must still be. But the facts were that neither Mac nor her property had actually come to any real harm.

He moved to sit on the side of his desk. 'At least you had the sense to call the police.'

'I'm not a complete moron!'

Jonas didn't think that Mac was a moron at all. All evidence was to the contrary. 'I don't recall ever saying otherwise,' he commented dryly.

'You implied it, with your "at least" comment!' She thrust her hands into the hip pockets of her denims, instantly drawing Jonas's attention to the full and mature curve of her breasts beneath the fitted black sweater. Making a complete nonsense of how he had mistaken her for a young girl at their first meeting two days ago.

She was different again today, he realised ruefully. No longer the waif or the femme fatale, but a beautiful and attractive woman in her late twenties. A man could never become bored with Mac McGuire when he would never know on any given day which woman he was going to meet!

He sighed. 'What conclusions did the police come to?'

She shrugged those narrow shoulders. 'They seem to think it was kids having fun.'

Jonas grimaced. 'Maybe they're right—'

'Kids don't just break in, they steal things,' Mac disagreed impatiently. 'I have a forty-two-inch flat-screen television set, a new Blu-ray Disc player, a state-of-the-art music system and dozens of CDs, and none of them were even touched.'

Jonas looked intrigued. 'So it was just your studio that was targeted?'

'*Just* my studio?' she repeated indignantly. 'You just don't understand, do you?' she added as she turned away in disgust.

The problem for Jonas was that he did understand. He understood only too well. Having seen Mac's work for himself on Saturday evening, he knew exactly how important her studio was to her. It was the place where she created beauty deep from within her. Where she poured out her soul onto canvas. To have that vandalised, wrecked, was the equivalent of attacking the inner, deeply emotional Mac.

His mouth firmed. 'But you believe *I'm* responsible for what happened?'

Mac turned to eye him warily as she once again heard that underlying chill in Jonas's tone, the warning against repeating her earlier accusations.

If Jonas wasn't responsible, then who was? Not just who, but why? Nothing of value had been taken. In fact, the living-area part of her home hadn't been touched. Only her studio had been vandalised. Surely whoever had done that would have to know her to realise that the studio was her heart and soul?

Which, as he didn't know her, surely ruled out Jonas

Buchanan as being the person responsible for the damage? After all, they had only met twice before this morning, and neither of those occasions had been in the least conducive to them gaining any personal insights about each other. Jonas certainly couldn't know how much Mac's studio meant to her.

She gave a weary shake of her head. 'I don't know what to believe any more...'

'That's something, I suppose,' Jonas commented dryly. 'Why don't we start with the premise that neither I nor anyone I employ had anything to do with the break-in, and go from there?' he suggested. 'Who else could have reason for wanting to cause you this personal distress? Perhaps an artist rival, jealous of your success? Or maybe an ex-lover who didn't go quietly?' he added.

Mac's eyes narrowed. 'Very funny!'

Strangely, Jonas didn't find his last suggestion in the least amusing. Especially when it was accompanied by vivid images of this woman's naked body intimately entwined with another man, that ebony hair falling about the two of them like a silken curtain...

He straightened abruptly and once again moved to sit behind his desk. 'I really am busy this morning, Mac. In fact I have an appointment in a little under five minutes, so why don't we meet up again at lunchtime and discuss this further?'

Mac eyed him suspiciously. 'You're inviting me out to lunch?' she repeated uncertainly, as if she were sure she must have misheard him.

No, Jonas hadn't been inviting her out to lunch. In fact, those earlier imaginings had already warned him that, the less he had to do with the volatile Mac McGuire, the better he would like it!

'On second thoughts it would be far more sensible if you were to talk to my secretary on your way out and make an appointment to come back and see me at a time more convenient for both of us.'

It would be more sensible, Mac agreed, but after arriving back late from the gallery on Saturday evening to find her studio in chaos, and then another hour spent talking to the police, to spend the rest of the weekend alternating between ranting at the mess and crying for the same reason, she wanted to sort this problem out once and for all. Today, if possible.

Her parents, safely ensconced in their retirement bungalow home in Devon, where they also ran a B&B in the summer months, already worried that their move to the south of England had left her living alone in London. They would be horrified to learn that she'd had a break-in at her home.

But was it a good idea for her to have lunch with Jonas Buchanan? Probably not, Mac acknowledged ruefully. Except that he had seemed sincere—no, furious, actually—in his denial that he was in any way responsible for the break-in.

If that were genuinely the case, then she probably owed him an apology, at least, for having come here and made those bitter accusations.

'Lunch sounds a better idea,' Mac contradicted his earlier suggestion. 'In fact, I'll take you out to lunch.'

Jonas raised mocking brows. 'Would that offer be the equivalent of wearing sackcloth and ashes?'

Mac felt the warmth of colour in her cheeks at his pointed suggestion that she should appear penitent for her behaviour.

'It means that for the moment I'm prepared to give you the benefit of the doubt regarding the break-in.'

'For the moment?' Jonas repeated softly, trying not to grit his teeth. 'That's very…good of you.'

'Don't push your luck, Jonas,' she snapped. 'I'm only suggesting this at all because this whole situation seems to be getting out of control.'

Jonas considered her between hooded lids. Mac really had behaved like a little hellion this morning by forcing her way into his office and throwing out her wild accusations. And if Jonas had any sense then he would tell her he would see her in court for even daring to voice those accusations without a shred of evidence to back up her claim. He certainly shouldn't even be thinking of accepting her invitation to have lunch.

Except that he was…

Mac intrigued him. Piqued his interest in a way no woman had done for a very long time. If ever.

All the more reason not to even consider going out to lunch with her then!

She was absolutely nothing like the women Jonas was usually attracted to. Beautiful and sophisticated women who knew exactly what the score was. Who expected nothing from him except the gift of a few expensive baubles during the few weeks or months their relationship lasted; if any of those women had ever harboured the hope of having any more than that from him then they had been sadly disappointed.

Jonas had witnessed and lived through the disintegration of his own parents' marriage. He had been twelve years old when he'd watched them start to rip each other to shreds, both emotionally and verbally, culminating in an even messier divorce when Jonas was fifteen.

He had decided long ago that none of that was for him. Not the initial euphoria of falling in love. Followed by a few years of questionable happiness. Before the compromises began. The irritation. And then finally the hatred for each other, followed by divorce.

Jonas wanted none of it. Would willingly forgo the supposed 'euphoria' of falling in love if it meant he also avoided experiencing the disintegration of that relationship and the hatred for each other that followed.

Mac McGuire, for all she was an independent and successful artist, gave every appearance of being one of those happily-ever-after women Jonas had so far managed to avoid having any personal involvement with.

'Well?' she prompted irritably at Jonas's lengthy silence.

He should say no. Should tell this woman that he had remembered he already had a luncheon appointment today.

Damn it, it was only lunch, not a declaration of intent!

His mouth thinned. 'I have an hour free between one o'clock and two o'clock today.'

'Wow,' Mac murmured, those smoky-grey eyes now openly laughing at him. 'I should feel honoured that Jonas Buchanan feels he can spare me a whole hour of his time.'

His eyes narrowed to icy slits as he retorted, 'When what I should really do is take your shapely little bottom to court and sue you for slander!'

Mac's eyes widened and hot colour suffused her cheeks at hearing Jonas claim she had a shapely little bottom, making her once again completely aware of his own dark and dangerous attraction…

If anything he seemed even bigger today, his wide shoulders and powerful chest visibly muscled beneath the tailored suit and silk shirt, his face hard and slightly predatory, and dominated by those piercing blue eyes that seemed to see too much.

Did they see just how affected Mac was by his dark good looks, and that air of danger?

Perhaps the two of them lunching together wasn't such a good idea, after all, Mac decided with a frown. She could always claim that she had remembered a prior engagement. That she had to go to the Lyndwood Gallery to check on how the exhibition was going—

'Jonas, I have the letter here from—' The blonde, blue-eyed woman who had entered from the adjoining office, and who Mac instantly recognised as being Jonas's PA, Yvonne Richards—the same woman who had visited Mac a couple of months ago in an effort to persuade her into agreeing to sell her home—came to an abrupt halt in the doorway to Jonas's office as she saw Mac there. 'I'll come back later, shall I?' She totally ignored Mac as she looked at Jonas enquiringly.

'No need, Yvonne; Miss McGuire was just leaving,' Jonas said as he stood up, obviously dismissing Mac.

The fact that was exactly what Mac had been about to do did nothing to nullify the fact that Jonas was trying to get rid of her! Without any firm arrangements having been made for them to meet later today to continue this discussion…

'There's an Italian restaurant two streets over from this one,' she turned to inform him briskly. 'I'll book a table for us there for one o'clock.'

'Perhaps you would prefer me to book the table for the two of you?' the blonde woman offered coolly. 'Mr Buchanan's name is known to the restaurant owner,' she added pointedly as Mac looked at her enquiringly.

Mac gave the other woman a narrowed-eyed glance as she heard the edge in her tone, recognising that Yvonne Richards, beautiful and in her late twenties, was obviously a typical case of the PA who believed herself in love with her boss. A crush that Mac doubted Jonas Buchanan was even aware of.

Mac gave the other woman a saccharin-sweet smile. 'That won't be necessary, thank you; I know Luciano personally, too.'

'Fine,' Yvonne Richards bit out before turning to her employer. 'I'll come back when you aren't so busy, Jonas.' She turned abruptly on her two-inch heels and went back into the adjoining office, the door closing sharply behind her.

Mac turned back to Jonas. 'I don't think your PA likes me!'

Jonas's mouth compressed briefly. 'She hasn't known you long enough yet to dislike you.' Before Yvonne had interrupted them Jonas had had every intention of refusing Mac's invitation to lunch, and he wasn't at all happy with the fact that, between them, Yvonne and Mac seemed to have arranged for him to have lunch at Luciano's at one o'clock today.

Mac gave an unconcerned grin, two unexpected dimples appearing in her cheeks. 'That usually takes a little longer than five minutes, hmm?'

'Precisely,' he growled.

She raised dark, mocking brows. 'Perhaps she just has a crush on you?'

An irritated scowl darkened Jonas's brow. 'Don't be ridiculous!'

Mac gave an unconcerned shrug. 'She seems—less than happy at the thought of the two of us having lunch together.'

'Will you just go away and leave me in peace, Mac?' Once again Jonas moved to sit behind his imposing desk in obvious dismissal. 'I'll see you later,' he added pointedly as Mac made no move to respond to his less-than-subtle hint.

'One o'clock at Luciano's,' she came back mockingly before turning and walking over to the door that led out to his secretary's office.

Jonas's scowl deepened as he found he couldn't resist the temptation to look up and watch Mac leave. To be fully aware of his own response, the stirring, hardening, heated pulsing of his thighs, as he watched the provocative sway of those slender hips and pert bottom beneath fitted jeans.

She was an irritation and a nuisance, he told himself firmly. Trouble.

With a very definite capital T!

CHAPTER FOUR

'THIS IS NICE.'

'Is it?' Jonas asked darkly as they sat at a window table in Luciano's. It was an obvious indication that Mac was indeed known personally to the restaurateur; Jonas had dined here often enough in the past to know that Luciano only ever reserved the window tables for his best and most-liked customers.

Mac was already seated at the table, and had been supplied with some bread sticks to eat while she was waiting, by the time Jonas arrived at the restaurant at ten minutes past one. Not that he had been deliberately late; his twelve-thirty appointment had just run over time.

Everything had seemed to go wrong after she had left his office this morning. His nine-thirty appointment hadn't arrived until almost ten o'clock—which was probably as well when Jonas had spent most of the intervening time trying to dampen down his obvious arousal for Mac McGuire!

He had also found himself closely studying Yvonne throughout the morning as he searched for any signs of that 'crush' Mac had mentioned. Rightly or wrongly, Jonas didn't approve of personal relationships within the work-place—and that included unrequited ones. Which meant, if Mac was right, he would have to start looking for another PA. But if anything Yvonne's demeanour had been slightly frostier than usual, with nothing to suggest she had anything other than a working relationship with him.

Resulting in Jonas feeling annoyed with himself for doubting his own judgement, and even more irritated with Mac for mischievously giving him those doubts in the first place!

Consequently, he was feeling irritable and bad-tempered by the time he sat down at the lunch table opposite his perkily cheerful nemesis. 'Let's just order, shall we?' he grated as he picked up the menu and held it up in front of him as an indication he was not in the mood for conversation.

Mac didn't bother to look at her own menu, already knowing exactly what she was going to order: garlic prawns followed by lasagne. As far as she was concerned, Luciano made the best lasagne in London.

Instead she looked across at Jonas as he gave every indication of concentrating on choosing what he was going to have for lunch.

Every female head in the Italian bistro had turned to look at him when he'd entered a few minutes ago and taken off his long woollen coat to hang it up just inside the door. They had continued to watch him as he made his way over to the window table, several women giving Mac envious glances when he'd pulled out the chair opposite her own and sat down.

Mac had found herself watching him too; Jonas simply was the sort of man that women of all ages took a second, and probably a third, look at. He was so tall for one thing, and the leashed and elegant power of his lean and muscled body in that perfectly tailored charcoal-coloured suit was undeniable.

His irritation told her that he was also not in a good mood. 'We don't have to eat lunch together if you would rather not?' Mac prompted ruefully.

He lowered his menu enough to look across at her with icy blue eyes. 'You would rather I moved to another table? That's going to make conversation very difficult, wouldn't you say?' he taunted.

Mac felt the warmth in her cheeks at his obvious mockery. 'Very funny!'

Jonas placed his closed menu down on the table. 'I want to know more about the break-in to your studio on Saturday night. Such as how whoever it was got inside in the first place?' he asked grimly.

Mac shrugged. 'They broke a small window next to the door and reached inside to open it.'

Jonas noticed that some of the animation had left those smoky-grey eyes, presumably at his reminder of the break-in. 'You don't have an alarm system installed?'

She grimaced. 'I've never thought I needed one.'

'Obviously you were wrong,' Jonas said reprovingly.

'Obviously.' Anger sparkled in those grey eyes now. 'I have to say that I've always found people's smugness after the event to be intensely irritating!' She was still wearing the black fitted sweater and faded denims of earlier, the silky curtain of her hair framing the delicate beauty of her face to fall in an ebony shimmer over her shoulders and down her back.

Jonas relaxed back in his chair to look across at her speculatively. 'Then hopefully I've succeeded in irritating you enough to have a security system installed. Or perhaps I should just arrange to have it done for you?' he mused out loud, knowing it would immediately goad her to respond with the information that he wanted.

'That won't be necessary, thank you; I have a company coming out to install one first thing tomorrow morning,' she came back sharply. 'Along with a glazier to replace the window that was broken.'

His eyes narrowed. 'You haven't had the glass replaced yet?'

'I just said I hadn't,' Mac bit back.

Jonas gave a disgusted sigh. 'You should have got someone out on Sunday to fix it.'

Mac's eyes flashed darkly. 'Don't presume to tell me what I should or shouldn't do!'

'It's a security breach—'

'Oh, give it a rest, Jonas,' she muttered wearily. 'I'm quite capable of organising my own life, thank you.'

'I'm seriously starting to doubt that.'

'Strangely, your opinion is of little relevance to me!' Mac snapped. 'When I suggested we have lunch to talk about this situation I wasn't actually referring to the break-in.'

Jonas managed to dampen down his impatience as he smiled up at Luciano as he appeared beside their table to personally take their order.

'I take it you don't have a date this evening?' He mockingly changed the subject once the restaurateur had taken note of their order and returned to his beloved kitchen a few minutes later.

Mac knew he had to be referring to the fact that there was garlic in both of the foods she had ordered. 'I take it that

you do?' she retorted, the Marie Rose prawns and Dover
sole he had ordered not having any garlic in at all.

'As it happens, no.' That blue gaze met hers tauntingly.
'Are you offering to rectify that omission?'

Mac frowned. 'You can't be serious?'

Was he? Having spent part of the morning in uncomfortable arousal because of this woman, Jonas had once again
decided that, the less he had to do with Mac the better it
would be for both him and his aching erection! A decision
his last remark made a complete nonsense of.

'Obviously not,' he muttered.

Mac looked across at him shrewdly. 'It sounded like you
were asking me out on a date.'

Jonas shrugged. 'You're entitled to your opinion, I suppose.'

'You "suppose"?' she taunted.

He scowled darkly. 'Mac, are you deliberately trying to
initiate an argument with me?'

'Maybe.'

Jonas narrowed his gaze. 'Why?'

'Why not?' Mac smiled. 'It's certainly livened up the
conversation!'

Jonas knew it had done a lot more than that. He was far
too physically aware of this woman already; he didn't need
to feel any more so. In fact, he was somewhat relieved when
the waiter chose that moment to deliver their first course
to them.

What the hell had he been doing, all but suggesting that
Mac ask him out on a date this evening? Meeting her for
lunch was bad enough, without prolonging the time he had
to spend in her disturbing company. In future, Jonas decided

darkly, he would just stick to taking out his usual beautiful and sophisticated blondes!

'The reviews of your exhibition in Sunday's newspapers were good,' he abruptly changed the subject.

She nodded. 'Your cousin was especially kind.'

'Amy is a complete professional; if she says you're good, then you're good,' Jonas said.

'I went to the gallery after seeing you this morning. It seems to be pretty busy,' Mac told him distractedly, still slightly reeling from what she was pretty sure had been an invitation on Jonas's part for them to spend the evening together too. An offer he had obviously instantly regretted making.

Which was just as well considering Mac would have had to refuse the invitation! Going to his office was one thing. Having lunch with Jonas so that they could discuss what was going on with her warehouse was also acceptable. Going out on a proper date with him was something else entirely...

In spite of the fact that Jonas Buchanan was so obviously a devastatingly attractive man, he simply wasn't Mac's type. He was far too arrogant. At least as arrogant, if not more so, as Thomas Connelly, the art critic who had considered her nothing but a trophy to parade on his arm six years ago.

She picked up her fork to deliberately spear one of the succulent prawns swimming in garlic, before raising it to her mouth and popping it between her lips. Only to glance across the table at the exact moment she did so, her cheeks heating with flaming wings of colour as she saw the intensity with which Jonas was watching the movement.

Dark and mesmerising, his eyes had become a deep and cobalt blue. There was a slight flush to his cheeks too, and those sculptured lips were slightly parted.

Mac shifted uncomfortably. 'Would you like to try one?'

That dark gaze lifted up to hers. 'What?'

She swallowed hard, feeling strangely alone with Jonas in this crowded and happily noisy restaurant. 'You seemed to be coveting my garlic prawns, so I was offering to let you try one...'

Damn it, Jonas hadn't been coveting the prawns on Mac's plate—he had been imagining lying back and having those full and red lips placed about a certain part of his anatomy as she pleasured him!

What the hell was the *matter* with him?

In the last fifteen years he had never once mixed business with pleasure. Had always kept the two firmly separate. Since meeting Mac he seemed to have done nothing else but confuse the two, with the result that he was now once again fully aroused beneath the cover of the chequered tablecloth. Hopefully there would be no reason for him to stand up in the next few minutes or his arousal would be well and truly exposed!

'No, thank you,' he refused quickly. 'I would prefer not to smell of garlic during any of my business meetings later this afternoon.'

Mac gave an unconcerned shrug of her shoulders. 'Please yourself.'

'I usually do,' Jonas said dryly.

'Lucky you,' she said.

Jonas considered Mac through narrowed lids. 'Are you saying that you don't?' he taunted. 'I thought all artists preferred to be free spirits? In relationships as well as their art?'

Mac didn't miss the contempt in his tone. Or the underlying implication that, as an artist, she probably slept around.

It would have been amusing if it weren't so obvious that Jonas had once again meant to be insulting!

Oh, Mac had lots of friends, male as well as female, both from school and university, but that didn't mean she went to bed with any of them. That she had ever been intimately involved with anyone, in fact.

After that fiasco with Thomas, Mac had become completely focused on what she wanted to do with her life. Which was to be successful as an artist in her own right.

From the time she was twelve years old, and her art teacher had allowed her to paint with oils on canvas for the first time, Mac had known exactly what she wanted, and that was to become a successful artist first, with marriage and children second. She had become slightly sidetracked from that ambition during that brief relationship with Thomas, but if anything the realisation of his arrogance and condescension had only increased that ambition.

'If you'll excuse me, I need to go to the ladies' room.' She placed her napkin on the table before pushing back her chair and standing up.

Jonas raised dark brows. 'Was it something I said?'

Mac frowned down at him. 'That necessitates my needing to go to the ladies' room?' she drawled derisively. 'Hardly!'

Nevertheless, Jonas was left sitting alone at the table feeling less than happy, both with himself, and with his earlier biting comment. He knew very little about her personal life—the fact that he had an erection every time he was in her company really didn't count! He certainly didn't know her well enough to have deliberately cast aspersions upon the way she might choose to live her private life.

He forced himself to continue eating his own food as he waited for Mac to return.

And waited.

And waited.

After over ten minutes had passed since she'd left the table, Jonas came to the uncomfortable conclusion that she might have walked out on both him and the restaurant!

Deservedly so?

Maybe. But that didn't make the experience—the first time that a woman had ever walked out on Jonas, for any reason—any more palatable than the prawns he had just forced himself to finish eating.

He stood up abruptly to place his own napkin on the tabletop and make his way across the restaurant to the door through to the washrooms, determined to see exactly how Mac had made her escape. Only to come to a halt in the doorway and feeling completely wrong-footed as he came face to face with Mac, who was standing in the corridor in laughing conversation with one of the waitresses.

She looked at him curiously. 'Is there a problem, Jonas?'

His eyes narrowed. 'Your food is getting cold.'

'Oh, dear.' The waitress gave an apologetic smile. 'I'll talk to you later, Mac,' she said, before hurrying off in the direction of the kitchen.

Leaving Mac alone in the hallway with an obviously seriously displeased Jonas.

Well, that was just too bad!

Jonas had been deliberately insulting before she left the table, and when she'd bumped into Carla as she was leaving the ladies' room Mac had felt no hesitation in stopping to chat; Jonas Buchanan could just sit alone at the table for a few more minutes and stew as far as she was concerned.

She raised dark brows as he stepped further into the otherwise deserted hallway and quietly closed the door behind him, enclosing the two of them in a strangely tense and otherwise deserted silence. Mac shifted uncomfortably as Jonas walked stealthily down that hallway towards her. 'I thought you said my food was getting cold?' she prompted, suddenly nervous.

'It's already cold, so a few more minutes isn't going to make any difference,' he dismissed softly.

Mac moistened dry lips as Jonas kept walking until he came to a halt standing only inches away from her. Very tall and large, his close proximity totally unnerving. 'Why do we need to be a few more minutes?' She glanced up at him uncertainly.

Jonas was enjoying turning the tables and seeing Mac's obvious discomfort—God knew she had already made his own life uncomfortable enough for one day! Since the moment he first met her, in fact. He had no doubt that leaving him sitting alone at a table in the middle of a crowded restaurant had been deliberate on her part.

A public restaurant wasn't the ideal place for what he now had in mind, either, but to hell with that—Jonas had realised in the last few seconds that he didn't just need to kiss Mac, it had become as necessary to him as breathing.

'Guess,' he murmured throatily as he stepped even closer to her.

Her eyes widened in alarm as she took several steps back until she found herself against the wall. 'Garlic breath, remember,' she reminded him hastily.

He gave an unconcerned shrug. 'That will just make you taste even better.'

'This is so not a good idea, Jonas,' she warned him desperately.

Jonas was all out of good ideas. At this precise moment he intended—needed—to go with a bad one.

His gaze held Mac's as he reached up to cup his hand against the silky smooth curve of her cheek and ran the soft pad of his thumb over her slightly parted lips, the warmth of her breath a caress against his own highly sensitised skin. An arousing caress that made his stomach muscles clench and his thighs harden.

He drew in a sharp breath as he stepped closer still and Mac instinctively lifted her hands to rest them defensively against the hardness of his chest, the warmth of those hands burning through the silk material of Jonas's shirt as he deliberately rested his body against hers.

Mac suddenly found herself trapped between the cold wall and the heat of Jonas's body, her hands crushed against his muscled chest as he slowly lowered his head with the obvious intention of kissing her.

She knew she should protest. That she should at least try to ward off this rapidly increasing intimacy.

And yet she didn't. Couldn't.

Instead her lips parted in readiness for that kiss, her breath arrested in her throat at the first heated touch of Jonas's lips against hers.

Oh, Lord…

Mac had never known anything like the sensual pleasure of having Jonas's mouth moving against hers, exploring, sipping, tasting, teeth gently biting before that kiss deepened hungrily, his body hard and insistent against hers as her hands moved up his shoulders and her fingers became entangled in the dark thickness of his hair as she pulled him even closer. Jonas pushed her against the wall and lowered his body until his arousal pressed into Mac, making her respond with an aching hotness that pooled between her thighs in a rush of moist and fiery heat, her breasts swelling, the rosy tips hardening to full sensitivity as they pressed against the lacy material of her bra.

Her fingers tightened in the silky softness of Jonas's hair as that heat grew, their mouths fusing together hungrily, Mac groaning low in her throat as she felt the firm thrust of Jonas's tongue enter her mouth. Hot, slow and deep thrusts matched by the rhythmic movement of his thighs into the juncture of her sensitive thighs.

Mac groaned again in pleasure as that hardness pressed against the swollen nub nestled there, creating an aching heat deep inside her before it spread to every part of her body, arousing her to an almost painful degree.

God, she wanted this man with a ferocity of need she had never imagined, never dreamt was possible. Here. Now. She wanted to strip off their clothes and have Jonas take her up against the wall, her legs wrapped about his waist as he thrust deep inside her to ease that burning ache.

As if aware of at least some of her need, Jonas moved his hand to curve about her left breast, the soft pad of his thumb unerringly finding the swollen tip and sweeping across it.

Mac whimpered as the pleasure of that caress coursed down to her thighs, and she wished Jonas could touch her there, too—

'Well, *really*!' a shocked female voiced gasped. 'This *is* a public restaurant, you know,' the woman added disgustedly as she walked past them to the washrooms. 'Why don't the two of you just get a room somewhere?' The door to the ladies room closed behind her with a disapproving snap.

Mac had wrenched away from Jonas the moment she'd realised they were no longer alone in the hallway, burying the heat of her face against his chest now to hide her embarrassment at being caught in such a compromising position.

In a public restaurant, for goodness' sake!

With Jonas Buchanan, of all people.

What could she have been thinking?

She hadn't been thinking at all, that was the problem. She had been feeling. Experiencing emotions, sensations, she had never known before.

If that woman hadn't interrupted them then Mac might just have gone through with that urge she'd had to start ripping Jonas's clothes from his body before begging him to ease the burning ache between her thighs!

Oh, God.

CHAPTER FIVE

'So, WHAT DO you think?' Jonas asked as he stepped back from Mac.

'What do I think about what?' She blinked up at him as she straightened away from the wall to push the tangle of her hair back from her face; her eyes fever bright, her cheeks flushed, and those sensuously enticing lips slightly swollen from the fierce hunger of their kisses.

A hunger that had made Jonas forget, not only who they were, but *where* they were. All that had mattered to him at that moment was tasting Mac, devouring those tempting red lips, pressing the heat of his body against hers, her fingers becoming entangled in his hair as she responded to his desire.

Jonas knew he hadn't been this physically aroused, so totally lost to reason, since he was an inexperienced teenager. And he didn't like the sensation of being out of control. He didn't like it at all.

His mouth twisted. 'The two of us getting a hotel room for the afternoon.'

Mac's eyes widened. 'Certainly not!' she exclaimed indignantly.

'Why not?' he taunted.

'Why not?' Mac repeated as she glared up at him. 'I have no idea what sort of women you usually associate with, Jonas, but I can assure you that I do not go to hotel rooms with men for the afternoon!'

'I wasn't suggesting you went with men plural, Mac, just me,' he drawled.

'I said *no!*' She was breathing heavily in her agitation, the fullness of her breasts rapidly rising and falling.

Something that Jonas was all too well aware of as he looked down at her and his still heavily roused manhood pulsed achingly in response. 'You want me, I want you, so why the hell not?' he rasped.

He would have felt happier about this situation if Mac had just said yes to the two of them going to a hotel for the afternoon. That way he would have found her less of an enigma than he did now. Less intriguing than he did now.

Because Mac had definitely returned his passion. Yet it was a passion she made it clear she had no intention of doing anything about, probably not now nor in the future. He already knew his own afternoon was going to be as uncomfortable as his morning had been, but how did Mac intend dealing with her own unsatisfied arousal?

'Unless you're trying to tell me you don't want me?' he murmured.

Mac wasn't sure which of her emotions was the strongest—the urge she had to slap Jonas's arrogant face or the one she had to just sit down and cry at her own stupidity.

Because he was right, damn him. She did want him. She had never physically wanted a man more, in fact, her whole body one burning ache of need. Something Mac knew was going to bother her long after he had gone back to his office to attend his afternoon meetings.

But she definitely wanted to slap him too. For bringing that physical awareness down to a purely basic level by suggesting they get a hotel room for the afternoon and satisfy those longings.

She really wasn't that sort of woman. She had never done anything so impulsively reckless as kissing a man so heatedly on the premises of a restaurant before, let alone gone to a hotel room with him, and she had no intention of doing the latter now with Jonas, either. Much as she might secretly ache to do so. It sounded wild. Liberating. Dangerously exciting…

She deliberately fell back on anger as the solution to her predicament. 'Whether I want you or not, an afternoon in a hotel bedroom with a man I barely know—and who I really don't want to know any better—is really not my thing,' she told him scornfully. 'If you're feeling frustrated, Jonas, then I'm sure there are any number of women you could call who would be only too happy to spend the afternoon satisfying you!'

Jonas's eyes narrowed to icy slits. 'I've never been that desperate for sex, Mac.'

Including sex with her, she knew he was implying. Which was no doubt true. Jonas was young, handsome and rich enough to attract any woman he decided he wanted. He certainly didn't need to trouble himself over one stubborn artist, who obviously irritated him as much as she aroused him.

And Mac had aroused him. She'd felt the hard evidence of that arousal pressed against her own thighs as Jonas kissed her.

Her mouth firmed. 'I suggest we just forget about lunch,' she said abruptly. 'I'm really not hungry any more, and I doubt you are either—'

'Not for food, anyway,' Jonas muttered.

'I—' Mac broke off suddenly as the woman who had interrupted them earlier now came back out of the ladies' room, her gaze averted as she passed them and returned to the dining room of the restaurant. Mac's embarrassment returned with a vengeance. 'Don't worry, I'll explain to Luciano that you had an appointment you had to go to rather than intending any slight to the preparation of his food.'

'I moved my afternoon around. My next appointment isn't for another hour,' Jonas told her.

Her eyes widened. 'You want us to go back to the table and finish eating lunch together?'

After what just happened between us? Jonas inwardly finished Mac's question. And the answer to that was no, of course he didn't want them to return to the table and carry on eating lunch together as if nothing had happened. But neither did he appreciate Mac dismissing him as if the last few minutes had never happened at all.

His mouth thinned. 'Obviously not,' he bit out tersely. 'I'll settle the bill and explain to Luciano that *you* had a previous appointment.'

Mac frowned. 'I asked you out to lunch—'

'I'm paying the bill, Mac,' Jonas repeated firmly.

Mac continued to look up at him frowningly for several long seconds before giving an impatient shrug. 'Fine. Whatever.' Her tone implied she just wanted to get out of here. Away from him. Now.

A need she followed through on as she turned swiftly on

her heel and marched down the hallway back into the restaurant, the door swinging closed behind her.

Jonas remained where he was for several more minutes after Mac had gone, eyes narrowed and his expression grim as he recognised that she was no longer just a problem on a business level, but had also become one on a personal level, too.

Perhaps one that would only be resolved once they had been to bed together...

Mac was barefooted and belatedly eating a piece of toast for her lunch when she went to answer the knock on her door later that afternoon, a brief glance through the spy-hole in the door showing her that she didn't know the grey-haired man standing at the top of the metal staircase dressed like a workman in blue overalls and a thick checked shirt. 'Yes?' she prompted politely after opening the door.

'Afternoon, love,' the middle-aged man returned with a smile. 'Bob Jenkins. I've come to replace ya window.'

Mac's brows rose. 'That's great!'

He was already inspecting the broken window next to the door. 'Had a break-in, did ya?' He gave a shake of his head. 'Too much of it about nowadays. No respect, that's the problem. Not for people or their property.'

'No.' Mac grimaced as she recalled the mess that had been left in her studio.

'It will only take a few minutes to fix.' Bob Jenkins gave her another encouraging smile. 'I'll just go and get my things from the van.'

Mac had made him a mug of tea by the time he came back up the stairs with his tools and a pane of glass that appeared to be the exact size of the one that had been broken. 'How did you know which size glass to bring?'

The glazier took a sip of tea and put the mug down before he began working on the window frame. 'The boss is pretty good at judging things like this,' he explained.

Mac sipped her own tea as she watched him work. 'Was that the man I spoke to on the telephone this morning?'

'Don't know about that, love.' Bob Jenkins looked up to give her a grin. 'He just told me to get over here toot sweet and replace the window.'

Mac had no idea why, but she had a sudden uneasy feeling about 'the boss'. Maybe because she didn't recall telling the man at the glazier company she had called this morning what size window had been broken. Or expected anyone to arrive from that company until tomorrow...

She eyed Bob warily. 'Exactly who is the boss?'

He raised grizzled grey brows. 'Mr Buchanan, of course.'

Exactly what Mac had suspected—dreaded—hearing!

After their strained parting earlier Mac hadn't expected to see or hear from Jonas ever again. Although technically, she wasn't seeing or hearing from him now, either; he had just arrogantly sent one of his workmen over to fix her broken window.

Why?

Was Jonas treating her like the 'fragile little woman' who needed the help of the 'big, strong man'?

Or was Jonas replacing the window because he knew that he—or someone who worked for him—was responsible for it being broken in the first place?

'Of course,' Mac answered the workman distractedly. 'If you'll excuse me, Bob?'

'No problem,' he assured her brightly.

Mac was so annoyed at Jonas's high-handedness that she didn't quite know what to do with all the anger bubbling inside her. What did he think he was doing, interfering in this way, when she had already told him that she had arranged for a glazier to come out tomorrow?

An arrangement he had instantly expressed his disapproval of. Enough to have arranged for one of his own workmen to come out and replace the window immediately, apparently! Were Jonas's actions prompted by a guilty conscience? Or by something else? Although quite what that something else could be Mac had no idea. It was enough, surely, that Jonas was sticking his arrogant nose into her business?

Too right it was!

'What can I do for you this time, Mac?' Jonas took his brief-case out of the car before locking it and turning to face her wearily across the private and brightly lid underground car park beneath his apartment building.

He had been vaguely aware, as he drove home at the end of what had been a damned awful day, of the black motor-bike following in the traffic behind him. He simply hadn't realised that Mac was the driver of that motorbike until she followed him down into the car park, stopped the ve-hicle behind his car and removed the black crash helmet to shake the long length of her ebony-dark hair loose about her shoulders. The black biking leathers she was wearing fitted her as snugly as a glove, and clearly outlined the full-ness of her breasts and her slender waist and hips. Jonas couldn't help thinking of how they were no doubt moulded to her perfectly shaped bottom, too!

But there was no way that Jonas could mistake the obviously hostile demeanour on her face for anything other than what it was as she climbed off the motorbike; her eyes were sparkling with challenge, the fullness of her lips compressed and unsmiling.

Jonas's afternoon had been just as uncomfortable as he had thought it might be. So much so that he hadn't been able to give his usual concentration to his business meetings.

What was it about this woman in particular that so disturbed him? Mac was beautiful, yes, but in a wild and Bohemian sort of way that had never appealed to him before. There was absolutely nothing about her that usually attracted him to a woman. She was short and dark-haired, boyishly slender apart from the fullness of her breasts, and not in the least sophisticated; she even rode a motorbike, for heaven's sake!

Jonas wasn't particularly into motorbikes, but even he recognised the machine as being a Harley, the chassis a shiny black, its silver chrome gleaming brightly. For what had to be the dozenth time, Jonas told himself that Mac McGuire was most definitely not his type.

So why the hell couldn't he stop thinking about her?

His eyes narrowed. 'Don't you think—whatever your reason for being here—that following me home is taking things to an extreme?'

Her mouth tightened further at the criticism. 'Maybe.'

He raised mocking brows. 'Only maybe?'

'Yes,' she admitted grudgingly.

He eyed her coldly. 'And so you're here because…?'

She glared at him. 'You sent a glazier to repair my window.'

'Yes.'

Her eyes widened. 'You aren't even going to attempt to deny it?'

Jonas grimaced. 'Presumably Bob told you I had sent him?'

'Yes.'

'Then what would be the point of my trying to deny it?' he reasoned impatiently.

Mac was feeling a little foolish now that she was actually face to face with Jonas. Anger had been her primary emotion, as she waited the twenty minutes or so it had taken Bob Jenkins to replace the window, before donning her leathers and getting her motorcycle out of the garage and riding it over to Jonas's office. Just in time to see Jonas driving out of the office underground car park in his dark green sports car.

Frustrated anger had made her decide to follow him home; having ridden back into the city for the sole purpose of speaking to him, Mac had had no intention of just turning round and going home without doing exactly that.

At least, she had hoped Jonas was driving home; it would be a little embarrassing for Mac to have followed him to a date with another woman!

The prestigious apartment building above this underground car park—so unlike her own rambling warehouse-conversion home—definitely looked like the sort of place Jonas would choose to live.

She stubbornly stood her ground. 'I told you I had a glazier coming out tomorrow.'

Jonas nodded tersely. 'And I seem to recall telling you that wasn't good enough.'

Her eyes widened. 'So you just arranged for one of your

own workmen to come over this afternoon instead? Without even giving me the courtesy of telling me about it?'

Jonas could see that Mac was clearly running out of steam, her accusing tone certainly lacking some of its earlier anger. He regarded her mockingly. 'So it would seem.'

'I—but—you can't just take over my life in this way, Jonas!'

He frowned. 'You see ensuring your safety as an attempt to take over your life?'

'Yes! Well…not exactly,' she allowed impatiently. 'But it was certainly an arrogant thing to do!'

Yes, she was definitely running out of steam… 'But I *am* arrogant, Mac.'

'It's not something you should be in the least proud of!'

He gave her an unapologetic, smile. 'Your objection is duly noted.'

'And dismissed!'

Jonas gave a shrug. 'I presume Bob has now replaced the broken window?'

Mac gave a disgusted snort. 'He wouldn't dare do anything else when "the boss" told him to do so "toot sweet".'

Jonas had to smile at her perfect mimicry of Bob's broad Cockney accent. 'Well, unless you want me to break the window again just so that you can have the satisfaction of having your own glazier fix it tomorrow, I don't really see what you want me to do about it.'

Those smoky-grey eyes narrowed. 'You think you're so clever, don't you?'

Jonas straightened. 'No, Mac, I think what I did was the most sensible course of action in the circumstances,' he stated calmly. 'If you disagree with that, then that's obviously your prerogative.'

'I disagree with the way you went about it, not with the fact that you did it,' she continued in obvious frustration.

He gave a cool nod. 'Again, your objection is duly noted.'

'Right. Okay.' Mac didn't quite know what to do or say now that she'd voiced her protest over the replacement of her broken window.

She should have just telephoned Jonas and told him what she thought of him rather than coming back into town to speak to him personally. She certainly shouldn't—as he had already pointed out so mockingly—have followed him home!

The wisest thing to do now would be to get back on her motorbike and drive back home. Unwisely, Mac knew she wasn't yet ready to do that...

Just looking at Jonas, his dark hair once again ruffled by the breeze outside, the hard arrogance of his face clearly visible in the brightly lit car park, was enough to make her knees go weak. To remind her of the way he had kissed and touched her earlier today. To make her long for him to kiss and touch her in that way again.

To make her question whether that wasn't the very reason she had come here in the first place...

Jonas had been watching the different emotions flickering across Mac's expressive face. First the fading of her anger, which was replaced by confusion and uncertainty. And now he could see those emotions replaced by an unmistakable hunger in those smoky-grey eyes as she looked at him so intently...

A hunger he fully reciprocated. 'I intend to have several glasses of wine as soon as I get up to my apartment—would you care to join me?' he offered huskily.

She visibly swallowed. 'That's probably not a good idea.'

Again, here and now, Jonas was more than willing to go with a bad idea. His body physically ached from the hours he had already spent aroused by this woman today; the thought of an evening and night suffering the same discomfort did not appeal to him in the slightest. Besides, he really did want to see her perfect little bottom in those skin-tight leathers! 'Half a glass of wine isn't going to do you any harm, Mac.'

'Isn't it?'

Maybe it was, Jonas acknowledged with dark humour. If he had anything to do or say about it. 'Scared, Mac?' he taunted.

Her cheeks became flushed. 'Now you're deliberately challenging me into agreeing to go up to your apartment with you!'

He gave her an amused smile. 'Is it working?'

Mac knew that her temptation to go up to Jonas's apartment with him had very little to do with annoyance. Just talking with him like this made her nerve endings tingle, the low timbre of his voice sending little quivers of awareness up her nape and down the length of her spine, the fine hairs on her arms standing to attention, and her skin feeling as if it were covered in goose-bumps. She also felt uncomfortably hot, a heat she knew had nothing to do with the leathers she was wearing to keep out the early evening chill, and everything to do with being so physically aware of Jonas.

All of which told Mac she would be a fool to go anywhere she would be completely alone—and vulnerable to her own churning emotions—with Jonas.

Except she ached to be alone with him.

She nodded abruptly. 'I— Fine. Will it be safe to leave my helmet down here with my bike?'

'I'm sure your bike and helmet will be perfectly safe left down here,' Jonas assured her.

The implication being that it was Mac's own safety, once she was alone with him in his apartment, that she ought to be worried about.

CHAPTER SIX

MAC TURNED TO look at Jonas as he fell into step slightly behind her as she crossed the car park to the lift that would take them up to his apartment. Only to quickly turn away again, her cheeks flaring with heated colour, as she saw the way he was unashamedly watching the gentle swaying of her hips and bottom as she walked.

He eyed her unapologetically as he stood beside her to punch in the security code that opened the lift doors and allowed the two of them to step inside. 'You shouldn't wear tight leathers if you don't want men to look at you!' He pressed the penthouse button.

Mac looked up at him reprovingly as the lift began to ascend. 'I wear them for extra safety if I should come off the bike, not for men to look at. And you know how hot *you* are on safety,' she prodded.

'Hot would seem to be the appropriate word,' Jonas teased.

Mac's cheeks felt more heated than ever at the knowledge that Jonas thought she looked hot in her biking gear. 'Perhaps we should just change the subject.'

'Perhaps we should.' He nodded, blue eyes openly laughing at her.

Mac turned away to stare fixedly at the grey metal doors until they opened onto the penthouse floor. The lights came on automatically as they stepped straight into what was obviously the sitting-room—or perhaps one of them?—of Jonas's huge apartment.

It had exactly the sort of impersonal ultra-modern décor that Mac had expected, mainly in black and white with chrome, with touches of red to alleviate the austerity. The walls were painted a cool white, with black and chrome furniture, with cushions in several shades of red on the sofa and chairs, and several black and white rugs on the highly polished black-wood floor.

Mac hated it on sight!

'Very nice,' she murmured unenthusiastically.

Jonas had seen the wince on Mac's face before she donned the mask of social politeness. 'I allowed an interior designer free rein with the décor in here when I moved in six months ago,' he admitted ruefully. 'Awful, isn't it?' He grimaced as he strode further into the room.

Mac followed slowly. 'If you don't like it, why haven't you changed it?'

He shrugged. 'I couldn't see the point when I shall be moving out again soon.'

'Oh?' She turned to look at him. 'Is that why you haven't bothered to put up any Christmas decorations, either?'

Jonas never bothered to put up Christmas decorations. What was the point? Only he lived here, with the occasional visitor, so why bother with a lot of tacky decorations that only gathered dust, before they had to be taken down again? For Jonas, Christmas was, and always had been, just a time to be suffered through, while everyone else seemed to overeat and indulge in needless sentimentality. In fact, Jonas usually made a point of disappearing to the warmth of a Caribbean island for the whole of the holidays, and, although he hadn't made any plans to do so yet, he doubted that this year would be any different from previous ones.

'No,' Jonas said shortly. Mac really did look good in those figure-hugging leathers, he acknowledged privately as once again he felt what was fast becoming a familiar hardening of his thighs. 'Come through to the kitchen and I'll open a bottle of wine,' he invited briskly before leading the way through to the adjoining room.

He had designed the kitchen himself, the cathedral-style ceiling oak-beamed using beams that had originally come from an eighteenth-century cottage, with matching oak kitchen cabinets, all the modern conveniences such as a fridge-freezer and a dishwasher hidden behind those cabinets, with a weathered oak table in the middle of the room surrounded by four chairs, and copper pots hanging conveniently beside the green Aga.

It was a warm and comfortable room as opposed to the coolly impersonal sitting-room. The kitchen was where Jonas felt most at ease, and was where he usually sat and read the newspapers or did paperwork on the evenings he was at home.

Although he wasn't too sure any more about inviting Mac McGuire into his inner sanctum…

'Much better,' she murmured approvingly. 'Did you design this yourself?'

'Yes.'

'I thought so.'

Jonas raised dark brows. 'Why?'

She gave an awkward shrug. 'It's—warmer, than the other room.'

He scowled. 'Warmer?'

'More lived-in,' she amended.

Jonas continued to look at her for several long seconds before giving an abrupt nod. 'Make yourself comfortable,' he invited and moved to take a bottle of Chablis Premier Cru from the cooler before deftly opening it and pouring some of the delicious fruity wine into two glasses.

Mac still wasn't sure about being in Jonas's apartment at all, let alone making herself comfortable. And from the frown now on Jonas's brow she thought maybe he was regretting having invited her, too.

She sat down gingerly on one of the four chairs placed about the oak table. 'I'll just drink my half a glass of wine and then go.'

Jonas placed the glass on the table in front of her. 'What's your hurry?'

She nervously moistened her lips with the tip of her tongue as he stood far too close to her, only to immediately stop again as she saw the intensity with which Jonas was watching the movement. 'I just think it would be better if I don't overstay my welcome.' Her hand was shaking slightly as she reached out to pick up the glass and take a sip of the cool wine.

Jonas smiled slightly. 'Better for whom?'

She lifted one shoulder delicately. 'Both of us, I would have thought.'

'Maybe we're both thinking too much,' he murmured broodingly. 'Have you eaten dinner yet?'

Mac looked at him sharply. 'Not yet, no.' Surely he wasn't

about to repeat his earlier suggestion that the two of them go out to dinner together?

'I only had a few prawns for lunch,' he reminded her ruefully. 'How about you?'

'I had a piece of toast when I got home. But I'm hardly dressed for going out to dinner, Jonas.'

'Who said anything about going out?' He looked at her quizzically.

Mac felt an uncomfortable surge—of what?—in her chest. Trepidation? Fear? Or anticipation? Or could it be a combination of all three of those things? Whichever it was, Mac didn't think she should stay here alone with Jonas in his apartment any longer than she absolutely had to.

'It's very kind of you to offer—'

'How polite you are all of a sudden, Mac,' Jonas cut in. 'If you don't want to have dinner with me then just have the guts to come out and say so, damn it!' His eyes glittered darkly.

She gave a pained frown. 'It isn't a question of not wanting to have dinner with you, Jonas—'

'Then what is it a question of?' he demanded harshly.

Mac swallowed hard. 'I'm not sure I belong here...'

Jonas scowled. 'What the hell does that mean?'

She gave an awkward shrug. 'I— This apartment is way out of my stratosphere. That bottle of wine you just opened probably cost what some people earn in a week.'

'And?'

'I am what I am. How I am. I hate dressing up in fancy clothes and "being seen".' She winced. 'I've already been through one experience where a man thought I would make a nice trophy to show off on his arm at parties—'

'And you think that's what I want, too?' Jonas asked.

Mac looked a little confused. 'I'm not really sure what you want from me.'

'Then that makes two of us,' Jonas told her with a sigh. 'For some inexplicable reason you have a strange effect on me, Mary "Mac" McGuire.' His gaze held hers as he reached out and took the wine glass from her slightly trembling fingers, placing it on the table beside his own before grasping Mac's arms to pull her slowly to her feet so that she stood only inches away from him.

Jonas looked down at her searchingly, noting the almost feverish glitter in those smoky grey eyes, the flush to her cheeks, and the unevenness of her breathing through slightly parted lips. Parted lips that were begging to be kissed.

His expression was grim as he resisted that dangerous temptation. 'I'm going through to my bedroom now to change out of my suit. If you decide you don't want to stay and help me cook dinner then I suggest you leave before I get back.' He released her abruptly before turning on his heel and going out of the room in the direction of his bedroom further down the hallway.

Mac was still trembling somewhat as she stood alone in the kitchen. She should do as Jonas suggested and leave before he came back. She knew that she should. Yet she didn't want to. What she wanted to do was stay right here and spend the evening cooking dinner with him before they sat down together to eat it in this warm and comfortable kitchen…

Except she knew that Jonas wasn't suggesting they just cook and eat dinner together. Her remaining here would mean she was also agreeable to repeating their earlier shared kisses.

Mac sat down abruptly, totally undecided about what to

do. She should go. But she didn't want to. She knew she shouldn't allow that explosive passion with Jonas at the restaurant to happen again. But she wanted to!

She was still sitting there pondering her dilemma when Jonas came back into the kitchen, her breath catching in her throat as she saw him casually dressed for the first time. The thin black cashmere sweater was moulded to wide shoulders and the flatness of his chest and stomach, jeans that were faded from age and wear rather than designer-styled to be that way sat low down on his hips and emphasised the muscled length of his legs, and his feet were as bare as her own had been earlier when Bob Jenkins had arrived at the warehouse to replace her broken window. They were long and somehow graceful feet, their very bareness seeming to increase the intimacy of the situation.

Jonas looked everything that was tall, dark, and most definitely dangerous!

Mac raised startled eyes. 'I decided to stay long enough to help you cook dinner at least.'

Jonas's enigmatic expression, as he stood in the doorway, gave away none of his thoughts. 'Did you?'

She stood up quickly, already regretting that decision as she felt the rising sexual tension in the room, her pulse actually racing.

Even breathing was becoming difficult. 'Would you like me to help prepare the vegetables or something?' she offered lamely.

Jonas very much doubted that Mac wanted to hear what he would have liked to ask her to do at this particular moment. He had never before even thought about sitting down on one of the kitchen chairs with a woman's naked thighs straddled either side of him as he surged up into the heat of her, but the idea certainly had appeal right now. Making love to Mac anywhere appealed to him right now!

'Or something,' he murmured self-derisively as he made himself walk across to the refrigerator and open the door to look inside at the contents. 'I have the makings of a vegetable and chicken stir-fry if that appeals?' He looked at her enquiringly.

'That sounds fine.'

Jonas was frowning slightly as he straightened. 'Wouldn't you be more comfortable out of those leathers? Unless of course you aren't wearing anything underneath?' he added mockingly. 'In which case, neither of us is going to be comfortable once you've taken them off!'

It was time to put a stop to this right now, Mac decided. They hadn't even got as far as cooking dinner yet and already Jonas was talking about taking her clothes off!

'Of course I'm wearing something underneath,' she said, scowling at Jonas's deliberate teasing, sitting down to remove her boots before unzipping the leathers and taking them off to reveal she was wearing a long-sleeved white t-shirt and snug-fitting jeans above black socks. 'Satisfied?' she challenged as she stood up to lay her leathers over one of the kitchen chairs and place her heavy boots beside it.

'Not hardly,' Jonas murmured.

'Jonas!'

'Mac?' He raised innocent brows.

She drew in a deep, controlling breath. 'Just tell me what vegetables you want me to wash and cut up,' she muttered bad-temperedly.

'Yes, ma'am!' he shot back.

To Mac's surprise they worked quite harmoniously together as they prepared and then cooked the food, sitting down at the table to eat it not half an hour later. 'You said you'll be moving from here soon?' she reminded Jonas curiously as she looked across the table at him.

He nodded as he put his fork down on his plate and drank some of his wine before answering her. 'By this time next year we should be neighbours.'

Mac's eyes widened. 'You're moving into the apartment complex next to me once it's finished being built?'

Jonas didn't think she could have sounded any more horrified if he had said he was actually moving in with her. 'That's the plan, yes,' he confirmed dryly. 'Unless, of course, you decide to sell and move out, after all.'

Her mouth firmed. 'No, I can safely assure you that I have no intention of ever doing that.'

Jonas frowned. 'Why the hell not?'

'It's difficult to explain.'

'Try,' he invited grimly.

Mac frowned. 'The warehouse belonged to my great-grandfather originally, then to my grandfather. Years ago my great-grandfather owned a small fleet of boats, for delivering cargos to other parts of England. Obviously long before we had the huge container trucks that clog up the roads nowadays.' She chewed distractedly on her bottom lip.

Jonas's gaze was riveted on those tiny white teeth nibbling on the fullness of her bottom lip, that ache returning to his thighs as he easily imagined being the one doing the biting...

For the moment Mac seemed unaware of the heated intensity of his gaze. 'I spent a lot of time there with my grandfather when I was a child, and when he died he left it to me,' she finished with a shrug.

Jonas forced himself to drag his gaze from the sensual

fullness of her lips. 'So you're saying you want to keep it because it has sentimental value?'

'Something like that, yes.'

'Your grandfather didn't want to leave the property to your parents?'

It really was difficult for Mac to explain the affinity that had existed between her grandfather and herself. How he had understood the love and affection she felt for the rambling warehouse beside the river. How living and working there now made Mac feel that she still had that connection to her grandfather. 'My parents had already moved out of London to live in Devon when my grandfather died, and so didn't want or need it.'

'No siblings for you to share with?'

'No. You?' Mac asked with interest, deciding she had probably talked about herself enough for one evening.

Jonas's mouth thinned. 'I believe my parents considered that one mistake was enough.'

Mac gasped, not quite sure what to say in answer to a statement like that. 'I'm sure they didn't think of you as a mistake—'

'Then you would be wrong, Mac,' he said dryly. 'My parents were both only nineteen when they got married, and then it was only because my mother was expecting me. She would have been better off—we all would have—if she had either got rid of the baby or settled for being a single mother.' He finished drinking the wine in his glass, offering to refill Mac's glass before refilling his own when she shook her head in refusal.

Mac had continued to eat while they talked, but she gave up all pretence of that after Jonas's comment that his mother should have got rid of him rather than marry his father!

Jonas looked bitter. 'I have no doubts that your own child-hood was one of love and indulgence with parents and a family who loved you?'

'Yes,' she admitted with slight discomfort.

Jonas gave a hard smile. 'Don't look so apologetic, Mac. It's the way it should be, after all,' he said bleakly. 'Unfor-tunately, it so often isn't. I believe it took a couple of years for the novelty to wear off and the cracks to start appearing in my own parents' marriage, then ten years or more for them to realise they couldn't stand the sight of each other. Or me,' he added flatly.

Mac gave a pained wince. 'I'm sure you're wrong about that, Jonas.'

'I'm sure your romantic little heart wants me to be wrong about that, Mac,' he corrected.

He meant his mockery of her to wound, and it did, but Mac's 'romantic little heart' also told her that Jonas's taunts hid the pain and disillusionment that had helped to mould him into the hard and resilient man he was today. That had made him into a man who rejected all the softer emo-tions, such as love, in favour of making a success of his life through his own hard work and sheer determination. That had made him into a man who didn't even bother to put up Christmas decorations in his apartment...

'Your parents are divorced now?' she asked.

'Yes, thank God,' he replied. 'After years of basically ignoring each other, and me, they finally separated when I was thirteen and divorced a couple of years later.'

Mac didn't even like to think of the damage they had done in those thirteen years, not only to each other, but most especially to Jonas, the child caught in the middle of all that hostility.

'Which one did you live with after the separation?'

'Neither of them,' Jonas bit out with satisfaction. 'I had my own grandfather I went to live with. My father's father. Although I doubt Joseph was the warm and fuzzy type your own grandfather sounds,' he added.

Mac doubted it too, if Jonas had actually called his grandfather by his first name, and if the expression on Jonas's face was anything to go by!

Jonas would have found Mac's obvious dismay amusing if it weren't his own childhood they were discussing. Something that was unusual in itself when Jonas usually went out of his way not to talk about himself. But it was better that Mac knew all there was to know about him now. To be made aware that falling in love and getting married wasn't, and never would be, a part of his future. Jonas had seen firsthand the pain and disillusionment that supposed emotion caused, and he wanted no part of it. Not now or ever.

'You said earlier that you didn't belong in these surroundings,' Jonas reminded her. 'Well, neither do I. My parents were poor, and my grandfather Joseph was a rough, tough man who worked on a building site all his life. I've worked hard for what I have, Mac.'

'I didn't mean to imply—'

'Didn't you?' He gave her a grim smile. 'I probably owe part of my success to the fact that my grandfather had no time for slackers,' he continued relentlessly. 'You either worked to pay your way or you got out. I decided to work. My parents had both remarried by the time I was sixteen and disappeared off into the sunset—'

'Jonas!' Mac choked as she sat forward to place her hand over his as it lay curled into a fist on the tabletop.

He pulled his hand away sharply, determined to finish

this now that he had started. Mac should know exactly what she was getting into if she decided to become involved with him. Exactly! 'In between working with my grandfather before and after school and cooking for the two of us, I also worked hard to get my A levels. Then I worked my way through university and gained a Masters degree in Mathematics before going into architecture. I worked my ba—'

He broke off with an apologetic grimace. 'I worked hard for one of the best architecture companies in London for a couple of years, before I was lucky enough to have a couple of my designs taken up by a man called Joel Baxter. Have you heard of him?'

Mac's eyes were wide. 'The man who makes billions out of computer games and software?'

'That's the one,' Jonas confirmed. 'Strangely, we became friends. He convinced me I should go out on my own, that I needed to take control of the whole construction of the building and not just the design of it, that I would never make money working for someone else. It was a struggle to start with, but I took his advice, and, as they say, the rest is history.' He gave a dismissive shrug.

Yes, it was. Mac was aware of the well-publicised overnight success of Buchanan Construction—which obviously hadn't been any such thing but was simply the result of Jonas's own hard work and determination to succeed.

She moistened dry lips. 'Are you and Joel Baxter still friends?'

Jonas's expression softened slightly. 'Yeah. Joel's one of the good guys.'

Mac brightened slightly. 'And your parents, surely they must be proud of you? Of what you've achieved?'

Jonas's eyes hardened to icy chips. 'I haven't seen either

one of them since my father attended my grandfather's funeral when I was nineteen.'

Mac looked at him incredulously. 'That's—that's unbelievable!'

He looked at her coldly. 'Is it?'

'Well. Yes.' She shook her head. 'Look at you now, all that you've achieved, surely—'

'I didn't say that they hadn't wanted to see me again, Mac,' Jonas cut in. 'Once Buchanan Construction became known as a multimillion-pound worldwide enterprise, they both crawled out of the woodwork to claim their only lost son,' he recalled bitterly.

Mac swallowed hard. 'And?'

'And I didn't want anything to do with either of them,' he said emotionlessly.

Mac could understand, after all that had gone before, why Jonas felt the way that he did about seeing his parents again. Understand his feelings on the subject, maybe, but accepting it, when the situation between Jonas and his parents remained unresolved, was something else. Or perhaps he considered that just not seeing or having anything to do with his parents was the solution?

She looked sad. 'They've missed out on so much.'

Jonas lifted an unconcerned shoulder. 'I suppose that depends upon your perspective.'

Mac's perspective was that Jonas's parents had obviously been too young when they married each other and had Jonas, but it in no way excused their behaviour towards him. He had been an innocent child caught up in the battleground that had become their marriage.

Was it any wonder that Jonas was so hard and cynical?

That he chose to concentrate all his energies on business relationships rather than personal ones?

'Don't go wasting any of your sympathy on me, Mac,' he grated suddenly as he obviously clearly read the emotions on her face. 'You told me earlier what you didn't want, and the only reason I've told you these about myself is so that you'll know the things *I* don't want.' He paused, his mouth tightening. 'So that you understand there would be no future, no happy ever after, if you chose to have a relationship with me.'

She raised startled eyes to look searchingly across the table at Jonas as he looked back at her so intensely. She saw and recognised the raw purpose in his gaze. The underlying warmth of seduction and sensuality in those hard and unblinking blue eyes.

CHAPTER SEVEN

THE CHAIR SCRAPED noisily on the tiled floor as Mac suddenly stood up. 'I think it's time I was going.'

'Running scared, after all, Mac?' Jonas mocked, watching her through narrowed lids as she turned agitatedly to pick up her leathers.

She dropped the leathers back onto the chair and faced him, her chin raised challengingly. 'I'm not scared, Jonas, I just don't think I can give you what you want.'

'Oh, I think you can give me exactly what I want, Mac.' He stood up slowly to move around the table to where she stood determinedly unmoving as she looked up at him. 'Exactly what I want,' he repeated as he reached out to curve his arms about her waist and pull her firmly up against him so that she could feel the evidence of what it was he wanted from her. All that Jonas wanted from her or any woman.

Mac gasped as she felt the hardness of his arousal pressed revealingly against her. She felt an instant echoing of that arousal in her own body as heat coursed through her breasts to pool hotly between her thighs.

God, she seriously wanted this man! Wanted him so

badly that she ached with it. Longed to strip the clothes from both their bodies and have him surge hard and powerfully inside her and make her forget everything else but the desire that had burned so strongly between them ever since they'd met again at her exhibition on Saturday evening.

She gave a desperate shake of her head. 'I don't do casual relationships, Jonas.'

His face remained hard and determined. 'Have you ever tried?'

She swallowed. 'No. But—' Her protest ceased the moment that Jonas's mouth claimed hers in a kiss so raw with hunger that she could only cling to the hard strength of his shoulders as she returned the heated hunger of that kiss.

Jonas felt wrapped in the luscious smell and heat that was Mac, even as his hand moved unerringly to that strip of flesh between her T-shirt and jeans that had been tantalising him all evening. He needed to know if those full breasts were bare beneath that thin cotton top, and the first touch of her creamy flesh against Jonas's fingertips made him groan low in his throat.

Mac was pure heat. Silk and sensuality as his hand moved beneath that T-shirt and up the length of her bare spine. Jonas felt the quivering vibration of her response in the depths of his body as he pressed her closer against him. He deepened the kiss, his arousal surging in response as his tongue moved skilfully across the heat of Mac's lips and then into the hot, moist vortex beneath.

She took him in, deeper, and then deeper still, as her hands moved up Jonas's shoulders to his nape, her fingers becoming entangled in the thickness of his hair as her tongue touched lightly against his, testing, questioning.

Jonas instantly retreated, encouraging, enticing, giving another low groan as that hot and moist tongue shyly followed.

He stroked her satiny flesh beneath her T-shirt, closer, ever closer to the firm mounds that he now knew without a doubt were bared to his touch, loving the way Mac arched into him as his hand moved to cup and stroke one of those uptilted breasts, capturing the soft cry that escaped her lips with his mouth as his fingers grazed across the swollen nipple.

Mac had never felt this way before and felt lost to everything but Jonas as he continued to kiss and touch her, mouth devouring hers, sipping, tasting her, with deep and drugging kisses that drove her wild with longing. While his tongue brushed lightly over the sensitivity of her lips and teeth, his hand— Oh, God, what the touch of Jonas's hard and slightly calloused hand against her naked flesh was doing to her...

Her whole body felt hot, sensitised, and she gasped and writhed, the moisture flooding between her thighs as Jonas rolled her nipple between thumb and finger. Gently, and then harder, the almost pleasure-pain like nothing Mac had ever experienced before.

Her neck arched when Jonas dragged his mouth from hers, his breath hot and moist against her skin as he left a trail of kisses across her cheek, the line of her jaw, before moving down her throat to the hollows beneath, tongue dipping, tasting, as he seemed to draw in the drugging scent of her arousal with his every breath.

Mac could only cling to the power of his shoulders as he swept her along in a tidal wave of desire so strong she felt as if Jonas were her only anchor. All that mattered. Her only reality.

Jonas had never wanted a woman as much as he did Mac. Had never hungered like this before. Had never needed to be inside any woman so badly that he literally seemed to blaze with that need, every cell and nerve in his body aching for her, robbing him of his usual self-control as he longed to feel her hands on him.

His mouth moved back to claim hers in a kiss that was almost savage, Mac offering no protest as Jonas grasped the bottom of her T-shirt to tug it upwards, only breaking that kiss long enough to pull the article of clothing over her head and throw it down on the floor.

He could barely breathe, his eyes glittering darkly blue as he looked down at her tiny breasts. Their nakedness peaked shyly through that long ebony hair. 'My God, you're beautiful,' Jonas groaned before lowering his head to capture one of those rosy red nipples into the heat of his mouth, intending to drink his fill, to wrest every last vestige of pleasure from her hot and delicious body.

Mac gasped at the first touch of Jonas's lips against her breast, her back tensing now as she arched into him, cradling his head to her as he drew her deeper, ever deeper into his mouth, tasting her sweetness, her heat, the heady smell of her arousal driving him mad with need.

He raised his head to look down at the nipple that had swollen in size, gaze intent as he turned the attention of his lips and tongue to her other breast. At the same time he released the fastening on her jeans to slip his hands beneath the material and grasp her hips before sliding further back to cup the perfectly rounded cheeks of her bottom encased in lacy panties.

Jonas looked up at Mac with darkened and hungry eyes. 'Touch me, Mac,' he growled. He deliberately, slowly, flicked his tongue against that hard and delicious nipple, watching her response as the pleasure vibrated, resonated through the whole of her body.

Mac had never felt so sensitised to the touch of another, so aroused and needy, her body a single burning ache as she moved eagerly to return those caresses, tugging Jonas's jumper up and off his body to reveal the hard and muscled perfection of his chest before she placed her hands flat against it. He stood immobile in front of her, that glittering blue gaze hidden beneath hooded lids, but the husky exclamation of pleasure he gave as Mac touched him for the first time encouraged her, incited her to explore all of that hard, silken flesh.

He felt like steel encased in velvet, the tiny nipples hidden amongst the light covering of chest hair standing to attention as Mac ran her fingers over them delicately. She wondered curiously whether Jonas would feel the same pleasure as she did if she were to kiss him there.

'Oh, yes, Mac!' Jonas moaned at the first flick of her tongue against that tiny enticing pebble, his hand moving to curve about her nape as he threaded his fingers in the dark tangle of her hair and held her against him, encouraging, demanding.

Mac felt empowered, exhilarated with the knowledge that she could give Jonas the same pleasure he gave her, continuing to flick her tongue against him there as her hands roamed restlessly across the broad width of his back and down the muscled curve of his spine.

Mac's mouth moved down his chest as her fingers moved lightly along the length of the erection pressing against his jeans, able to feel the heat of him through the material as he grew even harder as she touched him.

Jonas stood unmoving beneath the onslaught of those caresses, barely breathing, body tense, hands clenched into fists at his sides as he fought grimly to maintain control as Mac's lips and hands drove him almost wild with need. Knowing he was losing the battle as that image he'd had earlier, of him sitting on a chair with Mac's naked thighs wrapped about him, caused his thighs to throb and surge in painful need, his jeans too uncomfortable, too tight to contain him any longer.

'We need to be somewhere more comfortable,' he growled before he bent down and swung Mac up into his arms. He moved out of the warm kitchen, down the hallway to his bedroom, kicking the door closed behind them. He walked over to the bed and placed Mac on top of the downy duvet before turning to switch on the soft glow of the bedside light.

He stood looking down at her for several seconds, eyes dark as he looked at that cascade of straight ebony-black hair spread across his pillows, her eyes bright, cheeks flushed, lips slightly swollen from the hunger of their kisses, and then down to the swell of those perfect breasts.

Jonas drew in a harsh breath as he gazed at those orbs with their rosy-hued nipples jutting out firmly, and then down over the curving indentation of her narrow waist, a tantalising glimpse of her lacy panties visible beneath her unzipped jeans.

He sat on the side of the bed, his gaze briefly holding hers before lowering as he slowly tugged those jeans down to fully reveal those white panties with the soft curls dark behind the lace, and the long length of her legs.

Mac was barely breathing as she looked up into the dark

intensity of Jonas's face as his gaze slowly, hungrily, devoured every inch of her, from her head down to her toes.

His face was flushed as that glittering blue gaze returned to meet hers. 'I'm think I'm going to have to make love to you until you beg for me to stop,' he muttered gruffly.

Mac longed for that, ached for it, but at the same time she trembled at the depth of the desire she could feel flowing between them. 'I hope you aren't going to be disappointed,' she whispered.

Those blue eyes narrowed. 'Why should I be disappointed?'

Mac shook her head. 'I'm not experienced, and—I— I don't have any protection,' she warned, not wanting to break the spell of the moment, but only too aware now of the reason Jonas's parents had married each other. Of how much he would despise any woman stupid enough to make the same mistake with him.

'You aren't on the pill?' Jonas slid open the drawer in the bedside cabinet and took out a small foil packet.

Her cheeks were flushed. 'I— No, there's never been any need.'

Jonas looked at her suspiciously as an incredulous thought suddenly occurred to him. 'You can't possibly still be a virgin?'

'Why can't I? Jonas...?' Mac frowned her uncertainty as he stood up abruptly.

Jonas stared down at her disbelievingly—accusingly— for several long seconds, before turning away to run an agitated hand through the thickness of his hair. A virgin! Jonas couldn't believe it; Mac McGuire, a beautiful woman in her late twenties, who looked and dressed like a Bohemian, was a virgin!

He turned back. 'And exactly when were you going to tell me that interesting little piece of information?' he bit out angrily. 'Or were you just going to let me find out for myself once it was too late for me to do anything about it?'

Mac gave a dazed shake of her head. 'I don't understand,' she whispered.

Jonas glared at her. 'Virgin or not, you can't be that naïve!'

Mac was too stunned by the sudden tension between them to know what to think. 'I don't believe I'm naïve at all,' she said slowly as she sat up, her hair falling forwards to cover the nakedness of her breasts. 'I thought you re-alised after I told you about my one youthful disaster of a relationship—Jonas, what difference does it make whether or not I've had other lovers?'

'All the difference in the world to me,' Jonas assured her harshly.

Mac gave a pained frown as she wrapped her arms de-fensively about the bareness of her knees. 'But *why* does it?'

'Because I have no intention of being any woman's first lover, that's why.' His jaw was tightly clenched.

'All women have a first time with someone—'

'Yours isn't going to be with me,' he reiterated.

'Most men would be only too pleased to be a woman's first lover!' Tears of humiliation glittered in her eyes as she glared back at him and she resolutely blinked them away. She refused to cry in front of him!

'Not this man,' he said fervently.

Mac couldn't believe they were having this conversation. Couldn't believe that Jonas was refusing to make love to her just because she was a virgin!

'Why is that, Jonas?' she challenged. 'Do you think that

I'm making such a grand gesture because I already imagine myself in love with you? Or do you think I'm trying to trap you in some way?' Her eyes widened as she saw from the cold stiffening of Jonas's expression, the icy glitter of his eyes, that was *exactly* what he thought—and so obviously feared. 'You arrogant louse!' she scorned furiously.

'No doubt,' he acknowledged. 'But I'm sure you'll agree that it's better if this stops now?'

'Oh, don't worry, Jonas, it's stopped,' she said scathingly as she moved to sit on the side of the bed, grabbed up her jeans from the carpeted floor and started pulling them back on.

'I'm going back to the kitchen; I suggest you join me there once you've finished dressing. You might need this.' He took a black T-shirt out of the tall chest of drawers and threw it on the bed beside her before turning on his heel and leaving the bedroom, almost slamming the door behind him.

Mac stilled, unsure as to whether the tears now finally falling hotly and unchecked down her cheeks were of anger or humiliation, too confused still at the way their heated lovemaking had turned into an exchange of insults.

Did Jonas really imagine Mac was somehow trying to trap him into a relationship with her by giving him her virginity? Into making him feel responsible for her because he'd become her first lover?

If that was what he thought, what he was desperately trying to avoid, then Jonas didn't deserve her tears. He didn't deserve anything but her pity.

Unless you're in love with him, after all? a little voice deep within her wanted to know.

No. She was most definitely not. Mac had felt closer to Jonas this evening. Felt she understood him and his motivations better after hearing about his parents' marriage and his own childhood. And she had physically wanted him. That was undeniable. But none of those things added up to her being in love with him.

Not even a little bit? the same annoying voice persisted.

No, not even a little bit! she answered it firmly.

Jonas was arrogant. Cold. And his behaviour just now proved that he was also completely undeserving of her emotions or her body.

Jonas had pulled his jumper back on and was sitting at the oak kitchen table drinking some of the wine when Mac came back into the room, his gaze narrowing as he took in her appearance in his T-shirt. It was far too big for her, so long it reached almost down to her knees, the shoulder seams hanging halfway down her arms—and yet, somehow, she still managed to look sexy as hell.

Nothing at all like the virgin she was.

Jonas couldn't have known about her inexperience. He would never have guessed it from how she'd responded to him so passionately, so eagerly...

He scowled across at her broodingly. 'Having dinner together was obviously no more successful than our attempt at having lunch.' The food remained half eaten and cold on the plates.

Mac strode across the room to grab her own T-shirt from the back of the chair where Jonas had draped it. 'At least I know who to see now if I ever want to lose weight,' she retorted.

Jonas's jaw tightened. 'You're too thin already.'

Her eyes flashed a deep, smoky grey. 'I didn't hear you complaining a few minutes ago!'

He raised dark brows, his smile sardonic. 'I wasn't stating a preference now either, only fact.'

Mac wanted to slap that mocking smile off his face. No—she wanted to pummel his chest with her fists until she actually hurt him. As he had hurt her when he'd turned away from her so coldly.

She held her T-shirt protectively in front of her. 'Is there a bathroom I can use to change back into my own top?'

He kept one mocking brow raised. 'Isn't it a little late for modesty when I've already seen you naked?'

Her cheeks warmed hotly. 'Not completely!'

Jonas gave a shrug. 'The part you're going to expose, I have.'

Mac's mouth set determinedly. 'Would you just tell me where the bathroom is?'

'The nearest one is down the hallway, first door on the right,' he told her before turning away.

It was a cold and uninterested dismissal, Mac realised with a frown as she turned and walked out of the kitchen. Anyone would think that being a virgin at her age was akin to having the plague! Maybe in his eyes it was...

She wasted no time in admiring the luxurious bathroom as she quickly pulled off Jonas's overlarge T-shirt and replaced it with her own white one, a glance in the mirror over the double sink showing her that her hair was in too much of a mess for her to do any more than plait it loosely in an effort to smooth it into some sort of order.

Her face was very pale, her eyes huge and slightly red from the tears she had shed earlier, her lips full and swollen from the intensity of the kisses she had shared with Jonas.

Most of all she looked...sad.

Which wouldn't do at all, Mac decided as she set her

shoulders determinedly before leaving the bathroom to go back to the kitchen. She was a mature and confident woman—even if, horror or horrors, she was still a virgin!—and she intended to act like one.

Jonas was still sitting at the table surrounded by the remains of their meal, although the level of wine in his glass had definitely gone down in her absence.

Mac placed his T-shirt on the back of one of the other chairs. 'Thank you,' she said stiltedly, her face averted as she sat down to begin pulling on her leathers.

This, putting her clothes back on in a strained and awkward silence, had to be one of the most embarrassing and humiliating experiences of her entire life. More embarrassing than if she and Jonas had actually made love completely? Probably not, she acknowledged with a self-derisive grimace, as she could only imagine his reaction if he had discovered her virginity when it was too late for him to pull back.

Once again Jonas watched Mac broodingly through narrowed lids, easily able to read the self-disgust in her expression, the underlying hurt. Damn it, he had never meant to hurt her. Hadn't wanted to hurt her. He just knew he had nothing to offer a woman like Mac. Beautiful. Emotional. Virginal…

His relationships were always, *always* based on a mutual attraction and physical need. That desire definitely existed between himself and Mac, but the fact that she was still a virgin, and had been willing to give that virginity to him, had also warned him that if they made love together then she would probably want more from him than that. Much more.

Jonas didn't have any more than that to give. Not to Mac or any other woman. But that wasn't her fault.

'I'm sorry.'

She gave him a sharp glance as she straightened from lacing her boots. 'For what?'

Jonas grimaced. 'For allowing things to go as far between us just now as they did. If I had known—'

'If you had known I was a virgin then you wouldn't have invited me up to your apartment at all!' she finished knowingly as she stood to zip up her leathers.

Jonas winced at the bitterness he could hear in her tone. 'None of what happened was premeditated on my part—'

'No?' she challenged.

'No, damn it!' A scowl darkened his brow.

Mac shrugged. 'Don't worry about it, Jonas. Not all men are as fickle as you; I'm pretty sure I can find one who's more than willing to become my first lover. Maybe I'll come back once I have, and we can finish what we started?' she taunted.

Jonas pushed his chair back noisily to stand up. 'Don't be so stupid!' he rasped harshly.

Mac's chin tilted with determination as she looked up at him. 'What's stupid about it?'

'You can't just decide to lose your virginity in that cold-blooded way!'

'Why can't I?'

He shook his head. 'Because it's something too precious to just throw away. It's a gift you should give to a man you care about. That you love.'

Mac felt a clenching in her chest as she acknowledged that she *did* care about Jonas. She didn't think she was in love with him yet—it would be madness on her part to fall in love with him!—but she definitely cared about him.

About the hurt child he had once been, and the disillusioned man he now was.

She looked him straight in the eye. 'I believe that's for me to decide, Jonas, not you.'

'But—'

'I would like to leave now,' she told him flatly.

Jonas stared down at her in obvious frustration. 'Not until you promise me that you aren't going to leave here and do something totally reckless.'

'Like taking a lover?'

'Exactly!'

Mac gave him a pitying glance. 'I don't believe that anything I do in future is any of your business.'

His mouth was set grimly, a nerve pulsing in his tightly clenched jaw. 'If you're really that desperate for a lover—'

'Oh, I'm not desperate, Jonas,' she said coolly. 'Just curious,' she added, deliberately baiting him.

Jonas wanted to shake her. Wanted to grasp the tops of Mac's arms and shake her until her teeth rattled. Except that he didn't dare touch her again. Because he knew that if he did, he wouldn't be able to stop...

He sighed heavily. 'I thought you understood after the things I told you about my childhood. Mac, I'm not the man you need, and I never could be.'

She frowned. 'I don't believe I ever asked you to be anything to me,' she pointed out.

'But you would.' That nerve continued to pulse in his jaw. 'Perhaps you would enjoy the novelty of the relationship at first, the sexual excitement, but eventually you would want more than I have to give you.'

'You know what, Jonas,' she said conversationally, 'I think you're taking an awful lot for granted in assuming that I would have wanted to continue a—a sexual relationship with you after tonight. I mean, who's to say I would actually have enjoyed having sex with you? Or is it that you're under the illusion you're such a great lover that no woman could possibly be left feeling disappointed after sharing your bed?'

Jonas felt the twitch of a smile on his lips as Mac deliberately insulted him. 'That would be a little arrogant of me, wouldn't it?'

'More than a little, I would have said,' she shot back. 'So, how do I get out of here?' She moved pointedly across the room to stand beside the doorway out into the hallway.

This evening had been something of another disaster as far as he and Mac were concerned, Jonas acknowledged ruefully as he preceded her out of the kitchen and walked with her to the lift.

She grimaced once she had stepped inside the lift. 'I'm not sure if I said this before, but thank you for sending Bob over this afternoon to fix my window.'

Jonas had totally forgotten that was the original reason she had followed him home! 'But don't do anything like it again?' he guessed dryly.

'No.'

He nodded. 'That's what I thought. I—If I don't see you again before then—Merry Christmas, Mac.'

She eyed him quizzically. 'And I'd already marked you down as the "bah, humbug" type!'

'I am the "bah, humbug" type,' he admitted with a quirk of his mouth.

Mac nodded as the lift doors began to close. 'Merry Christmas, Jonas.'

Jonas continued to stand in the hallway long after she had

gone down to the car park and no doubt driven away on that powerful motorbike as if the devil himself were at her heels.

He liked Mac, Jonas realised frowningly. Liked the way she looked. Her spirit. Her independence. Her optimism about life and people in general. Most of all he admired her ability to laugh at herself.

Unfortunately, he also knew that allowing himself to like Mac McGuire was as dangerous to the solitary lifestyle he preferred as having a sexual relationship with her would have been.

CHAPTER EIGHT

IT WAS LATE in the morning when Mac parked her four-wheel-drive Jeep next to her motorbike in the garage on the ground floor of the warehouse after arriving back from a three-day pre-Christmas visit to her parents' home in Devon.

She had felt the need to get away for a while after the disastrous and humiliating end to the evening spent with Jonas at his apartment. And as the men had duly arrived the following day to install the alarm system to the warehouse, and the exhibition at the gallery was going well—Jeremy had informed Mac when she spoke to him on the telephone that the paintings were all sold, and the public were pouring in to see them before the exhibition came to a close at Christmas—she was free to do what she wanted for the next few days, at least.

Just as she had hoped, the time spent with her parents—the normality of being teased by her father and going Christmas shopping with her mother—had been the perfect way to put things in her own life back into perspective. For her to decide that her behaviour that evening at Jonas's apartment had been an aberration. A madness she didn't intend ever to repeat. In fact, she had come to the conclusion that ever seeing Jonas Buchanan again would be a mistake...

Which was going to be a little hard for her to do when he was the first person she saw as she rounded the corner from the garage!

Mac's hand tightened about the handle of the holdall she had used to pack the necessary clothing needed for her three days away, her gaze fixed on Jonas as she walked slowly towards him. She unconsciously registered how attractive he looked in a brown leather jacket over a tan-coloured sweater and faded jeans...

Any embarrassment she might have felt at seeing him again was forgotten as she realised he was directing the actions of the two other men, workmen from their clothing, who seemed to be in the process of building a metal tower beside the warehouse. 'What on earth are you doing?' Mac demanded.

'Oh, hell!' Jonas muttered as he turned and saw her, his expression becoming grim. 'I'd hoped to have dealt with this before you got back.'

'Hoped to have dealt with *what*? What on earth...?' Mac stared up at the wooden sides of the warehouse. Her eyes were wide with shock as she took in the electric-pink and fluorescent-green paints that had been sprayed haphazardly over the dark wooden cladding.

'It isn't as bad as it looks...'

'Isn't it?' she questioned sharply, the holdall slipping unnoticed from her fingers as she continued to stare numbly up at that mad kaleidoscope of colour.

'Mac—'

'Don't touch me!' She cringed away as Jonas would have

reached out and grasped her arm. 'Who—? Why—?' She gave a dazed shake of her head. 'When did this happen?'

'I have no idea,' Jonas rasped. 'Some time yesterday evening, we think—'

'Who is *we*?'

'My foreman from the building site next door,' he elaborated. 'He noticed it this morning, and when he didn't receive any reply to his knock on your door he decided to report it to me.'

Mac swallowed hard, feeling slightly nauseous at the thought of someone deliberately vandalising her property. 'Why would anyone do something like this?'

'I don't know.' Jonas sighed heavily.

'Could it be kids this time?'

'Again, I have no idea. These two men are going to paint over it. They should be finished by this evening.' He grimaced. 'I had hoped to have had it done before you got back—'

'I thought I had made it plain the last time we met that I would rather you didn't go around arranging things for me?' Mac reminded him coldly.

Jonas eyed her with a frown, the pallor of her cheeks very noticeable against the red padded body-warmer she wore over a black sweater and black denims. He didn't like seeing the glitter of tears in those smoky-grey eyes, either. But he liked the cold, flat tone of her voice when she spoke to him even less. 'Would you rather I had just left it for you to find when you got home?'

'I have found it when I got home!' Her voice rose slightly, almost shrilly.

Jonas shook his head. 'I wasn't expecting you to be back

just yet; I had hoped it would be later today, or even better, tomorrow morning.'

Those huge grey eyes settled on him suspiciously. 'How did you even know I had gone away?'

Jonas knew he could have lied, prevaricated even, but the suspicion he could read in Mac's expression warned him not to do either of those things. 'The Patels,' he revealed unapologetically. 'Once I had seen the mess, and you obviously weren't at home, I went to their convenience store and asked if they had any idea where you were.'

Those misty grey eyes widened. 'And they just told you I had gone away for a few days?'

He gave a rueful nod. 'Once I'd explained about the vandalism, yes.'

'Tarun always puts a daily newspaper by for me,' Mac muttered absently. 'I cancelled it while I was away.'

Jonas smiled. 'So he told me.'

She sighed and ran a hand through her hair. 'Nothing like this ever happened before I met you—'

'Don't say something you'll only have to apologise for later,' Jonas warned through suddenly gritted teeth.

'Even before,' Mac continued as if he hadn't spoken, 'when your assorted employees came here to try and persuade me into selling the warehouse, nothing like this happened. It's only since actually meeting *you*—'

'I said stop, Mac!' A nerve pulsed in his tightly clenched cheek.

Her gaze narrowed as she focused on him. 'Since meeting you, I've had my window broken and my home vandalised,' she said accusingly. 'And now some helpful soul has decided to redecorate the outside of the warehouse for me.

Bit too much of a coincidence, don't you think, Jonas?' Her eyes glittered with anger now rather than tears.

Jonas had known exactly where Mac was going with this conversation, and had tried to stop her from actually voicing those accusations.

Damn it, he had considered himself well rid of her once she'd left his apartment on Monday evening. He'd had no intention of going near her on a personal level ever again if he could avoid it. Unfortunately, he hadn't been able to avoid coming here, at least, once he'd received the telephone call earlier this morning from his foreman.

He certainly wasn't enjoying being the object of Mac's suspicions. 'Only if you choose to look at it that way,' he bit out icily.

She eyed him challengingly. 'Did you report this to the police?'

Jonas narrowed cold blue eyes. 'I have the distinct feeling that I'm going to be damned if I did, and damned if I didn't.'

Mac raised questioning brows. 'How so?'

'If I did report it then I was probably just covering my own back. If I didn't report it, then again, I'm obviously guilty.'

Mac was feeling sick now that the shock was fading and reaction was setting in. She didn't want Jonas to be in any way involved in this second act of vandalism. It was the last thing she wanted! It was only that the coincidence of it all was so undeniable…

She closed her eyes briefly before opening them again. 'Your men seem to have everything well in hand,' she acknowledged ruefully as she glanced up at the two men now scaling the metal tower with the familiarity of monkeys, pots of paint and brushes in their hands. 'Would you like to come upstairs for some coffee?'

Jonas raised surprised brows. 'Are you sure it's wise to invite the enemy into your camp?'

Mac straightened from picking up the holdall she had dropped minutes ago. 'Have you never heard the saying "keep your friends close, but your enemies even closer"?' she teased.

His mouth tightened. 'I'm not your enemy, Mac.'

'I wasn't being serious, Jonas,' she assured him wearily.

'Strange, I didn't find it in the least funny,' he muttered as he began to follow her up the metal staircase.

Those psychedelic swirls of paint were even more noticeable from the top of the staircase, evidence that the perpetrator had probably stood on the top step in order to spray onto the second and third floor of the building. They had certainly made a mess of the stained dark wood.

But why had they?

Was it just an act of vandalism by kids thinking they were being clever? Or was it something else, something more sinister?

Mac gave a disgruntled snort as she unlocked the door and entered the living area of the warehouse, dropping her holdall just inside the door before going over to the kitchen area to prepare the pot of filtered coffee.

She was so lost in thought that she didn't notice for several seconds that Jonas had closed the door behind him and come to a complete halt. She eyed him curiously. 'Is there something wrong?'

Jonas was completely stunned by the inside of Mac's warehouse. He had never seen anything like this before. It was—

'Jonas?'

He blinked before focusing on Mac as she looked across at him in puzzlement. 'I—' He shook his head. 'This is—'

'Weird?' she finished dryly as she stepped out from behind the breakfast bar that partitioned off the kitchen area from the rest of the living space. 'Odd? Peculiar? A nightmare?' she concluded laughingly.

'I was going to say *fantastic*!' Jonas breathed incredulously as he now looked up at the high ceiling painted like a night sky, with the moon and stars shimmering mysteriously in that darkness.

The rest of the living area was open plan, the four walls painted like the seasons; spring was a blaze of yellow flowers against burgeoning green, summer a deeper green and gorgeous range of rainbow colours, autumn covered the spectrum from gold to russet, and winter was a beautiful white landscape.

The furniture was a mixture of all those colours, one chair gold, and another terracotta, the sofa burnt orange, with several white rugs on the highly polished wooden floor, that flat-screen television Mac had once mentioned tucked away in a corner. The bedroom area was slightly raised and reached by three wooden steps, the cover over the bed a patchwork of colours, a spiral staircase in another corner of the room obviously going up to the studio above.

And in place of honour in front of the huge picture window was a real pine Christmas tree that reached from floor to ceiling, and was decorated with so many baubles it was almost impossible to see the lushness of the branches.

Jonas had never seen anything so unusual—or so beautiful—as Mac's warehouse home. Much as Mac herself was unusual and beautiful? he wondered...

He firmly closed off that avenue of thought as he turned to give her a rueful smile. 'No wonder you didn't like the décor in the sitting-room of my apartment.'

Mac brought over two mugs of coffee and put one of them down on the low bamboo tabletop before carrying her own over to sit down on the sofa, her denim-covered legs neatly tucked beneath her. 'Obviously I prefer to go with the rustic look!' she teased, sipping her coffee.

Jonas picked up the second mug and sat down in the terracotta-coloured chair facing her. 'Is the studio upstairs like this, too?'

'I'll show it to you, if you like.'

Jonas eyed Mac curiously as he sensed the reluctance behind her offer. 'You don't usually show people your studio, do you?' he guessed.

She grimaced. 'Not usually, no.'

And yet she was offering to show it to *him*…

Jonas wasn't sure if he felt privileged or alarmed at the concession, but his curiosity was such that he wanted to see the studio anyway. 'Perhaps after we've drunk our coffee,' he suggested lightly.

'Perhaps,' Mac echoed uneasily, not altogether sure what to do with Jonas now that he was here.

She had only invited him in for coffee because their earlier conversation had been deteriorating into accusations on her part and defensive warnings on Jonas's. But now that he was here, in the intimacy of her home, she was once again aware of that rising sexual tension between them that never seemed to be far from the surface whenever the two of them were together.

Jonas looked very fit and masculine in his casual clothes, and that overlong dark hair was once again slightly ruffled by the cold wind blowing outside, his face as hard and sculptured as a statue Mac had once seen depicting the Archangel Gabriel. As for those fathomless blue eyes…

She turned away abruptly. 'You never did tell me whether or not you had informed the police about this second incident of vandalism in just a few days?'

His mouth tightened. 'I did call them, yes. Two of them arrived about an hour ago and looked the place over. If I understood them correctly, they were of the opinion that the demolishing of the other warehouses around this one has left it rather exposed and so a prime target for bored teenagers wanting to cause mischief.'

Mac was pretty sure that he had understood the police correctly. 'And what's *your* opinion, Jonas?'

His eyes narrowed. 'I think it's more—personal, than that.'

She gave a rueful smile. 'We aren't back to that disgruntled ex-lover theory again, are we?' she said dryly.

Hardly, when Jonas now knew only too well that there had never been a lover in Mac's life, ex or otherwise! Not even the man who had wanted her to be a trophy on his arm to show off at parties…

He gave a tight smile. 'I prefer to go with the jealous rival theory.'

'We've only been out together once,' she taunted. 'And that was something of a disaster, if you remember? I doubt that would have made any of your other…*women friends* jealous of me.'

Unfortunately, Jonas remembered every minute he had ever spent in this woman's company. 'Very funny.' He scowled. 'I was actually referring to a professional rival of yours rather than a personal angle involving me.'

'That would make sense seeing as we don't have a *personal* relationship—from any angle,' she said cuttingly.

Jonas deliberately chose not to enter into any sort of argument as to what there was or wasn't between himself and Mac. 'I understand your exhibition has been a tremendous success—'

'Understand from whom?' Mac pounced on his comment.

'Mac, you were the one who asked for my opinion, so would you now just let me finish giving it instead of jumping down my throat after every sentence?' he snapped his frustration with her interruptions.

'Fine,' she sighed.

'Is there anyone you know, or can think of, who might be—less than happy, shall we say, at the success of your exhibition?'

'No, there isn't,' she answered snippily. Emphatically.

Which brought Jonas back to that frustrated ex-boyfriend again...

He looked at her through narrowed lids. 'Where have you been for the past three days?'

She looked startled. 'Sorry?'

'I asked where you've been for the past three days,' Jonas repeated firmly.

Mac gave an irritated frown. 'I can't see how that's any of your business!'

'It is if it has any bearing on the unwanted graffiti outside,' he reasoned.

'I don't see how it can have.' Mac sat forward and put her empty coffee mug down on the bamboo table. 'If you must know, I went to visit my parents in Devon,' she explained as Jonas continued to look at her questioningly.

'Oh.' He looked frustrated. 'As you said, that's not particularly helpful.'

It also wasn't the answer he had obviously been expecting. 'Where did you think I'd been, Jonas?' Mac asked.

'How the hell should I know?' he retorted tersely.

Was he being defensive? It certainly sounded that way to her. But why did it? Jonas had made it more than clear on Monday evening that he wasn't interested in becoming involved with her—or indeed with any woman who was so physically inexperienced!

Thinking about what had happened between the two of them that evening perhaps wasn't the right thing for her to do when they were sitting here alone in her home. Well... alone apart from the two men she could see outside the window painting the wooden cladding!

She stood up suddenly. 'I don't think we'll achieve anything further by talking about this any more today, Jonas.'

He looked up at her mockingly. 'Is that my cue to politely take my leave?'

Mac felt the warmth of the colour that entered her cheeks. 'Or impolitely, if you would prefer,' she said sweetly.

What Jonas would *prefer* to do was something he dared not allow himself.

The last few minutes spent here with her, in the warmth and beauty that she had made of her home, made him strangely reluctant to leave it. Or her. Just the thought of going back alone to the cold and impersonal sterility of his own apartment was enough to send an icy shiver of revulsion down the length of his spine.

What was it about this woman in particular that made Jonas want to remain in her company? That made him so reluctant to leave the warmth and vitality that was Mary 'Mac' McGuire?

'Have you ever done any interior designing other than your own?' he heard himself asking.

Mac raised an eyebrow. 'Not really. A room here and there for my parents, but otherwise no. Why?'

What the hell was he doing? Jonas wondered, annoyed with himself. The last thing he wanted—the *very* last thing—when he moved into his new apartment next year was a constant reminder of this unusual woman because he was surrounded by *her* choice of décor!

'No reason,' he replied coldly as he stood up decisively. 'I was just making conversation,' he explained. 'You're right, I have to get back to the office.'

Mac stood near the door and watched beneath lowered lashes as Jonas strode over to place his empty coffee mug on the breakfast bar, her gaze hungry as she admired the way his brown leather jacket fitted smoothly over the width of those shoulders and how his legs appeared so long and lean in his snug faded jeans.

She wasn't over him!

Mac had thought—and hoped—that three days in Devon would put this man and that mad desire she had felt for him on Monday evening into perspective. Looking at him now, feeling the wild beat of her pulse and the heated awareness washing over her body, she realised that all she had done was force herself not to think about him. Being with Jonas again, and once more totally aware of that unequivocally passionate response to him, showed her that she hadn't forgotten a thing about him since she'd last seen him.

She moistened dry lips, instantly aware of her mistake as she saw the way Jonas's dark gaze fixated on the movement as he walked slowly towards her. 'I really do need to go out and get some things in for dinner,' she said desperately.

Jonas came to a halt only inches away from her. 'Why don't I take you out to dinner this evening and you can do the food shopping tomorrow?' he prompted huskily.

Mac blinked her uncertainty, part of her wanting to have dinner with him this evening, another part of her knowing it would be reckless for her to even think of doing so. 'I thought we had already agreed that the two of us seeing each other again socially was not a good idea?'

'It isn't,' Jonas acknowledged wryly.

'Then—'

'I want to have dinner with you, damn it!' he bit out fiercely.

Mac gave a rueful smile. 'And do you usually get what you want, Jonas?'

'Generally? Yes. As far as you're concerned? Rarely,' he said bluntly.

Mac was torn. An evening spent alone, after being with Jonas again, now stretched in front of her like a long dark tunnel. Alternately, spending any part of the evening with him presented a high risk of there being a repeat of Monday evening's disaster...

'No,' she said finally. 'I—no.'

Jonas eyed her speculatively. 'That's a definite no, is it?'

'Yes.'

'Yes, that's a definite no? Or yes, I've changed my mind and would love to have dinner with you this evening, Jonas?' he drawled.

He was teasing her! It was so unexpected from this normally forcefully arrogant man that Mac couldn't stop herself from laughing softly as she gave a slight shake of her head. 'You aren't making this easy for me, are you?'

Jonas had no idea what had possessed him to make the invitation in the first place, let alone try to cajole her into accepting it. Especially when he knew that spending any more time with this woman was the very last thing he should do.

He had been telling himself exactly that for the past three days. To no avail, obviously, when the first time he set eyes on her again he was pressing her to have dinner with him!

Even now Jonas couldn't bring himself to retract the invitation. 'It can't be that difficult, Mac,' he cajoled. 'The answer is either yes or no.'

Mac looked up at Jonas quizzically, wondering why he had invited her out to dinner when he was so obviously as reluctant to spend time alone with her again as she was with him.

Except the two of them were alone right now…

Alone, and with the sexual tension between them rising just as obviously. The very air that surrounded them seemed to crackle with that awareness; she was so aware of it now that her heart raced and her palms felt damp.

She drew in a sharp breath. 'I think that has to be a definite no.'

'"I think" is surely contradictory to "definite"?' Jonas pressed.

Because Mac was having a problem *thinking* at all in Jonas's company!

Because she really wanted to say yes?

Maybe. No, definitely! But the part of her that could still reason logically—a very small part of her, admittedly!— knew it really wasn't a sensible thing for her to spend any more time in his highly disturbing company.

'I don't want to go out to dinner with you, Jonas,' she stated very firmly—at the same time aware of a sinking disappointment in the pit of her stomach. An ache. A hollowness that instantly made her want to retract her refusal. She bit her bottom lip, hard, to stop herself from doing exactly that.

Jonas looked down at Mac through narrowed lids, physically aware of everything about her; the slender and sexy elegance of her body, the long silky length of her ebony hair, the warm grey of her eyes, her tiny up tilted nose, the satiny smoothness of her cheeks, those full and sensuous lips—the bottom one firmly gripped between her tiny white teeth. Could that be in an effort to stop Mac from retracting her own refusal?

Implying she didn't *really* want to say no to his dinner invitation...

Jonas straightened. 'I'm not asking you out so that you can dress up and be a trophy on my arm, Mac,' he assured her gently. 'How about we eat here instead of going out? I'll come back at eight o'clock with a bottle of wine and a takeaway. Would you prefer Chinese or Indian?'

Mac's eyes widened. 'But I just said—'

'That you didn't want to go out to dinner,' he cut in. 'So we'll eat dinner here instead.'

She frowned. 'That wasn't quite what I meant.'

'I know that, Mac.' Jonas smiled.

'Then—'

'Look, we both know that we would actually prefer not to spend any more time together,' Jonas said neutrally. 'The problem with that is I can't seem to stay away from you. How about you?' he asked, eyes suddenly fierce with emotion in his otherwise calm face.

Mac realised from his careful tone and fierce expression that he disliked intensely even having to make that admission. That he was still as disturbed by their physical attraction to each other as she was. A physical attraction that was going precisely nowhere when he distrusted her sexual inexperience and she distrusted her own ability to resist him. To see him any more than was absolutely necessary would be absolute madness.

She drew herself up determinedly. 'I said no, Jonas, and I meant *no*!'

His mouth tightened, jaw clenched. 'Fine,' he said tersely. 'I'll wish you a pleasant evening, then.' He nodded abruptly before crossing to the door, closing it softly behind him as he left.

That hollow feeling deepened in Mac's stomach as she watched him go. She knew absolutely that the last thing she was going to have was a pleasant evening in any shape or form.

CHAPTER NINE

'I HAVE MISS MCGUIRE for you on line one, Mr Buchanan,' Mandy informed Jonas lightly down the telephone line when he responded to her buzz.

'Miss McGuire?' Jonas frowned as he suddenly realised Mandy was referring to Mac; he had ceased thinking of her as 'the irritating Miss McGuire' days ago!

He and Mac had only parted a few hours ago, and not exactly harmoniously, so why was she calling him at his office now? Had something else happened at her home?

Jonas put his hand over the mouthpiece to look across at Yvonne as she sat on the other side of his desk, the two of them having been going through some paperwork. 'Would you come back in fifteen minutes so we can finish up here?'

'Of course, Jonas.' She stood up smoothly. 'Are you having better luck persuading Miss McGuire into selling?' she paused to ask ruefully.

Jonas gave her an irritated look. 'It hasn't come into our conversation for some time,' he answered honestly. Part of him had forgotten why he had ever met Mac in the first place. Part of him wished that he never had.

'Oh.' Yvonne looked surprised. 'I thought that was the whole point of your—acquaintance?'

'Did you?' Jonas returned unhelpfully. Yvonne was a good PA, a damned good one, but even so that didn't give her the right to question any of his actions. 'If you wouldn't mind, this is a private call…?' he prompted pointedly, regretting the embarrassed colour that entered Yvonne's cheeks, but making no attempt at an apology as he waited for her to leave his office before taking Mac's call. 'Yes?' he said tersely, not sure who he was annoyed with, only knowing that he was.

Mac had been aware of each second she'd been kept waiting to be put through to Jonas—perhaps because he was unsure about taking her call?—and she could hear the displeasure in his voice now as she held her mobile to her ear with one hand and poured two mugs of coffee with the other. 'Have I called at a bad time?'

'No.'

Mac begged to differ, considering that long wait, and the impatience she could hear in Jonas's tone. She knew she shouldn't have telephoned him. Had tried to talk herself out of it. Wished now that she had heeded her own advice! 'I realised after you had left earlier that I hadn't… I just called to say thank you,' she said awkwardly. 'For everything you did for me this morning. Calling the police. Arranging to have the graffiti painted over.'

There was a brief silence before Jonas answered, his voice sounding less aggressive. 'Have Ben and Jerry finished the painting now?'

'Ben and Jerry? That's what they're called?'

'Yes,' Jonas answered dryly.

'Really?'

'Yes, really,' Jonas chuckled softly.

Mac felt slightly heartened by that chuckle. 'They've almost finished, yes. I was just making them both a mug of coffee.'

'That's very...kind of you.'

Mac bristled. 'You sound surprised?'

His sigh was audible. 'Let's try to not have another argument, hmm, Mac.'

'No, of course not.' She grimaced. 'Sorry.'

'Was that the only reason you called?' Jonas asked huskily.

Was it? Mac had convinced herself that it was before she made the call, but now that she had heard his voice again she wasn't so sure.

They had parted with such finality earlier. Leaving no room for manoeuvre. Something that had left Mac with a feeling of uneasy dissatisfaction.

'I think so,' she answered.

'But you're not sure?' he pressed.

'I am sure,' she said firmly. 'I just— Anyway, thank you for your help earlier, Jonas. It is appreciated.'

'You're welcome,' he said warmly. 'Have you had second thoughts about dinner?'

Second and third ones, Mac acknowledged ruefully. But all of them with the same conclusion—that a relationship between herself and Jonas was going nowhere. Except possibly to a broken heart on her part.

She wasn't sure when—or even how—the feelings she had for Jonas had sneaked up on her. She only knew that they had.

Quite what those feelings were, she had so far shied away from analysing; she only knew, after seeing him again this morning, that her three days away had achieved nothing and that she definitely felt something for him.

She felt energised in his company. A tingling awareness. An excited thrumming. Whether or not that was just a sexual excitement, Mac wasn't experienced enough in relationships to know. She only knew that the thought of never seeing him again, speaking to him again, was a painful one.

It made no difference to those feelings whatsoever that she knew there was no future for the two of them. Jonas undisputedly affected her in a way no other man ever had.

'I'll take it from your delay in answering that you have,' he drawled softly.

'I didn't say that—'

'In which case, Indian or Chinese?' he said authoritatively, rolling right over her vacillation, having no intention of letting her wriggle out of the invitation a second time. Or was it a third time? Whatever. For some reason, Mac had called him, once again opening the line of communication between them, and at the same time renewing Jonas's own determination to see her again. 'I'm waiting, Mac,' he added.

Her raggedly indrawn breath was audible. 'Indian. But—'

'No buts,' Jonas cut in forcefully. 'I'll be there about eight o'clock, okay?'

'I—Yes. Okay.'

Jonas only realised he had been tensed for another refusal as he felt his shoulders relax. 'We're only going to eat dinner together, Mac,' he mocked gruffly—not sure whether he was offering her that reassurance or himself!

Himself, probably, he accepted derisively. Mac had got under his skin in a way he wasn't comfortable with. So much so that he knew he shouldn't see her again. So much so that he knew he *had* to see her again.

She was a magnet he was inexorably drawn to. And resistance on Jonas's part was proving as futile as preventing the proverbial moth from being drawn to a flame...

'Very festive,' Jonas told Mac dryly later that evening once she had opened the door to his knock and he had stepped into the living area of the warehouse, the main lights switched off to allow for the full effect of the brightly lit Christmas tree. The smell of pine was thick in the air, and the branches were heavily adorned with decorations and glittering shiny baubles that reflected those coloured lights.

The dining table in the corner of the huge open-plan area was already set for two, with several candles placed in its centre waiting to be lit, and a bottle of red wine waiting to be opened.

Jonas turned away from the intimacy of that setting to look at Mac instead. Her hair was loose again this evening, and she had changed out of the black jumper, jeans and red body-warmer, into an overlarge thigh-length long-sleeved red shirt over black leggings, with calf-high black boots.

Jonas had spent the remainder of the afternoon telling himself what a bad idea it was for him to come here again this evening. One look at Mac and he didn't give a damn how bad an idea it was, he was just enjoying being in her company again.

'Here.' He handed her the bag of Indian food before thrusting his hands into his jeans pockets in an effort not to reach out, as he so wanted to do, and pull her close to him. Jonas knew that once he had done that he wouldn't want to let her go again. That he would forget everything else but having her in his arms…

Mac turned away from the stark intensity of Jonas's gaze to carry the bag of food over to the breakfast bar and take out the hot cartons before removing the lids with determined concentration, feeling strangely shy in his company now that she was aware of—if choosing not to look too closely at—the feelings she had for him.

'Ben and Jerry did a good job painting over the graffiti,' she told him conversationally as she carried the warmed plates and cartons of food over to the table on a tray.

Jonas shrugged. 'It's too dark for me to tell.'

Mac nodded. 'They were very efficient.' Her gaze didn't quite meet his as she straightened and turned, at the same time completely aware of how vibrantly attractive he looked in a blue cashmere sweater, the same colour as his eyes, and faded jeans of a lighter blue.

'Mac…?'

She raised her eyes to look at him before as quickly looking away again as she felt that familiar thrill of awareness down the length of her spine. 'We should sit down and eat before the food gets cold.'

Jonas frowned at the awkwardness he could feel growing between them. 'Mac, are you even going to look at me?'

She leant back against the table as she turned and raised startled lids, her eyes huge grey orbs in the paleness of her face, her expression pained. 'What are we doing, Jonas?' she groaned huskily.

He gave a rueful shrug. 'Eating dinner together, I thought.'

She shook her head. 'After agreeing only this afternoon that it was a *bad* idea!'

'No, *you* said it was a bad idea. I don't think you asked for my opinion,' Jonas recalled dryly. Although, if asked at the time, he would have said it was a bad idea, too! 'As you said, the food is getting cold, so I suggest that for now we just sit down and eat and think about this again later?' He moved to pointedly pull back one of the chairs for her to sit down.

Mac regarded him quizzically as she sat. 'You really do like having your own way, don't you?'

'Almost as much as you enjoy doing the exact opposite of what you know I want,' Jonas acknowledged with a quick smile as he sat down opposite her before picking up the bottle of wine and deftly opening it.

Mac chuckled softly. 'Interesting.'

'Irritating for the main part, actually,' Jonas admitted as he poured the wine into their glasses. He raised his own glass and made a toast. 'To—hopefully—our first indigestion-free meal together!'

Mac raised her glass and touched it gently against the side of Jonas's. 'To an indigestion-free meal!' she echoed huskily, not too sure about the 'first' part of the toast. It implied there might be other meals to come, and, as Mac knew only too well, she and Jonas always ended up arguing if they spent any length of time together.

Well…almost always. The times when they didn't argue were even more disturbing…

'You really do like Christmas, don't you?'

Mac looked up from helping herself to some of the food in the cartons to see Jonas was looking at her brightly decked Christmas tree. 'I would have said, doesn't everyone?' she replied. 'But I already know that you don't.'

'I wouldn't go that far,' Jonas said.

'No?' Mac eyed him interestedly.

He shrugged. 'I don't dislike Christmas, Mac, it's just a time I remember when my parents were forced to spend a couple of days in each other's company, with the result they usually ended up having one almighty slanging match before the holiday was over. As my grandmother died on Christmas Eve, Joseph wasn't particularly into celebrating it, either.'

'What about your cousin Amy and her family?'

'Amy always goes away with her partner for Christmas, and I'm not close to my uncle and aunt. What can I say?' he drawled at Mac's dismayed expression. 'We're a dysfunctional family.'

It sounded awful to Mac when she thought of her own happy childhood, and the wonderful memories she had of family Christmases, both in the distant past and more recently. 'Why did you call your grandfather Joseph?'

Jonas gave a humourless smile. 'Calling out "Granddad" on a building site didn't go down too well with him, so it became a habit to call him by his first name.'

Looking at Jonas now, so suave, so obviously wealthy from the car he drove and the penthouse apartment he lived in, it was difficult to envision him as a rough and tough teenager working on a building site.

Yet there were those calluses Mac had noticed on his palms three days ago. And there was a ripcord strength about Jonas that didn't look as if it came solely from working out in a gym. Wealthy or not, underneath all that suave sophistication, she realised he was still capable of being every bit as rough and tough as he had been as a teenager.

'What?' Jonas paused in eating his food to look across at her questioningly.

Mac shrugged. 'I was just thinking that maybe you should think about starting your own Christmas traditions.'

From the way Mac had been looking at him so searchingly Jonas was pretty sure that hadn't been what she had been thinking at all. Although quite what she had been thinking, he had no idea.

She was still something of an enigma to him, he recognised ruefully. There was no sophisticated game-playing with Mac. No artifice. As she had so emphatically told him, what you saw was what you got. And what Jonas saw he wanted very badly indeed…

He sighed. 'It's never seemed worth the bother when I only have myself to think about.'

Mac looked at him assessingly. 'I'm taking a bet that you usually go away for Christmas. Somewhere hot,' she qualified. 'Golden sandy beaches where you can sunbathe, and there are waiters to bring you tall drinks with exotic fruit and umbrellas in them. Somewhere you can forget it even is Christmas,' she teased.

'You would win your bet,' Jonas acknowledged with a smile.

She shook her head. 'I can't imagine ever going away for Christmas.'

Neither could Jonas when he could clearly see the distaste on Mac's face. 'What do you and your family do over Christmas?' he asked.

Those beautiful smoky grey eyes glowed. 'Nowadays we all converge on my parents' house in a little village called Tulnerton in Devon. My mother's parents, several aged aunts. All the presents are placed under the tree, and Christmas Eve we all have a family meal and then attend Midnight Mass at the local church together. When we get back Mum and I usually put the turkey in the oven so that it cooks slowly overnight and the house is full of the smells of it cooking in the morning when we sit down to open our presents. When I was younger, that sometimes happened as early as five o'clock in the morning,' she recalled wistfully. 'Nowadays it's usually about nine o'clock, after we've checked on the turkey and everyone has a cup of tea.'

Jonas's mouth twisted. 'The perfect Christmas indeed.'

Mac eyed him ruefully. 'To me it is, yes.'

Jonas reached out and placed his hand over hers as it rested on the tabletop. 'I wasn't mocking you, Mac,' he said gruffly.

'No?'

Strangely enough, no... It was all too easy for Jonas to envisage the Christmas Mac described so warmly. The sort of Christmas that many families strived for and never actually experienced. The sort of Christmas Jonas had never had. And never would have.

'There are no arguments?' he prompted.

Her eyes glowed with laughter. 'Usually only over who's going to pull the wishbone after we've eaten our Christmas lunch!'

His fingers curled about hers. 'It sounds wonderful.'

Mac was very aware of the air of intimacy that now surrounded the two of them. But it was a different type of intimacy from a physical one. This intimacy was warm and enveloping. Dangerous...

She removed her hand purposefully from beneath Jonas's to pick up her fork. 'I'm sure there must have been arguments; you can't put eight or ten disparate people in a house together for four or five days without there being the odd disagreement. I've obviously just chosen to forget them.' She grimaced.

Jonas looked across at her with enigmatic blue eyes. 'You don't have to make excuses for your own happy childhood, Mac.'

'I wasn't—'

'Weren't you?' he rasped.

Yes, she supposed she had been. Because Jonas's childhood had borne absolutely no resemblance to her own. Because, although he wouldn't thank her for it in the slightest, her heart ached for him. 'If you haven't made other plans yet, perhaps you would like to—' Mac broke off abruptly, her cheeks warming as she realised how utterly ridiculous she was being.

Jonas eyed her warily. 'Please tell me you weren't about to invite me to spend Christmas with you and your family in Devon.'

That was exactly what Mac had been about to do! Impulsively. Stupidly! Of course Jonas didn't want to spend Christmas with her, let alone the rest of her family; with half a dozen strangers there, as well as Mac herself, he would necessarily have to be polite to everyone for the duration of his stay.

Her cheeks were now positively burning with embarrassment. 'I think I feel that indigestion coming on!'

Jonas studied Mac through narrowed lids, knowing by her evasiveness that she *had* been about to invite him to spend Christmas with her and her family. Why? Because she actually wanted to spend Christmas with him? Or because she felt sorry for him and just couldn't bear the thought of anyone—even him—spending Christmas alone?

His mouth thinned. 'I don't recall ever saying that I'm

alone when I spend my Christmases sunbathing on those golden sandy beaches.'

'No, you didn't, did you?' The colour had left Mac's cheeks as quickly as it had warmed them, her eyes a huge and haunted grey as she gave a moue of self-disgust. 'How naïve of me.'

Jonas knew that he had deliberately hit out at her because pity was the last thing he wanted from her. From anyone. Damn it, he was successful and rich and could afford to do anything he wanted to do. He had never met refusal from any woman he'd shown an interest in taking to his bed. All the things he had decided he wanted out of life years ago when he left university so determined to succeed he had achieved.

Then why did just being with Mac like this, talking with her, make him just as aware of all the things he *didn't* have in his life?

Things like having someone to come home to every night. The same someone. To share things with. To laugh with. To make love with.

'Don't knock it until you've tried it,' Jonas drawled. 'In fact, why don't you consider giving the traditional family Christmas a miss this year and come away with me instead?' he asked as he looked at her over the top of his wine glass before lifting it and taking a deep swallow of the ruby-red liquid.

Mac stared at Jonas, absolutely incredulous that he appeared to be asking her to go away with him for Christmas.

CHAPTER TEN

WAS JONAS SERIOUS about his invitation? Or was he just playing with her, already knowing from her earlier remarks exactly what her answer would be?

One look at the unmistakable mockery on his ruggedly handsome face and Mac knew that was exactly what he was doing.

She stood up. 'It would serve you right if I said yes!' she snapped as she picked up her glass of wine and moved across the room to stand beside the Christmas tree.

'Try me,' Jonas invited as he relaxed back in his chair to look across at her thoughtfully. 'I assure you, if you said yes then I would book two first-class seats on a flight that would allow us to arrive in Barbados on Christmas Eve,' he promised huskily.

Mac looked at him scornfully. 'That's so easy to say when you knew before you even asked that I would refuse.'

'Did I?' He stood up to slowly cross the room, his piercing blue gaze easily holding hers captive as he came to a halt only inches away from her.

Mac stared up at him, her breathing somehow feeling constricted. She moistened her lips with the tip of her tongue. 'I had already told you that I couldn't imagine spending Christmas anywhere but at home with my parents.'

Jonas's dark gaze was fixed on those moist and slightly parted lips. 'I'm curious to know what your answer would have been if that family Christmas was taken out of the equation?'

Mac gave a firm shake of her head. 'I hate even the idea of spending Christmas on a beach.'

Jonas had no idea why he was even pursuing this conversation. Except perhaps that he wanted to know if Mac's invitation for him to spend Christmas with her family had been out of the pity he suspected it was, or something else... 'What if I were to suggest we went to a ski resort instead of a beach?'

She smiled slightly. 'I can't ski.'

'I don't recall saying anything about the two of us actually going skiing. I seriously doubt I would have any desire to leave our bedroom once we got there,' Jonas admitted wickedly.

Once again her cheeks coloured with that becoming blush. 'Wouldn't that rather defeat the object?'

He gave a shrug. 'Surely that would depend on what the objective was?'

Mac looked up at him and frowned. 'I believe we had this conversation three days ago, Jonas. At which time, I believe you made it *more* than clear that you're not at all interested in becoming my first lover.'

He hadn't been. He still wasn't. Except he had realised these last three days that he didn't like the thought of some other man being Mac's first lover either! 'Maybe I've changed my mind,' he replied guardedly.

'And maybe you just enjoying playing games with me,' Mac said knowingly.

'Mac, I haven't even begun to play games with you yet!' he teased. Although whether that teasing was directed at her or himself, Jonas wasn't sure...

He wanted to make love with this woman. He actually wanted it so badly he could taste it. Taste *her*.

Dear God, there were so many ways he could make love to this woman without actually taking her virginity. So many ways he could give her incredible pleasure. And she could give him that same pleasure in return.

But would it be enough to sate the ever-rising hunger inside him? Would touching Mac, caressing her, making love to her but never actually taking her, being inside her, ever be enough for him? Did he really have that much self-control?

Where she was concerned? Somehow Jonas doubted it! The only reason they hadn't already become lovers when she had been at his apartment was because of the realisation of the seemingly insurmountable barrier of her virginity.

Jonas moved away abruptly. 'You're right, this conversation is pointless. Christmas is still two weeks away—'

'And we may not even be talking to each other again by then!' Mac put in with black humour.

'Probably not,' he admitted. 'But even if we are, we still both know that you will be spending Christmas in Devon with your family and I will be sitting on a beach somewhere improving my tan.'

Mac didn't think that Jonas's tan needed improving; his skin was already a deep gold. And from the calluses on his hands and those defined muscles in his shoulders and chest, she didn't think that tan had been acquired sitting on a beach anywhere!

In fact, if she had arrived home a little later than she had this morning, then she was pretty sure that she would have found Jonas up that metal tower outside her home beside Ben and Jerry as he helped to paint over the graffiti. Jonas might now be rich and powerful, the owner of his own company for some years rather than an employee, but his rugged appearance and weather-hewn features were testament to the fact that he still enjoyed getting his hands dirty occasionally.

'I was totally sincere in my invitation for you to spend Christmas with my family, Jonas,' she said huskily.

His eyes were a hard and mocking blue. 'And what do you think your family would have made of you bringing a man home for the holidays?'

Mac's cheeks warmed as she easily imagined her father's teasing, and the whispered speculation of her aged aunts, if Jonas had accepted her invitation and accompanied her to Devon. 'Oh.' She grimaced. 'I hadn't really thought of that.'

'Exactly,' Jonas said, drinking the last of his wine before placing the empty glass on the table. 'It's probably time I was going.'

Mac blinked. 'It's still early.'

As far as Jonas was concerned, it was seriously bordering on being too late!

She looked so damned beautiful, so desirable with the coloured lights on the tree reflected in the glossy curtain of her long black hair, her eyes a deep and misty grey, her skin like a warm peach, and her lips—dear heaven, those full and pouting lips!

Jonas wanted to take those lips with his own, devour them, to kiss her and explore the hot temptation of her mouth until she felt the same need he did. If he didn't leave here soon, in the next few minutes, he wasn't going to be able to withstand that temptation at all.

'You didn't get to see my studio earlier; would you like to see it now?'

Jonas was jolted out of that rising fiery haze of desire to focus on Mac. 'Sorry…?'

She shrugged narrow shoulders. 'Obviously the studio is pretty empty at the moment with most of my recent work being at the exhibition, but you're welcome to take a look. If you would like to,' she added almost shyly.

Did he want to do that? He had evaded taking up the invitation earlier because he didn't want to find himself being drawn into Mac's world any more than he already was. To see where she had created the amazing paintings like the ones he had seen at the Lyndwood Gallery the previous week, and to feel himself being pulled even deeper into the intimacy of Mac's life.

He still wanted to avoid doing that, didn't he?

'I would like to,' Jonas instead heard himself accept gruffly.

Mac smiled. 'It's just up the spiral staircase.' She placed her glass down next to Jonas's on the table before turning to lead the way.

Jonas reached out and grasped her arm to look down searchingly into her face, sure by the way she avoided meeting his gaze, that she was already regretting having made the invitation. 'Don't take me up there if you would rather not, Mac…'

'I—no, it's fine,' she reassured him, not really sure that it *was* fine, but unwilling for Jonas to leave just yet.

Because she could sense the air of finality about him

now and she had the feeling that once he left this time he would ensure that it really was the last time she saw him.

Yet wasn't that what she wanted? Didn't she want Jonas out of her life? To never have to see and deal with this disturbing man ever again?

'It will only take a few minutes,' she told him briskly as she pulled out of his grasp and walked over and switched on the light overhead. She'd rather take him up the spiral staircase to her studio than answer any of her own soul-searching questions.

But she was completely aware of Jonas, every step of the way, as he followed behind her up that metal staircase...

Whatever he had been expecting Mac's studio to look like, after the warmth and colour of the living area below, it certainly wasn't the starkness of the pale cream colour-wash on the three bare brick walls. Or the fourth wall that faced towards the river completely glass, the ceiling also made up of glass panels, and revealing the clear star-lit sky overhead. The only furniture in the room was an old and faded chaise against one wall and a daybed beside another.

Mac's easel was set up near the huge glass window, and she strolled across the room to lightly lay a cover over the painting she was currently working on. 'I never allow people to see my work before it's completed,' she explained ruefully at Jonas's questioning look.

The surroundings weren't quite 'starving in a garret', but the studio was much more basic than Jonas had been expecting after the vividness of colours on the floor below. 'You prefer not to have any outside distractions when you're working,' he realised softly.

Mac turned to him with wide eyes. 'No...'

She hadn't expected him to have that insight, Jonas realised, wondering if anyone else had ever really understood how and why she worked in the surroundings she did. Surroundings that were unique in the way Mac had converted this warehouse to her own individual needs.

Another reason she refused to sell the warehouse to Buchanan Construction. The main reason probably; most of Mac's emotional links to her grandfather would be inside her rather than consisting of bricks and mortar.

This last realisation put Jonas in an untenable position.

Had she done that deliberately?

His mouth thinned as he turned to look at Mac. 'You brought me up here for a purpose.'

Mac briefly thought of denying it, and then thought better of it as she recognised the steely glitter in Jonas's eyes. 'I'm not sure I could work anywhere else,' she answered truthfully.

'Have you ever tried?' he gritted.

'No. But—' She moved her shoulders in an uncomfortable shrug. 'I just thought it might help if you understood I'm not just being bloody-minded by refusing to sell my home and my studio to you.'

'You thought by showing me this that I would back off,' Jonas guessed. 'I don't enjoy being manipulated, Mac,' he said coolly.

She frowned. 'I wasn't—'

'Yes, you were, damn you!' he burst out, suddenly explosive in his anger, taking the two long strides that brought him to within touching distance of her. 'This is just an artist's studio, Mac. It could be replicated just about anywhere.'

She shook her head. 'You're wrong. I've lived and worked here for the past five years—'

'And once this place has been knocked down you'll live

and work somewhere else for a lot longer than that!' he said grimly.

'I told you, that isn't going to happen—' Her protest was cut short as Jonas reached out to pull her into his arms before lowering his head and grinding his mouth fiercely down onto hers.

It was a kiss of punishment rather than gentleness, anger rather than passion, Jonas's arms like steel bands about her waist as he held her tightly against him, pressing her to his muscled body, making Mac completely aware of the pulsing hardness of his thighs.

She stood on tiptoe as her hands moved up his chest to his shoulders, and then into the dark thickness of the hair at his nape, her mouth slanting, lips parting beneath his as she returned the heat of that kiss.

Jonas was aware of his shift in mood as the angry need to punish her faded and passion and desire took over, groaning low in his throat as he began to sip and taste the softness of Mac's lips, his tongue stroking those lips as he tested their sweetness before moving deeper into the hot and welcoming warmth of Mac's mouth.

He could feel her delicacy beneath the restless caress of his hands down the length of her spine before he cupped her bottom to pull her up and into him, the soft and welcoming well between her thighs both an agony and an ecstasy as his arousal fitted perfectly against her.

He dragged his mouth from hers to breathe deeply against her creamy cheek. 'Wrap your legs around me,' he encouraged fiercely.

'I don't—'

'I promise I'll lift and support you, Mac,' he looked up to encourage hotly. 'I just need you to wrap your legs around me,' he exhorted her gruffly before burying his lips against the side of her neck.

Jonas's tongue was a fiery torment against Mac's skin, a rasping, arousing torment that made her feel weak and wanting even as she did as he asked. As promised, Jonas's hands beneath her bottom easily lifted and supported her as she raised up to curve her legs about him and instantly felt the press of his arousal against the centre of her parted thighs.

Her thin leggings and brief panties were no barrier to that firm and pulsating flesh as it pressed against her. Mac felt herself swell there, becoming damp, wet, so hot and aching as Jonas's mouth claimed hers once again.

She was barely aware of him carrying her across the room to press her against the wall, Mac only realising he had done so as the coldness of the brick against her back became a sharp counterpoint to the heated arousal of her breasts and thighs.

His arousal was more penetrating now, pressing into that welcoming well as Jonas moved against her rhythmically, each thrust of his body matched by the penetration of his tongue into the heated inferno of her mouth, so that Mac felt him everywhere.

Jonas wrenched his mouth from hers, breathing hard as he looked down at her with fiercely dark eyes. 'I'm going to pleasure you, Mac,' he promised gruffly as he carried her over to lay her down on the chaise. 'I'm going to make love to you until you beg me to stop,' he vowed as he knelt on the floor beside the chaise.

He pushed her shirt out of the way and took off her boots, then peeled away her leggings and panties before moving up to kneel between her parted thighs. 'You're so beautiful here, Mac,' he murmured throatily as he looked down at her hungrily. He reached out to touch her naked thighs, fingers gentle as he parted her ebony curls.

Mac moaned as she felt Jonas's fingers move against her in a light caress, heat coursing through her body as that pressure increased, that moan turning to a breathless keening as she felt a burning, aching pressure building inside her, demanding, wanting, needing—

'Jonas!' she cried out at the first intimate touch of his mouth against her, the moistness of his tongue a soft caress against her tender and aching skin.

Her hands moved restlessly, fingers threading into Jonas's hair with the intention of stopping that unbearable torment, but instead finding her fingers tightening her hold as she pressed him closer still, arching into him as she felt the probe of his fingers against her entrance, so close, so very close, and yet circling just out of reach.

'Yes, Jonas!' Mac groaned her torment as she pressed urgently against those tormenting fingers. 'Please…!'

God, how Jonas needed this, wanted this; the taste of Mac in his mouth and the feel of how hot and ready she was beneath his caressing hands.

He entered her slowly as he continued to use his tongue to flicker against her. His fingers began to thrust, slowly, gently to the rhythm of Mac's low encouraging groans as she moved urgently until her muscles tightened and she climaxed in long and beautiful spasms that caused her to cry out in mindless pleasure.

Mac had never felt anything like this in her life before, the pleasure so incredible it bordered on pain. Wave after wave of heat coursing, singing through her body as Jonas continued the relentless pressure of his lips and tongue until he had extracted every last vestige of her climax.

It seemed minutes, hours later, that Mac finally collapsed weakly back onto the chaise, her breath a choking sob, her body so alive to his every touch, so tinglingly aware, that she almost couldn't bear it.

Almost...

Jonas began to kiss his way up the flatness of her belly, unbuttoning her shirt to expose her naked breasts to the ministrations of the heat of his mouth, first one breast and then the other, the rasp of his jeans against her inner thighs as he lay half across her an added torment to her roused and sensitive body.

His hair looked so dark against the whiteness of her skin as Mac looked down at him, his lips fastened about one nipple as his fingers caressed its twin.

Incredibly Mac felt her pleasure rising again. More intense this time, deeper. Every touch, every caress causing her body to quiver in awareness. 'I want to touch you, too, Jonas.' She moved until she was sitting up slightly. 'I need to touch you,' she added achingly as he looked up at her, his eyes dark and heavy with arousal.

Jonas studied her searchingly; her eyes were fever bright, her cheeks flushed, her lips... He had never seen anything as sensual as Mac's pouting, full lips, could feel himself hardening to steel as he easily imagined those lips about him and her hair falling silkily across his hips and thighs as she pleasured him.

The image was so clear, so urgent, that Jonas offered no resistance as she sat up fully to push him down onto the chaise beneath her before unbuttoning and unzipping his jeans to slide them and his boxers far enough down his thighs to fully expose his hard and jutting erection. He groaned low in his throat as he saw the way Mac looked at him so hungrily before she reached out tentatively and wrapped her fingers about him.

She loved caressing him and learning what gave Jonas the most pleasure as her hand began to move up and down.

Jonas's hands clenched at his sides as that pleasure held him as tightly in its grip as Mac did. His focus became fixed on the expression on her face as she continued to touch him. The fascination. The pleasure. Then the eroticism of seeing the moist tip of her tongue moving over her lips before she slowly lowered her head towards him, before she finally took him into her mouth.

Jonas's back arched as he thrust up into that heat, the past week or so of wanting this woman, making love to her so far but never taking her, making it impossible for him to temper his own response. That response spiralled out of control as she took him deeper into her mouth before slowly drawing back. Then repeating it all over again. Setting a rhythm, a tormenting, heated rhythm that Jonas had no will or desire to resist.

Jonas became lost in that bombardment of sensations, breathing hard, and then not breathing at all when he felt his exquisite release in mindless, beautiful pleasure.

CHAPTER ELEVEN

MAC COULD FEEL and hear Jonas breathing raggedly beside her as her head lay against his chest. Jonas's arms were wrapped tightly about her as the two of them lay side by side on the chaise. Her thoughts were racing as she wondered what happened now. Now that Jonas knew her—and her body—more intimately than anyone else ever had. Now that she knew Jonas's body more intimately than she had any other man's...

That she had been able to give him the same pleasure he had given her filled her with an immense feeling of satisfaction. But it was a satisfaction tempered by uncertainty. By the knowledge that her emotions, while she didn't want to look at them too deeply here and now, were most definitely involved. And she had no idea whether or not she would ever see Jonas again after tonight...

Neither of them had spoken as they'd adjusted their clothing into some semblance of order before they lay down together on the chaise. Mac knew her own silence was because she felt a somewhat gauche awkwardness following the intensity of their lovemaking. But she had absolutely no idea what Jonas was thinking or feeling as he lay so silently beside her.

'This is usually the awkward part.' Jonas's chest rumbled beneath Mac's ear as he finally spoke.

Mac could feel the rapid beat of her own heart. The plummeting beat of her heart. Surely this could only be awkward if Jonas didn't intend seeing her again?

'Extracting oneself without embarrassment, you mean?' she guessed huskily.

'Something like that.'

He hadn't intended things to go as far between them as they had. He had wanted to make love to Mac, to give her pleasure. But he hadn't expected to receive that same pleasure back, or for that pleasure to be given so completely. So beautifully. So erotically he had been unable to stop himself from climaxing.

There had been many women in Jonas's life the last fifteen years. Or, rather, in his bed; he didn't allow any woman to actually be a part of his life.

In the past those relationships had always been based on Jonas's need for physical release, and the woman's need for a bed partner who was wealthy enough to treat them out of bed in the way they enjoyed, to be wined and dined and bought the odd piece of expensive jewellery. As far as Jonas was concerned, it had been a fair exchange of needs. Almost as cut and dried as a business proposition, in fact. Something he could definitely relate to.

He didn't understand this relationship with Mac at all…

In fact, Jonas shied away from even calling it that.

That they had met at all had been purely accidental, a business necessity. Their meetings since had, for the main part, been just as incidental. Oh, Jonas had known it was her exhibition he was attending, and after their unsatisfactory conversation a few days earlier he had enjoyed seeing her discomfort when he'd arrived at the gallery with Amy.

But the number of times the two of them had met since weren't so easily explained away.

His desire to see her again after tonight was even less so...

It would be insanity on his part to ask to see her again. A complication he didn't need in his life; Mac was nothing at all like any of the women he had known in the past. Jonas doubted he would be able to extricate himself from a relationship with her as easily as he had with those other women.

No, he couldn't see Mac McGuire again.

Not couldn't, *wouldn't*!

He had told Mac more about himself in the time he had known her than he had ever confided in anyone. Even Joel Baxter, who had become a good friend the past twelve years. He had allowed Mac to get below his defences, Jonas realised. To reach him, know him, better than anyone else ever had.

Sex was one thing, but it was definitely time to sever the unwitting friendship that had been developing between them.

Mac looked up just in time to see the grimness of his expression. And to guess the reason for it. Well, she might have been stupid enough to lose her heart to Jonas Buchanan, but that didn't mean she had lost her pride too!

'You needn't look so worried, Jonas,' she assured him dryly as she pulled out of his arms to stand up. Luckily her shirt was thigh length, long enough to hide her nakedness beneath. 'This evening was—different. But I'm in no hurry to repeat the experience.'

Jonas scowled darkly as he sat up and smoothed the untidy thickness of his hair back from his face. Hair that had felt silky and soft beneath Mac's fingers only minutes ago!

'Are you trying to tell me you didn't *enjoy* it?' he growled incredulously.

Mac raised a cool eyebrow. 'That would be rather silly of me, wouldn't it? No, Jonas,' she added firmly, chin raised. 'I'm not saying that at all. Only that while this evening was—pleasant, sexual gratification is no reason for the two of us to see each other again after tonight.'

It was exactly the same conclusion that Jonas had come to only minutes ago, but hearing her echo that conclusion so emotionlessly irritated the hell out of him. Mac thought the evening had been *pleasant*! Damn it, he had never, ever lost it in the way he had with her tonight. Had never allowed himself to lose control in the way he had earlier when Mac took him into her mouth.

Jonas could still feel that pleasure. The most gut-wrenching, soul-deep pleasure that he had ever known. He knew the memory of it was going to haunt his days and fill his nights for longer than he cared to think about.

He stood up, eyes glittering angrily. 'In other words, you've had your fun, and thanks for the experience?'

She eyed him mildly. 'You seem angry, Jonas. Isn't this what you wanted?'

Yes, damn it, of course it was what he wanted!

Jonas had wanted to be able to extricate himself from this situation with as little unpleasantness between them as possible. Except he had discovered it was something else entirely for Mac to want to do the same thing!

'Whatever,' he snapped coldly. 'I suggest—what the hell was that?' He scowled darkly as he heard a loud crashing noise coming from outside.

Mac looked totally bewildered. 'I have no idea…'

Jonas strode quickly over to the window that faced over the river, looking out into the darkness. He couldn't actually see anything, or anyone, and his car was still parked in the street below, but he was pretty sure that crashing noise had been the sound of glass breaking.

He turned quickly, his expression grim as he hurried over to the spiral staircase. 'I think your intruder is back!'

Mac had been rooted to the spot, shocked into immobility by the loud sound. But she moved now, hurrying over to stand at the top of the staircase and look down at Jonas as he reached the bottom step. 'You can't go out there alone, Jonas—'

He paused to look up at her. 'Of course I'm going out there,' he said.

'You can't.' Mac shook her head worriedly. 'What if they have a knife? Or—or a gun—'

'You've been watching too much television, Mac,' he said gently.

'There was a stabbing in this area only a couple of weeks ago,' she protested.

'Reportedly rival gangs sorting out the pecking order,' he reassured her.

'Yes, but—'

'Just put some clothes on and call the police, and then wait inside until I come back and give the all-clear,' Jonas told her grimly.

'But—'

'You are *not* to come outside, Mac,' he instructed firmly. 'Do you understand?'

Mac felt her cheeks warm with displeasure, both with Jonas's high-handed attitude and the reminder that she still didn't have all her clothes on. 'I'm not stupid, Jonas. Neither do I intend just cowering in here while you go outside and face goodness knows what!'

'You'll do as you're damn well told if you don't want me to come back and deal with you once I've dealt with what's going on outside!' he growled.

'You could try,' she seethed.

Jonas's mouth tightened as there was another sound of glass breaking. 'I really don't have time for this right now, Mac. Just do as I ask and don't complicate the situation by forcing me to worry about your safety when I should be concentrating on putting an end to this!' He didn't stay to argue with her any further before disappearing from the bottom of the stairs.

Mac heard the outside door closing seconds later, her heart pounding erratically as she quickly grabbed up her leggings and panties before hurrying down the metal staircase to use her mobile and call the police, her hand shaking so badly she could barely press the right three buttons.

She had to calm down. Had to at least try to be coherent when she gave the necessary information to the police.

Despite those inner warnings Mac knew she sounded slightly hysterical as she talked to the dispatcher who answered.

She hadn't just sounded hysterical, Mac acknowledged after she had ended the call and hurried over to the picture window to look outside. She had sounded frantic.

Because she didn't care who was outside, or what damage

they had done to her home this time. All she cared about was Jonas. That he should come back safely.

Mac might have been uncertain about her feelings for Jonas until tonight, but she had absolutely no doubts now that she had fallen totally in love with him...

Jonas knew he was white-faced by the time he wearily accompanied Mac back up the stairs and into the living area of her home almost an hour later.

Who would have guessed it?

Who could have known?

He gave a heavy sigh. 'I told the police I would join them down at the station as soon as possible.' He picked up his jacket and slipped it on, all without looking at Mac.

He couldn't look at her. Couldn't bear to see the accusation that was sure to be in her face.

It had all been his fault, he realised numbly. The initial break-in. The graffiti. The windows broken this evening on Mac's Jeep parked downstairs in the garage. All of it was Jonas's fault.

He hadn't known. Hadn't realised. Despite Mac's teasing remark earlier in the week, he had still never guessed that Yvonne had feelings for him; the sort of feelings that had prompted his PA into trying to scare Mac into selling the warehouse to Jonas.

'Drink some of this first.'

Jonas looked up to see that Mac had refilled his wine glass and now held it out to him. As if wine were going to erase the horror of finding Yvonne downstairs systematically breaking the windows on Mac's car. Or numb his disbelief at the conversation that had followed. The hysterical conviction Yvonne had that she was helping him.

That she loved him. Was sure the two of them were meant to be together.

All of it made worse by the fact that Mac had disobeyed his instruction by then and come downstairs to join him, hearing every word Yvonne said. Along with the police who had arrived only minutes earlier.

Nothing could ever erase the horror of any of that from Jonas's mind!

He grimaced. 'I don't think it's a good idea for me to arrive at a police station smelling of alcohol.'

Probably not, Mac acknowledged as she put the wine glass down on the table.

What an evening! She and Jonas had made love. Mac had realised—and still shied away from looking at it too deeply—that she was in love with Jonas. And now this.

By the time she had dressed and hurried downstairs to the garage, Yvonne Richards had been in full spate, professing her love for Jonas, explaining that she had only terrorised Mac because she wanted to help him. That she had only done those things in an effort to convince Mac into selling the warehouse to Buchanan Construction.

This whole evening had been surreal from start to finish. And it wasn't over yet!

'Would it help if I told the police I have no intention of pressing charges?' Mac asked softly; Yvonne Richards seemed more in need of psychiatric help than prosecution!

Jonas's expression was bleak. 'I have no idea.' He gave a slightly dazed shake of his head as he sat down suddenly. 'I— Do you think Yvonne has done anything like this before? Tried to "help me" like this before?' He frowned darkly as the possibility occurred to him.

Mac shrugged. 'Let's not even go there, Jonas. It's the

here and now that we have to deal with,' she added cajolingly. 'Perhaps I should come to the police station with you—'

'No!' Jonas refused harshly as he stood up. He felt humiliated enough for one evening, without Mac having to hear—yet again—how Yvonne had only done the things she had because she was in love with him.

How or why that had happened, Jonas had no idea. Yvonne had worked for him as his PA for almost two years now. She had proved to be particularly good at her job, and as far as Jonas was concerned the two of them had an excellent working relationship. Obviously there had been business trips they had taken together, as well as long hours spent alone together, but Jonas was sure there had never been the slightest suggestion on his part that the two of them had any sort of personal relationship.

He looked across at Mac. 'I've never given Yvonne the slightest encouragement to feel the way she says she feels about me.' He rubbed the back of his neck. 'To my knowledge I've never so much as touched her or spoken to her in a way that could possibly be misconstrued as sexual interest.'

Mac knew that her gaze didn't quite meet his. 'I'm sure you haven't—'

'Don't patronise me, Mac,' Jonas rasped harshly, eyes narrowing to steely slits. 'I do *not* have relationships with the people who work for or with me. Besides complicating things unnecessarily, it's bad business practice.'

'And why bother when there are so many other women willing to give you what you want?' she came back tartly.

'Was that comment really necessary?' Jonas snarled.

Was it? Probably not. But Mac was feeling less than composed herself after their lovemaking earlier this evening.

She and Jonas had made beautiful and erotic love to each other. At least…it was love on Mac's side. She doubted Jonas's feelings went any further than lust.

It just seemed too much to now learn that she had been terrorised this past week by another woman suffering from that same unrequited love for him!

Mac accepted that it wasn't his fault. Jonas had made it clear from the beginning that he didn't even believe in love, let alone a committed relationship, and so it wasn't his fault if the women he met were stupid enough to fall in love with him.

But that didn't mean Mac couldn't feel a little angry and resentful about it! 'You had better go,' she said distantly.

Jonas knew he had to go. That he should drive to the police station where they had taken Yvonne and try to make some sort of sense out of this ludicrous situation. He would just prefer not to leave things so strained between himself and Mac.

'I'll come back later—'

'I would prefer it if you didn't,' Mac cut in firmly. 'We have nothing else to say to each other, Jonas,' she reasoned as a scowl creased his brow.

'Don't you even want to know what's going to happen to Yvonne?' he asked tonelessly.

She shrugged. 'I'm sure the police will inform me if I need to be involved any further.'

In other words, Jonas realised darkly, Mac considered her 'involvement' with him to be at an end.

Like hell it was!

He reached out and gripped the tops of her arms. 'I'm coming back later, Mac,' he insisted determinedly. 'If nothing else, you and I need to talk about this evening—'

'There's nothing else to say.' Mac wrenched out of his grasp, her cheeks fiery red. Whether in temper or embarrassment, Jonas wasn't sure. 'I'm grateful for the experience, of course, but I certainly don't want to have a post-mortem about it!'

Temper, Jonas acknowledged. Maybe tinged with a little embarrassment...

He should just cut his losses. Take the opportunity Mac was giving him to extricate himself from this situation with a little grace allowed to remain on both sides.

Yet looking at her he couldn't help but remember how he had kissed her. Touched her. Pleasured her. Just as she had kissed and touched and pleasured him.

'I'm coming back later,' he repeated firmly.

'I'm going to bed as soon as I've locked up behind you and cleared away,' she argued just as stubbornly.

Jonas's mouth twisted. 'Then you'll just have to get out of bed and unlock the door and let me in again, won't you?'

Her mouth compressed. 'Don't you understand that I don't want you here, Jonas?'

'I would have to be pretty stupid not to realise that when you've said it three times in as many minutes,' he commented.

Mac had never felt so—so frustrated, so irritated with anyone in her life before. 'Isn't finding out one woman is in love with you enough for one evening?' she shot back.

'Low blow, Mac,' Jonas muttered between clenched teeth, his face paling one more.

It was a low blow. Not only that, it was spiteful when Jonas's shock earlier at learning of his PA's feelings for him had been self-evident. 'Sorry,' she murmured uncomfortably. 'I'm just not sure you should come back here later.'

'Why not?'

Mac moved away restlessly. 'Frankly, I find this whole situation embarrassing,' she admitted. 'I— We—Earlier—' She shook her head. 'Maybe you're used to these situations, Jonas, but I'm not.' And she never would be. Not if the cringing awkwardness she now felt with Jonas was any indication of how traumatic it was to be in the company of a man you had been intimate with. A man you were in love with but who didn't, and never would, love you back…

It was no good telling herself how stupid it was to have allowed her emotions to become involved with a man like Jonas. No good at all when she knew herself to be deeply, irrevocably, in love with him. In the circumstances, her only option had to be never to see him again!

'I really can't take any more tonight, Jonas,' she told him with quiet conviction. 'I just want to go to bed, fall asleep, and hope that when I wake up in the morning I'll find that this whole evening has been just a nightmare.'

Jonas had never heard any woman describe making love with him as a nightmare before, but there had been so many firsts for him with Mac already, why not add that one to the list?

His mouth firmed. 'I'm not quite sure what you're referring to by "these situations",' he said. 'However, I do accept—for now—that you feel you want some time alone.' He ran a hand impatiently through the dark thickness of his hair. 'If it's any consolation, this evening didn't turn out the way I expected it to, either.'

Mac gave a humourless smile. 'Nothing ever seems to turn out as "expected" between the two of us.' The fact that she had met the owner of Buchanan Construction at all, let alone made love with him, certainly shouldn't have happened.

'No,' Jonas acknowledged heavily as he studied her for several long minutes before turning sharply and walking over to the door. 'I'll ring you tomorrow.'

Jonas could ring all he wanted; Mac had already decided she wasn't going to be here.

No doubt her parents were going to think it a little odd when she turned up in Devon again so soon after her last visit, but what choice did she have? She couldn't stay in London after tonight. Well…she could. If she wanted to have another embarrassing conversation with Jonas like this last one!

'Fine.'

Jonas's eyes narrowed suspiciously on her suddenly ex-pressionless face. 'What aren't you telling me, Mac?'

She gave a brittle laugh. 'Nothing you want to hear, I assure you!'

Jonas continued to look across at her in utter frustration. Would he still be leaving like this if they hadn't heard the sound of glass breaking downstairs, if he hadn't discovered that it was one of his own employees causing the damage to Mac's property, scaring the hell out of her in the process, and if he didn't now have to go to the local police station and sort the mess out? If none of that had happened, would he now be joining Mac in her bed, or would he have left anyway?

It had certainly been his intention to leave before any of those things happened. For him to get as far away from her disturbing presence as possible. Now the only thing he wanted to do was crawl into bed with her and make love to her all over again. Which, in itself, was reason enough for him to get the hell out of here!

'Make sure you bolt and lock the door behind me,' he advised gruffly.

Mac waited only long enough for Jonas to close the door behind him before quickly crossing the room and doing exactly that, to then turn and lean weakly back against it as her legs threatened to buckle beneath her.

She *had* fallen in love with Jonas Buchanan.

A man who would never love her because he had no time for the emotion.

What was she going to do?

CHAPTER TWELVE

As it turned out, Mac wasn't able to leave London the following morning as planned, after all.

The telephone rang for the first time just after eight o'clock. Fearing, as promised, that it might be Jonas, Mac reluctantly answered the call, immensely relieved when it turned out to be the police asking if she would come down to the police station this morning so that they might talk to her.

Mac was only too happy to agree—the thought of not being at the warehouse to take Jonas's call, or at home if he actually came to the warehouse in person, was definitely an appealing one.

When she received a second telephone call a few minutes later, from Jeremy this time, asking her if she could call round to the gallery in the afternoon and meet a gallery owner from America who was interested in showing some of her work over there, she was only too happy to have an excuse not to be at the warehouse in the afternoon too.

Besides, the request from the police was one that Mac couldn't avoid or simply ignore, and the one from Jeremy was one she didn't want to avoid or ignore. The possibility of taking her work to America, too, would be a dream come true for her.

Consequently, Mac was forced to remain in London even though it was the last place she wanted to be. Forced to remain, perhaps, but at the same time given two legitimate reasons to avoid speaking to or seeing Jonas while she was here.

At least, until she returned to the warehouse at six o'clock that evening and once again found him sitting waiting for her at the bottom of the metal staircase leading up to her home!

Jonas stood up slowly as Mac came to a brief halt before she resumed walking cautiously towards him, her crash helmet tucked under her arm and her hair shaken loose about her leather-clad shoulders. 'You're a difficult woman to track down,' he commented ruefully.

She shrugged those narrow shoulders as she came to a halt in front of him. 'Is this something important, Jonas, or can it wait until another time? I'm rather busy this evening.'

Jonas's mouth thinned at her dismissive tone. He had spent hours at the police station the previous night, talking, explaining, in the hope of avoiding having the situation go any further than it already had. But it had taken until lunchtime today for the police to telephone and inform him they were prepared not to proceed any further with the case as long as Yvonne sought professional help for her behaviour. At the same time making it clear to him that Mac's refusal to press charges concerning the damage to her property had helped them to make that decision.

Trying to speak to Mac and thank her for her intervention had proved more difficult. She hadn't answered any of Jonas's telephone calls. She hadn't been at home when he'd called round earlier this afternoon. When he'd called at the warehouse a second time about an hour ago, and found she still wasn't at home, Jonas had just decided to sit and wait for her.

'Busy doing what?' he grated harshly.

Her eyes narrowed. 'I don't believe that is any of your business, do you?'

The fact that Mac now made no effort to walk up the steps and go into the warehouse indicated she had no intention of inviting him inside. 'It's too cold to stand out here talking.' The cold vapour on his breath gave truth to that statement.

Her chin rose stubbornly. 'I didn't invite you here, Jonas.'

He reached out and took a light hold of her arm. 'Perhaps not, but now that I *am* here you could be polite and invite me inside.'

Mac eyed him impatiently. 'Why change things now?'

Jonas gave her a humourless smile. 'Meaning we've never particularly bothered being polite to each other before?'

'Exactly!' she said. 'I really do need to shower and change, Jonas.'

'You're going out this evening?'

'Not that it's any of your business, but yes, I'm going out,' she snapped.

Jonas felt his hands clench in the pockets of his long woollen overcoat. 'With whom?'

'That's none of your business, either!' Grey eyes glittered with temper.

His jaw tightened warningly. 'I believe what we did last night made it my business.'

Mac tensed indignantly. 'Like hell it did!' She glared up

at Jonas, so angry she could have hit him. 'Last night was a mistake from start to finish. The finish obviously being the revelation that it was your own PA who was vandalising my home and property!'

Jonas scowled darkly. 'You're holding *me* responsible for that?'

'Who else?' Mac came back heatedly, knowing she wasn't being completely fair in that accusation, but feeling too unnerved by finding him here waiting for her to even try to rationalise or calm the situation down. 'There's bound to be some sort of reaction when you play games with people's emotions—'

'I've already told you I've never so much as said a word out of place to Yvonne!' A nerve pulsed in his jaw. 'As far as I'm concerned, she has only ever been my PA, never my mistress, and—'

'Jonas, I don't care what your relationship was with Yvonne Richards.' Mac smiled insincerely. 'I'm just relieved to have the whole sorry mess over and done with.'

His nostrils flared. 'You're including our own relationship in that statement?'

'We don't *have* a relationship, Jonas,' she said flatly.

'Last night—'

'We had sex,' Mac finished coolly. 'Interesting experience, but, as I told you at the time, one I'm in no particular hurry to repeat!'

Jonas eyed her frustratedly. He had sought her out today with the sole intention of thanking her for her help in regards to the situation with Yvonne, and then leaving without making any further arrangements to ever see or be with her again. That she was making it more than obvious she was just as anxious to be rid of him definitely rankled.

Which was pretty stupid of him! 'I just wanted to thank you for your help with Yvonne,' he explained.

'You could have done that over the telephone.'

'I wanted to thank you personally.' His eyes glittered. 'Besides, you weren't answering your phone.'

'I've been out all day.'

'Obviously.' Jonas looked at her broodingly as she made no answer, knowing he should leave, and that Mac herself was giving him the perfect opportunity to do exactly that. Except... 'So, are you going out anywhere interesting this evening?' he prompted lightly.

Her eyes narrowed. 'As I believe I've already told you—I'm not answerable to you for any of my actions, Jonas.'

No, and he had never wanted that from any woman, either. Had never asked for exclusivity from any of the women he had dated in the past. But just the thought of Mac going out with another man was enough to cause a red tide of—of what? What emotion was it that was driving him at this moment? Making it necessary for him to know whom she was seeing this evening?

He straightened. 'I'll leave you to get ready for your evening out then,' he bit out, tersely.

Mac's anger and resentment faded as she looked up at Jonas searchingly and acknowledged the finality she could hear in his tone. 'So this is finally goodbye, then?'

His mouth tightened. 'Only if you want it to be.'

Mac's eyes widened. 'If *I* want it to be?'

He shrugged. 'There's no reason why the two of us shouldn't continue to see each other.'

Not for Jonas, perhaps, but for Mac it would be excruciating to see him, be with him as she longed to be, and know that she loved him while all he felt for her was desire.

Knowing that once Jonas had completely sated that desire their relationship would come to an end. As all Jonas's other relationships had ended.

No, Mac's pride wouldn't allow her to take the little that he had to give for as long as he chose to give it. Even if her heart squeezed painfully in her chest at the very idea of never seeing or being with him again...

'Until you got tired of me, you mean?' she guessed shrewdly.

He gave her a half-smile. 'Or you tired of me.'

As if that was ever going to happen!

Mac had waited the whole of her twenty-seven years to meet the man she could love. That she *did* love. It was her misfortune that man happened to be Jonas. A man who didn't even believe in love, let alone in a happy-ever-after forever!

'I don't think so, thank you, Jonas,' she refused dryly.

He scowled darkly. 'Why the hell not?'

Mac shook her head. 'What would be the point? You have your life and I have mine, and the two have absolutely nothing in common.'

Jonas's jaw was clenched. 'Except we want each other!'

Mac smiled sadly. 'Wanting something doesn't mean it's good for you.'

His scowl deepened. 'What the hell does that mean?'

She gave a rueful grimace. 'It means that I know how much I enjoy chocolate, while at the same time accepting that eating too much of it wouldn't be good for me.'

'You're comparing a relationship with me to eating choc-olate?'

'It was just an example, Jonas,' she said. 'What I'm really saying is that ultimately the two of us wouldn't be good for each other.'

'We *are* good together,' he contradicted, his voice lowering huskily.

'I said we *wouldn't* be good for each other,' Mac reiterated clearly.

Jonas frowned. 'You can't possibly know that.'

Mac gave a humourless smile. 'Inwardly we both know it, Jonas.'

Yes, inwardly he did know it. Just as he knew Mac was everything that he had always avoided in the women he became involved with. Physically inexperienced and vulnerable. Family orientated. Warm. Emotional.

Most of all emotional!

In essence she represented everything that Jonas didn't want in his own life.

Yet at the same time, she was everything he *did* want…

He shifted uncomfortably. 'Admittedly, I can't give you romance and flowers, but—'

'I don't remember ever saying I wanted romance and flowers from you!' she cut in indignantly.

Jonas eyed her intently. 'Then what *do* you want, Mac?' he asked bluntly.

'From you?' she asked shortly. 'Nothing.'

'I doubt you would be this…angry, if it was nothing,' Jonas drawled ruefully.

'I'm not in the least angry, Jonas.' Mac sighed. 'At least, not with you.'

'Then who?'

She shook her head. 'You wouldn't understand.'

'Try me,' he invited huskily.

Mac gave a huff of laughter. 'We simply don't look at things the same way, Jonas.'

'Concerning what exactly?'

She almost smiled at the sudden wariness in his expression.

'Concerning everything that matters,' she elaborated. 'I don't need that romance and flowers that you mentioned but I do want my relationships to matter. *I* want to matter!'

'Didn't our lovemaking last night prove that you matter?' he asked.

Mac gave him a pitying glance. 'Last night proved only that you're physically attracted to me.'

'Don't all relationships start that way?'

'All *your* relationships certainly start *and* end that way! As any relationship with me would too,' she added quietly.

'You can't know that—'

'We both know that, Jonas,' she said wearily.

He couldn't let this go. 'You're making assumptions—'

'I'm being realistic,' Mac corrected firmly. 'I really don't want to have an affair with you, Jonas,' she stated honestly.

His mouth twisted. 'Why don't you just come right out and say that you're holding out for the whole package? Love and romance, followed by marriage?'

Mac felt the warmth in her cheek. 'I'm "holding out", as you put it, for exactly what you said I should hold out for last week—the right man to come along.'

'And obviously that isn't me!'

She swallowed down the sick feeling that had risen in her throat. 'Obviously, that isn't you. Don't you see, Jonas, you've allowed your childhood experiences to colour the rest of your life? To damage you rather than anyone else?'

'Are you a psychiatrist too now?' he sneered.

'No, of course not.' She sighed. 'I just think—you'll never be able to function emotionally until you confront the problem you have with your parents.'

'Forgiveness and all that?' he scorned.

'Yes,' she stated.

Jonas stared down at her for long, timeless seconds before breaking that gaze to glance up at the warehouse. 'Have you given any more thought to selling out to Buchanan Construction?'

Mac was thrown for a minute by the sudden change of subject. But only for a minute. 'None at all,' she said definitely.

'Because it isn't going to happen,' Jonas guessed easily.

Mac's chin rose challengingly. 'No.'

Which left Jonas and Buchanan Construction in something of a dilemma. The same dilemma, in fact, that Jonas had been in when he first met Mac over a week ago...

'That's your final word on that subject, too?'

'Absolutely my final word, yes.' She nodded.

Jonas drew in a harsh breath. 'Fine,' he said.

Mac eyed him uncertainly. 'Does that mean you accept my decision?'

He raised dark brows. 'What other choice do I have?'

None as far as Mac was concerned. 'You seemed so—determined to get me out of here a week ago...'

Jonas's smile was as lacking in humour as her own had been a few minutes ago. 'That was before Yvonne started her sick little game.'

'Oh.'

'And before I knew you...' Jonas added softly.

Before Jonas knew her? Or before he 'knew' her in the physical sense?

Did it really matter which, as long as he accepted that she wasn't going to sell the warehouse?

Mac straightened. 'I really do have to go now, Jonas.'

His expression was remote, those eyes a cold, remorseless blue as he nodded. 'Have a pleasant evening.'

Have a pleasant life, he might as well have said, Mac realised achingly.

Because she knew that after today he wanted no part of her or her life. Just as she knew it wasn't specifically her he wanted no part of; it was simply that the very idea of emotional entanglement with anyone was complete anathema to him.

Mac couldn't even imagine what it must be like to live without love in your life. The love of parents. Of family. Of friends. Of that certain special someone that you loved and who loved you.

Although, after today, Mac was going to have to learn to live without the last one herself…

'You too,' she muttered before turning and hurrying up the staircase, her hand shaking slightly as she unlocked the door before going quickly inside and closing it firmly behind her.

Without hesitation.

Without so much as a single backward glance.

Because she dared not look at him again. Knowing that if she did she wouldn't be able to stop herself from launching herself into his arms and agreeing to continue their relationship—that emotionless relationship that was all Jonas could ever give any woman—to its painful conclusion…

Mac lingered only long enough on this floor to drop her keys and helmet on the breakfast bar before hurrying over to switch on the lights to the floor above and ascending the spiral staircase up to her studio.

The canvas she had been working on the last few days still stood on the easel near the glassed wall, the thin cloth Mac had placed over it when she'd brought Jonas up here yesterday evening still in place. After last night she had stayed well away from her studio today, reluctant to see— to be—where the memories of that lovemaking with Jonas were so strong.

Mac crossed the room slowly now to stare at that blank cloth for several seconds before reaching out and removing it.

The background of the painting was there already in shades of blue, but the focus of the painting was only a pencilled sketch at the moment. Strong, abstract lines that nevertheless caught perfectly the wide brow, intensity of light-coloured eyes, high cheekbones either side of an aristocratic slash of a nose, and the mouth sculptured above that square and determined jaw.

Jonas.

Mac rarely painted portraits, and had no idea why she had felt compelled to do this one of him when those hard and handsome features were already etched deep, and for ever, into her soul. As was the love she felt for him.

Painfully.

Irrevocably.

Tears filled Mac's eyes as she continued to stare at that hard and beautiful face on the canvas.

And she wondered what she was going to do with this portrait of Jonas once it was finished.

CHAPTER THIRTEEN

'COME ON, DAD, if you don't hurry we're going to be late,' Mac encouraged her father laughingly as the family gathered in the hallway of her parents' bungalow on Christmas Eve to put on their warm coats and hats and scarves in preparation for going out into the cold and snowy evening. 'And you know how Mum hates to be late—' Mac abruptly broke off her teasing as she opened the front door and saw the person standing outside on the doorstep, one of his gloved hands raised as he prepared to ring the doorbell.

Oh, my God, it was Jonas!

Mac felt the colour drain from her face beneath the red woollen hat she wore. Totally stunned as she stared up searchingly into the grimness of Jonas's face. At the scowl between his brows, the guarded blue of his gaze as it met hers, his mouth and jaw set challengingly.

What on earth was he doing here, of all places?

'Jonas.' Mac's gloved fingers tightened painfully on the door as she moistened dry and slightly numbed lips.

He gave a slight inclination of his head before glancing at the people crowding the hallway behind her. 'I realise you weren't expecting me but—am I in time to join you all at church?' he asked huskily.

'I—yes. Of course,' Mac answered haltingly, her thoughts racing as she tried to make sense of Jonas being here at all.

Apart from the man sent by 'the boss' to collect her Jeep and have the windows repaired almost two weeks ago, Mac hadn't seen or heard from Jonas. Nothing. No telephone calls. No sitting on her metal staircase waiting for her to come home. Just an empty…nothing.

If it hadn't been for the continuous ache in her heart, and the vivid memories she had of their lovemaking, Mac might almost have thought that she had imagined him!

Or perhaps she was just imagining he was here now?

Hallucinating might be a better description!

After all, Jonas was sitting on a beach somewhere on a Caribbean island drinking tall drinks adorned with fruit and pretty coloured-paper umbrellas, possibly with a beautiful blonde at his side. Wasn't he?

'Get a move on, darling, or we're— Oh.' Mac's mother came to an abrupt halt beside her to stare up at Jonas with open curiosity.

Not a hallucination, then, Mac acknowledged with a nervous fluttering in her stomach. Jonas really *was* standing on the doorstep of her parents' bungalow at eleven o'clock at night on Christmas Eve!

The look of total disbelief on Mac's expressive face when she had opened the door and found him standing there might have been amusing if Jonas weren't already feeling so totally wrong-footed himself. If he hadn't already been deeply regretting his decision to come to Devon with the stupid idea of surprising her. But as he was feeling both those things he didn't find that look of embarrassed horror on Mac's face in the least reassuring!

'Mrs McGuire.' He extended his hand politely to the woman who, with her short bob of glossy black hair and smoky-grey eyes, bore such a startling resemblance to Mac that she couldn't possibly be anyone else but her mother. 'Jonas Buchanan,' he explained. 'I hope you don't mind my just turning up like this and joining you all for Midnight Mass? I'm—'

'A friend of mine from London,' Mac put in quickly as she moved to stand at Jonas's side before turning to face her family, linking her arm lightly with his as she did so, and looking very festive in a long white overcoat over a red sweater and black jeans. 'I'm so glad you could make it, after all, Jonas,' she assured huskily. 'Mum, Dad, this is Jonas Buchanan. Jonas, my parents, Melly and Brian.'

To give the two elder McGuires their due, they showed no surprise at finding a complete stranger standing on their doorstep at eleven o'clock at night on Christmas Eve, the tall and still-handsome grey-haired Brian moving forward to shake Jonas's hand warmly. 'The more the merrier,' he assured with genuine heartiness. 'I'm afraid we're already late so we'll have to make all the other introductions later,' he added with a rueful smile at the numerous members of Mac's family milling about in the hallway obviously ready to leave for church.

'I can take three other people as well as Mac in my car if that's of any help,' Jonas offered smoothly as Mac's family tumbled outside into the snowy night.

'Perfect,' the beautiful Melly McGuire accepted warmly. 'I won't have to drive the second car now and can have a glass of mulled wine with my mince pie after the service!'

Jonas was preoccupied for the next few minutes helping Mac settle three of her elderly aunts into the back of his car, but conscious all of that time of her puzzled gaze as it rested on him often.

Mac paused out on the icy road. 'Jonas, why aren't you sitting on a beach somewhere on that Caribbean island?' she prompted softly.

Good question.

One that Jonas felt required the two of them being alone when he answered it…

'Never mind,' Mac dismissed as she saw Jonas's hesitation. 'All that matters is you're here.'

He winced slightly. 'Is it?'

'Yes,' Mac answered firmly as she saw that her father had already reversed his car out onto the road and was waiting to leave. 'We had better go,' she said ruefully as she moved to sit in the passenger seat of Jonas's black Mercedes.

Surrounded as they were by so many members of Mac's family, there was absolutely no opportunity for a private conversation between the two of them as they drove the short distance into the village itself, attended the service in the church surrounded by berry-adorned holly and lit by dozens of candles, and then lingered afterwards to chat and enjoy that anticipated mulled wine and those mince pies.

But that didn't mean that Mac wasn't aware of Jonas's presence at her side for that whole time. That she didn't burn with curiosity to know why he was here. And if he intended staying. That her initial uncertainty at seeing him again hadn't begun to turn to hope…

That uncertainty returned with a vengeance once she and Jonas were finally alone in the sitting-room of her parents' bungalow a little after one o'clock in the morning, the rest of Mac's family having gone to bed. Her mother had already offered the suggestion, 'The small boxroom is empty if Jonas would like to stay for the rest of the Christmas holiday…'

'I did try to warn you,' Mac murmured ruefully as Jonas looked about the sitting-room with its numerous glittering Christmas decorations and enormous and heavily adorned tree with its dozens of presents beneath.

'It's wonderful,' Jonas murmured huskily, his gaze slightly hooded as it came back to rest on Mac as she stood across the room, her hands tightly clasped together in front of her. 'As is your family. I— Mac, I wanted to thank you for my Christmas present,' he said abruptly.

Ah.

Mac smiled a little. 'You didn't have to drive all the way to Devon on Christmas Eve to do that.'

'No.'

Mac shrugged. 'Besides, I had to somehow say thank you for all the help you gave me by having the warehouse painted and the windows on my Jeep fixed. I thought perhaps you might like to hang it in your offices somewhere? In the reception, maybe? A portrait of the head of Buchanan Construction,' she said offhandedly.

'A Mary McGuire portrait of the head of Buchanan Construction,' Jonas corrected softly.

'Well…yes,' she acknowledged awkwardly. 'Just think, if you ever fall on hard times, you'll be able to sell it!' she added jokingly.

Jonas had been surprised when the huge wooden crate was delivered to his office two days ago, stunned when he removed all the packaging and saw the portrait inside. Even so, he hadn't needed to look at the signature in the bottom right hand side of the painting to know it was Mac's work. The style and use of colour were unmistakable.

It was why she had painted it in the first place that Jonas wanted to know...

The last two weeks had been long and...difficult, for Jonas. For numerous reasons. Yvonne Richards. His parents. But most of all, because of Mac.

He hadn't been able to get her out of his mind. Not for a single moment of that time. Her beauty. Her laughter. Her warmth. Her smooth and satiny skin. Her perfume.

This past two weeks Jonas had remembered and relived every single moment he had ever spent with her.

As he had always known would happen, memories of Mac had filled his days and haunted his nights!

'I'm not sure I can allow you to give me such a valuable gift,' he told her gruffly.

Her cheeks flushed. 'I think that's for me to decide, don't you?'

And her temper, Jonas acknowledged ruefully; he hadn't forgotten that fiery temper. How could he, when she had been annoyed or angry with him about one thing or another since the moment they'd first met?

'Yes,' he acknowledged huskily.

Mac's eyes widened. 'Are you actually *agreeing* with me, Jonas?'

He chuckled softly at her obvious incredulity. 'Yes.'

'Well, there's a first!'

Jonas sobered. 'I'm agreeing with you on the understanding that I be allowed to give you something in return.'

Mac eyed him frowningly. Even dressed casually in a dark blue sweater and faded jeans, Jonas was still the most devastatingly handsome man she had ever met. Several other women in the church earlier tonight had obviously thought the same thing as they had eyed him covetously. Admiring glances that Jonas had seemed completely unaware of as he'd stood attentively at Mac's side, his hand resting lightly beneath her elbow.

She shook her head. 'I already told you, the portrait is a thank you for the way you helped me a couple of weeks ago.' It was also a way for Mac to avoid having Jonas's portrait hanging in her studio as a day-to-day reminder of the man she loved but who would never love her in return…

His mouth tightened. 'Help you wouldn't have needed if—'

'We really don't need to talk about that now, Jonas,' Mac rushed in.

'If you wish.' He gave an abrupt inclination of his head.

'I wish,' Mac confirmed firmly. 'What sort of thing are you giving me in return?' she asked warily.

Jonas thrust his hands into his jeans pockets as he shifted uncomfortably. 'I need to explain a few things first.' He frowned. 'I— You told me when we last met that I needed to confront the problem I have with my parents. That the feelings I have for them were—damaging, to me. That—'

'I seem to have made rather a lot of personal remarks that perhaps I shouldn't!' Mac interrupted uncomfortably. 'I was upset when I said those things, Jonas. You really shouldn't take too much notice of me when I'm upset. I inherited my Irish grandfather's sentimental temperament, I'm afraid.'

Jonas gave a twisted smile. 'The truth is the truth, whenever or however it's said.'

'Not if it's in the heat of the moment—'

'But you were right to say those things to me, Mac,' Jonas insisted softly. 'I *have* allowed my parents' disastrous marriage, my unhappy childhood, to affect the man I am now.' He looked her in the eye. 'I've been to see both my parents during the past two weeks—'

'You have?' Mac gasped.

He nodded. 'I've also met my stepfather and stepmother. I still have nothing in common with any of them,' he continued ruefully. 'But I was with them all long enough to know that both second marriages are happy ones. To learn that my parents no longer feel any animosity towards each other.' He sighed. 'I decided that if they can forgive each other for the past then surely I can forgive them too.'

Mac blinked back the tears that threatened to fall. 'I'm so glad, Jonas. For your sake.'

'Yes,' he said. 'Of course, I consider it completely your fault that this reconciliation has now presented me with another set of problems,' he added dryly.

'My fault?' she echoed. 'How?'

'I now have the diplomatic problem of avoiding offending either of my parents. For example, both sets of parents duly invited me to spend Christmas with them,' he drawled ruefully. 'To have accepted one would have insulted the other.'

Mac repressed a smile. 'So as it's my fault you thought you would come here and bother me instead?'

Jonas looked at her consideringly from beneath hooded lids. 'Am I bothering you, Mac?'

Of course having Jonas here was bothering her! Especially as, avoiding offending either of his parents aside, Mac still had no idea why Jonas had chosen to come here tonight of all nights.

Why he had attended church with her family. What he was still doing here…

She moistened her lips nervously. 'You could always

have gone to that beach in the Caribbean,' she reminded him huskily.

'No, I couldn't,' he denied quietly.

'No?'

'No.'

'Why not?' Mac breathed softly, the sudden tension between them so palpable she almost felt as if she could reach out and touch it.

'The only reason that matters,' Jonas murmured.

'Which is?'

He drew in a ragged breath, yet his gaze was clear and unwavering as it met hers. 'The only person I want to spend Christmas with has assured me that under no circumstances would she ever spend Christmas sitting on a beach anywhere!'

Mac couldn't breathe as she stared at him incredulously. *'Me?'* she finally managed to squeak.

Jonas gave a genuine smile. 'You.'

Mac stared at him with wide eyes. 'You want to spend Christmas with *me*?'

'And your family. If you'll allow me to,' he added uncertainly. 'Mac.' He crossed the room in two long strides so that he was now standing only inches away from her. 'I know that I'm— Well, I appreciate that my track record for long-term relationships is—'

'Non-existent,' she put in helpfully as a tidal wave of hope began to build inside her.

Jonas's mouth firmed. 'Non-existent,' he acknowledged. 'But that could be a good thing,' he continued encouragingly as he reached out and grasped both Mac's hands tightly in his. 'It means that I don't have any past relationships, any lingering feelings for another woman, to complicate things.'

That tidal wave of hope grew bigger still as Mac easily saw the lingering uncertainty in Jonas's eyes. 'Complicate what things?' she prompted.

'Ah.' He winced. 'Yes. I need my overcoat from the hall-way.' Jonas released her hands. 'Your Christmas present is in the pocket—'

'Family rule, no presents to be unwrapped until Christmas morning!' Mac protested before Jonas could leave the sitting-room.

He turned in the doorway. 'It already *is* Christmas morning, Mac,' he pointed out dryly. 'Besides, this present isn't gift-wrapped,' he added confidently.

Mac had no idea what was going on. Just now Jonas had seemed on the point of—well, on the point of something. And now he was totally preoccupied with giving her a Christmas present instead.

When the only Christmas present Mac wanted was Jonas himself!

Jonas returned from the hallway to find Mac still standing where he had left her. His heart pounded loudly in his chest as he walked over to join her, two folded sheets of paper in his hand. 'I'd like your input on this before I submit it for planning approval.' His expression was strained as he handed her the top sheet of paper.

Mac gave him an uncertain glance before she slowly unfolded the sheet of paper, a frown between her eyes as she looked up at him. 'I— It appears to be a building plan of the new apartment complex, one that rather tastefully incorporates my warehouse into the grounds...'

A nerve pulsed in the tenseness of Jonas's jaw. 'It *is* a building plan of the new apartment complex that—hopefully—tastefully incorporates your warehouse,' he confirmed huskily.

She refolded it carefully. 'And the other one?' She looked at the second sheet of design paper in Jonas's hand.

Jonas's fingers tightened perceptibly. 'These are some alterations to the original plan that don't include your warehouse in the grounds.'

Mac looked at him accusingly as she thrust the original sheet back into his hands. 'And *this* is the present you drove all this way to give me?' she exclaimed. 'You're unbelievable, do you know that, Jonas?' She looked thoroughly disgusted. 'You've come all this way just to have yet another attempt at trying to talk me into selling my home!' She moved away restlessly. 'The answer is no, Jonas. N. O. Is that clear enough for you?' Angry tears glistened in those smoky-grey eyes as she glared at him.

Well that went well, Jonas—*not*! he told himself, wincing. Self-confident to the point of arrogance usually, he had known before he came here tonight that he was somehow going to bungle this. Because it was more important than anything else had ever been in his life before. Because it mattered to him more than anything else ever had in his life before!

'I haven't asked the question yet...' he murmured softly.

'You don't need to,' Mac fired back. 'Just leave, Jonas. Go away and never come back. I never want to see—'

'Mac, will you marry me?'

'—or speak to you *ever*—' Mac abruptly broke off her tirade to stare across at him incredulously. 'What did you just say?'

Jonas swallowed hard. 'I asked if you would do me the honour of marrying me,' he repeated gruffly as he moved hesitantly towards her, the intensity of his gaze searching the paleness of Mac's face as he stood in front of her.

Exactly what she had thought he'd said!

She looked closely at his face, finally seeing the anxiety in those blue eyes, in his tensely clenched jaw and cheeks. 'Why?' she breathed.

Jonas gave a huff of laughter. 'Most women would have said, "No, thank you, Jonas," or, "Oh, Jonas this is so sudden." You, being you, ask me *why*!' He gave a rueful shake of his head.

Mac gave him an irritated glance. 'Well, it *is* rather sudden.'

'Not to me.' Jonas sighed. 'The two weeks since we were last together have been—' He shook his head. 'Hell, is the only fitting description I can think of,' he decided heavily.

'Why?'

'Again with the why!' He briefly raised his gaze to the ceiling. 'Mac, I didn't *want* to fall in love with you. It's the last thing I ever wanted! But you—' He sighed. 'You are the most infuriating, provoking, stubborn, irritating—'

'Do you think we could go back to the "I didn't want to fall in love with you" bit…?' Mac interrupted, her heart beating so loudly, so erratically, she was sure Jonas must be able to hear it too.

'—fascinating, warm, arousing, wonderful woman I have ever met!' Jonas finished. 'How could I not fall in love with you?' He shook his head as he once again reached out to grasp both Mac's hands in his.

Mac felt hot and cold all at the same time. 'You really love me?' she breathed dazedly.

'It's worse than that, I'm afraid,' Jonas muttered. 'Mac, this past two weeks I've come to realise that I want it *all* with you. Love. Marriage. Children. I want to be your last lover as well as your first. I want to wake up and find you beside me for the rest of my life. Most of all I want to be the man you deserve. The man you can love. Will you at least give me the chance to show you that I can be that man?' He looked down at her anxiously.

Jonas loved her! Wanted to marry her! Have children with her!

Mac released one of her hands from his to reach up tentatively and cup one hard and chiselled cheek. 'Are you sure about this, Jonas? Absolutely sure? Love, marriage, children—those things mean for ever to me, you know...'

His fingers tightened painfully about hers. 'I wouldn't settle for anything less!' he assured her fiercely. 'Mac, you totally misunderstood my motives for those two new sets of plans. The first one leaves the warehouse standing, yes, but the second one shows a completely different layout to the penthouse in the apartment complex.'

'Show me,' she encouraged huskily.

Jonas unfolded and smoothed out the second set of plans. 'You see here?' He pointed to the diagram. 'That wall is now completely glass, as is the ceiling in that room. It's a replica of your studio, Mac,' he explained gruffly. 'I went to see my parents because I love you. Because you were right about my needing to confront that situation, to deal with those ghosts from the past, before I could move on with my own life. You are my life, Mac. I'm asking you to give me the chance to show you that, to prove to you how much I love you. To show you how I will always love you, and only you. Exactly as you are,' he added emphatically.

'No dressing up and being a trophy on your arm, then?' she teased a little tearfully.

Jonas really did love her!

'As far as I'm concerned you can live in those damn-awful dungarees and never set foot outside the apartment again as long as I can be there with you. Mac, just give me the chance to show you how much I love you, to persuade you into falling in love with me, and I promise you won't ever have reason to regret it!' he vowed.

'Oh, Jonas,' she groaned.

He gave a pained wince. 'Is that a "no, thank you, Jonas," or a "Let me think about this, Jonas."?'

'It's an "I already love you, Jonas,"' Mac assured him emotionally as she moved into his arms.

'You *love* me?' There was a look of stunned disbelief on his face.

'So much that I really don't care where I live any more, either, as long as it's with you! Jonas, I love you so much that these past two weeks have been hell for me too. I love you, Jonas!' she repeated joyfully.

His arms moved about her like steel bands. 'Enough to marry me?'

'Enough to spend for ever, eternity, with you!' she assured him happily.

Jonas looked down at her searchingly for long, timeless minutes, his eyes blazing with his love for her as he saw that emotion reflected back at him. He buried his face in the perfume of her silky hair as he groaned. 'I can't believe that I let you walk away from me two weeks ago. That I almost lost you!'

'Just kiss me, Jonas,' Mac encouraged breathlessly.

'I intend to kiss you and love you for the rest of our lives,' he promised as his mouth finally claimed hers.

The rest of their lives sounded just perfect to Mac...

* * * * *

His Until Midnight
Nikki Logan

ABOUT NIKKI LOGAN

—

Nikki Logan lives next to a string of protected wetlands in Western Australia, with her long-suffering partner and a menagerie of furred, feathered and scaly mates. She studied film and theater at university, and worked for years in advertising and film distribution before finally settling down in the wildlife industry. Her romance with nature goes way back, and she considers her life charmed, given she works with wildlife by day and writes fiction by night—the perfect way to combine her two loves. Nikki believes that the passion and risk of falling in love are perfectly mirrored in the danger and beauty of wild places. Every romance she writes contains an element of nature, and if readers catch a waft of rich earth or the spray of wild ocean between the pages she knows her job is done.

DEAR READER,

Have you ever heard the saying "why let the truth get in the way of a perfectly good story"? A friend told me how she catches up, once a year, with a long-standing (male) friend in a gorgeous restaurant high above a beautiful Asian city. They spend a full lazy day catching up and sharing stories and squeezing a year's worth of friendship into that one day of the year and then they fly back to their respective countries. And it's entirely, completely, unquestionably wholesome.

So of course I had to go and ruin it.

The simple premise grabbed me and filled me to overflowing with those "what-ifs" that authors love. What if it wasn't completely wholesome? What if one of them was secretly attracted to the other one but never, ever planned to act on it? What if they did this for years and then one year *something changed...?*

And I realized that this story was really about the biggest *what-if* of all...one that we can all relate to. *What if* you'd turned right instead of left that day, or taken the bus instead of walking, or been brave enough to give your phone number to one man instead of his friend? What if you'd just grabbed opportunity by the shirt-collars the first time around? Where would you be today?

This is a story about the patience of Love, the beauty of Friendship and the magic of Christmas.

If you're reading it at Christmas, please accept my best wishes to you and your family for a wonderful and safe holiday season.

May love always find you,

Nikki

www.nikkilogan.com.au—A Romance with Nature

For Alex and Trev who let me turn their entirely platonic
annual tradition into something much more dramatic.
Thank you for the inspiration.

CHAPTER ONE

December 20th, four years ago
Qīngtíng Restaurant, Hong Kong

AUDREY DEVANEY FLOPPED against the back of the curved sofa and studied the pretty, oriental-style cards in her hands. Not the best hand in the world but when you were playing for M&M's and you tended to eat your stake as fast as it accumulated it was hard to take poker too seriously.

Though it was fun to pretend she knew what she was doing. Like some Vegas hotshot. And it wasn't too hard to imagine that the extraordinary view of Hong Kong's Victoria Harbour stretching out behind Oliver Harmer was really out of the window of some casino high-roller's room instead of a darkened, atmospheric restaurant festooned with pretty lanterns and baubles in rich, oriental colours.

Across from her, Oliver's five o'clock shadow was designer perfect and an ever-present, unlit cigar poked out of the corner of his grinning mouth—more gummed than smoked, out of respect for her and for the other patrons in the restaurant. It only *felt* as if he bought the whole place out each Christmas, it wasn't actually true. Though it was nice to imagine that they had the entire restaurant to themselves.

'Thank you, again, for the gift,' she murmured, letting the fringed silk ends of the cobalt scarf run between her fingers. 'It's stunning.'

'You're welcome. You should wear more blue.'

Audrey studied Oliver over her cards, wanting to ask but not entirely sure how to raise it. Maybe the best approach was the direct approach…

'You know, you look pretty good for a man whose wedding just fell through.'

'Good' as in *well*. Not 'good' as in *gorgeous*. Although, as always, the latter would certainly apply. All that dark hair, long lashes and tanned Australian skin…

He took his time considering his hand and then tossed three cards face down onto the ornate carved table. 'Dodged a bullet.'

That stopped her just as she might have discarded her own dud cards. 'Really? Last Christmas it was all about how Tiffany might be "the one".'

Not that she'd actually believed him at the time, but a year was the longest relationship she'd ever known him to have.

Maybe she was just in denial.

'Turns out there was more than one "one" for Tiffany.' The tiniest glimmer of hurt stained his eyes.

Oh, no. 'Who called it off?'

His answer came fast and sure. 'I did.'

Oliver Harmer was a perpetual bachelor. But he was also Shanghai's most prized perpetual bachelor and so she couldn't imagine the average woman he dated being too fast to throw away her luxury future.

But she knew from Blake how seriously Oliver felt about fidelity. Because of his philandering father. 'I'm so sorry.'

He shrugged. 'She was with someone when I met her; I was foolish to think that I'd get treated any different.'

Foolish perhaps, but he was only human to hope that he'd be special enough to change his girlfriend's ways. And if ever there was a man worth changing for... Audrey dropped two cards onto the table and Oliver flicked her two replacements from the top of the pack with confident efficiency before taking three of his own.

'What did she say when you confronted her?' she murmured.

'I didn't see any purpose in having it out,' he squeezed out past the cigar. 'I just cut her loose.'

Without an explanation? 'What if you were mistaken?'

The look he threw her would have withered his corporate opponents. 'I checked. I wasn't.'

'Checking' in Oliver's world probably meant expensive private surveillance. So no, he wouldn't have been wrong. 'Where is she now?'

He shrugged. 'Still on our honeymoon, I guess. I gave her an open credit card and wished her the best.'

'You bought her off?' She gaped.

'I bought her forgiveness.'

'And that worked?'

'Tiffany never was one for labouring under regret for long.'

Lord, he had a talent for ferreting out the worst of women. Always beautiful, of course and—*cough*—agile, but utterly barren on the emotional front. To the point that she'd decided Oliver must prefer them that way. Except for the trace of genuine hurt that had flitted across his expression...

That didn't fit with the man she thought she knew.

She studied the nothing hand in front of her and then tossed all five cards down on the table in an inelegant fold.

'Why can't you just meet a nice, normal woman?' she despaired. 'Shanghai's a big city.'

He scooped the pile of bright M&M's towards him—though not before she snaffled yet another one to eat—and set about reshuffling the cards. 'Nice women tend to give me a wide berth. I can't explain it.'

She snorted. 'It would have nothing to do with your reputation.'

Hazel eyes locked on hers, speculative and challenging. Enough to tighten her chest a hint. 'And what reputation is that?'

Ah...no. 'I'm not going to feed your already massive ego, Oliver.'

Nor go anywhere near the female whispers she'd heard about Oliver *'the Hammer'* Harmer. Dangerous territory.

'I thought we were friends!' he protested.

'You're friends with my husband. I'm just his South-East Asian proxy.'

He grunted. 'You only agree to our ritual Christmas catch-up for the cuisine, I suppose?'

'Actually, no.'

She found his eyes—held them—and two tiny butterflies broke free in her chest. 'I come for the wine, too.'

He snagged a small fistful of M&M's and tossed them across the elegant, carved coffee table at her, heedless of those around them sharing the Christmas-themed menu sixty storeys above Hong Kong.

Audrey scrabbled madly to pick them up. 'Ugh. Isn't that

just like a squazillionaire. Throwing your money around like it's chocolate drops.'

'Play your hand,' he griped. But there was a definite smile behind it. As there always was. Christmases between them were always full of humour, fast conversation and camaraderie.

At least on the surface.

Below the surface was a whole bunch of things that she didn't let herself look at too closely. Appreciation. Respect. A great, aching admiration for his life and the choices he'd made and the courage with which he'd made them. Oliver Harmer was the freest human being she knew. And he lived a life most people would hunger for.

She certainly did from within the boundaries of her awkward marriage. It was hard not to esteem his choices.

And then below all of that… The ever-simmering attraction. She'd grown used to it now, because it was always there. And because she only had to deal with it once a year.

He was a good-looking man; charming and affable, easy to talk to, easy to like, well built, well groomed, well mannered, but not up himself or pretentious. Never too cool to toss a handful of chocolates in a fine restaurant.

But he'd also been best man at her wedding.

Blake's oldest friend.

And he was pursued by women day in and day out. She would be two hundred per cent mortified if Oliver ever got so much of a hint of the direction of her runaway thoughts— not the least because it would just inflate his already monumental ego—but also because she knew exactly what he'd do with the information.

Nothing.

Not a damned thing.

He would take it to his grave, and she would never fully know if that was because of his loyalty to Blake, his respect for her, or because something brewing between them was just so totally inconceivable that he'd chalk it up to an aberrant moment best never again spoken of.

Which was pretty much the right advice.

She wasn't like the women he normally chose. Her finest day was the day of her wedding when she'd been called 'striking'—and by Oliver, come to think of it, who always seemed to say the right thing at the right moment when she was on rocky emotional ground. She didn't look as good as his women did in their finery and she didn't move in the same circles and know the same people and laugh overly loud at the same stories. She wasn't unattractive or dull or dim—she'd wager the entire pile of M&M's in front of her on the fact that she could outrank every one of them on a MENSA test—but she certainly didn't turn heads when she was in the company of the beautiful people. She lacked that…stardust that they had.

That Oliver was coated-to-sparkling in.

And in all the years she'd known him, she'd flat out never seen him with someone less beautiful than he was.

Clearly some scientific principle of balance at work there.

And when even the laws of nature ruled you out…

'All right, Cool Hand Luke,' she said, ripping her thoughts back to safer territory. 'Let's get serious about this game.'

That treacherous snake.

Audrey clearly had no idea whatsoever of Blake's latest conquest. Her face had filled just then with genuine sympathy about Tiffany, but nothing else. No shadows of pain at the mention of someone's infidelity, no blanching. No tears for a betrayal shared. Not that she was the tears-in-public type, but the only moisture in those enormous blue eyes was old-fashioned compassion.

For him.

Which meant that either Blake had lied and Audrey had no idea that her husband considered their marriage open, or she *did* know and Blake had worn her down to the point that she just didn't care any more.

And that awful possibility just didn't fit with the engaged, involved woman in front of him.

Oliver eyed her over his cards, pretending to psych her out and throw her game but really using the opportunity to study the tiniest traces of truth in her oval face. Her life tells. She wasn't flat and lifeless. She was enjoying the cards, the food, the conversation. She always did. He never flattered himself that it was him, particularly, that she hurried to see each year, but she loved the single day of decadence that they always shared on December twentieth. Not the expenditure—she and Blake were both on healthy incomes and she could buy this sort of experience herself if she really wanted to—it was the low-key luxury of this restaurant, this day, that she really got off on.

She was the only woman he'd ever met who got more excited by *not* being flashy with his money. By being as tastefully understated as she always was. It suited her down to the ground. Elegant instead of glitzy, all that dark hair twisted in a lazy knot on top of her head with what looked like bamboo spears holding it all together. The way her hands occasionally ran across the fabric of her tailored skirt told him she enjoyed how the fabric felt against her skin. That was why she wore it; not for him, or any other man. Not because it hugged the intriguing curve of her thighs almost indecently. The money Audrey spent on fashion was about recognising her equal in a quality product.

Whether she knew that or not.

Which was why he struggled so badly with Blake's protestations that Audrey was cool with his marital…excursions. He got that they didn't have the most conventional of marriages—definitely a meeting of minds—but she just didn't strike him as someone who would tolerate the cheapening of her relationship through his playing around. Because, if nothing else, Blake's sleeping around reflected on her.

And Audrey Devaney was anything but cheap.

'Oliver?'

He refocused to find those sapphire eyes locked hard on his. 'Sorry. Raise.'

She smiled at his distraction and then flicked her focus back down to her cards, leaving him staring at those long, down-curved lashes.

Did she know that her husband hooked up with someone else the moment she left town? Did that bother her? Or did she fabricate trips specifically to give Blake the opportunity, to give herself necessary distance from his infidelity, and preserve the amazing dignity that she wore like one of her silk suits. He'd never got the slightest sense that she evened the score while she travelled. Not that he'd necessarily know if she did—she would be as discreet about that as she was about the other details of her life—but her work ethic was nearly as solid as her friendship. And, as the lucky beneficiary of her unwavering loyalty as a friend, he knew that if Audrey was in Asia working then that was exactly what she'd be doing.

Working her silk-covered butt off.

And, if she wasn't, he'd know it. When it came to her, his radar was fine-tuned for the slightest hint that she was operating on the same wavelength as her husband.

Because if Audrey Devaney was *on* the market, then he was *in* the market.

No matter the price. No matter the terms. No matter what he'd believed his whole life about fidelity. He'd had enough hot, restless nights after waking from one of his dreams—riddled with passion and guilt and Audrey up against the cold glass of the window facing out over Victoria Harbour—to know what his body wanted.

'Call.' She tossed a cluster of M&M's onto the pile, interrupting the dangerous direction of his thoughts.

But he also knew himself pretty well. He knew that sex was the great equaliser and that reducing a woman that he admired and liked so much to the subject of one of his cheap fantasies was just his subconscious' way of dealing with the unfamiliar territory.

Territory in which he found himself fixated on the only woman he knew who was *genuinely* too good for him.

'Your game.' Oliver tossed aces and jacks purely for the pleasure of seeing the flush Audrey couldn't contain. The pleasure that spilled out over the edges of her usual propriety. She loved to win. She loved to beat him, particularly.

And he loved to watch her enjoy it.

She flipped a trio of fours on top of the mound of M&M's triumphantly and her perfectly made-up skin practically glowed with pleasure. Instantly, he wondered if that was what she'd look like if he pushed this table aside and pressed her back into the sofa with his lips against that confident smile and his thigh between hers.

His body cheered the very thought.

'Rematch,' he demanded, forcing his brain clean of smut. Pretty sad when throwing a card game was about as erotic as any dream he could conjure up. 'Double or nothing.'

She tipped her head back to laugh and that knot piled on the top and decorated with a bit of stolen airport tinsel wobbled dangerously. If he kept the humour coming maybe the whole thing would come tumbling down and he'd have another keeper memory for his pathetic fantasy-stalker collection.

'Sure, while you're throwing your chocolates away…'

She slipped off her shoes and pulled slim legs up onto the sofa as Oliver dealt another hand and, again, he was struck by how down to earth she was. And how innocent. This was not the relaxed, easy expression of a woman who knew her husband was presently shacked up with someone that wasn't his wife.

No question.

Which meant his best friend was a liar as well as an adulterer. And a fool, too, for cheating on the most amazing woman either of them had ever known. Just *wasting* the beautiful soul he'd been gifted by whatever fate sent Audrey in Blake's direction instead of his own all those years ago.

But where fate was vague and indistinct, that out-of-place rock weighing down her left hand was very real, and though her husband was progressively sleeping his way through Sydney, Audrey wasn't following suit.

Because that ring meant something to her.

Just as fidelity meant something to him.

Perhaps that was the great attraction. Audrey was moral and compassionate, and her integrity was rooted as firmly as the mountains that surged up out of the ocean all around them to form the islands of Hong Kong where they both flew to meet each December twentieth. Splitting the difference between Sydney and Shanghai.

And he was enormously drawn to that integrity, even as he cursed it. Would he be as drawn to her if she was playing the field like her selfish husband? Or was he only obsessed with her because he knew he couldn't have her?

That was more his playbook.

Just because he didn't do unfaithful didn't mean he was pro-commitment. The whole Tiffany thing was really a kind of retirement. He'd given up on finding the woman he secretly dreamed was out there for him and settled for one that would let him do whatever he wanted, whenever he wanted and look good doing it.

And clearly even that wasn't meant to be.

'Come on, Harmer. Man up.'

His eyes shot up, fearing for one irrational moment that she'd read the direction of his inappropriate thoughts.

'It's just one game,' she teased. 'I'm sure you'll take me on the next one.'

She was probably right. He'd do what he did every Christmas: give enough to keep her engaged and entertained, and take enough to keep her colour high with indignation. To keep her coming back for more. Coming back to him. In the name of her cheating bastard of a husband who only ever visited him when he was travelling alone—though he'd be sure to put an end to that, now—and who took carnal advantage of every opportunity when Audrey was out of the country.

But, just as he suppressed his natural distaste for Blake's infidelity so that he could maintain the annual Christmas lunch with his best friend's wife, so he would keep Blake's secret.

Not only because he didn't want to hurt gentle Audrey.

And not because he condoned Blake's behaviour in the slightest—though he really, really didn't.

And not because he enjoyed being some kind of confessional for the man he'd stood beside at his wedding.

No, he'd keep Blake's secret because keeping it meant he got to have Audrey in his life. If he shared what he knew she'd leave Blake, and if she left Blake Oliver knew he'd never see her again. And it was only as he saw her friendship potentially slipping away like a landslide that he realised how very much he valued—and needed—it.

And her.

So he did what he did every year. He concentrated on Audrey and on enjoying what little time they had together this one day of the year. He feasted like the glutton he was on her conversation and her presence and he pushed everything else into the background where it belonged.

He had all year to deal with that. And with his conscience.

He stretched his open palm across the table, the shuffled cards upturned on it. As she took the pack, her soft fingers brushed against his palm, birthing a riot of sensation in his nerve endings. And he boxed those sensations up, too, for dealing with later, when he didn't have this amazing woman sitting opposite him with her all-seeing eyes focused squarely on him.

'Your deal.'

CHAPTER TWO

December 20th, three years ago
Qīngtíng Restaurant, Hong Kong

BEHIND HER BACK, Audrey pressed the soft flesh of her wrists to the glassy chill of the elevator's mirrored wall, desperate to cool the blazing blood rushing through her arteries. To quell the excited flush she feared stained her cheeks from standing this close to Oliver Harmer in such a tight space.

You'd think twelve months would be enough time to steel her resolve and prepare herself.

Yet here she was, entirely rattled by the anticipation of a simple farewell kiss. It never was more than a socially appropriate graze. Barely more than an air-kiss. Yet she still felt the burn of his lips on her cheek as though last year's kiss were a moment—and not a full year—ago.

She was a teenager again, around Oliver. All breathless and hot and hormonal. Totally fixated on him for the short while she had his company. It would have been comic if it weren't also so terribly mortifying. And it was way too easy to indulge the feelings this one day of the year. It felt dangerous and illicit to let the emotions even slightly off the leash. Thank goodness she was old enough now to fake it like a seasoned professional.

In public, anyway.

Oliver glanced down and smiled at her in that strange, searching way he had, a half-unwrapped DVD boxed set in his hands. She gave him her most careful smile back, took a deep breath and then refocused on the light descending the crowded panel of elevator buttons.

Fifty-nine, fifty-eight...

She wasn't always so careful. She caught herself two weeks ago wondering what her best man would think of tonight's dress instead of her husband. But she'd rationalised it by saying that Oliver's taste in women—and, by implication, his taste in their wardrobes—was far superior to Blake's and so taking trouble to dress well was important for a man who hosted her in a swanky Hong Kong restaurant each year.

Blake, on the other hand, wouldn't notice if she came to the dinner table dressed in a potato sack.

He used to notice—back in the day, nine years ago—when she'd meet him and Oliver at a restaurant in something flattering. Or sheer-cut. Or reinforcing. Back then, appreciation would colour Blake's skin noticeably. Or maybe it just seemed more pronounced juxtaposed with the blank indifference on Oliver's face. Oliver, who barely even glanced at her until she was seated behind a table and modestly secured behind a menu.

Yet, paradoxically, she had him to thank for the evolution of her fashion sense because his disdain was a clear litmus test if something was *too* flattering, *too* sheer-cut. *Too* reinforcing.

It was all there in the careful nothing of his expression.

People paid top dollar for that kind of fashion advice. Oliver gifted her with it for free.

Yeah…his *gift*. That felt so much better on the soul than his *judgement*. And seasonally appropriate, too.

This year's outfit was a winner. And while she missed the disguised scrutiny of his greenish-brown gaze—the visual caress that usually sustained her all year—the warm wash of his approval was definitely worth it. She glanced at herself in the elevator's mirrored walls and tried to see herself as Oliver might. Slim, professional, well groomed.

Weak at the knees with utterly inappropriate anticipation. *Forty-five, forty-four…*

'What time is your flight in the morning?' His deep voice honey-rumbled in the small space.

Her answer was more breath than speech. 'Eight.'

Excellent. Resorting to small talk. But this was always how it went at the end. As though they'd flat run out of other things to talk about. Entirely possible given the gamut of topics they covered during their long, long lunch-that-became-dinner, and because she was usually emotionally and intellectually drained from so many hours sitting across from a man she longed to see but really struggled to be around.

It was only one day.

Twelve hours, really. That was all she had to get through each year and wasn't a big ask of her body. The rest of the year she had no trouble suppressing the emotions. She used the long flight home to marshal all the sensations back into that tightly lidded place she kept them so that she disembarked the plane in Sydney as strong as when she'd left Australia.

She'd invited Blake along this year—pure survival, hoping her husband's presence would force her wayward thoughts back into safer territory—but not only had he declined, he'd looked horrified at the suggestion. Which made no sense because he liked to catch up with Oliver whenever he was travelling in Asia, himself. Least he used to.

In fact, it made about as little sense as the not-so-subtle way Oliver changed the subject every time she mentioned Blake. As if he was trying to distance himself from the only person they had in common.

And without Blake in common, really what did they have?

Twenty-seven, twenty-six, twenty-five...

Breath hissed out of her in a long, controlled yoga sigh and she willed her fluttering pulse to follow its lead. But that persistent flutter was still entirely fixated on the gorgeous, expensive aftershave Oliver wore and the heat coming off his big body and it seemed to fibrillate faster the closer to the ground floor they got.

And they were so close, now.

Ultimately, it didn't matter what her body did when in Oliver's immediate proximity—how her breath tightened, or her mouth dried or her heart squeezed—that was like Icarus hoping his wings wouldn't melt as he flew towards the sun.

There was nothing she could do about the fundamental rules of biology. All that mattered was that it didn't show on the outside.

On pain of death.

Tonight she'd been the master of her anatomy. Giving nothing away. So she only had to last these final few mo-

ments and she'd be away, speeding through the streets of
Hong Kong en route to her own hotel room. Her cool, safe,
empty bed. The sleepless night that was bound to follow.
And the airport bright and early in the morning.

She should really get the red-eye next year.

It was impossible to know whether the lurch in her stomach was due to the arrest of the elevator's rapid descent or
because she knew what was coming next. The elegant doors
seemed to gather their wits a moment before opening.

Audrey did the same.

They whooshed open and she matched Oliver's footfalls
out through the building's plush foyer onto the street, then
turned on a smile and extended a hand as a taxi pulled up
from the nearby rank to attend them.

'Any message for Blake?'

She always kept something aside for this exact moment.
Something strong and obstructive in case her body decided
to hurl itself at him and embarrass them all. Invariably
Blake-related because that was about the safest territory
the two of them had. Blake or work. Not to mention the fact
that reference to her husband was usually one of the only
things that made a dent in the hormonal surge that swilled
around them when they stood this close.

The swampy depths of his eyes darkened for the brief-
est of moments as he took her hand in his large one. 'No.
Thank you.'

Odd. Blake hadn't had one, either. Which was a first…

But her curiosity about that half-hidden flash of anger
lasted a mere nanosecond in the face of the heat soaking
from his hand into the one he hadn't released anywhere
nearly as swiftly as she'd offered it. He held it—no caresses,
nothing that would raise an eyebrow for anyone watch-

ing—and used it to pull her towards him for their annual Christmas air-kiss.

Her blood surged against its own current; the red cells rushing downstream to pool in fingers that tingled at Oliver's touch stampeding against the foolish ones that surged, upstream, to fill the lips that she knew full well weren't going to get to touch his.

She thrilled for this moment and hated it at the same time because it was never enough. Yet of course it had to be. The sharp, expensive tang of his cologne washed over her catgut-tight senses as he leaned down and brushed his lips against her cheek. A little further back from last year. A little lower, too. Close enough to her pulse to feel it pounding under her skin.

Barely enough to even qualify as a kiss. But ten times as swoon-worthy as any real kiss she'd ever had.

Hormones.

Talk about mind-altering chemicals...

'Until next year,' he breathed against her ear as he withdrew.

'I will.'

Give my regards to Blake. That was what usually came after 'the kiss' and she'd uttered her response before her foggy brain caught up to the fact that he hadn't actually asked it of her this year. Again, odd. So her next words were stammered and awkward. Definitely not the cool, calm and composed Audrey she usually liked to finish her visit on.

'Well, goodbye, then. Thank you for lunch.'

Ugh. Lame.

Calling their annual culinary marathon 'lunch' was like suggesting that the way Oliver made her feel was 'warm'. Right now her body blazed with all the unspent chemis-

try from twelve hours in his company and her head spun
courtesy of the shallow breathing of the past few minutes.
Embarrassed heat blazed up the back of her neck and she
slipped quickly into the waiting taxi before it bloomed fully
in her face.

Oliver stood on the footpath, his hand raised in farewell as she pressed back against the headrest and the cab
moved away.

'Wait!'

She lurched against her seat belt and suddenly Oliver was
hauling the door open again. For one totally crazy, breathless heartbeat she thought he might have pulled her into his
arms. And she would have gone into them. Unflinchingly.

But he didn't.

Of course he didn't.

'Audrey—'

She shoved her ritualistic in-taxi decompression routine
down into the gap between the seat back and cushion and
presented him with her most neutral, questioning expression.

'I just... I wanted to say...'

A dozen indecipherable expressions flitted across his
expression but finally resolved into something that looked
like pain. Grief.

'Merry Christmas, Audrey. I'll see you next year.'

The anticlimax was breath-stealing in its severity and
so her words were little more than a disenchanted whisper.
'Merry Christmas, Oliver.'

'If you ever need me...need anything. Call me.' His hazel
eyes implored. 'Any time, day or night. Don't hesitate.'

'Okay,' she pledged, though had no intention of taking
him up on it. Oliver Harmer and The Real World did not

mix. They existed comfortably in alternate realities and her flight to and from Hong Kong was the inter-dimensional transport. In this reality he was the first man—the only man—she'd ever call if she were in trouble. But back home...

Back home she knew her life was too beige to need his help and even if she did, she wouldn't let herself call him.

The taxi pulled away again and Audrey resumed decompression. Her breath eased out in increments until her heart settled down to a heavy, regular beat and her skin warmed back up to room temperature.

Done.

Another year survived. Another meeting endured in her husband's name and hopefully with her dignity fully intact.

And only three hundred and sixty-five days until she saw Oliver Harmer again.

Long, confusing days.

CHAPTER THREE

December 20th, two years ago
Qīngtíng Restaurant, Hong Kong

OLIVER STARED OUT at the midnight sky, high enough above
the flooding lights of Hong Kong to actually see a few stars,
and did his best to ignore the screaming lack of attention
being paid to him by Qīngtíng's staff as they closed up the
restaurant for the night.

The arms crossed firmly across his chest were the only
thing keeping his savaged heart in his chest cavity, and the
beautifully wrapped gift crushed in his clenched fist was
the only thing stopping him from slamming it into the wall.

She hadn't come.

For the first time in years, Audrey hadn't come.

CHAPTER FOUR

December 20th, last year
Obsiblue prawn and caviar with Royale Cabanon Oyster
and Yuzu

'YOU'RE LUCKY I'M even here.'

The rumbled accusation filtered through the murmur of low conversation and the chink of expensive silverware on Qīngtíng's equally expensive porcelain. Audrey turned towards Oliver's neutral displeasure, squared the shoulders of her cream linen jacket and smoothed her hands down her skirt.

'Yet here you are.'

A grunt lurched in Oliver's tanned throat where a business tie should have been holding his navy silk shirt appropriately together. Or at the very least some buttons. Benefit of being such a regular patron—or maybe so rich—niceties like dress code didn't seem to apply to him.

'Guess I'm slow to learn,' he said, still dangerously calm. 'Or just naively optimistic.'

'Not so naive. I'm here, aren't I?'

'You don't look too pleased about it.'

'Your email left me little choice. I didn't realise how proficient you'd become in emotional blackmail.'

'It wasn't blackmail, Audrey. I just wanted to know if you were coming. To save me wasting another day and the flight from Shanghai.'

Shame battled annoyance. Yes, she'd stood him up last year, but she found it hard to imagine a man like Oliver left alone and dateless in a flash restaurant for very long. Especially at Christmas. Especially in a city full of homesick expats. She was sure he wouldn't have withered away from lack of company.

'And playing the dead best friend card seemed equal to your curiosity, did it?'

Because that was the only reason she was here at all. The relationship he'd had with her recently passed husband. And she'd struggled to shake the feeling that she needed to provide some closure for Oliver on that friendship.

His hazel eyes narrowed just a hint in that infuriating, corporate, too-cool-for-facial-expression way he had. But he didn't bite. Instead he just stared at her, almost daring her to go on. Daring her, just as much, to hold his glower.

'They got new carpet,' she announced pointlessly, thrilled for an excuse not to let him enslave her gaze. Stylised and vibrant dragonflies decorated the floor where once obscure oriental patterns had previously lain. She sank the pointed tip of her cream shoe into the plush opulence and watched it disappear into Weihei Province's best hand-tufted weave. 'Nice.'

'Gerard got another Michelin.' He shrugged. 'New carpet seemed a reasonable celebration.'

Somehow, Oliver managed to make her failure to know

that one of Hong Kong's most elite restaurants had re-carpeted sound like a personal failure on her part.

'Mrs Audrey...'

Audrey suppressed the urge to correct that title as she turned and took the extended hand of the maître d' between her own. 'Ming-húa, lovely to see you again.'

'You look beautiful,' Ming-húa said, raising her hand to his lips. 'We missed you last Christmas.'

Oliver shot her a sideways look as they were shepherded towards their customary part of the restaurant. The end where the Chinese version of Christmas decorations were noticeably denser. They racked up a bill this one day of the year large enough to warrant the laying on of extra festive bling and the discreet removal of several other tables, yet, this year, more tables than ever seemed to have been sacrificed. It left them with complete privacy, ensconced in the western end of the restaurant between the enormous indoor terrarium filled with verdant water-soaked plants and fluorescent dragonflies, and the carpet-to-ceiling reinforced window that served as the restaurant's outer wall.

Beyond the glass, Victoria Harbour and the high-tech sparkle and glint of hundreds more towering giants just like this side of the shore. Behind the glass, the little haven that Audrey had missed so badly last Christmas. Tranquil, private and filled with the kind of gratuitous luxury a girl really should indulge in only once a year.

Emotional sanctuary.

The sanctuary she'd enjoyed for the past five years.

Minus the last one.

And Oliver Harmer was a central part of all that gratuitous luxury. Especially looking like he did today. She didn't like to notice his appearance—he had enough ego all by himself without her appreciation adding to it—but, here, it was hard to escape; wherever she looked, a polished glass surface of one kind or another offered her a convenient reflection of some part of him. Parts that were infinitely safer facing away from her.

Chilled Cristal sat—as it always did—at the centre of the small table between two large, curved sofas. The first and only furniture she'd ever enjoyed that was actually worthy of the name *lounge*. Certainly, by the end of the day they'd both be sprawled across their respective sides, bodies sated with the best food and drink, minds saturated with good conversation, a year's worth of catching up all done and dusted.

At least that was how it normally went.

But things weren't normal any more.

Suddenly the little space she'd craved so much felt claustrophobic and the chilled Cristal looked like something from a cheesy seduction scene. And the very idea that she could do anything other than perch nervously on the edge of her sofa for the next ten or twelve hours…?

Ludicrous.

'So what are you hunting this trip?' Oliver asked, no qualms whatsoever about flopping down into his lounge, snagging up a quarter-filled flute on the way down. So intently casual she wondered if he'd practised the manoeuvre. As he settled back his white shirt stretched tight across his torso and his dark trousers hiked up to reveal ankles the same tanbark colour as his throat. 'Stradivarius? Guarneri?'

'A 1714 Testore cello,' she murmured. 'Believed to now be in South East Asia.'

'Now?'

'It moves around a lot.'

'Do they know you're looking for it?'

'I have to assume so. Hence its air miles.'

'More fool them trying to outrun you. Don't they know you always get your man…or instrument?'

'I doubt they know me at all. You forget, I do all the legwork but someone else busts up the syndicates. My job relies on my contribution being anonymous.'

'Anonymous,' he snorted as he cut the tip off one of the forty-dollar cigars lying on a tray beside the champagne. 'I'd be willing to wager that a specialist with an MA in identification of antique stringed instruments is going to be of much more interest to the bad guys than a bunch of Interpol thugs with a photograph and a GPS location in their clammy palms.'

'The day my visa gets inexplicably denied then I'll start believing you. Until then…' She helped herself to the Cristal. 'Enough about my work. How is yours going? Still rich?'

'Stinking.'

'Still getting up the noses of your competitors?'

'Right up in their sinuses, in fact.'

Despite everything, it was hard not to respond to the genuine glee Oliver got from irritating his corporate rivals. He wasted a fair bit of money on moves designed to exasperate. Though, not a waste at all if it kept their focus conveniently on what he *wasn't* doing. A reluctant smile broke free.

'I was wondering if I'd be seeing that today.' His eyes flicked to her mouth for the barest of moments. 'I've missed it.'

That was enough to wipe the smile clean from her face. 'Yeah, well, there's been a bit of an amusement drought since Blake's funeral.'

Oliver flinched but buried it behind a healthy draw from his champagne. 'No doubt.'

Well… *Awkward*…

'So how are you doing?' He tried again.

She shrugged. 'Fine.'

'And how are you really doing?'

Seriously? He wanted to do this? Then again, they talked about Blake every year. He was their connection, after all. Their *only* true connection. Which made being here now that Blake was gone even weirder. She should have just stayed home. Maybe they could have just done this by phone.

'The tax stuff was a bit of a nightmare and the house was secured against the business so that wasn't fun to disentangle, but I got there.'

He blinked at her. 'And personally?'

'Personally my husband's dead. What do you want me to say?'

All the champagne chugging in the world wasn't going to disguise the three concerned lines that appeared between his brows. 'Are you…coping?'

'Are you asking me about my finances?'

'Actually no. I'm asking you how you're doing. You, Audrey.'

'And I said *fine*.'

Both hands went up, one half filled with champagne flute. 'Okay. Next subject.'

And what would that be? Their one reason for continuing to see each other had gone trundling down a conveyor belt at the crematorium. Not that he'd remember that.

Why weren't you at your best friend's funeral? How was

that for another subject? But she wouldn't give him the satisfaction.

Unfortunately, for them both, Oliver looked as uninspired as she did on the conversation front.

She pushed to her feet. 'Maybe this wasn't such a—'

'Here we go!' Ming-húa appeared flanked by two serving staff carrying the first amuse-bouche of their marine-themed Christmas degustation. 'Obsiblue prawn and caviar with Royale Cabanon Oyster and Yuzu.'

Audrey got 'prawn', 'caviar' and 'oyster' and not much else. But wasn't that kind of the point with degustation—to over-stimulate your senses and not be overly bothered by what things were or used to be?

Culinary adventure.

Pretty much the only place in her life she risked adventure.

She sank politely back onto her sofa. It took the highly trained staff just moments to place their first course *just so* and then they were alone again.

Oliver ignored the food and slid a small gift-wrapped parcel across the table.

Audrey stared at the patched-up wrapping. Best he was prepared to do after she'd stood him up? 'Um…'

'I don't expect anything in return, Audrey.'

Did he read everyone this well? 'I didn't imagine we'd be doing gifts this year.'

'This was from last year.'

She paused a moment longer, then pulled the small parcel towards her. But she didn't open it because opening it meant something. She set it aside, instead, smiling tightly.

Oliver pinned her with his intense gaze. 'We've been friends for years, Audrey. We've done this for years, every

Christmas. Are you telling me you were only here for Blake?'

The slightest hint of hurt diluted the hazel of his eyes. One of the vibrant dragonflies flitting around the enormous terrarium matched the colour exactly.

She gifted him with the truth. 'It feels odd to be doing this with him gone.'

She didn't want to say *wrong*. But it had always felt vaguely wrong. Or her own reaction to Oliver certainly had. Wrong and dishonest because she'd kept it so secret and close to her heart.

'Everything is different now. But our friendship doesn't have to change. Spending time with you was never just about courtesy to a mate's wife. As far as I'm concerned we're friends, too.'

Pfff. Meaningless words. 'I missed you at *your mate's* funeral.'

A deep flush filled the hollow where his tie should have been. 'I was sorry not to be there.'

Uh-huh.

'Economic downturn made the flight unaffordable, I guess.' They would spend four times that cost on today's meals. But one of Oliver's strengths had always been courage under fire. He pressed his lips together and remained silent. 'Or was it just a really busy week at the office?'

She'd called. She knew exactly where he was while they'd buried her husband. 'Or did you not get my messages in time?'

All eight of them.

'Audrey...' The word practically hissed out of him.

'Oliver?'

'You know I would have been there if I could. Did you get the flowers I arranged?'

'The half-a-boutique of flowers? Yes. They were crammed in every corner of the chapel. And they were lovely,' honesty compelled her to admit. And also her favourites. 'But they were just flowers.'

'Look, Audrey, I can see you're upset. Can I please just ask you to trust that I had my reasons, good reasons, not to fly back to Sydney and that I had my own private memorial for my old friend back home in Shanghai—' Audrey didn't miss the emphasis on *'old'* friend '—complete with a half-bottle of Chivas. So Blake had two funerals that day.'

Why was this so hard? She shouldn't still care.

She shouldn't still remember so vividly the way she'd craned her neck from inside the funeral car to see if Oliver was walking in the procession of mourners. Or the way she'd only half attended to the raft of well-wishers squeezing her hand after the service because she was too busy wondering how she'd missed him. It was only later as she wrote thank-you cards to the names collected by the funeral attendants that she'd finally accepted the truth.

Oliver hadn't come.

Blake's best friend—their best man—hadn't come to his funeral.

That particular truth had been bitter, but she'd been too swamped in the chaos of new widowhood to be curious as to why it hurt so much. Or to imagine Oliver finding a private way of farewelling his old mate. Like downing a half-bottle of whisky.

'He always did love a good label,' she acknowledged.

A little too fondly as it turned out since Blake's thirst for good liquor was deemed a key contributor to the motor vehicle accident that took his life. But since her husband sitting in his den enjoying a sizeable glass or three with the evening newspaper had given Audrey the space and freedom to pursue things she enjoyed, she really couldn't complain.

The natural pause in the uncomfortable conversation was a cue to both of them to eat, and the tart seafood amuse-bouche was small enough that it was over in just mouthfuls.

Behind her, the gentle buzz of dragonfly wings close to glass drew her focus. She turned to study the collection that gave the restaurant its name. There were over one hundred species in Hong Kong—vibrant and fluorescent, large and small—and Qīngtíng kept an immaculate and stunning community of them in the specially constructed habitat.

She discreetly took several deep breaths to get her wayward feelings under control. 'Every year, I forget how amazing this is.'

And, every year, she envied the insects and pitied them, equally. Their captive life was one of luxury, with every conceivable need met. Their lives were longer and easier than their wild counterparts and neither their wetland nor food source ever dried up. Yet the glass boundaries of their existence was immutable. New arrivals battered softly against it until they eventually stopped trying and they accepted their luxurious fate.

Ultimately, didn't everyone?

'Give him a chance and the dragonfly curator will talk your ear off with the latest developments in invertebrate husbandry.'

His tone drew her eyes back. 'I thought you only flew down for the day? When did you have a chance to meet Qīngtíng's dragonfly guy?'

'Last Christmas. I unexpectedly found myself with time on my hands.'

Because she hadn't come.

The shame washed in again. 'It was…too soon. I couldn't leave Australia. And Blake was gone.'

He stared at her. Contemplating. 'Which one of those do you want to go with?'

Heat rushed up her neck.

'They're all valid.' His silence only underscored her lies. She took a deep breath. 'I'm sorry I didn't come last year, Oliver. I should have had more courage.'

'Courage?'

'To tell you that it was the last time I'd be coming.'

He flopped back in his chair. 'Is that what you've come to say now?'

It was. Although, saying it aloud seemed to be suddenly impossible. She nodded instead.

'We could have done that by phone. It would have been cheaper for you.'

'I had the Testore—'

'You could have come and not told me you were here. Like you did in Shanghai.'

Every muscle tightened up.

Busted.

She generally did her best to deal with Shanghai contacts outside Shanghai for a very specific reason—it was Harmer-country, and going deep into Oliver's own turf wasn't something she'd been willing to risk let alone tell him about. But how could he possibly know the population had swelled to twenty-five-million-and-one just that once? She asked him exactly that.

His eyes held hers. 'I have my sources.'

And why exactly were his sources pointing in her direction?

'Before you get too creeped out,' he went on, 'it was social media. Your status listed your location as the People's Square, so I knew you were in town.'

Ugh. Stupid too-smart phones. 'You didn't message me.'

'I figured if you wanted to see me you would have let me know.'

Oh. Sneaking in and out of China's biggest city like a thief was pathetic enough, but being so stupidly caught out just made her look—and feel—like a child. 'It was a flying visit,' she croaked. 'I was hunting a Paraguayan harp.'

Lord. *Not making it better.*

'It doesn't matter, that's in the past. I want to know why you won't be returning in the future.'

Discomfort gnawed at her intestines. 'I can't keep flying here indefinitely, Oliver. Can't we just say it's been great and let it go?'

He processed that for a moment. 'Do all your friends have best-by dates?'

His perception had her buzzing as furiously as the dragonflies. 'Is that what we are? Friends?'

'I thought so.' His eyes narrowed. 'I never got the sense that you were here under sufferance. You certainly seemed very comfortable helping me spend my money.'

'Oliver—'

'What's really going on, Audrey? What's the problem?'

'Blake's gone,' she pointed out needlessly on a great expulsion of breath. 'Me continuing to come and see you… What would be the point?'

'To catch up. To see each other.'

'Why would we do that?'

'Because friends nurture their relationships.'

'Our relationship was built on someone who's not here any more.'

He blinked at her—twice—and his perfect lips gaped. 'That might be how it started but it's not like that any longer.' An ocean of doubt swilled across the back of his gaze, though. 'I met you about six minutes before Blake did, if you recall. Technically, I think that means our friendship pre-dates Blake.'

That had been an excruciating six minutes, writhing under the intensity of the sexiest man she'd ever met, until his infinitely more ordinary friend had wandered into the Sydney bar. Blake with his narrower shoulders, his harmless smile and his non-challenging conversation. She'd practically swamped the man with her attention purely on reactive grounds, to crawl out from under Oliver's blistering microscope.

She knew when she was batting above her average and thirty seconds in his exclusive company told her Oliver Harmer was major league. Majorly gorgeous, majorly bright and majorly bored if he was entertaining himself by flirting with her.

'That doesn't count. You only spoke to me to pass the time until Blake turned up.'

He weighed something up. 'What makes you think I wasn't laying groundwork?'

'For Blake?'

His snort drew a pair of glances from across the room. 'For me. Blake's always been quite capable of doing his own dirty work...' As if it suddenly occurred to him that they were speaking of the dead, his words petered off. 'Anyway, as soon as he walked in the room you were captivated. I knew when I'd been bested.'

What would Oliver say if he knew she'd clung to Blake's conversation specifically to avoid having to engage with his more handsome friend again? Or if she confessed that she'd been aware of every single move Oliver made until the moment she left her phone number with Blake and fled out into the Australian night.

He'd probably laugh.

'I'm sure it did no permanent damage to your self-esteem,' she gritted.

'I had to endure his gloating for a week. It wasn't every day that he managed to steal out from under me a woman that I—' His teeth snapped shut.

'A woman that what?'

'Any woman at all, really. You were a first.'

She shook her head. 'Always so insufferable. *That's* why I gave my phone number to him and not you.'

That and the fact she always had been a coward.

He settled back into his sofa. 'Imagine how different things would be if you'd given it to me that day.'

'Oh, please. You would have bored of me within hours.'

'Who says?'

'It's just sport for you, Oliver.'

'Again. Who says?'

'Your track record says. And Blake says.'

Said.

He sat forward. 'What did he say?'

Enough to make her wonder if something had gone down between the two friends. She hedged by shrugging. 'He cared about you. He wanted you to have what he had.'

The brown flecks amid the green of his iris seemed to shift amongst themselves. 'What did he have?'

'A stable relationship. Permanency. A life partner.'

Would he notice she didn't say 'love'?

'That's rich, coming from him.'

'What do you mean?'

He glanced around the room and shifted uncomfortably in his seat before bringing his sharp, intent gaze back to her. Colour stained the very edge of his defined jaw. Audrey reached up to press her hand to her topknot to stop the lot falling down with the angle of her head. The pins really weren't doing their job so she pulled them out and the entire arrangement slid free and down to her shoulders.

His expression changed, morphed, as she watched, from something pointed to something intentionally dull. 'Doesn't matter what I mean. Ancient history. I didn't realise old Blake had such passion in him.'

'Excuse me?'

'Such possession. I always got the impression that your marriage was as much a meeting of minds as anything else.'

Heat raced up from under her linen collar. *What's wrong, Oliver, can't imagine me inspiring passion in a man?* 'You hadn't seen us together for years,' she said, tightly.

Why was that?

'My business relies on my ability to read people, Audrey. I hung out with you guys a lot those few years before your wedding. Before I moved to Shanghai. The three amigos, remember? Plenty of opportunity to form an opinion.'

Did she remember…?

She remembered the long dinners, the brilliant, three-way conversations. She remembered Oliver stepping between her and some drunk morons in the street, once, while

Blake flanked her on the *protected* side. She remembered how breathless she felt when Oliver would walk towards them out of the twilight shadows and how flat she felt when he walked away.

Yeah. She remembered.

'Then you must recall how partial Blake was to public displays of affection.' Oliver used to get so embarrassed by them, looking away like the fifth wheel that he was. Hard to imagine the confident man that he now was being discomposed by anything. 'Wasn't that sufficient demonstration of his feelings?'

'It was a demonstration all right. I always got the feeling that Blake specially reserved the displays of affection for when you were *in* public.'

Mortification added a few more degrees to the heat that was only just settling back under her jacket. Because that was essentially true. Behind closed doors they lived more like siblings. But what he probably didn't know was that Blake saved the PDAs up most particularly for when Oliver was there. Scent marking like crazy. As though he was subliminally picking up on the interest she was trying so very hard to disguise.

She breathed in past the tightness of her chest. 'Really, Oliver? That's what you want to do today? Take shots at a dead man?'

Anger settled between his brows. 'I want to just enjoy today. Enjoy your company. Like we used to.'

He slid the gift back across in front of her. 'And on that note, open it.'

She sat unmoved for a moment but the steely determination in his gaze told her that was probably entirely pointless. He was just as likely to open it for her.

She tore the wrapping off with more an annoyance she hoped he'd misread as impatience.

'It's a cigar.' And a pack of cards and M&M's. Just like three years ago. Her eyes lifted back to his. Resisted their pull. 'I don't smoke.'

'That's never stopped me.'

She struggled against the warm memory of Oliver letting her beat him at cards and believing she hadn't noticed. 'That was a great day.'

'My favourite Christmas.'

'Nearly Christmas.'

His dark head shook. 'December twenty-fifth has never compared to the twentieth.'

She sat back. 'What do you do on Christmas Day?'

'Work, usually.'

'You don't go home?'

'Do I go to my father's home? No.'

'What about your mum?'

'I fly her to me for Chinese New Year. A less loaded holiday.'

Audrey just stared.

'You're judging me,' he murmured.

'No. I'm trying to picture it.'

'Think about it. I can't go back to Sydney, I can't go to a girlfriend's place on Christmas without setting up the expectations of rings and announcements, and the office is nice and quiet.'

'So you work.'

'It's just another day. What do you do?'

'I do Christmas.' She shrugged.

But it wasn't anywhere near as exciting as flying to see Oliver. Or as tasty as whatever festive treat Qīngtíng had in store for her. And it didn't warm her for the rest of the year. It was roast dinners and eggnog and family and gifts that none of them needed and explaining ad nauseam every year why Blake wasn't there.

Here she'd got to split her focus between the beautiful skyline that was Hong Kong and Oliver. Depending on her mood.

Her eyes fell back on his gift. She picked up the cigar and clamped it between her teeth in a parody of him. Two seconds later she let it fall out again.

'Ugh. That's horrible.'

His laugh could have lit the other end with its warmth. 'You get used to it.'

'I can't imagine how.'

Yet somehow, while it tasted awful on her own lips, she caught herself deciding it might taste better on his. And then she had to fight not to stare there. Oliver made that a whole lot harder by leaning forward, picking up the cigar where she'd dropped it, rolling it under his nose and then sliding the sealed end between his teeth. Pre-loved end first.

Something about the casual intimacy of that act, of him putting her saliva into his mouth so effortlessly—as if they were a long-term couple perfectly used to sharing bodily fluids—sent her heart racing, but she used every ounce of self-control she had to keep it from showing as he mouthed it from the right to the left.

Not the worst way to end your days if you were a cigar— *Stop!*

Behind his easy smile his gaze grew unnaturally intent. And she grew inexplicably nervous.

'So,' he started, very much like one of his poker-plays, 'if we're not friends what are we?'

She choked slightly on her Cristal. 'Sorry?'

'I accept your assertion that we're not friends. But I wonder, then, what that means we are.'

Rabbit. Headlights. She knew it wasn't dignified and she knew exactly how that bunny felt, watching its fate career inevitably closer.

'Because there were two things that defined our relationship for me...' He used the word 'defined' as though it meant 'constrained'. 'One was that you were the wife of a friend. Now—tragically—no longer the case. And the other was that we were friends. Apparently also now no longer the case. So, tell me, Audrey—'

He leaned forward and swilled the liquid in his glass and his eyes locked on hard to hers.

'—where exactly does that leave us?'

CHAPTER FIVE

Lobster calamari tangle in braised southern ocean miniatures

TENSION BALLED IN amongst the food in Audrey's stomach. She should have seen this coming. He wasn't a gazillionaire for nothing; the acute sharpness of his mind was one of the things that she...appreciated most about Oliver.

She flattened her skirt carefully. 'We're...acquaintances.'

Excellent. Yes. A nice neutral word.

He considered, nodded, and she thought she was safe. But then his head changed—mid-nod—into more of a shake. 'No, see that doesn't work for me. I wouldn't normally spend this much time—' or this much money, presumably '—on a mere acquaintance.'

'Associates?' She hid the croak in a swallow of champagne.

'Definitely not. That suggests we do business. And that's the last thing on my mind when we're together. It's why I enjoy our Christmases so much.'

'Then what do you suggest we are?'

He thought about that. 'Confidantes.'

He'd certainly shared a lot of himself with her, but they both knew it didn't go both ways.

'How about cohorts?' she parried.

He scrunched his nose. 'More consorts. In the literal sense.'

No. That just put way too vital an image in her head. 'Sidekicks?'

He laughed, but his eyes didn't. 'What about soulmates?'

The words. The implication. It was too much.

'Why are you doing this?' Audrey whispered, tight and tense.

'Doing what?'

What was it exactly? Flirting? Pressing? She stared at him and hoped her face wasn't as bleak as her voice. 'Stirring.'

He drained the last of the Cristal from his glass. 'I'm just trying to shake you free of the cold, impersonal place you put yourself in order to have this conversation.'

'I don't mean to be impersonal.' Or cold. Though that was a term she'd heard before courtesy of Blake. In his meaner moments.

'I know you don't, Audrey. That's the only reason I'm not mad at you. It's a survival technique.'

'Uh-huh...' She frowned in a way she hoped would cover the fact he was one hundred per cent right. 'And what am I surviving?'

'This day?' He stared, long and hard. 'Maybe me?'

'Don't flatter yourself.'

Four staff with exquisite timing arrived with the second seafood plate of the degustation experiences ahead of them. Two cleared the table and two more lay down matching shards of driftwood, decorated with glistening seaweed, and nested in it were a selection of oceanic morsels. A solitary lobster claw, calamari in a bed of roe, a fan of some kind of braised whitebait and—

Audrey leaned in for a good look. 'Is that krill?'

Oliver chuckled and it eased some of the tension that hung as thick as the krill between them. 'Don't ask. Just taste.'

Whatever it was, it was magnificent. Weird texture on the tongue but one of the tastiest mouthfuls she'd ever had. Until she got to the lobster claw.

'Oh, my...'

'They've really outdone themselves with this one.'

The whole selection slid down way too easily with the frosty glass of Spanish Verdelho that had appeared in front of each of their dishes. But once there was nothing left on their driftwood but claw-husk and seaweed, conversation had no choice but to resume.

'Ask me how I know,' Oliver urged and then at her carefully blank stare he clarified. 'Ask me how I know what it is that you're doing.'

She took a deep slow breath. 'How do you know what I'm supposedly doing, Oliver?'

'I recognise it. From dealing with you the past five years. Eight if you want to go right back to the beginning.'

Oh, would that she could. The things she would do differently...

'I recognise it from keeping everything so carefully appropriate with you. From knowing exactly where the boundaries are and stopping with the tips of my shoes right on the line. From talking myself repeatedly into the fact that we're only friends.'

Audrey's heart hammered wildly. 'We are.'

He leapt on that. 'So now we *are* friends? Make up your mind.'

She couldn't help responding to the frustration leaching through between his words. 'I don't know what you want from me, Oliver.'

'Yes, you do.' He shifted forward again, every inch the predator. 'But you're in denial.'

'About what?'

'About what we really are.'

They couldn't be anything else. They just couldn't. 'There's no great mystery. You were my best man. You were my husband's closest friend.'

'I stopped being Blake's friend three years ago, Audrey.'

The pronouncement literally stunned her into silence. Her mouth opened and closed silently in protest. She knew something had gone down between them but...that long ago?

She picked up the M&M's. 'This long?'

'Just after that.' He guessed her next question. 'Friendships change. People change.'

'Why didn't you tell me?' she whispered. *And why hadn't Blake?* He knew that she saw Oliver whenever she went to Hong Kong. Why the hell wouldn't her husband tell her not to come?

He took a long breath. 'I didn't tell you because you would have stopped coming.'

Only the gentle murmur of conversation, the clink of silverware on plates and the hum of dragonfly wings interrupted the long, shocking silence. There was so much more in that sentence than the sum of the words. Two staff materialised behind them, unobtrusively cleared away the driftwood and shell remnants and left a small palate cleanser in their place. Then they were alone again.

'So, my comments today can't have been a surprise, then.' She braved her way carefully through the next moments. 'You knew I was going to end it.'

'Doesn't mean I'm going to acquiesce politely and let you walk off into the sunset.'

Frustration strung tight and painful across her sternum. 'Why, Oliver?'

He swapped the cigar from the left side of his mouth to the right. 'Because I don't want to. Because I like what we do and I like how I feel when we do it. And because I think you're kidding yourself if you don't admit you feel the same.'

The challenge—and the truth—hung out there, heavy and unignorable.

A nervous habit from her childhood came screaming back and, even though she knew she was doing it, she was helpless to stop her palms from rubbing back and forth along her thighs.

In desperation, she spooned up the half-melted sorbet and its icy bite shocked the breath right back into her. Oliver waited out her obvious ploy.

'I—'

Lord, was this wise? Couldn't she just lie and be done with it? But this was Oliver staring at her with such intensity and it didn't matter that he only saw her for ten hours a year, he could read her better than she could read herself.

'I enjoy seeing you, too,' she sighed. 'You know I do.'

'So why end it?'

'What will people say?'

Was that the first time she'd ever surprised him? Maybe

so, given how unfamiliar that expression seemed on his face. 'What people?'

'Any people.'

'They'll say we're two friends having lunch.'

And dinner and sometimes a late supper to finish up with, but that was besides the point. 'They'll say I'm a widow moving on before her husband's scent has even left the house.'

'It's just lunch, Audrey. Once a year. At *Christmas*.'

'As if the people I'm worried about would give a rat's what season it is.'

'What do you care what they say? You and I will both know the truth.'

She shot a puff of air between her lips. 'Spoken just like a man with more money than a small nation. You might not care about yours but reputations *mean* something to me.'

He shook his head. 'How is it any different than what we've been doing the past five years? Meeting, spending the day together.'

'The difference is Blake isn't here any more. He was the reason I came.'

He made it legitimate.

Now it was just…dangerous.

'Most women would be worried about *that* getting to the gossips. A married woman flying around the world to see a man that's not her husband. But you didn't care about it before you lost Blake—why do you care now?'

'Because now I'm—'

She floundered and he bent in closer to study her. 'You're what? The only thing that's changed in our relationship is your marital status.'

Her body locked up hard as awareness flooded his eyes.

'Is that it, Audrey? You're worried now because you're single?'

'How will it look?'

'You're a widow. No one will give a toss what you do or who you see. There's no hint of scandal for them to inhale.' But as she stared at him in desperate silence the awareness consolidated down into acute realisation. 'Or are you more concerned about how it will look, *to me*?'

Her pulse pounded against her throat. 'I don't want to give the wrong impression.'

'What impression is that?' Cool and oh, so careful.

'That I'm here because… That we're…'

He flopped back against the plush sofa, the cigar hanging limply from his mouth. 'That you're interested?'

'That I'm offering.'

Expressions chased across his face then like a classic flicker-show and finally settled on heated disbelief. 'It's lunch, Audrey. Not foreplay.'

That word on *those* lips was all it took; her mind filled then with every carnal thought about him she'd ever suppressed. They burst out just as surely as if someone took the lid off the tank holding all those dragonflies captive, releasing them to fill the room and ricochet off the walls. It took all her concentration to force them back into the lead-lined box where she usually kept them.

'Seriously, what's the worst that could happen? If I made a move on you, you'd only have to say no.'

Her lips tightened even further. 'It would be awkward,' she squeezed out.

His snort drew the glance of the maître d'. 'Whereas this conversation is such a pleasure.'

'I don't think your sarcasm is warranted, Oliver.'

'Really? Your inference is that I would make some kind of fool of myself the very moment you're available.' Disbelief was wiggling itself a stronghold in his features. 'How new do you imagine I am to women, Audrey?'

He was so close to the truth now, she didn't dare speak. But that just gave him an empty stage to continue his monologue. And he was getting right into the part.

'I'm curious. Do you see me as pathetically desperate—' his whisper could have cut glass '—or is it just that you imagine yourself as so intensely desirable?'

Hurt speared straight down into that place where she kept the knowledge that she was the last sort of woman he'd want to be with. 'Stop it—'

But no. He was in flight.

'Maybe it wouldn't be that way at all. I'm considered quite a catch, you know. They even have a nickname for me. Could your crazy view of the world cope with the fact that I could make a move and you wouldn't be *able* to say no? Or want to?'

There was no way on this planet that he wouldn't see the sudden blanche of her face. The blood dropped from it as surely as if the sixty floors below them suddenly vaporised.

And *finally* he fell silent.

Stupid, blind, lug of a man.

Audrey stood and turned to stare at the dragonflies, her miserable arms curled protectively around her midsection where the intense ache was still resident. It was that or fling her hands up to her mortified face. Beyond the glass, the other diners carried on, oblivious to the agony swelling up to press with such intent against her chest wall.

'Is that it?' Oliver murmured behind her after a mute eternity. 'Is that why you don't want to be here?'

Mortification twisted tighter in her throat. She raised a finger to trace the glass-battering of a particularly furious dragonfly wedged in the corner of the tank who hadn't yet given up on its dream of freedom. 'I'm sure you think it's hilarious.'

The carpet was too thick and too new to betray his movement, but she saw his reflection loom up behind her. Over her. He stopped just before they touched.

'I would never laugh at you,' he said, low and earnest. 'And I would never throw your feelings back in your face. No matter what they were.'

She tossed her hair back a little. Straightened a little more. She might be humiliated but she would not crawl. 'No. I'm sure you've had prior experience with the inconvenient attachment of women.'

That was what made the whole thing so intensely humiliating. That she was just one of dozens—maybe hundreds— to fall for the Harmer allure.

'I care for you, Audrey.'

...but...

It had to be only a breath away. 'Oh, please. Save it for someone who doesn't know you so well.'

The soberness in his voice increased. 'I *do* care for you.'

'Not enough to come to my husband's funeral.' She spun. Faced him. 'Not enough to be there for your *friend* in the hardest week of her life when she was lost and overwhelmed and so bloody confused.' She reached for her handbag on the empty seat at the end of the table. 'Forgive me for suspecting that our compassion-meters aren't equally calibrated.'

With a deft swing, she had the handbag and all its contents over her shoulder and she turned toward the restaurant's exit. Remaining courses, be damned.

'Audrey—' His heavy hand curled around her upper arm. 'Stop.'

She did, but only because she'd made quite enough of a scene for one lifetime. And this was going to be the last memory of her he had; she didn't want it to be hysterical.

'I think I should explain—'

'You don't owe me an explanation, Oliver. That's what makes this whole situation so ridiculous. You owe me nothing.'

He wasn't hers to have expectations of. He wasn't even her husband's friend any more. He was just an acquaintance. A circumstantial friend.

At best.

'I wanted to be there, Audrey. For you. But I knew what would have happened if I'd flown in.' He took her hands in his and held them gently between them. 'You and I would have ended up somewhere quiet, nursing a generous drink and a bunch of stories long after everyone else had gone home, and you would have been exhausted and strung out and heartbroken.' She dipped her head and he had to duck his to keep up eye contact. 'And seeing that would have broken my heart. I would have taken you into my arms to give you support and make all the pain just vanish—' he took a deep breath '—and we would have ended up in bed.'

Her eyes shot back up. 'That wouldn't have happened—'

His hands twisted more firmly around hers, but not to hold her close. He used the leverage to push her gently away from him. 'It would have happened because I'm a heartbeat and some sorely tested willpower from doing it right now. I *want* you in my arms, Audrey. I *want* you in my bed. And it has nothing to do with Blake being gone because I've wanted the same thing each Christmas for the last five years.'

Every muscle in her body tensed up and he knew it.

Amazing, excruciating seconds passed.

'But that's not who we are,' he went on. 'I know that. Reducing what we have to the lowest common denominator might be physically rewarding but it's not what our... *thing*...is worth. And so what we're left with is this awkward...awareness.'

Awareness. So he felt it, too. But it wasn't just awkward, it was awful. Because she suddenly got the sense that it made Oliver as uncomfortable as it made her. Not expressing it, just...feeling it.

'I value your friendship, Audrey. I value your opinion and your perception and your judgement. I get excited coming up here in the elevator because I know I'm going to be seeing you and spending a day with you picking through your brilliant mind. The only day I get all year. I'm not about to screw that up by hitting on you.'

Oh. A small part of her sagged. But was it relief or disappointment? 'I'm so sorry.'

'Why?'

The blood must have returned to her face if she could still blush. 'Because it's such a cliché.'

'It's flattering. The fact that a woman I value so highly finds things in me to value in return is...validating. Thank you.'

'Don't thank me.' That was just a little bit too close to patronising.

'Okay. I'll just be silently smug about it instead.'

The fact that she could still laugh, despite everything...

Yet, sure enough, the sound chuffed out of her. 'That seems more like you.'

They stood, nothing between them but air. And an emotional gulf as wide as the harbour.

'So now what?'

He considered her and then shook his seriousness free. 'Now we move on to the third course.'

CHAPTER SIX

Pineapple, hops, green tomato served in Brazil-nut-coated clusters

DID THE EARTH lurch on its axis between courses for the rest of Qīngtíng's chic clientele? None of them looked overly perturbed. Maybe this building was constructed to withstand earth tremors.

Because Oliver's entire existence had just shifted.

The two of them retreated to silence and polite smiles as a stack of curious, bite-size parcels were placed before them and the waiter announced in his accented English, 'Pineapple and green tomato clusters coated in Brazil nut.'

The parcels might have been small but he and Audrey each took their time first testing and then consuming the tart morsels. Buying time. Really necessary time. Because the last thing he felt like doing was eating.

He'd come *this* close.

He almost touched her, back then when she'd turned her blanched face away from him with such dismay. He almost pulled her back into his chest and breathed down onto her hair that none of it mattered. Nothing that had gone before had any relevance.

Their slate started today, blank and full of potential.

But that wasn't just embarrassment on her face. That was dread. She didn't *want* to be feeling any kind of attraction to him.

She didn't deserve his anger. He'd reacted automatically to the suggestion that he *was* as pitiful as he'd secretly feared when it came to her, but it wasn't Audrey's fault she'd pegged him so accurately. His anger was more appropriate directed at himself. *He* was the one who couldn't get another man's wife out of his head. *He* was the one who found himself incapable of being with a beautiful woman, now, and not wanting to peel back the layers to see the person inside. And *he* was the one who was invariably disappointed with what he found there, because they all paled by comparison.

Audrey was the best woman—the best human being— he knew. And he knew some pretty amazing people. But she was the shining star atop his Christmas tree of admired friends, just as glittering and just as out of reach.

And right up until a few minutes ago he'd believed she was safe territory. Because right up until a few minutes ago he had no idea that she was in any way into him. He'd grown so used to not acting on all the inappropriate feelings he harboured.

What the hell did he *do* in a world where Audrey Devaney was both single and into him?

'What happened with you and Blake?' she suddenly asked, cutting straight through his pity party. Her eyes were enormous, shimmering with compassion and curiosity. And something else… An edge of trepidation.

No. Not a conversation he could have with her. What would it achieve now that Blake was dead? 'We just…grew apart.'

Two pretty lines appeared between her brows. 'I don't understand why he didn't say something. Or suggest that I stop coming. For so long. That seems unlike him.'

'You'd expect him to force you to declare your allegiance?'

She picked her way, visibly, through a range of choices. 'He knew why I came here. He would have told me if it was no longer necessary.'

Necessary. The bubble of latent hope lost half of its air. The idea that she'd only been coming each year to please her husband bit deep. Attraction or no attraction.

'There must have been something,' she urged. 'An incident? Angry words?'

'Audrey, leave it alone. What does it matter now that he's gone?'

She leaned forward, over the nutty crumbs of the decimated parcels. 'I never did understand why you were friends in the first place. You're so different from Blake.'

'Opposites attract?' That would certainly explain his still-simmering need to absorb Audrey into his very skin. Too bad that was going to go insatiate. 'We weren't so different.' At least not at the beginning.

But, those all-seeing eyes latched onto the mystery and weren't about to let go. 'He did a lot of things that you generally disagreed with,' she puzzled. 'I'm trying to imagine what it would have taken to drive you away from him.'

Her unconscious solidarity warmed him right down to the place that had just been so cold. 'What makes you think it wasn't something *I* did?'

Her lips twisted, wryly. 'I knew my husband, Oliver. Warts and all.'

And that was about the widest opening he was ever going to get. 'Why did you marry him?'

The curiosity changed focus. 'Why do people usually marry?'

'For love,' he shot back. Not that he'd know what that looked like. 'Did you love him?'

And could she hear how much he was hoping the answer was 'no'?

'Marriage means different things to different people.'

Nice hedge. 'So what does it mean to you?'

She hesitated. 'I don't subscribe to the whole "lightning bolt across the crowded room" thing.'

It was true. There'd been no lightning bolt when she walked into the bar that first day. But when she'd first pinned him with her intellect and locked those big eyes on him just minutes later, he'd had to curl his fingers under the edge of the bar to keep from lurching backwards at the slam of *something* that came off her. Whatever the hell it was.

A big, blazing ball of slow burn.

'You don't aspire to that?' he dug.

'The great romantic passion? No.' A little colour appeared on her jaw. 'It hasn't been my experience. I value compatibility, shared interests, common goals, mutual respect, trust. Those are things that make a marriage.'

A hollow one, surely. Although how would he know? No personal experience to reference and a crap example in his parents' marriage, which barely deserved the title—just a woman living in the purgatory of knowing her husband didn't love her.

He risked a slight probe. 'Did Blake agree with that?'

She brought her focus back to him. 'I… Yes. We were quite sympathetic on a lot of things.'

Well, there was one area in particular that old Blake was definitely *un*sympathetic with Audrey.

Fidelity.

'You never looked at someone else and wondered what it might be like?' He had to know.

Her eyes grew wary. 'What *what* might be like?'

'To be with them. Did you never feel the pull of attraction to someone other than Blake and wonder about a relationship that started with good, old-fashioned lust?'

'You're assuming that *wanting* and *taking* are connected. It comes back to that mutual trust and respect. I just wouldn't do that to my partner. I couldn't.' Her eyes narrowed. 'I thought you, of all people, would understand that.'

A cold stone formed in his gut. *Of all people…* 'You're talking about my father?' They'd never discussed his father and so he knew whatever she knew had come from Blake. The irony of that…

'Was he very bad?'

He took a deep breath. But if sharing something with her, especially something this personal, was the only intimacy he was going to get from Audrey Devaney, he'd embrace it. 'Very.'

'How did you know what he was doing?'

'Everyone knew.'

'Including your mother?'

'She pretended not to.' For her son's sake. And maybe for her own.

'Did she not care?'

His stomach tightened at the memory of the sobbing he

wasn't supposed to have heard when she thought he was asleep. His jaw tightened. 'She cared.'

'Why did she stay?'

The sigh wracked his body. 'My father was incapable of fidelity but he didn't drink, he was never violent, he remembered birthdays and he had steady employment. He was, in all other ways, a pretty reasonable father.'

If you didn't count a little thing called integrity.

Part of Oliver's own attraction to Audrey had always been her values. This was not a woman who would ever have knowingly done wrong by the man she shared vows with. Just a shame Blake hadn't returned the favour.

'So she chose to stay.' And that had been a green light in his father's eyes. The ultimate hall pass.

'Maybe she didn't think she could do better?'

'Than a man who was ruthlessly unfaithful—surely no one would think that?' It hit him then how freely he was having this discussion. After so many years of bleeding the feelings out in increments.

She shook her head. 'I don't know that you'll ever be able to relate. Because of who you are. Successful and charming and handsome. It's not that easy for everyone else.'

His heart swelled that she thought him handsome enough to say it aloud. 'You think I don't have my demons?'

She stared at him. 'I'm sure you do. But doubting your worth is not one of them.'

She wasn't wrong. His ego had been described by the media as 'robust' and in the boardroom as 'unspeakable'.

'And can you, Audrey? Relate?'

She stared out across the harbour to the towering giants on the other side. But her head nodded, just slightly. 'When I got to upper school I'd gone from being the tubby, smart girl to the plain, smart girl. I didn't mind that so much as long as it also came with "smart" because that was my identity, that was where I got my self-worth from. Academic excellence.'

'I wish I'd known you then.'

Her laugh grated. 'Oh, no… The beautiful people and I didn't move in the same hemisphere. You would never have even seen me then.'

'That's a big assumption to make.' And kind of judgemental. Which wasn't like her at all.

She leaned forwards. 'For the first two years of high school boys didn't want to know me. I was invisible and I just got on with things, under the radar. And then one day I got…discovered. And that was the end of my cruise through school.'

'What do you mean "discovered"?'

'The same way species are discovered even though they've been there for centuries. I didn't change my hair or get a makeover or tutor the captain of the football team. It wasn't like the movies. One day I was invisible and the next—' she shrugged '—there I was.'

'In a good way?'

She took a healthy swallow of her wine. 'No. Not for me.'

The pain at the back of her eyes troubled him. 'What happened?'

'Nothing. At first. They just watched me, wherever I went. Like they weren't sure how to engage with me.'

They…like a pack.

'One of them asked me out to a movie once. Michael Hellier. I didn't know how to say no kindly so I said yes and it was all over the school in minutes. They hunted me down, then, the girls from that group, and they slammed me against the bathroom wall and told me I was fishing outside of my swamp.' She lifted her eyes. 'But he'd asked me, I couldn't just not turn up. So I went. I don't even remember what film we saw because all I could think about the entire time I was with him was those girls. I convinced myself they were spying from the back row. I barely spoke to him and I didn't even take off my coat even though I was sweating like crazy under it, and when he tried to put his arm around me I literally froze. I sat there, totally rigid for the entire movie, and the moment the credits rolled I stammered out my thanks and I ran out of the cinema.'

Oliver sat silently, the whole, miserable story playing out in his mind, his anger bubbling up and up as it proceeded.

She turned more fully towards him, eyes blazing. 'I enjoyed it, Oliver. The attention of those boys. I enjoyed that none of them quite knew how to deal with me. I enjoyed being a puzzle in their eyes and I enjoyed how it made me feel. The shift in power. It felt like vindication forevery tease I'd endured as a kid. As if "*See! I am worthy.*" I liked being visible. And I liked being sought after. I liked how fast my heart beat when I was near him because he was interested in me. And I totally played up to it.

'But I earned what happened to me.' She sighed. 'And I earned every cruel nickname they gave me after that. I tried to play a game I wasn't equipped for and I lost. I never made that mistake again. I never *reached* like that again. And after a while that starts to feel really normal. And so maybe something like that happened to your mother—'

God, he'd totally forgotten they'd been talking about Marlene Harmer.

'—something that taught her not to overreach.'

Or hope? Or expect more from people?

Or feel, maybe?

He asked the first thing that came to him. The thing he'd always, secretly, wanted to know. 'Is that why you chose Blake that day in the bar? Because some jerks in school taught you not to aim higher?'

The words hung, unanswered, between them. It was the first time either of them had ever acknowledged what had happened that night. How actively she'd focused her attention on Blake rather than on him. Almost to the point of rudeness.

And also hovering out there, in bright neon, was his presumption that Blake was somehow *less*. But deep down he knew that to be true—at least when it came to Audrey.

Audrey was never meant to be Blake's.

Not in a just world.

Indecision swam across her gaze, and he watched her trying to decide what was safe to reveal. When she did speak it was painfully flat and her eyes drifted slightly to his left. 'Blake was within reach.'

Low-hanging fruit.

Oliver flopped back against the rear of his sofa, totally lost for words, understanding, just a little bit, what Audrey had just said about vindication. He'd always wondered what drew Audrey to Blake instead of him that day, but such thoughts were arrogant and unkind given Blake was supposedly his best friend. So he'd swallowed them. Buried the question mark way down deep.

And now he had his answer.

An absurd kind of hope—totally at odds to the conversation they were having—washed through him.

Audrey didn't pick Blake because she deemed him the better man...

He was just the *safer* man.

Just like that, a whole side of her unfolded like spreading petals revealing an aspect to her he'd never suspected.

'It kills me to think that my mother would have harboured those kinds of feelings about herself and that my father would have reinforced them...'

Did she realise that when he said 'my mother' he really meant Audrey? And instead of his father, he meant himself? To imagine this extraordinary woman sitting in that bar all those years ago, smiling and chatting and sipping her drink and all the while going through a mental process that ended in her deciding she wasn't worthy—

She! The finest of women.

It killed him.

'You know her best,' Audrey murmured. 'I'm just hypothesising how she might have allowed that to happen. Everyone has a different story.'

Her furious back-pedalling made sense to him now. She'd exposed herself and so she was retreating to safer ground. But no, he wasn't about to let her do that. Not when he'd finally made some headway into knowing her.

Really knowing her.

He reached forward and took her hand. 'I wish I could impress upon her just how amazing a woman she is.'

She swallowed twice before answering. 'You could just tell her.'

'Do you think she'd believe me?' His thumb traced the shape of her palm. 'Or would she look for the angle?'

Hints of alarm etched across her expression. 'If you say it often enough eventually she'll have to believe you.'

Was it that simple? Could simple reinforcement undo the lessons—the experience—of years?

He released his breath slowly and silently. 'I would have seen you, Audrey. I give you my word.'

Because *she* was special, though, not because he was, particularly.

She tipped her head back towards the sofa-top. 'I could have done with a champion.'

Chivalrous wasn't exactly what he was feeling now, but he absolutely would have defended her against those who would have caused her this hurt. Who would have changed her essence.

He would have taken on half the school for her.

'And I could have done with your strength. And your maturity.'

She smiled, gently slipped her hand out from his and sat back against her seat. 'Really? Were you a wild child?'

Ah. Back to safety. Any topic other than her.

But he let her go, incredibly encouraged now that he'd picked up the key to getting inside her. Because the beautiful thing about keys was that you could use them as and when required. And in between you tucked them away somewhere safe.

This one he tucked away in a pocket deep inside his chest and he let her have the breathing space she obviously needed.

'Oh, the stories I could tell.'

'Go ahead.' She settled into her seat and seemed to have totally forgotten that less than half an hour ago she was heading for the door. 'We've still got five courses.'

Yep. That was what he had. Five courses and the rest of the day to make sure Audrey Devaney didn't disappear from his life forever.

CHAPTER SEVEN

Pomegranate, blood orange and Campari

HOW WAS IT possible that she'd just revealed more about herself in a few minutes to Oliver than she had in her entire marriage to her husband? Blake was all about the now; he lived for the moment, or planned for the future. But he spent no time looking back and he didn't ever show a particular interest in her past beyond what it meant for his present. They talked—a lot—and they shared ideas and grand schemes and they got excited about some and disappointed about others but it was never remotely personal.

She'd certainly never told him about those awful few months at school. He wouldn't have understood.

But if ever there was a man who should have not understood, he was sitting across from her today. Oliver with his comfortable background, his top-end schooling and his voted-most-likely-to-succeed status. Oliver *was* those boys from her past. He would have dated those girls that had slammed her up against the bathroom wall. He probably had!

He shouldn't have been able to empathise at all.

Yet he did. And it was genuine.

'Pomegranate, blood orange and Campari sorbet,' the maître d' announced, appearing at the side of their table with staff wielding another dish. In perfect synch, they positioned a fan of frosted antique tablespoons each packed with crushed ice and a ball of sorbet neatly balanced on the head of the spoon. They looked just like Christmas baubles sitting in snow.

'Thank you,' Audrey murmured, smiling as they left, bowing. After they'd gone, she added, 'They're very deferential to you, Oliver.'

'The quality of service is one of the things Qīngtíng is famous for.'

Mmm, still... 'They bow extra low to you.'

'I spend a fortune with them whenever I'm in Hong Kong.'

Suddenly the thought that he might come here with other people—maybe with other women—grew and flashed green in her mind. This was *their* place. It didn't exist when they weren't here, surely?

'Tell me about your year,' she blurted, to force the uncomfortable idea off her tongue before thought became voice. 'Did you ever hear from Tiffany?'

His lips twisted. 'She married someone else by Valentine's.'

'No! So fast? That's terrible.'

'He adores her and doesn't mind the lack of intelligent conversation. And she has more money than she can spend and a secure future. It was a good match.'

'Better than you?'

'Infinitely.'

'Why were you with her, Oliver? If she wasn't all that bright?'

His eyes shadowed and he busied himself with the sorbet. But he didn't change the subject and eventually he lifted his head to meet her eyes again. The faintest sheen dotted his tan forehead.

'Tiffany was engaging in her own way. I found her complete disregard for social convention refreshing. Besides, I get my intelligent conversation elsewhere so I didn't feel the lack.'

'You were going to *marry* her, Oliver. Grow old with her, maybe father her children. And you didn't look to her for meaningful conversation?'

His lips thinned. 'Intellect isn't everything.'

No. Everyone had different strengths. She knew that better than most. Yet…

'Oliver. This is *you* we're talking about. You would have wasted away without a mental match in life.'

'What if I couldn't find a match?'

She practically snorted her pomegranate ice. 'That's a big call, isn't it? To assume that no woman could be your intellectual match.'

His eyes blazed. 'Not mine, Audrey. *Yours.*'

Her antique spoon clattered back onto its saucer.

But he didn't shy away from her startled gaze. 'You set a high bar, intellectually. Diversity of knowledge, your wit, your life experience. That's hard to equal.'

'Wh…' What was she supposed to say to that? 'Why would you *try* to match it?'

He leaned forwards, leading with his hazel eyes. 'Because you're the woman against which I measure all others, intellectually. You're my gauge of what's possible.'

'Me?' Her squeak was hardly the poster child for mental brilliance.

'And I haven't found anyone like you, yet.' He studied her as she squirmed. 'That makes you uncomfortable?'

'Yes!'

'Because you don't agree with my assessment of your smarts or because you don't want to be my bar?'

Her heart thundered so hard at the back of her throat she thought he might hear it pulsing below her words. 'Because pedestals are wobbly at the best of times.'

'Or is it just knowing that I consider us a perfect intellectual match that makes you nervous?'

If he said *intellectual* one more time she would scream; it only served to remind her how not matched they were in other ways.

She took a long breath. 'I'm flattered that you think so.' But only because of how highly she esteemed his mind. But then she saw how incredibly *un*-uncomfortable he looked. The devil lurked behind that sparkle in his eyes.

Oh.

'You're teasing me.'

'Hand on heart.' His big fist followed suit and he shook his head. 'But I knew your modesty wouldn't allow you to believe it.'

'You must meet some extraordinary people.'

'None who I'd want to spend an entire day just talking to.'

She stared, crippled by the monument of that. 'No pressure, then.'

Two diners looked around at Oliver's bark of laughter. 'Yeah, the next word out of your mouth better impress.'

She consciously coordinated the muscles necessary to

breathe and then used the outward part of the breath to say, 'Euouae.'

Oliver blinked.

'It's a musical mnemonic to denote the sequence of tones in the Seculorum Amen.'

'See what I mean?' His smile broke out on one side of that handsome mouth. 'Who knows that?'

She blew out a long breath. 'It's also the longest word in the English language made up of only vowels.'

'Okay, now you're just showing off. Eat your sorbet.'

'Thank you, Oliver,' she said, as soon as her mind would work properly again. 'That's quite a compliment.'

'No, actually, it's a curse. I can't tell you how many dinners I've sat through waiting for something like Eweyouu—'

'Euouae.'

'—to casually come up.'

'Hopefully none of those meals were as long as this one, then.'

'I'm serious, Audrey; you've spoiled me for other women.'

And just like that she was speechless again. And her blood was back to its thundering.

Intellectually, she reminded herself. *Only in that one way.* Because the women Oliver Harmer chose had beauty and grace and breeding and desirability and experience and, Lord knew, more elasticity than she could ever aspire to.

'So, you just…lowered your bar?'

'I decided that I could get my fix of conversational stimulation every Christmas instead.'

'You're assuming that your wife would be happy for us still to meet each year. I'm not sure I would be if you were—' she nearly choked on the word '—mine.'

He shrugged. 'It wouldn't be negotiable.'

'Famous last words. What would happen when you were completely smitten with her and she turned her big violet eyes up to you and let them fill with tears and begged you not to go?'

'Really? Violet.'

'I'm sure she'd be exceptional.'

He gave her that point. 'I'd hand her a Kleenex and tell her I'd see her later that evening.'

'And if she let her robe fall open and seduced you into staying?'

His eyes darkened. 'Then I'd cancel the car and take the chopper to make up the lost time.'

'And if she threatened you with divorce?'

'Then I'd call my lawyer and let him deal with the weeping,' he huffed, eyes rolling. 'Do you imagine I'm so easily manipulated, Audrey?'

No. She couldn't imagine him falling for any of that.

'So what if the woman that loved you sat you down and stoically explained how much it hurt her that you got from someone else something she couldn't give you.'

His pupils enlarged and then the deepest of frowns surrounded them. 'God, Audrey...'

Had he never thought about what it might do to the woman 'lucky' enough to get him? She much preferred to think that a woman he chose would select door number four. The vaguely dignified option. Of course, the alternative would be to say nothing and just *ache* every year as December twentieth approached.

Yeah, that had worked really well for her.

He blew air from between tight lips and forked his fingers through his hair.

'You see my point?' she murmured.

'So you're basically dooming me to a bachelor's life forever, then? Because I've been looking, Audrey, and you're
not out there.'

'I'm just saying you can't have Frankenstein's bride.'

He tipped his head.

'You don't want a regular woman with flaws and room
for improvement. You want the intelligence of one woman,
the courage of another, the serenity of a third. And you want
it all wrapped up in a beautiful exterior.'

'She doesn't have to be beautiful.'

Pfff. 'Yes, she does, Oliver. You only date stunning
women.' The Internet was full of pictures of him with his
latest arm decoration.

'You think I'm that shallow?'

All right then… 'When was the last time you were seen
in public with a plain, ordinary woman?' she challenged.

And he shot back, fast and sure. 'I have lunch with one
every Christmas.'

The air whooshed out of her, audibly. But it wasn't indignation and she didn't flounce out. She sat as straight
and dignified as she could and opened her mouth to say
something as witty as he probably expected. But absolutely
nothing came to her.

So she just closed it again.

He swore. 'Audrey, I'm sorry. I spoke carelessly. That
was supposed to be a compliment.'

Because he deigned to lower himself long enough to eat
in public with a less than beautiful woman? 'Your flattery
could do with some refinement, then,' she squeezed out.

'You are so much more than the particular arrangement
of your features. I see all the things you *are* when I look at
you, not the things you *aren't*.'

Clumsy, but at least he wasn't patronising her with claims of inner beauty.

'Please, Audrey. You're the last person on this planet that I would want to hurt. Or that I'm fit to judge. My social circle tends to fill with beautiful stars on the rise. I don't date them for the pleasure of sitting there looking at them. I date them to see what else they have going for them.'

It wasn't all that inconceivable. She could well imagine the facility with which a stunning woman would find herself with access to the kind of people Oliver mixed with. Where else was he going to meet women? And she absolutely couldn't blame them for being drawn to him, once there. He was Oliver Harmer.

He took her hand across the table. 'It's really important to me that you don't think I'm that kind of man.'

And it wasn't as if he were giving her a news flash. She detached her hand from his under the pretence of wiping her mouth with her napkin and sighed. But she wasn't about to be a princess about this. She was a big girl.

'I wake up to myself every day, Oliver. I know where my virtues lie.' Or didn't.

'I would give every cent I have—' The greenish-brown of his eyes focused in hard but as he spoke he turned away, so that the words were an under-breath jumble. And something in his expression made her really want to know what came next.

'Every cent, what?'

'For you to recognise your strengths.'

Had even the kitchen staff stopped to listen? Every sound that wasn't Oliver's low voice seemed to have vanished. But something stopped her from letting his words fill her heart with helium.

'I don't need you to do this, Oliver.' In fact she really would rather he didn't. 'I don't care what you think of my appearance.'

'Of course you do. Because you're human and because I just reinforced all those jerks at your school with my stupid, careless words.' He stood and pulled her to her feet. '*I* care what you think of *my* appearance.'

It was such a ludicrous concept—not that he cared, but that there was any question about how good he looked—she actually laughed. Out loud. 'No, you don't.'

'I changed three times before coming here today.'

She looked him over, some of her pre-shock spirit returning. 'And this was your best effort?'

The lips that gaped at her then were stained slightly red with pomegranate ice and looked more than a little bit like they were flush from kissing. 'This is all brand-new gear!'

'Oh, you shopped too? Wow.' Her umbrage eased a bit more.

'And I didn't shave this morning because you once said you liked stubble. Four years ago.'

A reluctant laugh tumbled out of her. 'Oh, that's just sad, Oliver.' It didn't matter why he was demeaning himself to stave off her further embarrassment, she was just very grateful that he was. She peered up at him. 'I know what you're doing.'

'What am I doing?'

'You're lying. To make me feel better.'

His eyes narrowed as he towered over her. 'Is it working?'

'Yes, actually.' Purely based on the fact he cared enough to try. He'd meant what he said but he hadn't meant it to be hurtful.

He took half a step closer. 'Great then.'

'Besides, you always look good. You don't have to try.'

'Small mercy. There are plenty more ways that I feel deficient around you, Audrey.'

The wealthiest and most successful man she knew? 'Like how?'

Indecision carved that handsome face. 'I live in fear that I'll glance up suddenly and catch you looking at me with the kind of patient, vacant tolerance I give most of my dates.'

'You think I'm humouring you?'

His shrug only lifted one big shoulder. 'You only came here at all because of Blake. Maybe it's all Christmas charity.'

The thought that she'd caused someone to question themselves the way she had—even someone as profusely confident as Oliver—made her squirm. Though she knew the ramifications of correcting him were steep.

'I'm still here, aren't I?'

He knuckled a loose piece of her hair more securely behind her ear. 'Ah, but you came to say goodbye.'

'I did,' she breathed. That was totally her plan when she walked in. Until something had changed without her consent. 'So why haven't I?'

His eyes glittered and his hand turned palm side up and curled around her cheek. 'Something else I'd give my fortune to know.'

A steam train thundered through her brain. 'You're rapidly running out of fortunes.'

'Benefit of a double-A credit rating.' His thumb crept across to trace the shape of her bottom lip. 'I can get more.'

'What are you doing?' she whispered, and he knew exactly when to drop the game.

'Everything I can before you tell me to stop.'

She absolutely should. They were in a public place and this was *'The Hammer'*, notorious player and corporate scourge of Asia. And more to the point, this was Oliver. She had no business letting him this close, no matter how much the furthest corner of her soul tried to tell her differently.

It didn't matter that she was no longer anyone's wife. It didn't matter that he was the one controlling the lazy drag of his fingers and therefore any resulting public exposure. Those things only made it more dangerous. More ill advised.

But as his hazel eyes blazed down on her and his big, smooth thumb pressed against the flesh of her lips she struggled to remember any of those things.

And her mouth opened.

CHAPTER EIGHT

Baked scallops, smoked eel with capsicum salsa and a Parmesan and dill crust.

'STOP.'

She wasn't inviting him in. She was locking him out. Of course she was. This was Audrey.

Oliver drew his hands back into his own personal space and stepped away from her, more towards the wall-that-would-be-a-window. The soothing, ancient presence of the mountains far behind Victoria Harbour anchored him and stopped his heart from beating clear through his chest and then through all that glass into the open air of the South China Sea.

'Shorter than I'd hoped,' he murmured at the vast open space. Yet so much further than he'd ever imagined he'd get.

'We're in a public restaurant, Oliver.'

'I have a suite just upstairs.' As if that were really what stopped her.

But she ignored the underlying meaning. Again, because

she was Audrey. The woman had more class than he could ever hope to aspire to.

'I thought we were on the top floor?' she said, smoothing her skirt and keeping the conversation firmly off what had just happened. All that…touching.

'The top public floor. There's a penthouse.' Technically part of the sixtieth floor but a half-dozen metres higher.

'And you have it?'

He turned and faced her. And the music. 'It came with the restaurant.'

Her brows dipped over slightly glassy eyes. He loved that he'd made them that way. But then they cleared and those fine brows lifted further than he imagined they could go. 'You *bought* the restaurant?'

'I did.'

She shook her head. 'What's the matter? No good restaurants closer to Shanghai?'

'I like this one.'

And Qīngtíng had the added advantage of being saturated in echoes of his time together with Audrey. And when she didn't come last year he began to believe that might be all he'd ever have of her.

Memories.

'Clearly.' And then her innate curiosity got the better of her. 'What did it cost?'

God, he adored her. So classy and yet so inappropriate at the same time. Absolutely no respect for social niceties. But he wasn't ready to put a price tag on his desperation just yet. Bad enough that his accountant knew.

'More than you can imagine. It wasn't on the market.' He'd just kept offering them more until they caved.

Understanding filled her eyes. 'That's why you seemed

so familiar with the dragonfly keeper. And why they bow so low for you.' And why he got to call the chef *Gerard*. 'You're their boss.'

'They treat everyone that well,' he defended. Badly.

'Why did you buy it?'

Uh…no. Not something he was going to admit to the woman who'd made it clear she wasn't after anything more with him. In words and, just moments ago, in deed.

He cleared his throat. 'It's a fantastic investment. The return is enormous.' As much an unexpected bonus as the big, luxurious, lonely suite right above their heads. 'Do you want to see it?'

She turned her confusion to him.

'The penthouse. It's pretty spectacular.'

'Is it…? Are you…?' She took a deep breath. 'Will you be sleeping there tonight?'

Was that her subtle way of asking whether there was a bed up there? 'You're safe with me, Audrey.'

Heat flared at her jaw. 'I know.'

Though, hadn't he been the one to instigate the touch-a-thon just now? 'It's so much more than a bedroom. It's like a small house perched atop this steel mountain.' She didn't have a prayer of hiding the spark of interest. So he went for the kill shot. 'Every window gives you a different view of Hong Kong.'

She was inordinately fond of this city, he knew. In fact, pretty much anything oriental. It made him wonder what she'd thought of Shanghai; if she'd liked it as much as he did.

And why, exactly, was that important…?

Indecision wracked her face. She wanted to see it, but she didn't want to be alone with him away from the security of a restaurant full of unwitting chaperones. So who did she trust less—him or herself?

Her eyes flicked to her left as two restaurant staff approached from the direction of the beautifully disguised kitchens and placed their next dish on the table.

'Oh, great!'

Audrey hadn't been quite that animated about the arrival of the previous dishes. But she certainly rushed back to her seat with enthusiasm now. Oliver half smiled and followed her.

'Scallops and smoked eel swimming in a sea of capsicum with a Parmesan and dill crust,' Ming-húa announced before departing. Each dish composed of an enormous white shell in which three tender scallop and eel pairs sat, awash, in a red liquid salsa. A two-pronged splade balanced across each one.

'Did Blake burn you financially?' Audrey asked, breathless, as she tucked into her scallops.

It was absolutely the last thing he expected her to say, although retreating behind the memory of her departed husband shouldn't have surprised him.

'No. Why?'

'I figured money would have to be the only thing big enough to drive a wedge between the two of you.'

Oliver moderated a deep breath. She wasn't going to let this go. 'Look, Audrey…Blake and I were friends for a long time and people change in that time. Values change. The more time we spent apart, the less we had in common.'

Except for Audrey. She was their constant.

'I just don't understand why he would have kept it a secret, unless it was a big deal of some kind.'

Even in absentia, he was still lying to cover his old

friend's ass. But it was more than that. Hadn't she just shared the misery of her childhood, all those issues with self-worth? What would it do to her to learn her husband was a serial adulterer?

The burning need to protect her surged through him. 'Let it go, Audrey.'

But something was clearly troubling her. She was eating the scallop as though it were toast. Biting, chewing and swallowing with barely any attention on the succulent food. 'What values?'

He faked misunderstanding.

'You said that values changed with time. What values changed between the two of you, if it wasn't about business?'

'Audrey—'

'Please, Oliver. I need to know. Was it your values?'

'Why do you need to know?'

She eyed him as she slipped the last succulent morsel between her lips. 'Because a few years before he died, he changed. And I want to know if it's connected.'

Dread pooled in his belly. 'Changed how?'

'He just...' She frowned, trying to focus what was obviously a lot of thoughts all rushing her at once. 'He became...affectionate.'

The second surprise in his day. 'Affectionate?'

'He grew all touchy-feely. And he'd never done that before.'

'You got worried because he got *more* intimate with you?' Exactly what kind of a marriage had they had?

'It was just notable by its sudden presence.' She cleared her throat. 'And it escalated every November. Like clockwork.'

The weeks leading up to her annual pilgrimage to Hong Kong. Overcompensating for the fact that he was lining up to betray her in the most fundamental way possible, probably.

'So I thought…that is, I wondered…' She closed her eyes and took a long slow breath. 'I thought it might have been related to me coming here. That he was struggling with it.'

'But he was the one who encouraged you.'

'I know, that's the part I don't understand. But I knew he had problems with how I was with you when we were all together and so I thought maybe he believed—'

She snapped her mouth shut.

How I was with you… Oliver filed that one away for later dissection. 'He believed what?'

'That there was something going on.' She flushed. 'With us.'

There were no words. Oliver could only stare. She was so very far off the mark and yet so excruciatingly close to the truth.

'But there wasn't,' he hedged.

'Blake didn't know that.' She threw her hands up. 'It's the only thing I can think of to explain it.'

Is it really, Audrey?

It wasn't until she spoke that he realised he had—aloud. 'What do you mean?'

Crap. 'I mean there could be dozens of other alternatives. Blake knew he could trust you with his life.'

That was what made his betrayal all the more vile.

'I thought, maybe he confronted you with it and, knowing how you felt about your father, you might have been insulted and the two of you might have fought…?'

Maybe that was what her subconscious wanted her to believe.

'He didn't confront me.' That much he could safely say. Blake was the confront*ee* not the confront*er*.

'Oh.' Those two appealing little forks appeared between her brows again. 'Okay.'

She was out of ideas. Oliver knew he could just change the subject and she'd go with that because that brilliant mind of hers was flirting around the edges but was determined not to see the possibility of truth. And who could blame her?

But would it eat at her forever?

She lifted the half-shell and used the splade to scoop up some of the rich, vibrant sauce. Her frown didn't dissipate even as she sipped at her dish.

No. She wasn't going to let her curiosity die with her husband. She was just going to let it fester and worsen her deeply suppressed self-doubt as only secrets could. But telling her the truth wouldn't achieve much better.

Except maybe bring it all out into the light where she could deal with it. Surely something like that lost some of its power when it was exposed to the light. Rather than poisoning as a fear. If Audrey knew nothing, he'd have been content to leave it that way but she knew enough that she would eventually work her way around to the truth or, if not that, then her subconscious would whisper cruelly in her ears forever. Or she'd hear it from someone else instead of in the protective company of a friend.

He studied her strong face and made his decision.

'It was guilt, Audrey.' The splade froze halfway to her mouth. 'If Blake changed then he was overcompensating because he knew what was going to happen the moment you left the country.'

Those enormous blue eyes grew. 'What do you mean?'

He took a deep breath and trashed the memory of a dead man.

'Your husband had affairs, Audrey. Lots of them. Every year while you were here with me.'

The effusive apologies of the staff for what was essentially her own mistake bought Audrey a few precious moments to get her act together. Immaculate girls in exotic Chinese silk dabbed and pawed at the ruined linen of her outfit where the splade, the shell and its entire remnant contents had tumbled out of her deadened fingers.

Oliver watched her with concern through the chaos and all the bodies.

She'd never had so many hands on her breasts and thighs at one time. How ironic to consider that in the same moment as discovering that her husband—who'd barely troubled himself to pay more than businesslike attention to the private parts of her body—was apparently sleeping all around town the moment she left the country.

Betrayal stung, heated and raw in that place behind her heart she never let anyone go.

And tears stung just as angry in her eyes.

'Ming-húa—' Oliver barked and then spoke quietly to the maître d', who then rattled a fast command to his staff who, in turn, scattered on individual errands. One left a clean towel with Audrey but it wasn't going to do much against the red stain that spread like a chest-wound down her cream front.

'Come on,' Oliver said, pulling her to her feet. 'You can change upstairs.'

Code for *I'm taking you somewhere you can have your meltdown in private.*

She let him pull her towards the exit, his hand hot and secure around her ice-cold one. But as they got to the elevators he led her, instead, up a carpeted circular staircase, which opened discreetly onto one side of the public restaurant lobby.

At the top of the stairs, the furnishings changed slightly to the polished floor and neutral décor so popular in this part of China. It actually felt quite welcoming since her home in Australia was much the same. Executive beige. Blake's taste, not hers. All very stylish but totally without soul.

Like their marriage.

Oliver swiped a keycard through the scanner and swung open a pair of big, dark doors into an amazing space.

The view shouldn't have stolen her gaze so immediately considering it was only a half-floor higher than the restaurant they'd spent all afternoon in, but the penthouse sat squarely on the top of the building and its windows wrapped around three-hundred-and-sixty degrees of amazing view. Some of it was the much taller buildings around them and the patches of mountainside in between, but the majority was the towering chrome and glass forest that was the buildings of Central Hong Kong and, across the harbour, Kowloon.

It didn't matter that the living area wasn't large because it had the most spectacular back yard she'd ever seen.

Pity she was in no mood to enjoy it.

'Tell me,' she gritted the moment the door closed behind her.

But Oliver waited until he'd removed her dripping jacket and folded it on the non-porous safety of the slate bench top in the open-plan kitchen. Short of removing her blouse and skirt, too, there wasn't much else he could do to clean her up.

Audrey folded her arms across her damp front and walked to the enormous window to just…stare.

'He called them his Christmas bonus.' Oliver sighed behind her.

Pain lanced through her. That was just crass enough for Blake, too. 'Who were they? Where did he find them?'

'I don't know, Audrey.'

'How long have you known? The whole three years?'

'The first year I thought maybe he'd grow out of it. But when he did it again the following year, I realised it wasn't a one-off. So I confronted him about it.'

She squeezed her hands around her elbows. 'So…five years in total? Also known as *our whole marriage*?'

Her voice shook on that and she saw him behind her, reflected in the glass of the balcony, his head bowed. The most defeated she'd ever seen him.

'I'm so sorry, Audrey. You don't deserve this.'

'Why didn't you tell me sooner?' she whispered.

'Because I knew how much it would hurt you.'

She spun. 'You preferred to leave me in a marriage where I was being made a fool of?'

'I couldn't be sure you didn't know.'

She couldn't prevent the rise in her voice. 'You thought I might *know* and *stay*?'

Like his mother? Was that what his upbringing taught him?

'I couldn't be sure,' he repeated. 'It's not an easy subject to raise.'

Which would explain why half their day had gone by before he elected to mention it.

'Is *this* why you didn't come to his funeral?'

'I've explained why—'

'Right. In case you couldn't keep your hands off me.' She snorted. 'I didn't actually believe you about that.' The hurt she was feeling had to go somewhere, and Oliver was right there.

'Well, you should, because I meant every word. Why do you think I sent your favourite flowers and not his? I wanted to be there for *you*.'

'Just a shame that Blake didn't share your enthusiasm for me or he may not have felt the need to stray.'

Ugh. Even the word sounded so wretched. And even though her head knew that *Blake* was the one who'd been so sad and weak, it didn't stop her from feeling like the pathetic one.

'So you and he…' Oliver risked.

She spun around. 'Did we have a rich and fulfilling sex life? Apparently not. I knew I didn't rock his world but I didn't realise I'd driven him to such desperate lengths.'

'It wasn't you, Audrey.'

'It was at least half me!'

He crossed to her, took her hands from around her ruined blouse and cupped them. 'It wasn't you at all.'

'Well, it wasn't Don bloody Juan. He seems to have had no problems in that regard.'

'I swear to you, Audrey, there was nothing you could have done differently.'

'How would you know? Did he—?' *Oh, God.* 'Did he talk to you about our sex life, or lack thereof?'

Yeah, that would be the final humiliation. Oliver could add *dud lay* to her mounting debit column.

'No. He did not. But he did talk quite freely about his other...encounters. Until I shut that down.'

She sunk onto an ottoman and buried her face in her hands. 'I feel like such a fool. How could I not have seen?'

'He didn't want you to see.'

'Then how could I not have guessed?' She shot back up onto her feet. 'We lived such separate lives but I was with him every day—surely I should have at least suspected?'

'Like I said, you look for the best in people.'

'Not any more,' she vowed.

'Don't.' He crossed to stand in front of her. 'Don't let him change you. Your goodness is why people will judge him for this, not you.'

People? Her face came up. 'How many people know?'

He dropped his eyes to the carpet. 'A few. I gather he wasn't all that subtle.'

A sudden image of Blake with a buxom post-adolescent on each arm strolling through inner Sydney filled her mind and thickened her throat. Everything she wasn't. Young, stacked, lithesome and probably the kind of performer in bed that she could never hope to be.

And so public... Maybe he wanted to be caught? Wasn't that what the experts said about men who had affairs? And maybe she would have caught him out if she'd been paying the slightest bit of attention to her marriage.

Reality soaked in as the tears dried up. She'd set herself up for this the day she gave her work and her friends and her hobbies more importance than her marriage.

She straightened on a deep inward breath.

'Audrey...' Oliver warned, his voice low. 'I know what you're doing.'

She tossed back her hair. 'What am I doing?'

'You're tallying up the ways this is your fault.'

He knew her so well. How was that possible?

'Do I need to say it again?' he growled.

'Apparently you do.'

He stared at her, indecision scouring that handsome face. Then he stepped forward and took her hands again, squatting in front of her. 'Audrey Devaney, this was *not* your fault.'

He spoke extra-slowly to get through her hysteria.

'There was nothing in this world that you could have done to change this—' he tightened his hold on her hands so much she actually glanced down at his white knuckles '—short of changing gender.'

Her tear-ravaged eyes shot back up to his one more time. Utterly speechless. But then denial kicked in.

'No—'

'I think he'd known a really long time,' he went on, calmly. 'I think he knew when we were growing up, I think he knew when you guys first started dating and I think he knew when he walked down the aisle with you. But I also think he just couldn't be on the outside what he didn't feel on the inside. Not long term.'

'You're defending him?'

'I'm defending his right to be who he truly was. But, no, I'm not defending his actions. Cheating is cheating and he was hurting someone I care deeply about. That is why I ended my friendship with him.'

'And he knew that?'

'He got a very graphic farewell visit.'

'You were in Sydney? Why didn't you tell me?' Although the answer to that was ridiculously patent. To someone whose brain cells weren't in a jumbled pile. 'Sorry. Don't answer that.'

Just then the tiniest knock came at the big brown doors. Almost like a kitten scratching. Oliver crossed to it and pulled one open and one of the stunning staff from earlier drifted in. She held a neat fold of gorgeous blue silk, threaded through with silver.

'A change of clothes for you,' Oliver explained. 'Your suit will be laundered onsite and returned to you before you leave tonight.'

The girl smiled, revealing flawless, tiny teeth to go with the hourglass figure and hand-span waist, and nudged the clothes towards her. Audrey felt foolish being treated with such kid gloves, so she took the clothes, thanked the girl and turned to go find a bathroom.

'Second on the right,' Oliver called after her.

It was a matter of only minutes for her to strip out of her ruined business suit and into the dress that the girl had clearly picked up in the boutiques on street level. Three-quarter length, with the high collar and short sleeves typical of Chinese fashion and accentuating every curve. The depth of the blue was truly stunning and the threads of silver cast a glow that refracted up to include her face.

Which only served to highlight the tear-struck devastation there. As if things weren't bad enough.

She sagged down onto the broad bath edge and slumped, exhausted, against the cool of the tiled wall.

Blake's secret life certainly explained a lot. His at times enigmatic behaviour, which she'd chalked up to business tensions. His emotional detachment, never rude but always

a few degrees…separated. And their lacklustre—and downright perfunctory—sex life.

Technically correct but lacking any real heart.

Turned out there was a very good reason for that.

And *she* wasn't *it*.

Her relief at that far eclipsed the shock of discovering her
husband was gay. How sad that Blake hadn't ever managed
to reconcile that part of his life. That he felt the need to lie
to everyone around him even while it ate him up inside.

And how sad that she couldn't have been there for him
in his struggle. Because she would have. Her feelings for
him might not have been traditional or immense but they
were genuine, even when she didn't always like the things
he did. If he'd confided in her, she totally would have supported him. Even as she left him.

Because hiding inside a marriage was no way to be
happy.

Audrey looked back up into the mirrors lining the far
side of the bathroom and practically heard them whisper…

Hypocrite.

She'd held onto her fair share of secrets, too, within their
marriage. Not quite as destructive as Blake's, but then again
her secrets weren't quite as colossal as his.

She tilted her head slightly back in the direction of the
living room. Towards Oliver.

Not quite.

Thanks to China and its quirks, Audrey knew exactly
what she'd find under the bathroom sink. A small refrigerator loaded with bottles of water and, on the left, a stack of
dampened, refrigerated towels. Manna during Hong Kong's
steamy wet season. Stocked just because during the dry. A
lifesaver now.

She pressed the topmost wet towel to her flushed face, trying to restore some semblance of order.

'Audrey?' Oliver murmured through the door.

She opened it just a crack.

'I thought you might want this?' He squeezed her purse through to her.

'Thank you. Um...here...' She bundled up her skirt and blouse and passed the whole wad back through the gap. 'So she doesn't have to wait.'

As his fingers closed around the clothes they brushed against hers, static sparking in their wake. Except it couldn't be static because she was standing on tiles and the corridor was bamboo-floored. She curled her fingers back into her palm as she pulled it back into the bathroom.

Oliver murmured and was gone.

It took two more towels and some hasty repair work with the travel make-up from her purse until she felt vaguely presentable again. She combed through her chaos of hair, pulled the snug blue dress down the few inches it had ridden up with all her fussing and turned to the door.

Ready or not.

CHAPTER NINE

Ginger fingers with lemon spritzer

'HOW ARE YOU DOING?'

It took Oliver a moment to speak after she emerged and when he did there was a hint of tightness to his voice. Uncomfortable at the idea of picking up the conversation where they left off, perhaps, given how hysterical she'd been.

Well, that was over.

The beautiful hostess had departed with her things and so they were alone again, but Audrey wasn't about to resume their previous discussion. She ignored his question and wandered straight past him into a kitchen that looked as if it had been shipped direct from a magazine. And also as if it had never made so much as a cup of coffee. And why would it when the residences in this building were fully serviced by maids and room service?

'Why do you suppose they need two sinks?' she mused.

Excellent. Displacement conversation.

There were dual sinks on opposite sides of the kitchen.

Neither of them overlooked the magnificent view, so they clearly weren't for standing at doing dishes.

Oliver moved up behind her. 'Maybe the wealthy entertain a lot? Need the catering facility?'

She turned. 'You say that like you're not one of them.'

'Entertaining is really not where I spend my money.'

'You entertain me every Christmas.'

'You're an exception to the rule.' He watched her as she trailed a finger along the granite bench tops, drifting slowly amongst all the polished surfaces. 'That dress looks—'

He struggled for words and she hoped whatever he was trying not to say wasn't *ridiculous*. Or *absurd*. Or *try hard*.

'—like it's part of your skin. It fits you perfectly.'

It shouldn't, given she was taller by a foot than the average Chinese delicacy. She glanced down at her legs where the dress stopped awkwardly halfway up her calves. 'I think it's supposed to be longer.'

'It doesn't matter. It looks right on you.'

She bowed in a parody of the cultural tradition and as she came up she saw the burst of dark intensity in his gaze. She swallowed with some difficulty. 'That's because you haven't seen me try to sit down in it, yet.'

But that wasn't nearly as difficult as she feared. The dress shifted and gave in all the right places as she sank down onto the edge of the expensive nine-seat sofa running around the far edges of the living space.

'Are we going to ignore it, Audrey?' Oliver said, still standing a few feet away.

It. The proverbial elephant in the room. 'I'm not sure there's much more to say.'

His eyes narrowed. 'Just like that? You've filed it away and dealt with it already?'

No, she'd filed it away *un*-dealt with. As was her wont. She smiled breezily. 'I really don't want to have to reapply my make-up a second time.'

Oliver stared down on her. 'It bothers you that little?'

Oh, where to begin answering that question? Her tight smile barely deserved the title. 'Many things about what he did will always bother me. It bothers me that I misread our marriage so much. It bothers me that he respected it little enough to cheat in the first place. It bothers me that he respected *me* little enough to do it and be so public about it.'

'But not that it was with men?'

She stared. 'You said it yourself. It wasn't *me*. It wasn't Audrey Devaney that he felt the need to stray from; it wasn't *his wife* that he couldn't stomach. It was all of us. My whole gender. There's no better or cleverer or funnier or sexier woman that might have been more suitable than me. His choice means my only lack was a Y chromosome.'

'You don't lack anything, Audrey.'

Get real.

She leaned forward. 'You know my school experience. That led me to bury myself in study during university and not long after graduating I met Blake.' And Oliver, but that wasn't going to help make her point. 'So my entire sense of who I am romantically—' she couldn't even bring herself to *say* 'sexually' '—was from him.'

A man who was just going through the motions for appearances' sake.

'I thought it was *me*. I thought I was to blame for the lack of passion in our marriage. That I didn't inspire it, that I wasn't worth it.'

That she couldn't feel it.

She shuddered in a breath. 'All those tears you just witnessed thirty minutes ago, all that devastation…? That was because the only man I've ever been intimate with preferred other women to me. Because that's how much of a dud I was in bed. But here I sit, just twenty minutes later, tearless and comparatively whole. I'm not mourning my marriage, I'm not cursing Blake's cheating, I'm not even cursing him.' She lifted wretched eyes to his. 'What does it say about me that my first reaction on hearing about all those men was *relief*? Vindication. Because that meant it wasn't *me*. That maybe I'm not broken.'

'I think it says you're human, Audrey. Which I know won't please you. You're a perfectionist and you like things to be orderly.' He peered down on her. 'And you're certainly not broken.'

She shot to her feet. 'Words. How would you know? Maybe a hotter woman might have been able to satisfy him.'

Oliver smiled. 'Pretty sure it doesn't work like that.'

'My point is that Blake is still my only reference point. So, really, we know nothing. I could still be a dud.'

Jeez, with self-belief like that who needed enemies?

Oliver folded his arms and calmly watched her pace. 'You haven't been involved with anyone else since he died? It's been eighteen months.'

'I've been too busy shoring up my life,' she defended, instantly conscious that maybe it was just further evidence of her lameness. Shoring up her life and conveniently returning directly to type. Her barricaded-up, risk-averse type.

'Audrey, think. You're missing something obvious—'

'Apparently I've been missing it for years!' That her husband wasn't into women. She spun on him. 'And why the hell does this amuse you?'

'—*I'm* attracted to you.'

Pfff. 'You just think the dress is hot.'

Yet her pulse definitely spiked at his words. But, once again, words were cheap.

'I do think the dress is hot but she had a similar one on, too—' he nodded to the front door where the beautiful china doll had just departed '—and I wasn't attracted to her. And you weren't wearing it earlier and I was definitely attracted to you then.'

'You're Oliver—*The Hammer*—Harmer. You'd be attracted to anyone.'

His fists curled that little bit tighter. 'You're going to need to find one slur and stick to it, Audrey. Either I'm guilty of swimming too exclusively down the beautiful end of the gene pool or I'll do anything in a skirt. Which is it?'

'I didn't say you couldn't slum it from time to time.'

That actually seemed to make him mad. For the first time today. 'I think you'd say anything to win an argument.'

Yep. He absolutely had her number there.

Well… Whatever. 'You being attracted to me is a comment on your general randyness not on my abilities—' or otherwise, a little, inner voice whispered '—in the sack.'

He laughed but it no longer sounded amused. 'Careful, Audrey. That sounds an awful lot like a challenge.' He stepped closer.

She tossed her head. 'How like you to read it that way.'

'Why are you so angry at me?'

'Because you're here,' she yelled. 'And because you kept this from me for so long. And because you're—'

Part of the bloody problem.

If not for the extraordinary chemistry she'd always felt around Oliver she might never have noticed it missing from her marriage. But she forced those words back into her throat before they spilled out, and let the tension out on a frustrated grunt instead.

'Because I'm what?'

'You're pushing me.'

'I'm trying to support you. I'm listening. And letting you vent. How is that pushing?'

'You're riling me up intentionally.'

'Maybe that's because I know what to do with you when you're angry. I felt powerless when you were so upset. I've never seen you like that before.'

And she'd be damned sure he never would again. Her chest heaved beneath the sensual silk. And some of her confusion billowed out.

'But that fire in your eyes and the sharpness of your words...? *That* I know.' He slid one arm around behind her and pulled her hard up against his chest. 'That and this feeling that I get when you're on fire.'

He took her hand and pressed it over his left pectoral muscle. His heart hammered wildly beneath it. 'Feel that? That's what you do to me. So please don't tell me I'm not attracted to you.'

She bent back as far as she could in his hold. Eyed him warily. Even as her own pulse began to gallop. 'You're just mad,' she muttered.

'Woman, you have no idea.'

He released her then and turned and crossed to the window. 'Audrey. You kill me. You have so much yet you don't value it. You don't see it.' He plunged both hands into his pockets as if to keep himself from reaching for her again. 'And I sit here every damned Christmas, wanting you, and wondering if you'd recognise the signs, if you had even the slightest clue that you were affecting me that way.'

Silence fell heavy and accusatory. But his outburst was enough to finally get the message through.

He was serious. He was actually drawn to her.

What the hell did she do with that?

'I'm sorry, Oliver.'

He turned back, all the anger gone now. 'I wasn't angling for an apology. I'm angry *for* you, not *at* you. That everything in life has led you to have such little faith in yourself despite all the amazing things you are. And I'm mad at myself that—despite everything my head tells me, despite the total lack of signals from you—my body just doesn't get the message.'

Her chest tightened like a fist.

No, he wasn't angry. He was hurting.

A lot.

'You never let on.'

'If there's one thing I'm good at, it's command over my baser instincts.'

She wet her lips and chewed them a little bit. This was Oliver: a man she cared for and respected. A man she'd been harbouring any number of inappropriate thoughts about for years. And he was telling her that the attraction was mutual.

'How could there be signals…?' she started.

He raised a hand to stop her. 'I understand, Audrey—'

'No, you don't. I meant how could I give you signals, when I was married and I knew how strongly you felt about fidelity? Above all else, I didn't want you to think badly of me.'

Not you.

He stared. 'Why would I?'

'You would have. If you could have seen into my head and read my thoughts sometimes when I was with you.'

Or lots of times when she wasn't.

He hadn't been moving before but somehow his body grew more still. Still and dangerously alert. 'What are you saying?'

'I'm saying that the absence of signals is a reflection of my great need for your good opinion.' She took a deep breath. 'Not my actual feelings.'

The shame in his gaze dissipated, heated and evaporated by the desire that took its place. But still he didn't move.

'You're not married now,' he murmured. 'And I'm hardly in a position to judge you given some of the fantasies I had when you were my friend's bride.'

Her breath tightened and ran out.

He was right. There was nothing stopping them. Blake was gone, and any loyalty she'd ever felt for him had dissolved the moment she discovered his serial infidelity. Oliver wasn't seeing anyone. She wasn't seeing anyone. They were both here in this amazing, private place. And she wouldn't see him again for twelve months.

And no one but them would know.

There was no reason in the world that she shouldn't cross the empty space between them and put her hands on Oliver Harmer as she'd been dreaming of for years.

And that freedom was completely and utterly terrifying.

She crossed to the window, instead, stared out at the view. All those millions of people just going about their business, oblivious to the torment happening at the top of one of the hundreds of buildings lining their harbour.

'Did you just weird yourself out?' he murmured from behind her.

Right behind her.

He read her like a book. There wasn't a person alive who

knew her as well as this man she only saw once a year. She smiled. 'Sure did.'

She could feel him there, his heat reaching out for her, but not touching. Just…teasing. Tormenting. Tantalising.

But she couldn't turn around to save her life. She clung to the ant-sized community far below them and used them as her anchor. Before she floated up and away on this bliss.

'It doesn't have to be weird,' he whispered. 'We're still the same people.'

That was exactly what made it weird. But also so very exciting. As her pounding pulse could attest.

'But you have to want it,' he breathed. 'And you have to think about it. I need you to make the conscious decision.'

'You want me to make the first move?' Please, no… surely?

'I want you to be certain.' His words brushed her ear.

She steadied herself with hands on the window, either side of her body, her hot palms instantly making a thermal handprint on the cool glass.

'What if I'm no good?' She hated how tiny her voice sounded.

The chuckle that rumbled in his chest so close behind her was almost close enough to feel. 'Audrey, I'm not even touching you and it's already good.'

He leaned more of his weight into her, pressing her to the window and the hard tension in his body gave his words veracity. The contrast of the cool glass to her front and his big, hot body at her back made her breath shudder in her throat.

'Let me show you.' His knuckle came up to stroke her hair back from her face, back over her shoulder. And it was that—more than anything he could have said or done—that convinced her.

Because those big, tan, confident fingers…?

They were trembling like an autumn leaf.

Her eyes fluttered shut and she forced all the doubts and fears and questions out of her mind and just let herself *feel*. The moment she tipped her head, exposing more of her throat above the delicate collar hem of the dress, Oliver dropped his lips straight onto her skin, hot and self-assured.

Her legs practically gave way. If not for the press of his body sandwiching her to the glass window she would have slid in a heap onto the expensive bamboo parquetry. Air shuddered in and out of her on inelegant gasps as his mouth and chin nuzzled below the blue and silver collar, then around to the front of her throat, lathing her collarbone. His hands covered hers on the glass and twisted them down to trace, with him, the silken length of her body.

His knuckles brushed the sides of her breasts, her waist, the swell of her hips, leaving her trembling and alive. Then he released her hands and one of his slipped around to press against her belly while the other traced down the outer curve of one buttock. Beneath its underside.

Her eyes flew open.

'Just feel it,' he murmured against her skin. 'Just be brave.'

The strange choice of words was lost again in the excruciating sensations of his lips back on her throat. They climbed up behind her ear, lingered there a moment and then drifted forward, across her jaw, along her cheek. Searching. Seeking. And when they reached what they were seeking Audrey was more than ready for them.

His mouth pressed against hers on a masculine, throaty sigh, and she twisted slightly in his hold to improve her purchase and meet his exploration with her own.

Wave after wave of vertigo washed over her as she stood, pressed against nothing but open sky and man, all the air in her body escaping out to mingle with Oliver's. She clung to his lips as though they were the only thing stopping her from plunging sixty storeys.

He tasted exactly as she'd dreamed—decadent and masculine and delicious.

He felt just as she'd always imagined—hard and hot and in control.

But so, so much better. Like nothing she'd ever experienced in her life.

Be brave, he'd said. This was what he meant. Take a chance.

Embrace the risk.

She twisted fully in his grasp, pressing her back to the glass, and slid her arms up around his bent neck.

And she kissed him back for all she was worth.

Things really took off then. Oliver slid his foot between her feet and nudged them apart, making room for the expensive fabric of his thigh. That pressed against her everywhere she'd started to ache but it also took over the important job of holding her up, which freed his hands to roam the front of her body where they'd been unable to go moments before.

One plunged up into her hair and the other trailed its way up to a breast. And he relieved her of another ache, there, with a gentle squeeze.

He ripped his mouth from hers as fast as his hand snatched away from her breast. 'You're not wearing a bra?'

Confusion dazzled her, but she answered, 'It was in the pile you sent for cleaning.' Some of the salsa had soaked through onto it. Which was a ridiculous thought to be having just now.

'That's going to make it a bit harder,' he gritted, blazing the words along the neglected side of her throat.

It was all she could do to harness enough air to keep speaking. 'Make what harder?'

'Stopping.'

'Why would you stop?'

Why *in this world*...?

'Because we're about to have company.'

She ripped her ear away from where his hot lips were torturing them. Company wasn't *just the two of them*. Company wasn't *no one will know*. Company was public. And she was standing with her skirt half hiked up sandwiched between Oliver and the window in the direct eyeline of the door.

He stepped back, but not without reluctance.

'What company?'

'I asked for the next dish to be served up here.'

'Why the hell would you do that?'

Well...wasn't she quite the lady when in the throes of carnal disappointment?

Moisture from her swollen lips glinted on his as he smiled. 'I didn't know this was going to happen. I thought you might have appreciated the privacy.'

She tugged her skirt down. He stepped back.

Looks like stopping is all taken care of. 'I would love privacy right now.'

'You don't have to eat it. We can resume the moment they're gone.' His gaze grew keen. 'If that's what you want.'

Was that what she wanted? Yes, right now it really was. Right now, she was numb all over except for some very dissatisfied, very grumpy, very pointed points of focus that couldn't really think of anything other than resuming. But in five minutes…who knew? By then her brain might have kicked back in and reminded her of all the reasons this was a bad, bad idea.

In five minutes this could all be over.

You have to be certain. That was what he'd said, and maybe this was what he'd meant. That she needed to be certain in the cold, hard light of reality, not the hot, fevered place he'd just taken her.

On cue, the door sounded slightly. She spun to face back out of the window, tugging her dress unnecessarily into position and pretending she'd just been admiring the view, not the sensation of Oliver's hand on the screaming flesh of her breast. Behind her, Oliver accepted the meal with thanks and closed the door quietly.

Then there was silence. So much silence that Audrey eventually turned around.

He stood, staring at her silhouette, the loaded tray balanced in his arms, a question on his face.

Giving her the choice.

Another bonus of being rich, he could ignore the just-delivered food, spend the evening trying out every soft surface in the place—and a few of the harder ones—and nothing would ever be said. At least not aloud.

If only the rest of the world worked that way.

Her pulse hadn't even had time to settle, yet. How could she make a good decision with it still screaming around her body with a swag of natural chemicals in tow?

She made her choice, curling one arm across her torso. 'What's under the lid?'

'Fingers of chilled ginger specially prepared.' If he was disappointed, he didn't let it show particularly. He quirked one eyebrow, deliciously, and wet the lips that had just done such gorgeous damage to hers. 'Want a taste, Audrey?'

Okay, so he wasn't going to let her go easily.

She smoothed her dress once again and then crossed to the oversized dining table and slid into the seat at one corner. With no chair at the end he would either have to sit next to her or across from her. One was too close but she wouldn't have to look into those all-seeing eyes. The other...

Of course he chose that one, sinking into the seat immediately opposite.

'Stop thinking,' he murmured as he lifted the lid off the delivered tray and spread the contents between them on the table.

'I'm not.'

'You are. And you're partitioning. I can see it happening.' He served up the fanned palate cleanser. 'You're separating the parts of what just happened into acceptable and unacceptable and you're locking them in different boxes.'

She kept her eyes averted.

'But I'm curious to know what you put where.'

She lifted her gaze for an answer.

'Where did you file being here, with me, alone in this suite?'

She took a deep, slow breath. 'Being here is necessary. And sensible.' And therefore completely defensible.

'What about being in that dress?'

'The dress is beautiful. It makes me feel beautiful.' The door was wide open for him to say '*you are beautiful*'. But he didn't. Part of her was pleased that he didn't resort to trite niceties. A smaller part cried just a little bit.

He leaned back in the expensive chair and considered

her. 'What would you change? If you could? If money was no object.'

She considered. The shape of her eyes wasn't anything to write home about unaided, but they came up pretty well under skilfully applied make-up. And their colour was harmless enough. Her lips were even and inoffensive, not too small, and they sat neatly under a long straight nose. Even that couldn't be called a problem, particularly.

It was just all so...lacklustre.

'My jaw's a bit square.'

He shook his head once. 'It's strong. Defined.'

'You asked me what I'd change. That's something.'

'It gives you character.'

She laughed. 'Yep. Because all women hunger to have a face "with character".'

'You can have character and still be beautiful. But okay, what else?'

She sighed. 'It's not a case of individual flaws. It's not like I could get a brow-lift or have my ears pinned and I'd feel reborn. It's just that I don't have...' She considered her wording options. 'There's no *standout* feature in my appearance.'

'I could name three.'

'Ha ha.'

'I'm serious. Want to hear them?'

She took a deep breath. Part of her wanted to watch him flounder, to make him own his lies. But a deeper part again wondered if he might see her differently from what she saw in the mirror. Curiosity won.

'Sure.'

'Your cheekbones,' he started, immediately, as though he'd been waiting years to say it. 'You don't highlight them,

but you don't need to. And when you smile and your muscles contract their angle seems to intensify.'

She lifted one brow. 'Good to know.'

'And that's number two, despite the sarcasm. Your face
is rich with…intelligence. You always look so switched on,
so intent. That stands out for me, big time.'

'I have a smart face?'

'Anyone can have a garden-variety pretty face…'

She processed that. His body language said he was serious, but she wasn't about to make a fool of herself by getting
all hot and bothered by his praise. 'Wow, I'm very curious
to know what could possibly top a "smart" face…'

He didn't hesitate. 'Your body.'

Not what she was expecting. And the intent fixation of
his gaze was just a little bit disconcerting. 'Please don't
call me athletic.'

'No?' Which meant he'd been about to.

'That's code for "shapeless and flat-chested".'

'Only if you're looking for offence.' He considered her
and his eyes darkened before he spoke. 'Here's what athletic means to me.'

He leaned slightly forward.

'Malleable. Flexible.' Every word was more of a breath.
'Resilient. Strong. It's a body that won't break easily under
duress.'

The air flowing in and out of her lungs seemed to divest
itself of oxygen and she had to increase her respiration to
compensate. Her undisciplined imagination filled with images of the kind of duress he might be referring to. And
ways of applying it.

'I think of endurance and fortitude—'

'Is everything about sex with you?' she breathed.

Pot. Kettle. Black.

'Who says I'm just talking about sex? What about a long, healthy life? What about childbirth? What about long hikes out there—' he indicated the steep slope of Hong Kong's wilderness trails on a distant green mountain '—and stretching out, long and straight on this sofa watching a movie? A man might see the surface details with his eyes, but his biology is naturally drawn to the kind of mate that will live as long as he does.'

The picture he painted was idyllic and she got the sense that that was exactly what he saw when he looked at her.

Potential.

Not flaws.

Awkwardness—and awareness—surged around them. She never was good with compliments, but there was also the sense that maybe he'd given the subject of her figure a whole lot more thought than just a few seconds.

'Although, yeah, it's definitely the kind of body that tends to make a man start thinking about getting sweaty.' Those thoughts reflected darkly in his eyes. 'And that's a whole other body part paying attention.'

Audrey grabbed the levity like a life raft on the sea of unspoken meaning on which she'd suddenly found herself adrift. 'That's what I figured.'

He joined her in that life raft. 'What can I say? I'm a man of very few dimensions.'

Not true. Not at all. And she was just beginning to get a sense of how much she'd yet to learn about him. And about how long that could take.

'I wish you could see yourself as I see you,' he murmured.

She shrugged. 'I don't lose sleep over it or anything.'

'I know. But I'd love to watch you walk into a room, full of knowing self-confidence instead of doubt.'

She knew exactly what he was talking about. Somewhere along the line she learned to downplay her strengths, maybe to fly under the radar. 'Confidence attracts you?'

'Completely.'

'Is that what the beautiful women are all about?'

'It's not their aesthetics I'm drawn to.'

No. She was starting to realise how shallow her accusation that *he* was shallow really was.

'But sadly the confidence doesn't always hold up. Some of them were the most fragile women I've ever met.'

'Maybe you just expect too much?' she risked.

'By knowing what I want?'

'By expecting it all. And maybe they got the sense that they were failing to measure up to some undefined standard.'

He stared at her. 'Law of averages. If one woman can have everything I want, then there has to be another.'

She had *everything* he wanted? That was a whole lot more than just intellectual compatibility. Her heart thumped madly. 'And yet I lack the confidence you look for. So incomplete, after all.'

'I said you don't see it, not that you don't have it. You could own any room you walked into if you could just tap into your self-belief.'

If only it were *as easy* as turning on a tap. 'A few more conversations like this one and maybe I will.'

He looked inordinately pleased to have pleased her. 'I live to serve.'

The intensity of his gaze reached out and curled around

her throat, cutting off most of her air. 'Really? Then how about serving me another finger?'

Oliver finished his dish way ahead of Audrey. She stalled, wiping up every drop, using it as a chance to cool things off as much as the ginger had. One part of her hungered for more of the physical sensation she'd enjoyed before the food came. Exactly as stimulating as the gastronomic marathon they were undertaking. But another part—the sensible, logical part—knew that there was much more going on with her than just Oliver's desire for some activity of the *athletic* kind.

And *more than* was a big mental shift to be making in one day. Particularly when she'd come here today all ready to say goodbye.

To cut off her supply.

'I think maybe we should head back downstairs,' she murmured.

That surprised him. 'Now?'

She folded her napkin neatly and placed it next to her licked-clean plate on the expensive table. 'I think so.'

'Safety in numbers, Audrey?'

'What happened before was—' *amazing, unprecedented, unforgettable* '—compelling, but I don't think we should necessarily pick up where we left off.'

It was too dangerous.

'You seemed as *compelled* as I was. Can you just walk away from it?'

'I… Yes. The timing is all wrong.'

'We're both single. We're alone in an executive suite looking out over one of the world's most beautiful views. We have the whole evening ahead of us. And it's Christmas. How could the timing be better?'

His knowing eyes saw way too much. Like just how much of a liar she was. 'I just learned my husband was cheating on me...' she hedged.

'I assumed you'd slipped into revenge sex mode.'

'You think me that much of a user?'

'Are you still a us*er* if the us*ee* is fully aware of what you're doing? I'd be delighted to be exploited for any revenge activity whatsoever.' He held his hands out to the side. 'Do your worst.'

Impossible man. And impossible to know if he was serious or joking, or some complicated combination of the two. 'That wouldn't be particularly mature, Oliver.'

'Sometimes the body knows better than the brain what it really wants. Or needs.'

'You think I *need* a good roll in the hay?' Did she strike him as that uptight?

'Who says I'm talking about you?'

Oh, please. 'Like you didn't have sex twice this week already.'

'I did not.'

'Then last week.'

He stared at her. Infuriatingly unabashed.

'Earlier in the month, then.'

'Nope.'

The mere concept of a celibate Oliver was fascinating. But she wasn't going to allow even intrigue. 'Well, that explains today's detour from the norm. You're horny.'

'Any detour we take today—' she didn't fail to notice his use of the future tense '—won't be due to lack of self-control on my part.'

'So bloody cocky,' she muttered, pulling the dishes together into an easy-to-collect pile for the hotel staff. 'And presumptuous if you think I lack self-discipline.'

It was another of the virtues she was prepared to own.

'Far from it. The moment I let you shore up your resolve, I'm screwed. You'll set your mind to leaving and I'll never see you again.'

A raw kind of tragedy lurked behind his eyes. 'So...you're keeping me off kilter, just to be safe?'

'Trying to.'

Huh. It was working. 'How is confessing that going to help your cause?'

'I'm trying something new. Something that goes against everything my instincts tell me.'

She narrowed her eyes at him.

'Honesty.'

'You're always honest with me.'

'I don't lie. That's not the same as being honest. There's a lot I don't say, rather than have to lie to you.'

'Like not telling me about Blake?'

'Like not telling you how badly I want you every time I see you.'

Air shot into her lungs in a short, sharp gasp.

'That's right, Audrey. Every single time. And it's not going to go away just because you refuse to think about it.'

Her chest pressed in on itself. 'I assume you don't want to go back downstairs?'

'I do not.' His gaze was resolute. 'We're too close.'

'Close to what?'

'Close to everything I've wanted for years.'

Wanted. Her, on a plate. It was still too inconceivable to trust. 'Regardless of what I want?'

'If I thought you didn't want it I'd be holding the door open for you right now and calling up the elevator.'

A fist squeezed around her larynx.

'But you do. You just need to let yourself have it.' He glowered down on her. 'And believe you deserve it.'

She curled her arms around the sensual silk of her loaned dress and remembered instantly how much better his arms had felt doing the same thing just minutes ago. *Deserve it?* Did he know what he was asking her to set aside? Years of careful, safe emotional shielding?

Of course she wanted to sleep with him. It seemed stupidly evident to her. But *dare* she? Could she do it and not be crippled by old doubts? Could she do it and not want more? Because he wasn't offering *more*. He was offering *now*.

And right now she had allure working very much in her favour.

'The Audrey of your imagination must be spectacular,' she whispered, enjoying the solar flare that erupted in his smouldering gaze. 'But, seriously, what if I'm just ordinary?'

Or worse. Was that something she could bear him knowing?

He stepped closer and slid his big hand around her cheek. 'Honey, I'm that keyed up I may not even notice what you're doing.'

A choked kind of laugh rattled through her. Bless Oliver Harmer and his gift for putting her at ease. 'You're supposed to say, "You couldn't possibly be, Audrey".'

'You *couldn't* possibly be, Audrey,' he repeated, all seriousness. 'But I'm done enabling you. If you want to know for sure you're going to have to take a step. Take a risk.' He lowered his hand between them and stretched it towards her, his eyes blazing but steady. 'And take my hand.'

She stared at those long, talented, certain fingers. No trembling now.

If she slid her own in between them she was changing her life, going boldly where she'd never gone before.

A one-night stand.

Sex with Oliver.

That couldn't be undone. And it probably wouldn't be repeated; after all, they only saw each other once a year and a lot could change in twelve months.

Revenge sex, he'd joked. But was it so very funny? She certainly had enough to feel vengeful for. She'd wasted years being modest and appropriate and not throwing herself across the table at a scrumptious Oliver every year out of loyalty to a man who was betraying everything she'd ever stood for. Who couldn't wait for her to leave the country so he could express the man he really wanted to be.

Wasn't she due a little bit of payback?

And wouldn't that moment when Oliver strained over her just as he had in her most secret fantasies…wouldn't *that moment* undo everything that had gone before it? Wouldn't she be reborn?

Like a phoenix out of the ashes of her ridiculous, restrained life.

His fingers twitched, just slightly, out there all alone in the gulf of inches between them and the simple movement softened her heart.

This wasn't sleazy. This wasn't some kind of set-up or test and there wasn't a bunch of schoolgirls waiting to slam her up against the bathroom wall for daring to reach.

This was Oliver.

And *he* was reaching for *her*.

She lifted her eyes, fastened them to his cautious hazel depths and slid her fingers carefully between his.

CHAPTER TEN

*Lavender-cured crocodile, watermelon fennel salad
served with a lime emulsion*

'Again?'

Audrey's beautiful, sweat-slicked chest rose and fell right in Oliver's peripheral vision as she sprawled, wild and indelicate, across his bed, eyeing him lasciviously.

His laugh strangled deep in his throat. 'I won't be doing it again for a little bit, love.'

'Really? You're not a three-times-a-night kind of guy?'

He rolled over and stared at her. 'Have you never heard of recovery? Any man who can go three times in a row didn't do it thoroughly the first time.'

And she'd been done *extremely* thoroughly.

The second time, anyway.

Their first time had been hot, and hard and slick and they didn't even make it off the sumptuous sofa. He'd been joking about being so keyed up, but it had taken a gargantuan effort on his part to keep things at a pace that wouldn't scare her off forever.

Or shame him.

The second time they'd turned nomad; roaming from surface to surface, view to view, stretching out the torture, exploring and learning the geography of each other's bodies, knocking vases off tables and sending light fittings swinging. He'd been determined to make a slightly better—and lengthier—showing than the almost adolescent fumblings on the sofa, and Audrey had risen to the challenge like the goddess she was, matching him move for move, touch for touch.

Until they'd finally collapsed in a heap on the penthouse's luxurious master bed where he really got to show her how he'd earned his nickname.

He rolled his exhausted head towards her. 'You were kidding, right?'

'Hell, yes. I'm numb.'

There we go... That was what a man liked to hear. He flipped his arm with the last remnants of energy he had and patted her unceremoniously on her perfect, naked bottom.

'Take that, Blake,' she said, after the giggles had subsided.

Audrey giggling. Wasn't that one of the heralds of the apocalypse?

'Hell hath no fury...' But it wasn't about vengeance, he knew that. This was much more fundamental.

'It wasn't me,' she whispered to the ceiling. And to every demon still haunting her.

He gave her a gentle shove with his own damp shoulder. 'Told you.'

'Yeah, you did.'

'Do you believe me now?'

'Yeah.' She sighed. 'I do.'

Then more silence.

Oliver studied the intricate plasterwork above them and mulled over words he'd never needed—or wanted—to utter. Found himself inexplicably nervous and utterly shamed of his own cowardice.

So...now what happens?

That was what he wanted to know. Half dreading and half breathless with anticipation at the answer. Because this— what they'd just shared—would be a crime to walk away from. He'd just had his deepest desire handed to him on a plate. Writhing under him.

Yet, he didn't do long-term. He didn't dare. Would he even know how? He'd lost years waiting for a woman with the right combination of qualities to come along. Goodness and curiosity and brilliance and elegance and wild, unbridled sensuality all bundled into one goddess.

He just wasn't going to find a woman on the planet better suited to being his.

Which meant he could *have* this remarkable gift that the universe had provided, but he couldn't *keep* it.

Because Audrey was far too precious to risk on someone as damaged as him.

Sex changed people. Women especially. Women like Audrey doubly especially. She wasn't a virgin, but he'd put good money on tonight being the first good sexual experience she'd had—again that sad, needy little troll deep inside him waved its club-fists triumphantly—and transformative experiences tended to make women start thinking of the future. Planning.

And he didn't do futures. He just couldn't.

There was more than one way of cheating in a relationship. He might never have been actually unfaithful to any of the women he'd been involved with, but he'd been false with every single one of them by not telling them they weren't measuring up to the bar set by a woman they'd never meet. By not telling them that what was between them was only ever going to be superficial.

By not telling them he wasn't in it for keeps.

He could dress it up whatever way he wanted—persevering, giving them a chance, getting to know one another—but the reality was from the moment he first realised they weren't the one, the rest of their time together was one big cheat.

As unfaithful and as unkind as his father. To every single one of them.

And so he'd come to specialise in short-term. He reserved his longest relationships for women who didn't change from first date to last. Predictable women who weren't looking for more. They got entire months.

Audrey wasn't the sort of woman you just kissed and farewelled after a few hot weeks. Look at the lengths he'd already gone to not to farewell her *at all*.

Audrey was someone he cared about deeply. And what happened from here was going to be critical to her remaining someone he was allowed to care deeply about. Because not caring for her was simply not an option. He couldn't even imagine it.

But using her—hurting her—wasn't going to work, either. He'd grown up witness to what it did to a woman to be in a relationship with a man incapable of loving just her.

It rotted her slowly from the inside out.

Bad enough imagining Audrey decaying in her sham of a marriage, but to think of himself being responsible for it… Watching her eyes getting dimmer and dimmer as he emotionally checked out of their relationship.

As he always did.

No. That was not something he was prepared to do to a woman he considered perfection. Who he actually cared for. Who he might love if he had any idea what the hell that meant.

And given his genetic make-up, the chances of him finding out any time soon weren't high.

But lying here drowning in *what-ifs* wasn't going to get them anywhere. Better to get it out in the open. Talk it through. Deal with whatever angst came.

Just ask!

'So what happens now?' he ground out. The longest four words of his life.

'Depends on what time it is.'

Okay. Uh, *not* what he was expecting. He craned his neck to check his TAG. 'Coming up to six p.m.'

Which meant she'd been here for eight hours already.

She rolled over, folding her arms under her as she went and boosting her breasts up into tantalising pillows. 'We still have half a degustation to enjoy.'

The little troll's fists fell limply by his side. She was thinking about food? While he was lying here doing a great impersonation of an angsty fourteen-year-old? 'Really? This hasn't been an adequate substitute?'

Her Mona Lisa smile gave nothing away. 'You said yourself we need to recharge. Might as well stretch our legs and eat while we do that.'

Stretch their legs. As if they'd just had a busy afternoon at their desks. He studied her for signs of weirdness—more than the usual amount—but found none. Her eyes were clear and untroubled.

'You're actually hungry?' Oh, my God, she actually was. Audrey Devaney might just be the perfect woman.

'Ravenous,' she purred. "That was quite a workout.'

No wonder he adored her. 'You want to be served up here?'

A hint of shadow crossed her expression. 'No. Let's go back downstairs.' But then she sagged and her warm lips fell against the cooling sweat of his shoulder. 'In just a minute or two.'

She was pretty hungry but, more than anything, Audrey wanted to walk back into this public restaurant with Oliver.

With Oliver.

Just for the sheer pleasure of doing it. Nothing but her dress had changed for the restaurant patrons or the staff because most of them probably assumed she and Oliver were already sleeping together. But *she'd* changed. *She* would know what it was like to have the best sex of her life with a man like Oliver Harmer, right over their very heads, and then casually stroll back in for the next course.

It was more decadent a sensation than if they'd served her palate cleanser smeared on Oliver's naked torso.

She stumbled over that image slightly and the fingers curled around hers tightened.

'Okay?'

She threw her gratitude sideways on a breathy acknowledgement. Lord, when had she become so...Marilyn Monroe?

She glanced awkwardly to the other tables for a half-heartbeat. Did she look like a woman who was quite accustomed to having exquisite sex between courses? *Could* she look like that? And it was, hands down, the best sex she'd ever had. With her husband. With anyone else. Even on her own. Her body was still swollen and sensitive and really, really pleased with itself.

What if she looked as smug as she felt?

'Are you sure you're okay?'

'I don't know what the etiquette is,' she admitted, dragging her focus back to their private little corner by the dragonflies as they approached. Were the insects this vivid and lively before or was everything just super-sensory right now?

'To what?'

'To walking into a room after our…bonus course.'

His chuckle eased a little of her nerves. 'I don't think there are any rules for that. You're going to have to wing it.'

'I feel—' *transformed* '—conspicuous.'

'If people are looking at you it's because of the dress, Audrey.'

Right. Not some tattoo on her forehead that said, 'Guess where she's just had her mouth.'

She sank, on instinct, towards her comfortable sofa and Oliver tugged on their still-entwined fingers as he kept moving.

Oh. *Together.*

How odd that—despite everything they'd done with each other and been to each other over the past hours—it was *this* that felt taboo. Like crossing over to the dark side. She joined Oliver on his sofa, facing the other way for the first time in five years, while he scanned her for the first sign of trouble.

She must look as if she was ready to bolt from the room.

She stretched, cat-like, back into his sofa. 'This is quite comfortable, too.'

'I've always liked it.'

Her bottom wriggle dug her a little deeper. 'I think you had the better end of the deal, actually.'

'I would definitely say so, today.'

Sweet.

Terrifying…but sweet.

Oliver did little more than flick his chin at a passing server and the man reappeared a moment later with two glasses of chilled white wine. Audrey smiled her thanks before sweeping her glass up and turning her attention again to the busy dragonflies in the tank that usually sat behind her, and, through its glass sides, the bustling kitchen on the far side of the restaurant.

'I always thought you were terribly sophisticated, knowing the timing of everything in a Michelin-starred restaurant,' she murmured. 'But you were cheating. You can see them coming.'

'It seems it's a night for exposing secrets.'

That brought her eyes back to his. 'Yes indeed.'

'Do you want to talk about it?'

It.

'I don't want to ruin it.' Or jinx it. 'But I don't want you to think I'm avoiding conversation, either.'

'Would you like to talk about something else?'

Desperately. 'What?'

He cupped his wine and leaned back into the corner of the sofa more comfortably. 'Tell me about the Testore.'

The instruments she hunted were certainly something she could get excited about. And talk about until his ears bled. 'What would you like to know?'

'How was it stolen?'

'Directly from the cabin of a commercial airline between Helsinki and Madrid, while the owner used the washrooms.'

'In front of a plane full of people?'

'The cabin was darkened. But Testores get their own seat when they fly so it's unusual that no one saw it being removed. Someone would have had to lean right over into the window seat.'

'Wow, it's that valuable? How did they get it off the plane without being seen?'

'No one knows. We have to assume one of the ground crew was paid off. The plane's cabin security picked up a shadow lingering by the seats and taking it but it was too dark to identify even gender. And short of paying for a seat for the instrument *and* one for a bodyguard I'm not sure what the owner could have done differently. She had to pee. They searched the plane top to bottom.'

The public areas, anyway.

'So how did you begin tracking it down?'

This was what she did. This was what she loved. It wasn't hard to relax and bore Oliver senseless with the details of her hunt for the cello.

Except that he didn't bore easily, clearly. Forty minutes later he was still engaged and asking questions. She'd kicked off her shoes again and tucked her feet up under her, feeling very much the Chinese waif in her silken sheath, helping herself to finger-sized portions of the crocodile and watermelon that was course number seven.

'Can you talk about all of this? Legally?' Oliver queried.

'I haven't told you anything confidential. It's all process.' She smiled. 'Plus I think I can trust you.'

His eyes refocused sharply, as if he had something to say

about that, but then he released her from his fixed gaze and reached, instead, to trace the line of her arm with a knuckle. 'Your patience amazes me. And that you're so close to finding it when you started with practically nothing.'

Oh, he had no idea how patient she could be. Just look how long she'd endured her feelings for him. Or how long she could endure his tantalising touch before shattering.

Apparently.

'It's taken all year but we're just one step behind them now. The plan is to get ahead and then we have them. The authorities just have to wait for them to deliver it up.'

'Why don't these people just take it and go to ground for a decade? Put it in a basement somewhere? Hoard it?'

'Criminals aren't that patient for their money and, besides, their industry is full of loose lips. You steal something like a Testore and don't keep it moving and one of your colleagues is just as likely to steal it out from under you.'

'I really don't see the point.'

'Neither do I,' she admitted. 'Why have lovely things if you never see them?'

'I'm surprised the bad guys haven't tried to buy you off.'

'Oh, they've tried.' She smiled. 'My sense of natural justice is just too strong. And I view the instruments a bit like children. Innocent victims. Stolen. Abused. All they want to do is go home to the person that loves and values them and keeps them safe and fulfils their potential.'

Because wasn't that what life was all about? Fulfilling your potential.

The brown in his eyes suddenly seemed more prominent. And chocolaty. And much closer. Which one of them had moved so subtly? Or had they both just gravitated naturally together?

'Want to hear something dumb?' he murmured.

'Sure.'

'That's how I feel about the companies I buy.'

She flicked an eyebrow. 'The near-crippled companies you get for a song, you mean?'

He smiled. 'They're innocent victims, too. In the hands of people that don't value them and don't understand how to make them strong.'

'And you do?'

'I'm like you—a facilitator. I have the expertise to recognise the signs of a flailing business and I gather them up, strengthen them and get them to the people who can give them a future.'

'That's a very anthropomorphic belief.'

'Says the woman who thinks of a cello like a trafficked child.'

She smiled. He was right. 'You don't ever break them up?'

'Not unless they're already falling to pieces.'

That was her greatest fear. Finding an instrument that someone took to with a sledgehammer rather than relinquish. Because some people were just like that: if they couldn't have it, no one would.

'I'm guessing that the people you buy them from don't see it that way.'

He shrugged. 'Hey, they're the ones selling. No one's forcing them.'

'I guess I hadn't realised how similar our jobs are. Though I get the feeling yours has a lot more facets.' Like a diamond. It was certainly worth a whole heap more.

Oliver studied her as he finished the last of the watermelon. 'That wasn't so bad, was it?'

'What?'

'Having a conversation.'

'We've had lots of conversations.'

'Yet somehow that feels like our first.'

It did have that exciting hum about it. 'I miss conversation.'

'Blake's been gone a while.'

'I never really talked with him. Not like this.' Not like Oliver. 'So it's been a couple of years.'

'Did you move to Antarctica when I wasn't looking? What about your friends?'

'Of course I have friends. And we talk a lot, but they've all known me forever and so our conversation tends to be about…you know…stuff. Mutual friends. Work. Dramas. Clothes.'

'That's it?'

'That's a lot!' But those steady hazel eyes filled her with confidence. 'I'm not… I don't share much. Often.' And she could never talk about Oliver. To anyone.

'You share with me.'

'Once a year. Like cramming.' Did that even count?

Nothing changed in his expression yet everything did. He studied her, sideways, and then reached out to drag soft knuckles across the back of her hand. 'You call me up whenever you want. I'd love to talk to you more often. Or email.'

The cold, hard wash of reality welled up around her.

Right. Because she was leaving in the morning. As she always did. Flying seven thousand kilometres in one direction while he flew twelve hundred in the other. Back to their respective lives.

Back to reality. With a phone plan.

'Maybe I will.'

Or maybe she'd chalk tonight up to a fantastic one-night stand and run a million miles from these feelings. That could work.

A murmuring behind them drew Oliver's gaze.

'Hey, it's starting.'

No need to ask what 'it' was. Her favourite part of December twentieth. Her favourite part of Christmas. Oliver pulled her to her feet and she padded, barefoot, on the luxury carpet to the enormous window facing Victoria Harbour. Below them Hong Kong's nightly light show prepared to commence.

Both sides of the harbour lit up like a Christmas tree and pulsed with the commencement of music that the Qīngtíng suddenly piped through their sound system. Massive lighting arrays, specially installed on every building the length of both sides of the waterfront, began to strobe and dance. It wasn't intended to be a Christmas show but, to Audrey, it couldn't be more so if it were set to carols. She couldn't see a light show anywhere without thinking about this city.

This man.

Oliver slipped her in front of him between the window and the warmth of his body and looped his arms across her front, and she knew this was the light show she'd be remembering on her deathbed.

Emotion choked her breathing as she struggled to keep the rise and fall of her chest carefully regulated. Giving nothing away. The beautiful lights, the beautiful night, the beautiful man. All wrapped around her in a sensory overload. Wasn't this what she'd wanted her whole life? Even during her marriage?

Belonging.

Never mind that it was only temporary belonging; she'd take what she could get.

'I missed this so much last year,' she breathed.

His low words rumbled against her back. 'I missed you.'

The press of her cheek into his arm was a silent apology. 'Let's just focus on tonight.'

She wasn't going to waste their precious time dwelling on the past or dreaming of endless combinations of futures. She had Oliver right here, right now; something she never could have imagined.

And she was taking it. While she could.

'What time does Qīngtíng close?'

His body tensed behind her. 'Got a flight to catch?'

She turned her head, just slightly—away from the light show, away from the other patrons, back towards him. 'I want to be alone with you.'

'We can go back upstairs.'

She took a breath. Took a chance. 'No, I want to be alone, here.'

Okay, that was definitely tension radiating on the slow hiss he released as a curse.

Too much? Had she crossed some kind of he-man line? She turned back to the view as though that was all they'd been discussing. As though it were that meaningless. But every cell in her body geared for rejection and made her smile tight. 'Or not.'

Oliver curled forward, lips hard against her ear. 'Don't move.'

And then he was gone, leaving her with only her own, puny arms to curl around her torso.

Ugh. She was so ill equipped for seduction.

And for taking a risk.

It was only moments before he returned, assuming his previous position and tightening his hold as though he'd never been gone. So... Maybe okay, then? It wasn't a total retreat on his part. The show went on, spectacular and epic, but all Audrey could think about was the press of Oliver's hips against her bottom. His hard chest against her back and how that had felt pressing onto her front not too long ago.

Light show? What light show?

At last, she recognised the part of the music that heralded the end of the nightly extravaganza and she tuned in once again to the sounds around her, reluctant to abandon the warm envelope of sensory oblivion she'd shared with Oliver in the dark.

Like insects scuttling away from sudden exposure, a swarm of staff whipped the restaurant's dishes and themselves back behind closed doors as the lights gently rose. The maître d' spoke quietly in turn to the six remaining couples and each of them collected up their things, curious acceptance on their faces, and within moments were gone.

'Oliver—?'

'Apparently your wish is my command.'

Her mouth gaped in a very unladylike fashion. 'Did you throw them out?'

'A sudden and unfortunate failure in the kitchen and a full return voucher for each of them. I'm sure they're thrilled.'

'Considering they were nearly on their last course—' and considering what Qīngtíng's degustation cost '—I'm sure they are, too.'

He led her back to his sofa.

Ming-húa appeared with a full bottle of white wine, an elegant pitcher of iced water and a remote control and placed all three on the table before murmuring, 'Goodnight, Mr Harmer. Mrs Audrey.'

And then he was gone back through the kitchen and out whatever back-of-house door the rest of the staff had discreetly exited through.

She turned her amazement to him in the luminous glow of the dragonfly habitat.

'Just like that?'

'They'll get it all cleaned up before the breakfast opening.'

Uh-huh. Just like that. 'Do you always get what you want?'

'Mostly. I thought you wanted it, too.'

'Wanting and getting aren't usually quite that intrinsically linked in my world.'

'Have you changed your mind?'

'Well…not exactly…' Although her breathless words were easier to own in the dark with the press of his body for motivation.

He leaned back into the luxury sofa and threw her a knowing look. 'You're all talk, Devaney.'

'I am not. I'm just thrown by the expedience with which that was…dealt with.'

'Careful what you wish for, then, because you might get it.'

Alone again.

Audrey glanced around the stylish venue. Then at the door. Then at Oliver.

His eyes narrowed. 'What?'

'I just need a minute…'

She pushed again to her bare feet and strolled casually

to the far side of the restaurant, and considered it before turning.

'Lost something?'

'I'm just seeing how the other half live.'

She peered out of the glass. Their view was definitely better in the dragonfly corner. Although it was, of course, exactly the same. Except Oliver was part of her view over there.

He chuckled and settled back to watch her. She hiked the sensuous fabric of her loaned dress up her legs slightly and then *cantered*—there was no other word for it—around the restaurant usually bustling with people.

'You're mad,' he chuckled, struggling to keep his eyes off her bared legs.

'No, I'm snoopy.'

She stuck her head inside the servery window and checked out the glamorous kitchen. No food left out overnight but definitely a clean-up job for someone in the morning. An industrial dishwasher did its thing somewhere in the corner, humming and churning in the silence.

On a final pass by his sofa, Oliver stretched up and snagged her around the waist, dragging her, like the prey of a funnel-web spider, down into the lair of his lap. Her squeal of protest was soaked up by the luxurious carpet and furnishings.

'Do they have security cameras?'

'Do you imagine they're not fully aware of why I sent them home early?'

The idea that they were all stepping out into the street, glancing back up at the top of their building and imagining—

Heat rushed up where Oliver's lazy strokes were already

causing a riot. 'There's a big difference between knowing and seeing. Or sharing on YouTube.'

'Relax. Security is only on the access points, fire escape and the safe. The only audience we have are of the invertebrate variety.'

Her eyes went straight to the pretty dragonflies now extra busy in their tank, as though they knew full well when the staff left for the evening and were only just now emerging for their nightly party.

Oliver reached with the hand not doing such a sterling job of feeling her up and pressed the small, dark remote control. The restaurant lights immediately dimmed to the preset from the light show.

'There you go. We'll be as anonymous as your Testore thief on their flight.'

Lying here in the dark, lit only by the dragonflies and the lights of Hong Kong outside, it was easy to imagine they were invisible.

'So—' he settled her more firmly against his body and made sure that they were connecting in dozens of hot, hard places '—you were saying? About being alone?'

'We have such a short time,' she whispered. 'I didn't want to share you with a crowd.'

A shadow ghosted across his eyes before they darkened, warmed and dropped towards her. 'The feeling is entirely mutual.'

His lips on hers were as soft, as pliable as before, but warmer somehow and gentler. As if they had all the time in the world instead of just a few short hours. She kissed him back, savouring the taste and feel of him and taking the time neither of them had taken upstairs. He didn't escalate, apparently as content to enjoy the moment as she was.

She hadn't indulged in a good old-fashioned make-out session since her teens. And even that hadn't been all that good, truth be told.

But neither of them were superheroes. Before long, her breath grew as tight as the skin of her body and a suffusing kind of heat swilled around and between them. Oliver shed his dinner coat and Audrey scrunched the long, silk dress higher up her thighs in a sad attempt at some ventilation where it counted.

'I feel like a kid,' he rasped, 'making out in the back of his parents' car.'

'Except you know you'll be scoring at the end of the night.' And he already had, twice.

He smiled against her skin. 'With you I'm not taking anything for granted.'

She levered herself up for a heartbeat, let some much-needed air flush in between their bodies and then resettled against him. 'Come on. We both know I'm a sure bet.'

His head-back laugh only opened up a whole new bit of flesh for her to explore and so she did, dragging aching lips down his jaw and across his throat and Adam's apple. He tasted of salt and cologne. The best dish yet.

They lay like that—wrapped up in each other, all hands and lips, getting hot and heavy—for the better part of an hour. Long enough for the ice in the wine bucket to mostly melt away and Audrey to drink the entire contents of the still water Ming-húa had delivered.

'I hope you're not going to get too drunk to be any good to me,' she teased, when Oliver reached for the wine bottle. But he just winked, placing it on the table, and then dunked his glass straight into the fresh, melted ice in the bucket.

'Someone's drunk all the water,' he pointed out. 'And you have to stay hydrated in a marathon.'

'Is that what we're doing? An endurance event?'

'Well, I sure am.' He tossed the water back in one long swallow and a rivulet escaped and ran down his jaw. When his mouth returned to hers it was fresh and straight-from-the-ice-bucket cool.

It didn't last ten seconds.

They kissed a while longer but, even with her eyes closed and her mind very much otherwise occupied, she could feel the subtle shift of Oliver's body as he leaned towards the table. A moment later, he pulled his mouth from hers and placed a half-melted ice block on her swollen lips.

Her whole body lurched as he ran the icy surprise over her top lip and then her lower one, and she lapped at the trickle of melted water that ran into her mouth, smiling as he departed for her chin. Then her throat. Then around to the thumping pulse-point at the top of her jaw. His lips trailed a heartbeat behind the melting cube, kissing off the moisture as the ice liquefied against her scorching skin until it was completely gone.

Four cool fingers slid up her thigh and tucked under the hem of her underwear while his other hand made a complete mess of her hair.

'Those girls at school must have known what they were doing,' he murmured hard against the ear he was lavishing.

'What do you mean?' She could barely remember them, and that was saying something.

'Even as kids, they must have known a threat when they saw one. That you were capable of this.'

His fingers moved further into her underwear. Into her. She arched into his touch. 'Such shamelessness?'

Greenish-brown eyes blazed into hers. 'Such potential passion. And, yeah, a hint of shamelessness. No wonder the boys finally caught on.'

She couldn't tell him she was packing a lifetime into this one night of the year. That she was hanging *way* outside her comfort zone because she knew she'd be spending the rest of her life safely inside it. Because how was she ever going to find something like this again, now that she'd tasted it?

Outside this day—outside this building—the real world ruled. It was a place where the kind of secret emotions she'd always harboured for sexy Oliver Harmer had no place being aired. And definitely not being indulged.

This was a 'what happens at Christmas stays at Christmas' kind of arrangement.

Casual and easy and terribly grown-up.

And the clock was ticking.

She moved against him to give him better access.

She'd grown lazy harbouring the feelings deep inside, exploiting the fact that he was *safe* to have feelings about as long as she was married. Like some kind of Hollywood star that it was okay to pant after because you knew you'd never, ever be acting on it. She held them close to her chest—clutched desperately, really—and enjoyed the sensations they brought. Enjoyed the what-if. Enjoyed the secret fantasy.

Careful what you wish for, he'd said.

But while she didn't dare indulge the emotional part, she was free to feed the physical part. The safe part. And Oliver was clearly very much up for the same with the hours they had left.

Because what happened here, inside the walls of this building, had nothing to do with the real world. And maybe it never had. Perhaps it had always been their weird little Cone-of-alternate-reality-Silence.

Maybe that was what made it so great.

'The synapses in your brain are smouldering,' he breathed, sniffing in amongst her hair. 'Stop overthinking this.'

'I can't help it,' she gasped. 'I'm a thinker.'

'Everyday-Audrey is a thinker. Go back to during-the-light show-Audrey. She was an impulsive and impressive doer.'

There you go. He saw it, too. There was a different set of rules for this day compared to the three hundred and sixty-four around it.

She twisted in his hold and it only pulled her dress up higher. But since both of them would have much preferred her to be out of it, that wasn't really a problem.

'You're right,' she said, settling more fully against him. 'Enough of the thinking. Let's go back to the feeling.'

Oliver pulled her more fully on top of him and studied her flushed face and shambolic hair.

'Best view ever,' he murmured.

'That's a big call given what's outside the window.'

He craned his neck towards the view. 'Good point. Change of plans.' His warm hand slid into hers. 'And change of view.'

She struggled to her feet alongside him, and Oliver led her, hand in hand, to an expensive, stuffed smoking chair by the window. One she'd always imagined him sitting in while he waited for her to arrive.

He twisted it square on to the view and sat before reaching for her.

'Where were we?'

'Here?' From first-sex to chair-sex in just a few hours. Alice was well and truly down the rabbit hole tonight.

'I wanted this upstairs. I've wanted it for years. You against that view. This is close enough.'

Her skin immediately remembered the cold press of glass against her hot breasts as he'd leaned on her from behind, upstairs, and her nipples hardened. There might not be the same drop sensation here on the chair a few feet back from all that glass and sky, but her stomach was doing enough flip-flops to qualify.

He took her hand and pulled her towards his lap. As she had on the sofa, she shimmied her silk dress higher to get her knees either side of his and then braced herself there.

'God, you're beautiful,' he breathed. 'Lit by all the lights of Hong Kong. It's like a halo.'

Was there a smoother-talking man in all this world? But her body totally fell for it, parts of her softening and throbbing an echo to the honey in his voice and the promise in his eyes. She lowered herself onto his lap.

One masculine hand slid, fully spread, up the tight, silk fabric of her stomach and over her breasts while the other followed it on the other side of her body, trailing the line of the dress's zip like someone following a rail line to the nearest town. At its end point he snagged the slider and lowered it and her loaner dress immediately loosened. It was a matter of moments before the hand at her breasts curled in the sensuous fabric and gently pulled it down her arms, revealing her uncovered breasts, and letting the beautiful fabric that he'd heated with his mere touch bunch, forgotten, around her waist.

'Oliver…' she breathed.

Two hands slid up her naked back holding her close as his

body closed the gap between theirs and his mouth moved immediately to her breast, dined there, sucking and coiling and working his magic against the sensitive pucker of nipple.

Her skin bloomed with gooseflesh.

She twisted against the excruciating pleasure and indulged herself by doing something she'd always dreamed of—burying her fingers deep in his dark hair. Over and over, curling and tangling and tugging; luxuriating as he tortured the breasts that had barely seen sun with the rasping caress of stubble.

Her legs officially gave out, but the warmth of his lap was waiting to catch her.

As soon as she pressed down into him, his mouth came away, sought hers out and clung there, rediscovering her before dropping again to the other breast.

Behind him, the polished glass of the dragonfly habitat reflected them both against the beauty of the city skyline. She, a half-naked silhouette balanced wantonly on Oliver's lap, and he, pressed powerfully to her chest, with the stunning beauty of the Hong Kong skyline stretching out behind them. She looked wild and provocative and utterly alien to herself.

This is what Oliver sees.

This was how he saw her.

Liberation rushed through her. She didn't look ridiculous. She didn't look all wrong teetering on the expensive chair. Or not enough like the beautiful people he mixed with. She looked *just like* a beautiful person. She looked absolutely, one hundred per cent right bedded within Oliver's embrace.

They fitted together.

Deep in her soul, something cracked and broke away on

a tidal surge of emotion. Part of a levee wall, a giant fragment of whatever powerful thing had been holding back all her feelings all this time.

They *belonged* together.

And finally they were.

Oliver's silhouette hands released her at the back and reached up to pull the struggling pins from her hair, sending it tumbling down over her bare shoulders, tickling the tops of her bared breasts. His hands framed her face and drew her gaze back down to his, hot and blazing and totally focused.

Those eyes that promised her the world. Promised her forever.

And he was the only man she could imagine delivering it.

His lips, when she met them, were as hot and urgent as the touch that skittered over her flesh, and while she was distracted with that he levered them both up long enough to get his wallet out of his trousers pocket, fumbled in it for a moment then threw the whole thing on the floor.

'How many of those do you have?' she breathed, needing the moment of sanity to ground her spinning mind. Nothing like a condom to bring things screaming back to reality.

'Just the one.'

Disappointment warred with pleasure. *One* was a very finite number. The two he'd used upstairs came from a stash in the en suite cabinet, which might as well be back in Shanghai for all the use it was to them at this moment. Upstairs was a whole world away. But *one* also meant he didn't carry a string of *twelve* in case he found himself on a desert island with a life raft full of flight attendants.

Which was strangely reassuring.

As though *one* made tonight somehow less casual, for him.

But clarity streamed in with the fresh air. That was crazy

thinking. The fact he had a condom at all made it casual. The fact she was leaving for another country in a few hours made it casual. The fact Oliver didn't do relationships made it casual.

But whatever it was. She still wanted it. Come what may.

And she was taking it.

She lowered herself to mere millimetres from his lips and breathed against them. 'Don't break it.'

His chuckle was lost in the resumption of their hot kiss and her brain had to let go of such trivialities as what happened with the condom as it focused on the rush of sensation birthed by his talented fingers and lips. The strength with which he pulled her against his hard body. The expediency with which he solved the barriers of fabric between them. She pressed back up onto her knees to give him room to manoeuvre beneath her and then he shifted lower in the chair just slightly—just enough—and used one hand at her coccyx to steady her while another worked at the wet juncture of her thighs to guide her down onto the rigid, strength of him.

'So damned beautiful…'

His choked words only made her hotter. As it had been the first time, and the second, it was again now—like pulling on a custom-made kid glove. They fitted together perfectly. More perfectly than before, if that was possible, because gravity gave her extra fit. She rose up on her knees again, repositioned, and then sank fully down onto him, heavy and certain.

His throaty, appreciative groan rumbled through them both. Had there ever been a more heartening sound? How was it possible to feel so small and feminine and so strong and powerful at the same time? Yet she did, balanced on him like a jockey on a thoroughbred, with just as much control of the powerful beast below her through the subtle movements of her body.

She tipped her pelvis on a series of rocks and let the choked noises coming from his throat set the tempo. Steady, heavy, slow.

His head pressed back against the armchair as she ground against him, and Audrey curled forwards to trail her mouth across the exposed strength of his throat, exploring the hollow below it. Her position meant her breasts hung within easy reach of his taskless hands so he pressed them both against her flesh—as though they were the fulsome mounds he'd always secretly coveted, as though they were all his big hands could manage—circling his palms in big, hard arcs that mirrored the rhythm of her hips.

The desperate roughness of her want.

'Oliver…'

As her speed increased so did their breathing, and she arched back in his hold. In the terrarium glass, dragonflies buzzed around her reflection like fluorescent faeries…or like living sparks generated by the extraordinary friction of their bodies. Oliver's hands tightened and rubbed her straining breasts and every quivering massage told her how much closer to the edge he was getting. His excitement fuelled hers.

She was doing this to him.

Her.

As she watched the lithe undulations of their silhouette, tight heat coiled into an exquisite pain where they fused together and the armchair rocked with the combined momentum of their frantic bodies.

Up…

Up…

She tipped her head back and vocalised—an expressive, inarticulate, erotic kind of gurgle—as the fibres of her muscles bunched and readied themselves deep inside.

'Now, beautiful,' he strained on a grimace, meeting her with the powerful upwards slam of his own hips. 'Come for me now.'

Her eyes snapped down to his—unguarded and raw— she let her soul pour out of them.

And then her world imploded.

As if the top storeys of their hotel had just *sheared away* in a landslide, and she went careening down to the earth far below on a roller-coaster tide of molten, magnificent mud. Punishing and protective. Weakening and reinforcing. Twitching and spasming. Utterly overwhelming.

She opened her eyes just in time to see them reflected in the tank, as glittering and ancient as the creatures flying around in it, and just in time to see the torsion of Oliver's big body beneath hers as he came right after her.

A pained stream of air, frozen on the prolonged first consonant of an oath and lasting as long as his orgasm, squeezed out between his lips and teeth. She fell forward into him, weakened, and the change of angle where they were still joined—where he was still so sensitive—caused a full-body jerk in his and the oath finally spilled across his talented lips, loud and crude.

And almost holy.

'Potty mouth,' she gasped against his sweat-dampened ear when she could eventually re-coordinate the passage of air in and out of her lungs.

His breath came in heaves and he swallowed several times before finally making words. 'I have no dignity with you.'

A place deep inside her chest squeezed as hard as the muscles between her legs just had.

...with you.

But she'd been protecting herself for too long to indulge the pleasure for more than a moment before she bundled the thought down where all the others milled, unvoiced, and focused instead on the decadent honey slugging through her veins and the punishing tenderness of flesh she'd finally used as nature intended.

'My God.'

Such simple words but there was something in them, something super powerful in the fact that she almost never invoked the 'g' word. But it belonged here with them today. Because what had just happened between them was as reverential as anything she could imagine.

She twisted sideways and squeezed down next to Oliver as he shuffled over in the big chair, both of them taking a moment to right themselves and their underwear.

Undignified, he had said and he wasn't wrong, but, strangely, dignity had no place here tonight. Neither of them required it and neither of them mourned its absence. Audrey curled into his still heaving body.

'Thank you,' she breathed and felt more than saw the questioning tilt of his head. 'You're very good at this.'

Tension drummed its fingers everywhere their bodies met. Odd, considering she'd given him a compliment.

'We're good *together*,' he clarified.

Her own throaty chuckle was positively indecent. 'I could learn so much from you.'

It was hard to know whether his resulting silence was discomfort at the suggestion of a future between them or something else. But his tone, when he eventually spoke, wasn't harsh.

'I'm like a theme-park ride to you, aren't I?'

'Best ever.'

Fastest, highest, most thrilling. And most unforgettable.

His smile was immediate, but there was an indefinably sad quality to the sigh just before he spoke. 'Come on. Let's move back to the lounge. Will your legs work?'

The idea of stretching out with Oliver as they had earlier, of falling asleep in his arms, was too tempting. She practically rolled off the chair. 'If they won't, I'll crawl.'

Nope. Not one shred of dignity. But when they had so little time together, and when she might well not see him again for twelve months—or at all—really what did it matter?

It was his pedestal, not hers.

She might as well throw herself off it before she tumbled off.

CHAPTER ELEVEN

Salted caramel chocolate ice cream topped with gold leaf

'AUDREY DEVANEY, YOU are such a paradox,' Oliver murmured from his position sitting knees up on the floor beside the sofa a deeply unconscious woman was presently stretched out on. He stroked a strand of dark hair away from her sleep-relaxed mouth.

That mouth.

The one he wanted to go on kissing forever. The one he'd pretty much given up hope of ever getting closer than a civil, social air-kiss to.

The one he'd bruised with his epic hours of worship.

She was like a wild creature released from captivity. Joyous and curious and adventurous yet heartbreakingly cautious. Running wild, tonight, in her attempt to experience everything she'd missed in life.

She was gorging on new experience. They both were.

But just for different reasons.

For Audrey...? She *was* on a theme park ride. The sort of thing you only did once a year but you had a blast while you were doing it. Whatever she lacked in experience, she made up double in raw enthusiasm and natural aptitude.

And for him…?

He knew that the moment she walked out of that door, this amazing woman would be lost to him. Away from the hypnotic chemistry that pulsed between them, her clever mind would start rationalising their night together, her doubts would skitter back to the fore, her busy life and her old-school common sense would have her filing their hours together away as some kind of treasure to be brought out and remembered fondly. Hotly, if he was any judge.

But very definitely in the past.

He traced the fine line of her cool arm with a fingertip.

And that was probably all for the better given he had no kind of future to offer her and she was absolutely not the booty-call type. If he were another kind of man he would happily spend eternity sharing her interests, respecting and trusting her. All the things she valued in a relationship.

If he were that man.

But he wasn't. He'd proposed to Tiffany because he was tired and she was there, and because she was the kind of woman who would have cheated on him long before he could ever cheat on her. *When, not if.*

Because genes would out. His inability to find a woman he could stick to was proof positive.

That was the kind of man he was.

He sure as hell wasn't the kind who could be trusted with what he'd seen in Audrey's eyes back on that chair. The look she was too overwhelmed to disguise. Or deny. The un-veiled look just before she shattered into a hundred pieces in his lap. That was not the look of a woman for whom this wasn't a big deal. It was not the look that belonged with the words she was saying.

It was a glimpse of the real Audrey.

And of what he really wanted. What he never knew, until tonight, *that* he wanted.

And what he damn well knew he couldn't have.

Tonight, he got a glimpse of something deeper than just sexy or smart or unattainable. Something much more fundamental.

Audrey's soul communicating directly with his.

That moment when it crashed headlong into his and its eyes flared with surprise and it whispered, incredulously, *Oh, that's right. There you are.*

He wasn't prepared to even put a name to the sensation. Not when a candle could burn longer than the time they had left together. Walking away tomorrow—today, really—was going to hurt her. But short-term pain had to be better than a lifetime of it, right?

But he was weak enough and selfish enough that he wanted to be the man against whom *she* measured all others. He wanted a place in her heart that nothing and no one could touch. Not some future man, not some future experience. A place she would smile and ache when she accessed it, the way he did with his memories of her. The smiles and the aches that sustained him through the year between her visits.

The bittersweet memories that would sustain him through his whole damn life.

And so, as ridiculous and pointless as it probably was, he wasn't letting her out of his sight until the law said he had to. He was going to keep her with him until morning, he was going to drive her back to her hotel and then deliver her to the airport and even the flight gate, personally. He was going to pour everything he wanted to say to her but couldn't into their last hours together and he was going to show her the kind of night a woman would find impossible to forget.

Because if he wasn't going to have her in his life he would damn well make sure he endured in her memory. Haunted it like some sad, desperate spectre. Made an impression on her heart.

A dent.

Hell, he'd take a scratch. She'd spent so long protecting it he wouldn't be surprised to find her heart was plated in three-inch steel. That was what would get her through the disappointment of them parting in seven hours.

Audrey murmured and resettled in her sleep, her fingers coming up to brush her lips as if feeling the memory of his kiss. A tiny frown marred her perfect skin.

But he was no masochist. He would take these last hours before Audrey climbed on her plane in the knowledge that, quite possibly, it was all she was ever going to give him. And he'd keep her close and make it special and live off the memories of it forever.

Too many parts of him needed this night too badly not to.

'Wakey-wakey, beautiful.'

Audrey's lashes fluttered open and it took a moment for her to orient herself against the odd sight that filled her field of vision. It looked like a giant tongue, curled back onto itself and with an ornate, gold insect perched on the top.

'Did a dragonfly escape?' Actually, there were two of them. The first one's twin sat on a matching dish across the table. Really, really spectacular escapees.

'Final course,' Oliver murmured from somewhere behind her.

She lifted her head and the world righted. She was stretched out on the sofa where they'd moved, exhausted, with Oliver's coat draped modestly over her bare legs.

She struggled into a sitting position, wriggling her skirt back down. 'I thought everyone had gone?' She hoped to heaven that was true and no one was in the kitchen while they got all Kama Sutra on the armchair.

'Looks like they didn't want us to miss out on the pièce de résistance. I found it in the kitchen cold room with a note on it saying "eat me".'

Well, that was about perfect for this whole Alice in Wonderland evening. If she grew until she banged her head on Qīngtíng's ornate ceiling she couldn't have felt more transformed than she did by the night's events.

Emotionally, spiritually.

She was leaving Hong Kong a changed woman.

She swung her legs off the sofa and blinked a few times to regain full consciousness. 'What time is it?'

'Half past five.'

A.M.? They'd lost precious hours to sleeping. She twisted to look behind her. Oliver knelt behind the sofa, his chin resting on the beautifully embroidered back. He looked as if he'd been there a while. He also looked extremely content.

And extremely gorgeous.

The cold, hard light of morning sat awkwardly on her, though. Flashes of how she'd behaved over by the window. The Audrey she'd never suspected was in there. The Audrey only Oliver could have freed.

'What have you been doing?'

'Just watching you sleep.'

She frowned and scrubbed at gritty eyes before remembering the face full of make-up she was probably no longer wearing. Her fists dropped. 'Stalker.'

His soft laugh caressed her in places she'd never felt a laugh before. 'I didn't do it the whole time. I've made a few calls, cleaned the kitchen up a bit—'

Presumably how he'd found the ice cream…

'—and sorted us for breakfast.'

He'd made calls? Done business while she was in a sex-induced coma?

Way to strip the special from something there, Oliver. 'Do you not need sleep?'

'I have the rest of the year to sleep.'

Elation tangled in her chest with disappointment. On one hand, that was tantamount to saying he also didn't want to miss a moment of their day. On the other hand, it said she was definitely getting on that flight at ten this morning.

Had she imagined last night would change anything? He'd made her no promises. If anything he'd forced her to verbalise what they both knew. That this was a time-limited, once-in-a-lifetime offer. No coupon required. She'd gone out of her way not to look too closely at *why* it was happening. She'd just thrilled at the fact it was happening and let the fantasy get away with her. Let herself be whoever she wanted to be.

And last night she'd wanted to be *that* woman. The one who could keep up with a man like Oliver and walk away, head high in the morning.

Regardless of how she felt inside.

And if nothing else Audrey Devaney was a woman who always—always—made the beds she'd lain in. And so she did what always worked for her in moments of crisis—especially at five-thirty a.m.

She ignored it.

She picked up one of the plated dark tongues instead. 'What is this?'

'Chocolate caramel ice cream.'

An understatement if the rest of the evening's astonishments were anything to go by. This was bound to be so much more than just ice cream. 'Why is there a dragonfly on it?'

'It's gold leaf. Qīngtíng's signature dish.'

She peered at the extraordinary craftsmanship. An intricate and beautiful dragonfly perfectly rendered in real gold leaf. No wonder the chef hadn't wanted them to miss it.

'I don't know whether to eat it or frame it,' she breathed, after a long study.

'Eat it. I suspect it's too fine to last long.'

Eating gold. That was going to take a little getting used to. Just like the sudden intimacy in Oliver's gravelly voice. He moved across from her, sat on *her* sofa, and watched her as she sliced her splade down across the back of the decorative insect and took a chunk out of the perfect curl of ice cream.

Salty, caramely, chocolaty goodness teased her senses into full consciousness.

'This is sublime.' Then something occurred to her. 'Is this breakfast?'

Why the heck not when the rest of the past twenty-four hours was Lewis Carroll kind of surreal? Ice cream and gold for breakfast fitted right in.

'This is the end of dinner. Breakfast will be in about ninety minutes.'

Breakfast meant sunrise. And sunrise meant it was time to go back to the real world. Audrey was suddenly suffused with a chill that had nothing to do with the delicious creamy dessert. She laid the splade across her barely touched dish.

'How long before dawn?'

His eyes narrowed. 'Sun-up is at six fifty-eight a.m.'

'That's very precise.'

'It's the winter solstice. A big deal in China.'

Right. Not like he'd been counting the minutes. 'What will we do until then?'

'Why, what happens at daybreak? You planning on doing a Cinderella on me?'

Did he know how close he was to the truth?

'As it happens you won't be able to,' he went on. 'We're going to be somewhere special at sunrise. Somewhere you'd struggle to run away from.'

The most special place she could imagine being as the sun crept over Hong Kong's mountains was back upstairs in that big, comfortable bed wrapped in Oliver's arms and both of them sleeping right through breakfast in satiated slumber.

A girl could dream.

'Sounds intriguing,' she said past the ache in her heart.

'I hope so. I had to pull a few strings to make it happen.'

Was he throwing a bunch of people out of another restaurant? 'You're not going to tell me?'

'No. I'd like it to be a surprise. Though I should ask… Can you swim?'

It was a necessary question.

Forty minutes later, Audrey stood on the pier at Tsim Sha Tsui staring at a gracious, fully restored Chinese junk.

'I've seen this at night going up and down the harbour,'

she breathed, walking the boat's moored length, running her hand along the one-hundred-and-fifty-year-old dark hull timbers. Its bright-red sails were usually illuminated by uplights and seemed to those on shore to glow red fire as it drifted silently across the water. This morning, though, no glowing sails, just a network of pretty oriental lanterns throwing a gentle light across the deck cluttered with boating business but devoid of any people.

'That's our sunrise ride.'

She was glad she was still in her silk dress for this, but she was also glad for the drape of Oliver's coat around her shoulders. As soon as she'd stepped out of the car he'd arranged for the slow drive to the Kowloon pier, the cool bite of morning had made itself known. But she tried to keep her appreciation purely functional and not fixate on the smell and warmth of gorgeous man as it soaked into her skin.

On board, they passed the first quarter-hour exploring the rigging and construction of the small junk and appreciating the three-hundred-and-sixty-degree views and the sounds of the waking harbour. But as the sky lightened and the vessel swung in a big arc to drift back up the waterfront again Oliver moved them to the upper deck, really the old roof of the covered lower deck, and propped them up against the mast of the fully unfurled centre sail.

A basket appeared courtesy of a fleet-footed, bowing crewman, filled to overflowing with fresh fruits and gorgeous pastries with a thermos of fragrant coffee. Oliver pressed his back to the mast, then pulled Audrey into the V of his legs and, between them, they picked the delicious contents of the basket clean as the sun rose over the mountainous islands of Hong Kong. The fiery orb first turned the harbour and everything around it a shimmering silver and then a rich gold before finally settling on a soft-focus blue.

The sounds of traditional oriental music drifted across the harbour as they passed a group of workers doing dawn t'ai chi by the water.

'What do you think?' he murmured.

The canvas above them issued an almost inaudible hum as it vibrated under the strain of the morning breeze. The same breeze that gave them motion. 'I think it's spectacular. I've always wanted to sail on this boat.' She twisted more towards him. 'Thank you.'

His lips fell on hers so naturally. Lingered. 'You're welcome.'

Yet it wasn't the same as the many—many—kisses they'd shared tonight because it wasn't really *tonight* at all. It was now *today*. And it was daylight and the real world was waking around them—solstice or not—and getting on with their lives.

Which was what they needed to do.

They'd been doing the whole *make-believe* for long enough.

'You've sure raised the bar on first dates,' she breathed without thinking, but then caught herself. 'I mean…any date.'

Discomfort radiated through his body and into hers. 'It's a kind of first date.'

No, it wasn't. The awkward tension in his voice was a dead giveaway.

'First implies there'll be more,' she said, critically light. 'We're more of an *only* date, really.'

And, importantly, it was the *end* of the only date. After breakfast she really needed to be thinking about picking up her stuff from the hotel and getting out to the airport over on Lantau. Before she made more of a fool of herself than she already had.

Before she curled her fingers around his strong arms and refused, point-blank, to let go.

'You don't see there being more?'

It was impossible to know what his casual question was hoping to ferret out. A yes or a no. It was veiled enough to be either.

Every part of her tightened but she kept her voice light. Determined to be modern and grown-up about this. 'We live in different countries, Oliver. That makes future dates a bit hard, doesn't it?'

'What we live in is a technological age. There are dozens of ways for us to stay connected.'

Not physically. And that was what he was talking about, right? Even though she got the sense he was speaking against his own will. 'I'm not sure I'm really the sexting type.'

Huh. She all but felt it in the puff of breath on the back of her neck.

'So…that's it? One night of wild sex and you're done?'

She twisted in his arms and locked her eyes on his. 'What were you hoping for, two nights? Three?' She held his gaze and challenged him. 'More?'

His face grew intensely guarded.

Yeah. Just as she thought.

'We have until ten,' he reminded her.

'What difference will a few more hours make?'

'Look what a difference the first few made.'

True enough. Her life had turned on its head in less than twelve hours. 'But what difference will it *make*? Really?'

Heat blazed down on her. 'I didn't expect you to be scrabbling to get away from me.'

She sat up straighter, pulled away a few precious inches. 'I'm not scrabbling, Oliver. I'm just being realistic.'

'Can't you be realistic on the way to the airport?'

She studied him closely. His face gave nothing away. Again, part of his success in the corporate world. 'Right down to the wire?'

'I just… This haste is unsettling.'

'You've never tiptoed out of a hotel room at dawn before?'

'Yeah I have, and I know what that means. So I don't like you doing it to me.'

'Oh.' She shifted away and curled her legs more under her. 'You don't like being revealed as a hypocrite.'

'Is it hypocrisy to have enjoyed our night together and not want it to end?'

'It has to end,' she pointed out. But then she couldn't help herself. Maybe he knew something she didn't. 'Doesn't it?'

If he clenched his jaw any tighter it was going to fracture. 'Yeah, it does.'

'Yeah,' she repeated. 'It does.' Because they were only ever going to be a one-off thing. A question answered. An itch scratched. 'Sydney's waiting for me. Shanghai's waiting for you.'

Except of course that he was on the phone this morning making up for time lost to their…adventures. So, Shanghai didn't really need to wait all that long at all, did it?

Was the morning after always this awkward? She could totally understand why he might have snuck out in the past to avoid it.

'Did you make plans for the next few hours?' she tested.

'I did.'

'And you didn't want to run them past me, first? What if I had Testore business this morning?'

Okay, now they just sounded like a bickering couple. But the line between generous and controlling wasn't all that thick. And bickering gave all the simmering pain somewhere to go.

He had enough grace to flush. 'Do you?'

She let out a long, slow breath. Maybe it would be smarter to say yes. To get off this boat and hurry off to some imaginary appointment. But he'd done this lovely thing… 'No. I took care of it all earlier in the week.'

He nodded. Then sagged. 'It was supposed to be the perfect end to the—' he bit back his own words and straightened '—to a nice night.'

Nice. Ouch.

'We're on a one-hundred-and-fifty-year-old private junk on Victoria Harbour at sunrise on the winter solstice. You've done well, Oliver.'

He stared out at a ferry that rumbled past them. Its wake slapped against the junk's hull like lame applause. He sighed. 'So, you want to head back in?'

She probably should.

'I don't want this to end any sooner than it has to.' She caught and held his gaze despite the ache deep in her chest. 'But I do respect that it does have to.'

Denial was one thing… Delusion was just foolish.

She settled back against his legs. 'We'll head back when we're due.'

It took him a while to relax behind her, but she felt the moment he accepted her words. His body softened, his hand crept up to gather her wind-whipped hair into a protected ponytail that he gently stroked in time with the sloshing of the waves. She sank back into his caress.

As if she'd been doing it always.

As if she always would.

Her friend. With shiny, new, short-term benefits.

Maybe that was just what they'd be now. Not that he'd offered anything other than a vague and unplanned cyber 'more'. She tried to imagine dropping into Shanghai for a quickie whenever she was in Asia and just couldn't. That wasn't her. Despite all evidence to the contrary, overnight. Despite the woman she'd seen reflected in the dragonfly terrarium.

Which was not to say her body wasn't *screaming* at her to be that person, but last night was really about years of long-ing finally being fulfilled. And it was all about fairy tales and chemistry and the loudly ticking approach of dawn. It had nothing to do with reality. Living together day to day, or the occasional fight, or morning breath or blanket hog-ging, or making the mortgage or any of the many unroman-tic things that made up a relationship.

It was what it was. A magical storybook ending to an unconventional friendship.

More than magical, really. It was dream-come-true coun-try.

And everyone knew that anything that seemed too good to be true…probably was. But she'd take it while it was on offer—including the next few hours—because she was un-likely to see its equal again in her life.

Ever.

CHAPTER TWELVE

Sulewesi coffee beans with eggnog and nutmeg

COLLECTING AUDREY'S THINGS and checking out of her hotel room while most people were still asleep took an easy fifteen minutes and then they were back in the limo and heading out to Stanley on the southern-most tip of Hong Kong island. Within the half-hour Oliver was pulling back a chair for her on the balcony of a one-hundred-and-seventy-year-old colonial hotel with views of the South China Sea stretching out forever, and with the single morning waiter much relieved they were only there for coffee.

Albeit a pricey coffee from one of the most exclusive plantations on the planet.

Audrey smiled at him—pretty, but each one getting progressively emptier as the morning wore on. As though she were already on that jet flying away from him.

'Eggnog, Oliver? At eight in the morning?'

'Eggnog *coffee*. And it's Christmas.'

And he wanted to spring into her mind whenever she smelled cinnamon. Or a coffee bean. Or the ocean.

'Can I ask you something?' she said after stirring hers for an age.

He lifted his eyes.

'Is this hard for you?'

Her clear, direct eyes said *be honest* and so he was. Or as honest as he knew how to be, anyway. 'You leaving in a few hours?'

'All of it. Knowing what to do. Knowing how to deal with it. Or is this just par for the course in your life?'

He took a deep breath. Whatever he said now would set the tone for how the rest of the morning went. How they parted. As friends or something less. Carelessness now could really hurt her. 'You think that last night happens for me all the time?'

'It might.'

'It doesn't.'

'What was different?'

He fought to keep his expression more relaxed than the rest of his tight body would allow. 'Fishing for compliments?'

His cowardice caused a flush of heat in her alabaster cheeks. Of course she wasn't. She was Audrey.

'I don't know how to go back from here, Oliver. And I know that we can't go forward.'

'Depends on how you define forward.'

'I define it as progress. Improvement.' She took a breath. 'More.'

A rock the size of his fist pressed against the bottom of his gut. *Forward* just opened up too much opportunity for hurt for her. This was Audrey. With all kinds of strength yet as fragile as the gold leaf they'd eaten back at the restaurant. She deserved much better than a man who had no ability to commit.

He wasn't about to risk her heart on a bad investment. On *more*.

'Then no. We can't go forward.'

Those enormous, all-seeing eyes scrutinised him but gave nothing away. 'Yet we can't go back.'

'We're still friends.'

'With benefits?'

'With or without. I'll always count you as a friend, Audrey. And I don't have many of those.'

'That's because you don't trust anyone.'

'I trust you.'

Her eyes reflected the azure around them. As crisp and sharp as a knife.

'Why do you?'

'Because you've never lied to me. I'd know if you did.'

'You think so? Maybe I'm just really good at it.' Because she'd been lying for eight years denying the attraction she felt for him and he'd missed that. 'So, do I see you more or less in the coming year? What's the plan?'

Less than once? Was she talking about not coming next Christmas? A deep kind of panic took hold of his gut and twisted. The same agony he'd felt last year when she didn't show. He struggled against it.

'What makes you think I have a plan?'

'Because you're you. And because you had hours while I was sleeping to come up with one.'

He shrugged, a postcard for nonchalance. 'You weren't interested in sexting.'

How could she find it in herself to laugh while he was so tight inside? Even if it was the emptiest he'd ever heard from her. 'I'm still not.' She locked eyes with his. 'So am I right to sleep with other men, then?'

The blood decamped from his face so fast it left him dizzy. 'I didn't realise there was a queue.'

She leaned onto her elbows on the table. 'Just trying to get my parameters. Will you be sleeping with anyone?'

'Audrey...'

'Because Christmas is a long time off.'

Wow, he was like a yo-yo around her. Excited now that Christmas—a Christmas that might include both of them— was back on the radar. But the roller coaster only decreased his control of this situation.

'Warming to your newfound sexuality?'

Her eyes finally grew as flat and lifeless as he feared they would around him. 'Yes, Oliver. I want to give it a good workout with anyone I meet. Maybe even the waiter.'

He stared her down. 'Sarcasm does not become you.'

She lifted both brows.

'What the hell do you want from me, Audrey?'

'I want you to say it out loud.'

'Say what?'

'That this is it. That there is no more. I need to hear it in your voice. I need to see the words forming on your lips.'

There wasn't enough air to speak. So he just stared.

'Because otherwise I will wait for you. I'll hold this amazing memory close to my heart and, even though I won't want it to, it will stop me forming new relationships because I'll always be secretly hoping that you're going to change your mind. And call. Or drop by. Or send me air tickets. And I'll want to be free for that.

'So you need to tell me now, Oliver. For real and for certain. So there is no doubt.' She took the deepest breath her twisted chest could manage. 'Should I be planning to spend any more time with you this year?'

'Have I offered you a future?'

A punch below her diaphragm couldn't have been more effective. But it didn't matter that she couldn't answer, because Oliver's question was rhetorical.

They both knew the answer.

'I don't do relationships, Audrey. I do great, short, blazing affairs. Like last night. And I do long hours at the office and constant travel. My driver sees more of me than most of my girlfriends do.'

Did he use the present tense on purpose?

'But I'm the woman against whom you measure others.' The words that had been so romantic last night sounded ludicrous in the cold, hard light of rejection.

'You are. You always will be.'

'But that's still not enough to pierce your heart?'

'What do hearts have to do with anything? I respect you and I care for you. Too much to risk—'

'To risk what?'

'To risk you. To risk hurting you more than I already have.'

'Shouldn't that have been something you thought of before you let things get hot and heavy between us? Do you imagine this doesn't hurt?'

Shame flitted behind his eyes. 'You knew the score.'

'Yes, I did. And I went ahead anyway.' More fool her. 'But something changed in me in that stupid armchair this morning. I realised that one day every eight years is not enough for me. I realised I *am* good enough for you. I am just as valuable and worthy and beautiful as any of the other women in your life. And most importantly I am not broken.'

He didn't respond, and the old Audrey crept back in for a half-heartbeat. 'Unless you're a much better liar than I believed?'

No. You couldn't fake the facial contortions and guttural declarations Oliver had made. They were real.

A fierce conviction suffused his face. 'You are not broken.'

'So how do you feel that some other man is going to enjoy the benefits of your…training? How will you feel when you imagine me with my thighs wrapped around a stranger instead of you? When I let someone other than you deep inside me? When I choke on someone else's name?'

His nostrils flared and he gritted words out. 'Not great. But you're not mine to keep.'

'I could be.' All he had to say was 'stay'.

'No.'

'Why?'

'Because I don't want you to be mine.'

I don't want you. Something ruptured and flapped wildly deep in her chest. 'You wanted me last night.'

'And now I've had you.'

Her stomach plunged. Was that it? Question answered? Itch scratched? Challenge conquered? 'No. I don't believe you. You respect me too much.'

'You were a goddess, Audrey. Chaste and unattainable.'

And now she was what…? Fallen? But then something sank through the painful misery clogging her sense. One word. A word she'd used herself. On herself.

Unattainable.

And she realised.

'You thought I was safe.'

His eyes shifted out to sea.

'You thought I was someone you could just quietly obsess on without ever having to risk being called on it. Someone to hang this ideal of perfection on and excuse your inability to commit to anyone else, but utterly, utterly safe. First I was married and you could hide behind a ring and your own values. Then you thought I wasn't interested in that kind of relationship with you and so you just got to brood about it like some modern-day Heathcliff, torturing yourself with my presence once a year.'

Something on the distant horizon sure had his focus...

'But what's a man to do when the woman he's been wanting for so long throws herself at you? You broke your own rule.'

His gaze snapped back to hers. 'I should have been stronger. You were vulnerable.'

'Oh, please, I think we've established that there is no pedestal strong enough to take me and all my foibles. I was pissed off but I wasn't vulnerable. I knew exactly what I was putting my hand up for. And you made a move long before you told me about Blake. So it was hardly reactionary.'

'It was weak.'

'Damn straight it was. And it still is if you're unwilling to just say "it's been fun, but it's over".'

'That's what you want?'

'That's what I need if I'm not to spend the next twelve months suffering death by a thousand cuts. Because if you don't say it—*and mean it*—I won't believe it. I know myself too well.'

He marshalled himself visibly. 'It *was* fun, Audrey. And it *is* over. Last night was a one-time thing. And it's not because of any lack on your part or because it didn't measure up compared to anyone else. It's because that's how I roll. I don't do relationships and nothing and no one can really change a man's nature.'

'Not even a paragon?'

He shuddered a deep breath and his voice gentled. 'Not even a paragon.'

'So what will you do for the rest of your life? Be alone?'

'I'll find another Tiffany.'

'Someone to *settle* for?'

'Someone I can't hurt.'

What did that *mean*? 'You think the Tiffanys of this world don't have feelings?'

'She was as hard as I am.'

That stopped her in her tracks. 'Why do you think you're hard?'

'Because I can't—' But he wouldn't let himself finish that sentence.

Love? Was that what he'd refused to say aloud? Well, she wasn't about to be the first. 'You think you *can't* be in a relationship just because you *haven't* been in a successful one?'

'I'm not afraid to acknowledge my weaknesses, Audrey. I just don't do commitment.'

She sat back hard into her bamboo-woven chair. 'What if it's weakness not to even try?'

Two lines cut deep between his eyebrows. 'It's not just about me. It's not some lab experiment or computer formula. There's another person there. A living breathing feeling person existing in a marriage that's not healthy for them.'

Marriage? Wait… How had they got there?

'But it's okay if she's…hard?' she said. Wasn't that the word he'd used?

'If she knows the score. Accepts it.'

'Accepts what?'

'The limitations of the relationship.'

'Oliver, I really don't understand—'

'Do the maths, Audrey,' he grated. 'You're a smart woman.'

She was, but clearly not in this. 'Are you talking about a relationship without commitment?'

'Commitment *traps.*'

She flopped back into her chair. 'Who? You?'

'Her.'

Wait… 'Is this about your mother?'

'She was trapped with a worthless human being because of her feelings for him.'

'She made a conscious choice to stay, Oliver.'

'There was no choice. Not back then.'

Did he fear love because he'd seen his mother suffer at the hands of an unfaithful husband? 'I can't imagine her being a weak woman.'

He blinked at her. 'What? No.'

'Then she made her own choices. Informed choices. She stayed because she wanted to. Or she decided he was worth it.'

'If not for me she could have walked. Should have.'

Did he hear his own Freudian slip? He blamed his mother for toughing it out with a serial cheater. 'It was the eighties, Oliver, not the fifties. She could have left him, even with a child in tow. Plenty of women did.'

'She wanted me to have a father.'

'Then that was her conscious decision. And it was a noble one. She loved him. And you.'

There. She said it aloud. The L word.

'Love trapped her.'

There was that word again. Maybe it wasn't about the love, maybe it was about the trapping.

'So, this is about your father?'

'If she'd cared as little as he obviously did the whole thing wouldn't have hurt her so much.'

Someone I can't hurt.

Oh.

A wash of dreadful awareness pooled in her aching chest and gut. She had to force the words across her lips. 'You don't want to repeat your parents' marriage. Where one person has feelings the other doesn't.'

This was his way of telling her he didn't—couldn't—love her. And this was why another Tiffany was a better bet for him.

'I don't ever want you to feel the way she felt.'

Trapped. In a one-sided relationship.

'You assume it would be that way.'

'I know myself.'

He meant he knew his feelings. But she was desperate enough to push. 'So you just avoid any kind of commitment just in case? What if I'm the exception?'

'You deserve someone who can be everything you are.'

'Yet, apparently, this paragon is still not worthy. Except for a bit of wham-bam-thank-you-ma'am.'

'You're the best person I know,' he muttered.

Oh, please... 'You just defiled the best person you know. I'd hate to see how you treat everyone else.'

She pushed her half-finished coffee away and stumbled to her feet. Correction, half-drunk but most definitely finished.

Like this relationship.

'This is what's going to happen now,' she began, working hard to keep the thick clag of pain from her voice. 'You are going to call your car around and tell him to take me to the airport. We will drop you back at your hotel on the way and all of this will be a surreal memory by morning.'

She omitted the part about her crying all the way back to Australia and never having another relationship again in her life. That didn't seem conducive to a dignified exit.

'I'm coming to the airport...'

She stopped and glared at him. 'Because this isn't hard enough?'

'Because it's over for me, then, too. I need to see you walking away.'

'Why, Oliver? Why not just let me go? Do the right thing.'

'I'm already doing the right thing. One day I hope you'll believe that.'

She knew she could hold it all together back to the harbour, but could she do it all the way over to Lantau? And then waiting for her flight to board?

She turned from him and walked towards the stairs, not even sure she could hold it together as far as the top tread. Behind her, he murmured into his phone, and as her foot touched the last flight, the limo pulled up outside the charming old building.

She crawled in without a word.

Oliver followed.

They sat as far apart as the spacious back seat would allow.

All the way back to Central Hong Kong Audrey peered out of the window at the complicated mix of green, verdant hills and dense, crowded, multicultural residential areas. Chances were good she'd be back in Hong Kong on a future instrument hunt but she knew she'd only ever have flying visits. This was no longer a place of pleasure.

It was now wrecked.

She swallowed past the thick lump resident in her throat.

As they approached the Western Harbour tunnel over to Kowloon and Mainland China she glanced east and saw the same junk they'd breakfasted on puttering between bigger vessels in the busy harbour, her sails ablaze. Filled with other people who would imagine it as *their* special thing. Only to discover it wasn't special at all.

Just like this whole experience.

Perhaps she'd projected too much of her own feelings onto Oliver. Perhaps she'd been foolish to indulge them after they'd come back down to the restaurant. *She'd* reignited things between them then, not him. She had to own that. She'd thought she was capable of handling a one-night stand but that was when it was *circumstance* keeping them apart, not some ill-defined deficiency on her part.

Whatever it was that meant Oliver couldn't imagine himself loving her as much as she—

Across the car, he seemed to flinch as though he could hear her thoughts and knew what was going to come next.

—loved him.

Her stomach plunged and she blamed the tunnel that sank deeper under Victoria Harbour. There really was no question: she'd adored Oliver Harmer for years. The only mystery was when, exactly, it had graduated into love. Her body had recognised it in the wee hours of this morning, when his hands were in her hair and he was buried deep in her and his eyes blazed up at her in a way that was so close to *worship*...

She didn't have any experience in what love looked like

but she'd felt so certain that it looked just like that. That moment where her soul and his connected. Her subconscious had named it even if she hadn't.

But what would she know?

Maybe he always looked like that when he came?

What if she was exactly as ill equipped to be with a man like Oliver as she'd always feared? What if the whole night had just been one big try-hard exercise on her part and he was just trying to extract himself from an uncomfortable situation?

What if she'd overreached after all?

The tears she'd done such a good job of holding back refused to let that last thought go unanswered. They spilled silently over her lids, along her lashes and then down her cheeks. She let them run, only the tunnel walls to witness.

But the spill became a river and the river a trembling torrent, and as they surfaced out of the tunnel and merged onto Highway 5 she couldn't disguise what was happening any longer.

'Audrey—'

Her hand shot up in warning to him as her body doubled over at the combined pain of his rejection and the humiliation of this moment. Only the glass of her window stopped her from crumpling right over and she pressed her forehead against its cool reassurance.

The minute strength she had left was in her silence and so she still didn't give the slightest voice to the sorrow.

'Audrey...'

No. Not compassion, not from Oliver. She struggled against him when he moved closer and slid one arm around her shoulders, but her pathetic resistance was no match for his gentle strength.

'Shh...'

He pulled her against his chest, into his arms and just held her. No platitudes. No promises. No lies. Just silent compassion.

And that made it all so much worse.

She was losing the man she loved and her best friend all at the same time.

The last of her resilience gave way on a hoarse, horrible sob and she buried her shame into his chest. She cried as they passed Stonecutter's Island. She cried as they crossed onto Tsing Yi. She cried as they rose on a suspension bridge high above the water and breached the two-kilometre ocean passage to Lantau. She cried right past the turnoff to the most magical theme park in China and she cried the full length of Highway 8.

And the whole time, Oliver just stroked her hair, fed her tissues and held her.

For the last time, ever.

A voice crackled on the intercom and she recognised the name of Hong Kong's primary airport. That and the interrupting voice was enough to lurch her up out of Oliver's gentle hold and back to her far corner where she pressed a series of fresh, folded tissues to her stinging, swollen eyes.

And still Oliver didn't speak.

What was there to say?

She'd just melted down on him for the second time in twenty-four hours. He'd already said he didn't know what to do with her when she was like this. And Hong Kong's traffic meant it was a long ride with a hysterical woman.

Tough luck, buddy. This one's all on you. This was his decision. This was his issue.

'I don't want you to come in,' she gritted between pats. 'At the airport.'

'I need to see you to your gate.'

To make sure she actually left? She half turned her head to beg him, 'And I'm asking you to do what *I* need, not what *you* need.'

His silent stare bored into the back of her head. 'Okay, Audrey.'

'Thank you.'

The limo negotiated the tangle of taxis, buses and private cars clogging the airport's approach until it began moving up the causeway. That seemed to press Oliver into action at last.

'Don't you think it would be easier for me to just go with the flow,' he bit out. 'To just say "see you in Sydney" and to swing by when I'm in town for a hot hook-up? I didn't want to be that man.'

That brought Audrey's gaze back around to his. 'Should I applaud?'

'I'd like you to understand. My motives if not my reasons.'

'You're avoiding commitment. Seems patently clear.'

He exhaled on a hiss. 'I'm avoiding—' He cut his own words off. 'I didn't want to hurt you, Audrey. I *don't* want to. I'm sorry, but, as bad as we both feel, ultimately it will be better this way.'

'You have nothing to apologise for, Oliver. You've lived up to your reputation and given me a night I will never forget. For so many reasons.' Her smile was tight. 'I get it, I really do.'

'Do you?'

'I'm going to go back to Sydney, throw myself into my

work and concentrate on low-hanging fruit from now on.' That was a lie, she wasn't going to be interested in fruit of any kind for a long, long time.

'Audrey, don't do that to yourself. This is about me, not you.'

He seemed to wince at the triteness of his own words.

'You're right. This is about you and your inability to let go of the past. This is about you being so afraid that you'll end up like your father you're avoiding any kind of commitment at all. You dress it up in chivalry and concern for me, but, let's be honest, this is all about you.'

His eyes grew as hard as his clenched jaw.

The limo pulled up to the concourse and Audrey had her door open practically before it had stopped. Oliver leapt out after her as the driver came around to the rear for her case.

'I've held a candle for you since I met you, Oliver. You were everything that I wanted and believed I didn't deserve. You came to be symbolic in my life of my own deficiencies and I wore them like a badge of shame.

'But you know what? I *don't* deserve the man you are. You are the one that doesn't measure up, Oliver Harmer. You are so fixated on not being the serial cheat your father was, you can't see that you've become exactly like him, ravaging from woman to woman spreading the misery around.

'Well, I'm done doubting myself.' She poked his chest. 'I'm awesome. And clever. And pretty. And loyal.' Every poke an accusation. 'And the best friend a person could have. I would have been fierce and proud by your side and someone you could face life with, head-on. But that honour is going to go to someone else and I'm not going to be able to find him while you're still in my life.'

She let her expressive hands drop by her sides. As dead

as she felt. 'So this is it, Oliver. After eight years. No more card games, no more conversations, no more long, lazy lunches that you can cling to in lieu of a real relationship with a real woman.' Her shoulders shuddered up and then dropped. 'No more Christmas. If I'm not in your life then I'm out of it. You don't get to have it both ways.' She settled her bag more firmly between them. 'Please don't email me. Or call. Don't send me a birthday card. Don't invite me to your wedding with whichever Tiffany you find next.'

Fortunately, she'd used up all her tears coming across the causeway. Oliver wasn't so lucky and the glitter of those hazel eyes just about broke her heart anew.

Audrey swung her bag around, smiled her thanks to the driver trying so very hard not to listen, and then forced her eyes back onto Oliver before whispering tightly, 'But I *beg* you not to settle for a loveless life. That is not what your mother sacrificed her life to teach you.'

And then she turned and he was gone from her vision.

From her life.

But never, ever, ever from her heart.

CHAPTER THIRTEEN

December 20th, this year

THE PERFECT, PRACTISED English washed over him as Oliver stared out across Victoria Harbour at the building that housed Qīngtíng and the penthouse at its very top, absently rolling an uncut cigar between his fingers. He had no trouble picking the restaurant out; he'd grown proficient at spotting it from any of Kowloon's major business centres courtesy of his hours of distracted staring.

Even with his lawyer and partner here, he should have been attending. This deal was too important to insult with his inattention the very people he wanted to buy out. But the fact they were speaking in English instead of requiring him to negotiate in Mandarin meant they were already deferring. And that meant they had already decided to sell.

The rest was just a dance.

Meaning his attention was that much freer to wander across the harbour and up sixty storeys of steel.

His brain made him schedule a day full of Hong Kong meetings today, the twentieth, but his heart insisted they be here, in Kowloon, in full view of Qīngtíng across the harbour. As if he'd somehow know if a miracle occurred and Audrey turned up. As if his eyes would make her out, standing, arms folded around herself, against that wall of window. A distant speck against a sea of silver and chrome.

A point of business required him to refocus, but the moment it was addressed he let his gaze wander back to the restaurant, let his mind wander back to last Christmas. That extraordinary, dreamlike twenty-four hours.

He'd been as good as his word and never contacted Audrey again. No emails, no phone calls, no letters, no messages. Well, not the sort she'd warned him against, anyway. He always had a talent for loopholes.

But it had been purgatory this past year. What a fool he'd been to imagine he could just go back to his life in Shanghai and work her out of his system and get by on a steady diet of memories. He'd had to work at it—really freaking work—just to get through those first weeks. Then months. Then seasons.

And now the year had passed and the moment he'd dreaded was here.

The moment Audrey *didn't* come to Christmas.

Again.

She'd hit him with some home truths that day at the airport. Hard, overdue, unpleasant words that he'd promptly blocked out. It took him weeks to begin to digest them. First he'd used his anger to justify letting her leave. Then he rationalised and remembered how much pain she'd been in and how much courage it must have taken to stand there and let him have it with both barrels.

And finally he saw the sense of her words and, as if letting the words in made them material, he suddenly saw evidence of her truth everywhere he went. Getting in his face.

Mocking him.

His failure to form successful relationships *was* all about him. And he *had* used his friendship with Blake as a protective screen from behind which he indulged his feelings without having to own them.

And once the denial started to drop he saw more and more. How he'd lied to himself all this time believing it was his high standards that made it impossible for him to connect to just one woman. Hardly surprising he could never find her when that was the last thing his subconscious wanted.

He was no more honest with himself about why it didn't work out than he was with them.

But that was not the sort of epiphany a man could simply *un*see. So he began dating again, testing the theory, testing himself, hunting for someone who could offer him the same soul-connection that Audrey had offered that night in the chair. That she'd been offering him for years. Hungry to find what he'd had a taste of.

And it just wasn't there.

Even though—this time—he was genuinely open to finding it. And being unable to find someone as good as Audrey didn't get any more comfortable for being in the cold light of reason.

At least, before, he'd had all his denial to keep him company.

And so he'd thrown a lifebuoy out, courtesy of a favour someone owed him, and just hoped to heaven that Audrey was in a perceptive mood when the unsigned Christmas parcel was delivered last week. And receptive. Or even rabidly furious, as long as it was an emotion strong enough to bring her back to Hong Kong.

Back to the restaurant.

Back to him.

Because he had an apology to deliver. And a friendship to try and save. And possibly a fragile, wounded spirit to save, too.

Behind him, the massive boardroom doors snicked softly and opened. Jeannie Ling murmured in the ear of the man closest to the door and he nodded then tapped a few keys into his tablet surreptitiously.

Seconds later Oliver's smartphone vibrated.

He glanced down disinterestedly at the subject line of his partner's email:

Ph. Msg-urgent

But then his body was up and out of his chair even before his mind had fully registered the words and phone number on the next line, and he was halfway to the door before any of the ridiculously wealthy and overly entitled people in the room realised what was happening.

Pls call Ming-húa

He hadn't come.

Audrey stared into the busy, oblivious world of Qīngtíng's dragonflies and cursed herself for the ideological fool she was.

Of course he hadn't come. He'd moved on. The online gossip sheets made that patently clear. In fact he'd probably moved on by last Christmas. Whatever they'd shared here in Hong Kong was ancient history. Solstice fever. Even the restaurant had gone back to being what it was. Just a place you went to eat food.

She glanced over towards the restaurant's festively decorated glass wall. The smoking chair was no longer resident.

Their chair.

Hastily removed as a bad memory, probably. Or quite possibly a hygiene issue.

Heat flooded her cheeks but the dragonflies didn't much care. They went about their business, zipping around, feeding and frolicking and dipping their many feet in the crystalline water that circulated through their beautiful, make-believe world. Only a single individual battered against the corner of the terrarium, repeatedly. Uselessly.

She knew exactly how it felt.

Most of what she'd done this past year was useless battering. Existing, but not really living. Punctuated by insane bouts of emotional self-harm whenever her discipline failed her and she'd do the whole stalker number online and search out any clues about Oliver.

What he was up to. *Who* he was up to. Whether he was okay.

Of course, he always was.

On her weak days, she imagined that Oliver never contacting her again was him honouring her request, respecting her, and she'd get all sore and squishy inside and struggle with the reality that it was over. But on her stronger days she'd accept the reality—that not contacting her was probably a blessed relief for a man like The Hammer and that there was nothing to really *be* over.

Nothing had even started.

If you didn't count the wild sex.

She'd vacillate between bouts of self-judgement for her stupidity, and fierce self-defence that she'd fallen for a man like him, convincing herself that it was possible for someone to be a pretty good *guy* without necessarily managing to always be a good *person*.

Except that, like it or not, he'd been more than pretty good. Oliver was exceptional. In so many ways. And knowing that only made his inability to love her all the more brutal.

What the hell was she thinking coming here? She could have done what she needed to do by email.

Almost as she had the thought, a flurry of low voices drew her focus, through the terrarium, past the dragonflies, over to the restaurant's glamorous entrance.

To the man who'd just burst in.

Oliver.

Her whole body locked up and she mentally scrabbled around for somewhere to hide. Under her sofa. In the lush terrarium planting with the dragonflies. Anywhere other than here, with the terrified-bunny look on her face, peering at him through the glass like the coward she wanted so badly not to be.

It took his laser-focus only a heartbeat to find her.

His legs started moving. His eyes remained locked on hers as he powered around the outside of the terrarium and stopped just a metre away. His intent gaze whispered her name even though no air crossed his lips.

'Explain,' she gasped aloud, before she did something more ill-advised.

Not, *'Hello Oliver,'* not, *'How dare you look so good after such a crap year?'*; not even, *'Why are you here?'* All much more pressing issues.

'Explain what?' he said, infuriating in his calmness. As if this weren't the biggest deal ever.

'Why my Testore trail leads to you.'

His steady eyes didn't waver. 'Does it?'

'Why the instrument I've been slowly working my way towards for two years suddenly turns up in a luggage locker at Hongqiao train station.'

He stepped one pace closer. 'Asia's biggest train station. I imagine that's not the only secret it's harbouring.'

Both arms folded across her chest. 'Shanghai, Oliver.'

'Coincidence.'

'What did you do?' Every word a bullet.

He studied the dragonflies for distracted moments and when he brought his eyes back to hers they were defiant. 'I made a few phone calls. Called in a few favours.' He shrugged. 'It's not like I donated a kidney.'

She peered at him through narrowed eyes. 'You just happened to be owed a favour by the exact someone who knew where the Testore was?'

He sized her up, as if trying to determine how far he could take the nonchalance. 'Look...I called in a marker with a colleague, they called one in from someone else and it reverse dominoed all the way up to someone who knew the right people to ask.'

'And then what?'

'Then I bought it.'

'A million-dollar instrument?'

'Can you put a price on a trafficked child?'

Ha ha. 'You realise you're an accessory to a crime, now?'

His eyes grew uncertain for the first time since he'd walked in the door and he frowned. 'I hoped I'd get bonus points for repatriating it.'

But she wasn't ready to give him those points yet. 'You perpetuated the problem by rewarding the syndicate for their crime. Now they'll go out and steal another cello.'

'Is that really what's bothering you, Audrey? Wasn't it more important to get the cello back into safe hands than to arrest whatever mid-level thug with a drug-debt they'd have made take the fall?'

Did it matter how the Testore was recovered or what favours were exchanged and promises made? Or did it only matter that its rightful owner literally broke down and sobbed when it was returned to her, triggering Audrey's own tears—tears she'd thought she'd used completely up?

Maybe it only mattered that Oliver had cared enough to try.

'What's bothering me is why you did it.' And by 'bother' she meant 'making my chest ache'.

'Because I could.' He shrugged. 'I have connections that you would never have had access to.'

'A million dollars, Oliver.' Plus some change. 'Excessive, even for you.'

'Not if it helped you out.'

Blinking didn't make the words any easier to comprehend—or believe—but this was not the time to let subtext get the better of her. 'I'm amazed that you have any fortune at all if you make such emotionally based decisions.'

'I don't, generally. Only with you.'

'Did you think I wouldn't figure it out?' That an anonymous key in a Christmas parcel leading her to a Shanghai train station wouldn't be clue enough?

'I knew you would.'

'So did you think I'd gush with gratitude?'

'On the contrary. I hoped it might piss you off enough to get on a plane.'

Manipulated again. By the master. She shook her head.

'Well, here I am. Hope you don't want your million bucks back.'

'Forget the money, Audrey. I sold one of my company's nine executive apartments to raise the cash. It had only been used twice last year.'

The world he lived in.

'What if I'd just taken the cello and run?'

That resulted in insta-frown. 'Then I'd have been no worse off.'

Ugh. 'This was a mistake.'

'Audrey—' his voice suspended her flight after only two steps '—wait.'

She ignored his command. 'Thank you for doing my job for me. I'll put a good word in with the authorities for you.'

'You're leaving?'

'Yes. I shouldn't have come at all.'

What she should do was get back onto her ridiculously expensive short-notice flight and head back to her ridiculously expensive Sydney house. Blake's house that she'd not had the courage or energy to move out of. The house and the life she hated.

He stepped round in front of her. 'Why did you?'

Because she was slowly dying inside knowing she'd never see him again? Because she'd managed the first six months on pride and adrenaline but now there was nothing left but sorrow. Because she was addicted.

'No idea,' she gritted. 'Let me rectify that right now.'

He sprinted in front of her again. 'Audrey, wait, please just hear me out.'

'Didn't we say enough at the airport?' she sighed.

'You said quite a lot but I was pretty much speechless.'

Seriously? He got her back here to have the last word?

'Ten minutes, Audrey. That's it.'

It was impossible to be this close to those bottomless hazel eyes and not give him what he was asking. Ten minutes of her time. In return for a million-dollar cello.

She crossed her arms and settled into the carpet more firmly. 'Fine. Clock's ticking.'

'Not here,' he said, sliding his hand to her lower back and directing her towards the door.

She stopped and lurched free of his hot touch. 'No. Not upstairs.' That had way too many memories. Although, reasonably, there were just as many down here.

But at least, here, there was an audience. Chaperones.

What are you afraid of? he'd once challenged her. *Me or yourself?*

He just stared, a stoic plea in his eyes.

'Oh, for God's sake, fine!' She swivelled ahead of him and marched back out into the elevator lobby then up the circular stairs off to the side. The plush carpet disguised his footfalls but she could feel Oliver's closeness, his eyes on her behind.

'You've lost weight,' he announced.

She froze. Turned. Glared.

Yes, she'd bloody well lost weight and she really didn't have much to spare. Now her 'athletic' was more 'catwalk' than she'd have liked. Especially for preservation of dignity. She didn't want him knowing how tough she'd been doing it.

His hands immediately shot up either side of him. 'Right, sorry…keep going. Ten minutes.'

At the top, he passed her and ran his key card through the swipe and the big doors swung open just as they had last year. She followed him into the luxurious penthouse—

—and stopped dead just a few feet in, all the fight suck-ing clear out of her.

Over by the window, over where he'd first touched her with trembling hands all those long, lonely nights ago, a new piece of furniture had pride of place overlooking the view.

An overstuffed smoking chair.

Their chair.

The sight numbed her—emotionally and literally.

'Why is that here?' she whispered.

He seemed surprised by the direction of her gaze. 'I had it brought up here. I like to sit on it, look out. Think.'

'About what?'

'A lot of things.' He took a breath. 'Us, mostly.'

She turned wide eyes on him 'There is no "us".'

His shoulders sagged. 'There was. For one amazing night. I think about that, and I miss it.'

Every muscle fibre in her body tightened up, ready for the 'but'.

He stepped closer. 'I sit in that chair and I think about you and I miss *you*.'

'Careful,' she squeezed out of an airless chest. 'I might get the wrong idea and let my *feelings* get away with me.'

When had she become so angry?

He took her hand, seemed surprised by its frigidity, and led her to the luxurious sofa circling the raised floor of the formal area. The sofa that they'd made such fast, furi-ous love on that first time. She pulled her fingers free and crossed to the chair, instead, curling her hands around its ornate back, borrowing its strength. Using it as a crutch.

Exactly the way her memories of it had been this past year.

'I need you to know something,' he said. 'Quite a few somethings, actually.'

She straightened, listening, but didn't turn around. The Hong Kong skyline soothed her. Speaking of things missed...

'I started wanting you about ten minutes after you walked into that bar all those years ago.' The greenish-brown of his eyes focused in hard. 'Then in the years that followed, I would have given every cent I had to wake up to you just once instead of clock-watching as midnight approached and waiting for the moment you'd flee down the stairs until the following Christmas.'

Her breath slammed up behind the fist his words caused in her chest until she remembered that 'wanting' was not the same as *'wanting'*.

One was short-term and easily addressed, apparently. Maybe that was why he'd lured her back here. Round two.

'I was captivated from the first time you locked those expressive eyes and that sharp mind on me. You were a challenge because you seemed so disinterested in me and so interested in Blake and that just didn't happen to me. And I'd sit there, enduring Blake's hands all over you—'

'Embarrassed by it.'

'Not embarrassed, Audrey. Pained. I hated watching him touch you. I hated thinking you preferred his company, his touch, to mine. And that was when I realised there was more than just ego going on. That I didn't just *want* you. I had *feelings* for you.'

Her fingers curled into the brocade chair-back and she whispered, 'Why did you send me the key, Oliver?'

'Because you were right and because I wanted to tell you that, face to face, and I thought it would get your attention.'

'Right about what?'

'All of it. The Heathcliff thing. It was so much easier to

be consumed with longing and never have to face the reality of what that actually meant. And then to disguise that with work and endless other excuses. You were my best friend's wife. As unattainable as any woman could possibly be. Completely safe to fixate on.

'I convinced myself that my inability to connect to women—just one woman—was about having high standards. It was easy to find them wanting and easier still to disregard them because they failed to measure up to this totally unattainable idyll I had. The idea of you.'

He came around in front of the chair, folded one knee on its thick cushion to level their heights and met her eyes. 'I would find fault with the relationships before they got anywhere near the point of commitment purely to avoid having to face that moment.'

The anguish in his face wheedled its way under her skin and she itched to touch him. But discipline, for once, did not fail her. 'Which moment?'

'The moment where I realised that I wasn't actually capable of committing to them. That I was no more capable of being true to someone than my father. So I'd get out before I had to face that or I chose women who would cheat on me first.'

Oh, Oliver...

'I counted myself so superior to him all this time—me with my rigid values and my high moral ground—but the whole time I was terrified that I had inherited his inability to commit to someone. To love just one someone.' He lifted harrowed eyes to hers. 'And that if ever I let myself, then I'd be exposed as my father's son to someone to whom it would really matter.'

He stroked her cheek.

'But then I had you. In my arms. In my bed. And every single thing I'd ever wanted was being handed to me on a platter. The woman against whom every other woman I'd ever met had paled. It was all so suddenly *real*, and there was no good reason for us not to be together—in this chair, in this room, in this town and beyond it. I panicked.'

'You told me you couldn't see yourself loving me. You were quite clear.' Saying it aloud still hurt, even after all this time.

'Audrey.' He sighed. 'My father took my mother's love for him and used it to bind her in a relationship that he didn't have to work for. He didn't value it. He certainly didn't honour it. What if I did that to you?'

'What if you didn't? You aren't your father, Oliver.' No matter what she'd said in anger.

'What if I am?' Desperation clouded his eyes. 'Your feelings were going to force me into discovering. That's why I pushed you away.'

Just twelve months ago she'd stood here, in this penthouse, terrified that she was somehow deficient. And Oliver had proven her wrong. And in doing so changed her life. Now was her chance to return the favour.

'You are not broken, Oliver Harmer. And you are as much your mother's son as you are your father's. Never forget that.'

He suddenly found something in the giant Christmas tree in the corner enormously fascinating, as if he couldn't quite believe her words were true.

'Could she love?' Audrey pressed.

'Yes.'

'Then why can't you?'

Confusion mixed in with the anguish. 'I never have.'

'Have you not? Truly?' She straightened and locked her eyes. 'Can you think of no one at all?'

He stood frozen.

She kept her courage. 'It can be easy to overlook. I once loved someone for eight years, almost without realising.'

His skin blanched and it was hard to know whether it was because she'd used the L word in connection with him or because she'd used the past tense.

'When did you realise?'

She ran her hands across the back of the chair's fine embroidered fabric. 'Out of the blue, this one time, curled up in a chair.'

He still just stared. Silence ticked on. She forced herself to remain tough.

'So, was that what you wanted to tell me?' she checked. *'It's not you it's me?'*

'It *is* me, Audrey. But no, what I really wanted to do was apologise. I'm sorry I let you leave Hong Kong believing there was anything you could have done differently or anything you could have been that would have made a difference.'

And his guilt was apparently worth a rare cello.

Her lips tightened. 'You know, this seems to be the story of my life. Last time it was my gender, this time there was nothing I could have done differently short of *caring less*.'

'This is nothing like Blake.'

'I'm not ashamed of my feelings. And I'm not afraid of them either. Unlike you.'

His eyes tarnished off as she watched. 'Meaning?'

'Exactly what I said. I think you are afraid of the depth of your feelings. Because feeling makes you vulnerable.'

'What I'm afraid of is hurting you.'

'Isn't that my risk to take? Just as it was your mother's choice to stay with your father.'

Two deep lines cut down between his brows. 'You can't *want* to make that choice.'

'I wouldn't if I believed that you've inherited anything more than eye colour from your father. You dislike him too much. If anything I'd expect you to grow into the complete opposite of him just out of sheer bloody determination.'

'I saw what losing his love did to my mother.' Tense and tight but not angry. 'How vulnerable it made her.'

'Don't you trust me?'

'You know I do.'

'Then why do you think I would hurt you?' she begged. 'I chose to be vulnerable with you last Christmas because I couldn't think of a single person in the world that I trusted more with my unshielded heart.'

'I'm afraid I might hurt *you*.'

'By possibly abandoning me at some point in the future?'

'I saw what it did to my mother.' For the first time, the tension in his face hinted at hostility. Except, now, she knew that was what fear looked like on him. 'And I felt what it did to me.'

She sucked in a breath, loud and punctuated in the frozen moments of silence before he crossed to the edge of the sofa. He pulled a hanging tinsel ball into his hands and punished it with attention.

'You?' she risked.

He spun. 'My father opted out of his *family*, Audrey, not just his marriage. He abandoned me, too.'

'But he didn't abandon you. He's still there now.'

Bleak eyes stared out of the window. 'Yeah, he did. He just couldn't be arsed leaving.'

For a heartbeat, Audrey wondered if she'd pushed him too far, but then that big body slumped down onto the sofa, head bowed.

She crossed to his side, sat next to him, curled her hand over his and said the only thing she could think of. 'I'm sorry.'

He shook his head.

She turned more into him. 'I'm sorry that it happened. And I'm sorry that it has affected you all this time. Love is not supposed to work that way.'

As her arms came up he tipped down into them, into her hold and slid his own around her middle. She embraced him with everything she had in her. This was Oliver after all, the man she loved.

And the man she loved was hurting.

He buried his face in her neck and she rocked him, gently. One big hand slid up into her hair, keeping her close, and she felt the damp of tears against her neck.

'You can love, Oliver,' she said, after minutes of silent embrace. 'I promise. You just need to let yourself. And trust that it's safe to do it with me.'

His silence reeked of doubt.

She stroked his hair back. 'Maybe your love is just like one of the companies you rescue. Broken down by someone who didn't value it and treat it right. So maybe you just need to get it into the hands of someone who will nurture and protect it. And grow it to its full potential. Because you have so much potential. And so do we.'

His half-smile, when he sat up straighter, told her exactly how lame that analogy was. But too bad, she was committed to it now.

'Someone like who?'

'Someone like me. I'm looking to diversify my portfolio, as it happens.'

'Really?'

She shrugged. 'I had a bad investment myself not so long ago, something that could have been very different if I'd given it the time and focus it deserved. But I've learned from my mistakes and know what to do differently next time.'

His smile twisted. 'Well, no one's perfect.'

'So how about it? Think I might be the sort of person you'd trust a damaged company to? I come highly recommended for my work in the recovery of trafficked stringed instruments.'

He nodded and pressed a grateful kiss to her forehead. 'Very responsible. And honourable.'

'And I have federal security clearance,' she breathed as he pressed another one to her jaw. 'They don't give those to just anyone. At all.'

His nod was serious. 'Hard to argue with Interpol.'

'And...um...' She lost her train of thought as his lips found the hollow between her collarbones. 'I have a blue library card. It means I can take books out of the reference section.'

Kiss. 'Persuasive.'

'And I'm not *him* any more than you are.' The lips stopped dead, pressed into her shoulder. 'So if I'm willing to take a risk on you despite the fact you've already hurt me once, the least you can do is return the favour.'

He pulled away to stare into her eyes for the longest time.

Then, in the space between breaths, the cool damp of his butterfly kisses became the warm damp of his mouth working its way up her throat. Her jaw. Roaming. Exploring. Rediscovering.

'I never should have let you go,' he breathed, hot against her ear, right before tonguing her lobe.

She twisted into him, seeking his lips. 'You had to. So I could come back to you, again.'

And then they were kissing. Hot and hard and frantic. Slow and deep and healing.

'I don't want to love anyone else,' he grated, twisting her under him and pressing her into the sofa with his strength. 'I don't want to trust anyone else. Only you, Audrey. It was only ever you.'

He stroked her hair back and applied kiss after kiss to her eyelids, cheekbones, forehead. Worshipping with his mouth. She reached up and stilled his hands, stilled his lips with her own and caught his eyes and held them.

'I love you, Oliver. I always have. I always will. And my love makes me stronger and better whether we're together or not.'

He twisted so that they faced each other on the spacious couch. 'I don't ever want to go hours without you, let alone months. Not again.'

'Then that's how we'll do it,' she breathed. 'One day at a time. Until days have become weeks and weeks years, and before you know it we'll have been together, in love, as long as we were apart, in love.'

'I can't imagine what it would have been like being alone without loving you all those years. How desolate it would have been.'

Loving you...

There was such veracity in the way it just slipped out in the middle of that sentence. As though it had always been a part of his subconscious and they weren't the most important words she'd ever heard.

Her laugh was five-eighths sob.

Something occurred to him then. 'Imagine if we'd never met. If you'd gone to the bar next door that day. I wouldn't have had you to keep me sane all this time.'

'Imagine if I'd been braver that first day and actually managed a proper conversation with you.'

'I never would have let you go,' he vowed.

'We'd be an old married couple by now.'

His smile bit into her ear. 'We'd be the horniest married couple Hong Kong had ever seen.'

She lifted her head. 'Hong Kong?'

'We'd have lived here, wouldn't we?'

Audrey considered that. 'Yeah, I think we would. Maybe you would have bought this penthouse anyway.'

'I bought the restaurant for you, after you didn't come, so I would always have you.'

'A little excessive, really.'

He huffed. 'A little desperate.'

She traced his lip with her tongue tip. 'I love you, desperate.'

'I love you, period.'

Okay, so she didn't mind hearing it formally, too. She would never, ever tire of hearing it.

They studied each other, drowning in each other's depths and tangling their fingers.

'I have a gift for you,' he said almost sheepishly as he crossed to the expensive tree in the corner.

'The cello wasn't enough?'

He handed her the parcel, small and suspiciously square and faultlessly gift-wrapped. 'I would have sent it to you if you hadn't come.'

'The paper is too perfect to ruin—'

He took the parcel from her and tore the beautiful bow off the top, then handed it back. Problem solved.

Inside a distinctive jeweller's box taunted her. 'Oliver...'

'Don't panic. It's not a ring,' he assured. 'Not this time.'

Not this time...

A tiny leather tie lifted off the clasp and let her open the box. She couldn't help the soft gasp. Inside, resting as though it had just alighted on the black silk pillow, was an exquisite stylised dragonfly necklace, its tiny white-gold body encrusted with gemstones and its fine wings a mix of aquamarine and laser-cut sapphire. At its head, a woman's torso carved from jade, bare-breasted and beautiful.

'That reminded me of you,' he murmured, almost apologetic. 'Wild and stylish and natural all at once. I had to have it.'

Tears welled so violently it was almost impossible to appreciate the handcrafted beauty. 'It's...'

Were there enough words to sum up what this meant to her? Such a personal and special gift. More meaningful than any cello. Or restaurant. Or penthouse.

This was up there with the chair for things she'd run back into a burning high-rise for. She pressed herself into his arms, the jeweller's box curled into one of the fists she snaked around his neck.

'It's perfect,' she breathed against his ear. 'Thank you.'

Her teary kiss was more eloquent than she could ever be and so she buried herself in his chest, crawling onto the sofa with him and letting the thrum of her heartbeat against his communicate for her. He draped the dragonfly around her neck and it nestled down between her breasts. Over her heart.

Oliver busied himself playing with it, alternating between stroking it and the breasts either side of it. Slowly the dragonfly heated with the warmth coming off her.

'Do you think Blake sensed it?' she said, after some time, to distract herself from his talented fingers. 'How drawn to each other we were?'

'What makes you ask that?'

'He was always so uptight when I was around you. I figured maybe he could sense my attraction.'

'Are you kidding? You have the best poker face in the world. I had no clue and I was perpetually on alert for the slightest sign.' She frowned and he kissed it away. 'I think it's more likely he could sense my attraction. I'm a mere grasshopper to your sensei of emotional discipline.'

'But why would he care if you were attracted to me, given what we now know?'

'Dog in a manger?' Oliver nibbled his way up her shoulder blades. 'Maybe he resented my attention to his property.'

As tempting as it was to drop the conversation and find out where all that nibbling would lead to, something in her just wouldn't let it go. 'It wasn't resentment. It was envy.'

He grinned and it just needed an unlit cigar to be perfect. 'Maybe it wasn't about you? I *am* pretty sexy…'

He laughed but Audrey sat up on her elbow, considered him. 'And Blake *was* pretty gay.'

'No, Audrey. I was kidding.'

Her whole body tingled with revelation. 'He was jealous *for* you, not *of* you. That makes so much more sense.'

Something final clicked into place. How flustered Blake used to get if she came to dinner looking hot. It wasn't attraction, it was anger—that Oliver might grow interested.

And all the random, unprovoked touching…that must have been designed to get a reaction out of Oliver, not her.

Maybe Blake had loved his best friend for more years than she had.

'He wanted you,' she said. 'And you wanted me. And he saw that every single time we were all together.'

There was a weird kind of certainty in the thought. No wonder he thought there was something going on in Hong Kong. He knew the truth. He just knew it much earlier than either of them.

'Poor Blake,' she whispered. 'Trapped behind so many masks. And you and I were supposed to be together all along.'

There was just no question. Again, that strange cosmic rightness.

'We may be slow,' he said, burrowing into the place below her ear, 'but we got there.'

'Promise me no masks between us, Oliver. Ever. Promise me we'll go back to Audrey and Oliver who can talk about anything, who will share anything. Even the tough stuff.'

He kissed his way to her lips, then, seeing how very serious she was about that, he rested his chin on her forehead and placed his hand on her heart. 'I give you my solemn oath, Audrey. Whenever we have something tough to discuss we'll curl up in that chair and talk it out and we won't leave it until we're done. No matter what.'

Her eyes shifted right. 'Our chair?'

'Our chair.' He lifted his chin to stare into her eyes. 'Why?'

'I was hoping it could be used more for evil than for good,' she breathed. 'And it has been a very, very long time between chairs.'

Desire flooded Oliver's gorgeous gaze. 'Fortunately, it's a multipurpose chair. But, come on.' He pulled her to her feet and towards the window. 'Let's make sure it's *fit* for purpose.'

* * * * *

The Most Expensive
Night Of Her Life

Amy Andrews

ABOUT AMY ANDREWS

———

Amy Andrews has always loved writing, and still can't quite believe that she gets to do it for a living. Creating wonderful heroines and gorgeous heroes and telling their stories is an amazing way to pass the day. Sometimes they don't always act as she'd like them to—but then neither do her kids, so she's kind of used to it. Amy lives in the very beautiful Samford Valley, with her husband and aforementioned children, along with six brown chooks and two black dogs.

She loves to hear from her readers. Drop her a line at amyandrews.com.au.

DEAR READER,

I've always had a secret hankering to do a bodyguard story. I just adore the trope. And, while this book isn't a typical bodyguard scenario, I hope you like my take on it—because I've had Ava and Blake in my head in various incantations for a long time now, and it was great to finally get them down on paper.

I had a lot of fun taking megarich, megaspoiled supermodel Ava and shoving her on a tiny canal boat in the UK with the only man on the planet who seems immune to her charms. I had even more fun needling private, serious, returned soldier Blake with the temptation of a woman who has absolutely no problem with baring acres of skin or leaving her lingerie all over his floating home.

I'm pleased I let Ava and Blake marinate, though. Had I written their story years ago, I don't think they'd have had the emotional complexity they do today. Because underneath Ava's hard, demanding surface is a woman who can't trust. And beneath Blake's tough, pragmatic shell is a man whose physical limitations cripple him emotionally.

Which only makes their happy-ever-after even more rewarding!

I hope you enjoy their journey to love. Oh, and London at Christmas!

Love,

Amy xx

To the Kohli family, our lovely UK friends—
Amanda, Nick, Lauren and Matthew.

Even though we live on opposite sides of the world,
your friendship warms our hearts.

CHAPTER ONE

A ROADSIDE EXPLOSION in the darkest depths of a war zone three years ago had left Blake Walker with a finely honed sense of doom. Today that doom stormed towards him on a pair of legs that wouldn't quit and a ball-breaking attitude that was guaranteed to ruin his last day on the job.

Ava Kelly might be one of the world's most beautiful women but she redefined the term *diva*.

Doing this job for her had been a freaking nightmare.

'Blake!'

Her classy Oxford accent grated and Blake took a deep breath. He went to the happy place the army shrink had insisted he find—which at the moment was anywhere but here.

Last day, man, keep yourself together.

'Ava,' he greeted as she stopped on the opposite side of the beautiful maple-wood island bench in the kitchen where he was poring over some paperwork. He'd polished the top to glass-like perfection with his own two hands. 'Problem?'

'You could say that,' she said, folding her arms and glaring at him.

Blake did not drop his gaze and admire how the arm-crossing emphasised the tanned perfection of her cleavage. Even if it was on open display in her loosely tied gossamer gown that reeked of a designer label and through which her itty-bitty, red bikini could also be clearly seen.

He did not think about how wet she was underneath it. About the water droplets that dripped off the ends of her slicked-back hair or trekked down the elegant line of her throat to cling precariously to her prominent collarbones before heading further south.

Blake did not look.

Blake was in a good place in his life. He was fit and healthy after a long period of being neither. He was financially secure. He had direction and purpose.

He could get laid any night of the week with just one phone call placed to any of half a dozen women. He didn't need to ogle the one in front of him.

She was trouble and he'd already had too much of that.

Instead he thought about the month-long holiday he started tomorrow—no braving a clutch of paparazzi every morning, no twelve-hour days and, most importantly, no divas.

'Something I can help with?' he asked.

'Yes,' she said, raising her chin to peer down her nose at him in that way he'd got used to the last few months. 'You can ask your salivating apprentice—' she jerked her thumb in the direction of the male in question '—to put his eyes back in his head and keep his mind on the job. My friends aren't here to be gawked at. They come into the privacy of *my* home to get away from objectification.'

Blake glanced over at the three women frolicking in the fully glassed indoor pool that ran alongside the magnificent internal open-air courtyard. They were all tall, tanned and gorgeous and if they were friends of Ava's then they were no doubt models too. Between them there were only twelve triangles of fabric keeping them from being totally naked.

He glanced at Dougy, who was installing some sophisticated strip lighting down the outside of the glass and steel staircase that led from the courtyard to a mezzanine level for sunbathing. Ava was right: he was barely keeping his tongue inside his head. Not that Blake could really blame him. This had to be every young apprentice's wet dream. And he was like a kid in a candy shop.

Sunlight flooded the courtyard through the open glass roof above reflecting off the stark white décor, dazzling his eyes. For a moment Blake tuned out Ava's disapproval and admired what they'd achieved—outside a semi-detached, early-nineteenth-century terraced house, inside a vibrant contemporary home full of light and flair.

'Well?' Ava's huffy demand yanked him back to the conversation.

'Dougy,' Blake said, in no mood to humour her as her gown slipped off her right shoulder exposing more of her to his view. He kept his gaze firmly fixed on the smattering of freckles across the bridge of her perfect little snub nose placed perfectly in the middle of her delicate kitten-like face.

'His name's Dougy.'

'Well, do you think you could rein *Dougy* in? He's acting like some horny teenager.'

Blake sighed. Why was it he liked project management again? He made a note to tell Charlie no more divas. Their business was going gangbusters—they could afford to be choosey.

'Ava,' he said patiently, 'he's nineteen. He *is* a horny teenager.'

'Well, he can be that on his own time,' she snapped. 'When he's on my time, I expect him to have his head down and do the job I'm paying him for. And so should you.'

Blake contemplated telling Ava Kelly to quit her bitching and let him worry about his employees. Dougy was a good apprentice—keen and a hard worker—and Blake wasn't about to make an issue out of what was, to him, a non-issue. But he figured no one had ever used the B word around Ms Kelly—*not to her face anyway*—and he wasn't going to be the first.

Hell, what she needed was a damn good spanking. But he wasn't about to do that either.

The job was over at the end of the day, they were just putting the finishing touches to the reno, and he could suck up her diva-ness for a few more hours.

Blake unclenched his jaw. 'I'll talk to him,' he said through stiff lips.

Ava looked down her nose at him again and sniffed. 'See that you do.'

Then she spun on her heel and marched away. He watched as the edges of her gown flowed behind her like tails, her lovely ankles exposed with every footfall. Higher up his gaze snagged on the enticing sway of one teeny-tiny red triangle.

The end of the day couldn't come soon enough.

A couple of hours later Blake answered the phone to his brother. Blake rarely answered the phone while at a job site but he always picked up for Charlie. His brother might have been younger but he'd been the driving force behind their design business and behind dragging Blake out of the maudlin pit of despair he'd almost totally disappeared into a few years back.

Blake owed Charlie big time.

'What's up?' he asked.

'Joanna rang. She's really upset. One of their biggest supporters is pulling out due to financial issues and she's freaking out they won't be able to continue to run their programmes.'

Joanna was their sister. She'd been widowed three years ago when her husband, Colin, a lieutenant in the British army and a close friend of Blake's, was killed in the same explosion that had injured him. They'd been in the same unit and he'd been Col's captain. And he'd promised his sister he'd look out for her husband.

That he'd bring him home alive.

Not a promise he'd been able to keep as it turned out.

She and three other army wives had started a charity soon after, which supported the wives, girlfriends and families of British servicemen. They'd done very well in almost two years but fighting for any charity backing in the global financial situation was hard—losing the support of a major contributor was a real blow.

And losing Col had been blow enough.

Blake understood that it was through the charity that Joanna kept him alive. It kept her going. It was her crutch.

And Blake understood crutches better than anyone.

'I guess we're in a position with the business now to become patrons ourselves,' Blake said.

'Blake!'

The muscles in Blake's neck tensed at the imperious

voice. He took a deep breath as he turned around, his brother still speaking in his ear.

'We can't afford the one million quid that's been yanked from their coffers,' Charlie said.

Ava went to open her mouth but Blake was so shocked by the amount he held his finger up to indicate that she wait without realising what he was doing. 'Joanna needs a *million* pounds?'

He watched Ava absently as Charlie rattled off the intricacies. By the look on her face and the miffed little armfold, she wasn't accustomed to being told to wait. But *holy cow*—one million pounds?

'I need you to move your car,' Ava said, tapping her fingers on her arm, obviously waiting as long as she was going to despite Charlie still yakking in his ear. 'I'm expecting a photographer from a magazine and your beat-up piece of junk spoils the ambience a little.'

Blake blinked at Ava's request. She'd never seemed more frivolous or more diva-ish to him and he was exceptionally pleased this was the last time he'd ever have to see her.

Yes, she was sexy, and in a parallel universe where she *wasn't* an elite supermodel and he *wasn't* a glorified construction worker he might have even gone there—given it a shot.

But skin-deep beauty left him cold.

He quirked a you-have-to-be-kidding-me eyebrow but didn't say a word to her as he spoke to Charlie. 'I've got to go and shift my *piece of junk car*.' He kept his gaze fixed to her face. 'We'll think of something for Joanna. I'll call you when I've finished tonight.'

'Who's Joanna?' Ava asked as Charlie hit the end button.

Blake stiffened. He didn't want to tell Little-Miss-I've-got-a-photographer-coming Ava anything about his private life. But *mind your own business* probably wasn't the best response either. 'Our sister,' he said, his lips tight.

'Is she okay?'

Blake recoiled in surprise. Not just that she'd enquired about somebody else's welfare but at the genuine note of concern in her voice. 'She's fine,' he said. 'The charity she runs has hit a bit of a snag, that's all. She'll bounce back.'

And he went and shifted his car so he wouldn't besmirch her Hampstead Village ambience, the paparazzi blinding him with their flashes for the thousandth time.

It was close to nine that night when Blake—and *the diva*—were satisfied that the job was finally complete. The evening was still and warm. Tangerine fingers of daylight could be seen streaking the sky through the open glass panels over the courtyard. Blake was heartened that the long-range weather forecast for September was largely for more of the same.

Perfect boating weather.

Dougy and the other two workers had gone home; the photographer had departed, as had the paparazzi. It was just him and Ava signing off on the reno. Dotting all the i's and crossing all the t's.

They were, once again, at the kitchen island bench—him on one side, her on the other. Ava was sipping a glass of white wine while something delicious cooked on the state-of-the-art cooktop behind him. She'd offered him a beer but he'd declined. She'd offered to feed him but he'd declined that also.

No way was he spending a second longer with Ava than he absolutely had to.

Although the aromas of garlic and basil swirling around him were making him very aware of his empty stomach and his even more empty fridge.

He was also very aware of her. She'd pulled on some rag-gedy-arsed shorts and a thin, short-sleeved, zip-up hoodie thing over her bikini. The zip was low enough to catch a glimpse of cleavage and a hint of red material as she leaned slightly forward when she asked a question. But that wasn't what was making him aware of her.

God knew she'd swanned around the house in varying states of undress for the last three months.

No. It was the way she was caressing the bench-top that drew his eye. As he walked her through the paperwork the palm of her hand absently stroked back and forth along the glassy maple-wood. He'd learned she was a tactile person and, despite his animosity towards her, he liked that.

She'd handed the décor decisions over to a high-priced consultant who had gone for the typical home-and-garden, money-to-burn classy minimalist. But it was the accesso-ries that *Ava* had chosen that showed her hedonistic bent. Shaggy rugs, chunky art, the softest mohair throws in vi-brant greens and reds and purples for the lounges, beaded wall hangings, a collection of art deco lamps, layers and layers of colourful gauzy fabric falling from the ceiling in her bedroom to form a dazzling canopy over her girly four-poster bed.

Even the fact that she'd chosen a wooden kitchen amidst all the glass and metal told him something about her. He'd have thought for sure she'd have chosen black marble and acres of stainless steel. But clearly, from the smell of din-ner, Ava loved to cook and spent a lot of time in the kitchen.

Blake wasn't much of a cook but he loved wood. The

family business, until recent times, had been a saw mill and his earliest memories revolved around the fresh earthy smell of cut timber. His grandfather, who had founded the mill fifty year prior, had taught both him and Charlie how to use a lathe from a very early age and Blake had been hooked. He'd worked in the mill weekends and every school holidays until he'd joined up.

He'd personally designed, built and installed the kitchen where they were sitting and something grabbed at his gut to see her hand caressing his creation as she might caress a lover.

'So,' he said as their business concluded, and he got his head back in the game, 'if you're happy that everything has been done to your satisfaction, just sign here and here.'

Blake held out a pen and indicated the lines requiring her signature. Then held his breath. Tactile or not, Ava Kelly had also been demanding, difficult and fickle.

He wasn't counting his chickens until she'd signed on the dotted lines!

Ava glanced at the enigmatic Blake Walker through her fringe. She'd never met a man who wasn't at least a little in awe of her. Who didn't flirt a little or at least try it on.

But not Blake.

He'd been polite and unflappable even when she'd been at her most unreasonable. And she knew she'd been unreasonable on more than one occasion. *Just a little.* Just to see if he'd react like a human being for once instead of the face of the business—composed, courteous, respectful.

She'd almost got her reaction this afternoon when he'd been on the phone and she'd asked him to shift his car. The tightening of his mouth, that eyebrow raise had spoken volumes. But he'd retreated from the flash of fire she'd seen in his indigo eyes and a part of her had been supremely disappointed.

Something told her that Blake Walker would be quite magnificent all riled up.

Charlie, the more easy-going of the brothers, had said that Blake had been in the army so maybe he was used to following orders, sucking things up?

Ava reluctantly withdrew her hand from the cool smoothness of the bench-top to take the pen. She loved the seductive feel of the beautiful wood and, with Blake's deep voice washing over her and the pasta sauce bubbling away in the background, a feeling of contentment descended. It would be so nice to drop her guard for once, to surrender to the cosy domesticity.

To the intimacy.

Did he feel it too or was it just her overactive imagination after months of building little fantasies about him? Fantasies that had been getting a lot more complex as he had steadily ignored her.

Like doing him on this magnificent bench-top. A bench-top she'd watched him hone day after day. Sanding, lacquering. Sanding, lacquering. Sanding, lacquering. Layer upon layer until it shone like the finest crystal in the discreet down lights.

Watching him so obviously absorbed by the task. Loving the wood with his touch. Inhaling its earthy essence with each flare of his nostrils. Caressing it with his lingering gaze.

She could have stripped stark naked in front of him as he'd worked the wood and she doubted he would have noticed.

And for a woman used to being adored, being ignored had been challenging.

Ava dragged her mind off the bench-top and what she was doing to an unknowing Blake on top of it. 'I'm absolutely…positively…one hundred per cent…' she punctuated each affirmation with firm strokes of the pen across the indicated lines '…happy with the job. It's *totally fab*. I'm going to tell all my friends to use you guys.'

Blake blinked. That he hadn't been expecting. A polite, understated thank-you was the best he'd been hoping for. The very last thing he'd expected was effusive praise and promised recommendations to what he could only imagine would be a fairly extensive A list.

He supposed she expected him to be grateful for that but the thought of dealing with any more Ava Kellys was enough to bring him out in hives.

'Thank you,' he said non-comittally.

She smiled at him as she pushed the papers and the pen back across the bench-top. Like her concern earlier it seemed genuine, unlike the haughty *can't-touch-this* smile she was known for in the modelling world, and he lost his breath a little.

The down lights shone off her now dry caramel-blonde hair pulled into some kind of a messy knot at her nape, the fringe occasionally brushing eyelashes that cast long shadows on her cheekbones. Her eyes were cat-like in their quality, both in the yellow-green of the irises and in the way they tapered down as if they were concealing a bunch of secrets.

Yeh, Ava Kelly was a *very* attractive woman.

But he'd spent over a decade in service to his country

having his balls busted by the best and he wasn't about to line up for another stint.

Blake gathered the paperwork and shoved it in his satchel, conscious of her watching him all the time. His leg ached and he couldn't wait to get off it.

He was almost free. She was almost out of his life for good.

He picked up the satchel and rounded the bench-top, his limp a little more pronounced now as stiffness through his hip hindered his movement. He pulled up in front of her when she was an arm's length away. He held out his hand and gave her one of his smiles that Joanna called barely there.

'We'll invoice you with the final payment,' he said as she took his hand and they shook.

She was as tall as him—six foot—and it was rare to be able to look a woman directly in the eye. Disconcerting too as those eyes stared back at him with something between bold sexual interest and hesitant mystique. It was intriguing. Tempting...

He withdrew his hand. *So not going there.* 'Okay. I'll be off. I'm away for a month so if you have any issues contact Charlie.'

Ava quirked an eyebrow. 'Going on a holiday?'

Blake nodded curtly. The delicate arch of her eyebrow only drew his attention back to the frankness in her eyes. She sounded surprised. Why, he had no idea. After three months of her quibbles and foibles even a saint would need some time off. 'Yes.'

Ava sighed at his monosyllabic replies. 'Look, I'm sorry,' she said, picking up her glass of wine and taking a fortifying sip. Something had passed between them just now and suddenly she knew he wasn't as immune to her as she'd thought.

'I know I haven't exactly been easy on you and I *know* I can be a pain in the butt sometimes. I can't help it. I like to be in control.' She shrugged. 'It's the business I'm in... people demand perfection from me and they get it but I demand it back.'

Ava paused for a moment. She wasn't sure why she was telling him this stuff. Why it was important he understand she wasn't some prima donna A-lister. She was twenty-seven years old—had been at the top of her game since she was fourteen—and had never cared who thought what.

Maybe it was the gorgeous wooden bench-top he'd created just for her? The perfection of it. How he'd worked at it and worked at it and worked at it until it was flawless.

Maybe a man who clearly appreciated perfection would understand?

'I learned early...very early, not to trust easily. And I'm afraid it spills over into all aspects of my life. I know people think I'm a bitch and I'm okay with that. People think twice about crossing me. But...it's not who I really am.'

Blake was taken aback by the surprise admission. Surprised at her insight. Surprised that she'd gone through life wary of everyone. Surprised at the cut-throat world she existed in—and he'd thought life in a warzone had been treacherous.

In the army, on deployment—trust was paramount. You trusted your mates, you stuck together, or you could die.

'Of course,' he said, determined not to feel sorry for this very well-off, very capable woman. She wanted to play the poor-little-rich-girl card, fine. But he wasn't buying. 'Don't worry about it. That's what you pay us for.'

Ava nodded, knowing that whatever it was that had passed between them before was going to go undiscovered. Clearly, Blake Walker was made of sterner stuff than even she'd credited him with. And she had to admire that. A man who could say no to her was a rare thing.

'Thanks. Have a good holiday.'

Blake nodded and turned to go and that was when it happened. He'd barely lifted his foot off the ground when the first gunshot registered. A volley of gunshots followed, slamming into the outside façade of Ava's house, smashing the high windows that faced the street, spraying glass everywhere. But that barely even registered with Blake. Nor did Ava's look of confusion or her panicked scream.

He was too busy moving.

He didn't think—he just reacted.

Let his training take over.

He dived for her, tackling her to the ground, landing heavily on the unforgiving marble tiles. Her wine glass smashed, the liquid puddling around them. His bad leg landed hard against the ground sucking his breath away, his other cushioned by her body as he lay half sprawled on top of her.

'Keep your head down, keep your head down,' he yelled over the noise as he tucked her head into the protective hollow just below his shoulder, his heart beating like the rotor blades of a chopper, his eyes squeezed shut as the world seemed to explode around him.

Who in the hell had she pissed off now?

CHAPTER TWO

EVERYTHING SLOWED DOWN around her as Ava clung to Blake for dear life. Her pulse wooshed louder than Niagara Falls through her ears, the blood flowing through her veins became thick and sludgy, the breath in her lungs felt heavy and oppressive, like stubborn London fog.

And as the gunfire continued she realised she couldn't breathe.

She couldn't breathe.

Her pulse leapt as she tried to drag in air, tried to heave in much-needed oxygen. She tried to move her head from his chest, seek cleaner air, but he held her firm and panic spiralled through her system. Her nostrils flared, her hands shook where she clutched his shirt, her stomach roiled and pitched.

Then suddenly there was silence and she stopped breathing altogether, holding her breath, straining to hear. A harsh squeal of screeching tyres rent the pregnant silence, a noisy engine roared then faded.

Neither of them moved for a moment.

Blake recovered first, grabbing his leg briefly, checking

it had survived the fall okay before easing off her slightly. 'Are you okay?'

She blinked up at him, dazed. 'Wha...?'

Without conscious thought Blake undertook a rapid assessment. She had a small scratch on her left cheekbone with a smudge of dried blood but that wasn't what caused his stomach to bottom out. A bloom of dark red stained her top and his pulse accelerated even further.

'Oh, God, are you hit?' he demanded, pushing himself up into a crouch. He didn't think, he just reached for her hoodie zipper and yanked it down. Just reacting, letting his training taking over. The bullets had hit the building high but they'd penetrated the windows and in this glass and steel interior they could have ricocheted anywhere.

'Did you get hit?' he asked again as her torso lay exposed to him. He didn't see her red bikini top or the body men the world over lusted after; he was too busy running his hands over her chest and her ribs and her belly, clinically assessing, searching for a wound.

Ava couldn't think properly. Her head hurt, her hand hurt, she was trembling, her heart rate was still off the scale.

'Ava!' he barked.

Ava jumped as his voice sliced with surgical precision right through her confusion. 'I think it's...my hand,' she said, holding it up as blood oozed and dripped from a deep gash in her palm, already drying in sludgy rivulets down her wrist and arm. 'I think I...cut it on the wine glass when it smashed.'

Blake allowed himself a brief moment of relief, his body flooding with euphoria as the endorphins kicked in—*she wasn't hit*. But then the rest of his training took over. He reached for her injured palm with one hand and pulled his mobile out of his back pocket with the other, quickly dialling 999.

An emergency call taker asked him which service he wanted and Blake asked for the police and an ambulance. 'Don't move,' he told her as he awkwardly got to his feet, grabbing the bench and pushing up through his good leg to lever himself into a standing position. He could feel the strain in his hip as he dragged his injured leg in line with the other and gritted his teeth at the extra exertion.

'I'll get a cloth for it.'

Ava couldn't have moved even if her life depended on it. She just kept looking at the blood as it slowly trickled out of the wound, trying to wrap her throbbing head around what had just happened. She could hear Blake's deep voice, so calm in the middle of the chaos, and wished he were holding her again.

He returned with a clean cloth that had been hanging on her oven door. He hung up the phone and she watched absently as he crouched beside her again and reached for her hand.

'Police are on their way,' he said as he wrapped the cloth around her hand, 'So's the ambulance.' He tied it roughly to apply some pressure. 'Can you sit up? If you can make it to the sink I can clean the wound before the paramedics get here.'

'Ah, yeh... I guess,' Ava said, flailing like a stranded beetle for a moment before levering herself up onto her elbows, then curling slowly up into a sitting position. Her head spun and nausea threatened again as she swayed.

'Whoa,' Blake said, reaching for her, his big hand covering most of her forearm. 'Easy there.'

Ava shut her eyes for a moment concentrating on the

grounding effect of his hand, and the dizziness passed. 'I'm fine now,' she said, shaking off his hand, reaching automatically for the back of her head where a decent lump could already be felt. She prodded it gently and winced.

'Got a bit of an egg happening there?' Blake enquired. 'Sorry about that,' he apologised gruffly. 'I just kind of reacted.

Ava blinked. Blake Walker had been magnificent. 'I'm pleased you did. I didn't know what was happening for a moment or two. Was that really gunfire?'

Blake stood, using the bench and his good leg again. 'Yep,' he said grimly. A sound all too familiar to him but not one he'd thought he'd ever hear again. Certainly not in trendy Hampstead Village. He held his hand out to her. 'Here, grab hold.'

Ava didn't argue, just took the proffered help. When she was standing upright again, another wave of nausea and dizziness assailed her and she grabbed him with one hand and the bench with the other. She was grateful for his presence, absorbing his solidness and his calmness as reaction set in and the trembling intensified. His arm slid around her back and she leaned into him, inhaling the maleness of him—cut timber and a hint of spice.

She felt stupidly safe here.

'Sorry,' she murmured against his shoulder as she battled an absurd urge to cry. 'I don't usually fall apart so easily.'

Blake shut his eyes as she settled against him. Her chest against his, their hips perfectly aligned. She smelled like wine and the faint trace of coconut based sunscreen. He turned his head slightly until his lips were almost brushing her temple. 'I'm guessing this hasn't been a very usual day.'

Her low shaky laugh slid straight into his ear and his

hand at the small of her back pressed her trembling body a little closer.

'You could say that,' she admitted, her voice husky.

And they stood like that for long moments, Blake instinctively knowing she needed the comfort. Knowing how such a random act of violence could unsettle even battle-hardened men.

The first distant wail of a siren invaded the bubble and he pulled back. 'The cavalry are here,' he murmured.

Blake stuck close to Ava's side, his hand at her elbow. 'Watch the glass,' he said as a stray piece crunched under his sturdy boots. Her feet were bare, her toenail polish the same red as her bikini.

He could hear the sirens almost on top of them now, loud and urgent, obviously in the street. He flicked on the tap and removed the cloth. 'Put it under,' he instructed. 'I'll go get the door.'

An hour later Ava's house was like Grand Central Station—people coming and going, crossing paths, stepping around each other. Uniformed and plain-clothed police went about their jobs, gathering evidence. Yellow crime-scene tape had been rolled out along the wrought-iron palings of her front fence and there were enough flashing lights in her street to outdo Piccadilly Circus in December. They reflected in the glass that had sprayed out onto the street like a glitter ball at some gruesome discotheque.

And then there was the gaggle of salivating paparazzi and the regular press who'd been cordoned off further down and none too happy about it either. Shouting questions at whoever happened to walk out of the house, demanding answers, calling for an immediate statement.

Safely inside, Ava felt her head truly thumping now. They'd been over what had happened several times with several different police officers and her patience was just about out. Her agent, Reggie Pitt, was there—a pap had rung him—to *protect her interests*, but it was Blake she looked to, who she was most grateful to have by her side.

'Is there anyone you know who'd do this to you or has reason to do this to you?' Detective Sergeant Ken Biddle asked.

Blake frowned at the question. The police officer looked old as dirt and as if nothing would surprise him—like one or two sergeant majors he'd known. But Blake had felt Ava's fear, felt the frantic beat of her heart under his and didn't like the implication.

'You think there's *any* reason to shoot up somebody's house and scare the bejesus out of them?' he growled.

The police officer shot him an unimpressed look before returning his attention to Ava. 'I mean anyone with a grudge? Get any strange letters lately?'

Ava shrugged. 'No more than usual. All my fan mail goes to Reggie and he hands anything suss on to you guys.' Reggie nodded in confirmation of the process.

Blake stared at her. '*You* get hate mail?'

Ava nodded. 'Every now and then. Pissed-off wives, guys who think I've slighted them because I didn't sign their autograph at a rope line, the odd jealous colleague. Just the usual.'

'But no one in particular recently?' Ken pressed.

Reggie shook his head. 'No.'

'We'll need to see them all.'

Reggie nodded. 'You guys have got a whole file of them somewhere.'

Ken made a note. 'I'll look into it.'

'Excuse me,' a hovering paramedic interrupted. 'We'd really like to get Ms Kelly to the hospital to X-ray her head and get her hand stitched up.'

The police officer nodded, snapping his notebook shut. 'Do you have somewhere you can stay for a while? I would advise you not to return here while the investigation is being carried out and the culprits are still at large. Hopefully we can close the case quickly but until then lying low is the best thing that you can do.'

Reggie shook his head. 'Impossible. She's up for a new commercial—she has a call back in LA in two days. And she's booked on half a dozen talk shows in the US next week to promote her new perfume.'

Blake bristled at the agent's obvious disregard for his client's safety—wasn't he supposed to put Ava first? But the police veteran was already on it.

'Cancel them.'

Reggie, who was a tall, thin streak with grey frizzy hair and round wire glasses sitting on the end of his nose, gawped like a landed fish. 'You don't just cancel, Detective Sergeant' he said, scandalised.

'Look, Mr Pitt, in my *very* long experience in the London Metropolitan Police force I can tell you that the best way to avoid trouble is to not go looking for it. Your client enjoys a high public profile, which, unfortunately, makes her *very* easy to find. Every pap in London knows where she lives, for example.'

'I'll get her a private security detail,' Reggie blustered.

'That is of course your prerogative,' the policeman conceded. 'But my advice would still be to lie low, which, by the way, would also be the advice any security person worth their salt would give you.'

Blake decided he liked Ken Biddle after all. He seemed solid. He obviously knew his stuff and didn't suffer fools gladly. And he clearly thought Reggie was an A-grade fool.

Reggie shot the police officer an annoyed look before turning to Ava. 'I'll get you booked into a hotel, darling. Get some security organised first thing in the morning.'

Blake also decided Reggie was an A-grade fool. 'I don't think you're listening, *mate*,' Blake said. 'I think the detective sergeant knows what he's on about. It sounds like it might be best for her to go dark for a while.'

'Ava, darling,' Reggie appealed to her. 'I think they're making a mountain out of a molehill.'

'Someone freaking shot up her house,' Blake snapped. 'Aren't you supposed to have her best interests at heart?'

'It's in Ava's best interests to keep working,' Reggie said through gritted teeth.

Ava's head was about to explode as they discussed her life as if she weren't there. Her hand throbbed too and she felt incredibly weary all of a sudden. She just wanted to lie down somewhere dark and sleep for a week and forget that somebody had shot up her house. Her beautiful, beautiful house.

'Do you think I could just go to the hospital and get seen to first?' she interrupted them.

It was all the encouragement the paramedic needed. 'Right. Question time is over,' he said, stepping in front of them all, and Ava could have kissed him as he took over as efficiently as he'd bandaged her hand earlier. 'We're taking her to the nearest hospital.'

Reggie shook his head. 'No. Ms Kelly sees a private physician on Harley Street.'

The paramedic bristled. 'It's nine o'clock at night. Ms Kelly needs an X-ray, possibly a CT scan. She needs a hospital.'

'The nearest hospital is fine,' Ava assured the paramedic, before Reggie could say any more.

'Are you okay to walk to the ambulance?' the paramedic asked her.

Ava nodded. 'I can walk.'

Blake checked his watch. He could be home and officially on holidays within half an hour. He could almost taste the cold beer he had waiting in his fridge to celebrate the end of having to deal with Little-Ms-Red-Bikini.

Except Ava Kelly looked far from the diva he'd pegged her as right now.

She looked pale and shaken, her freckles more pronounced. The small cut on her cheekbone was a stark reminder of what had happened to her tonight and part of him felt wrong walking away. Leaving her in the clutches of her shark-like agent. He hesitated. She wasn't his responsibility; he knew that. He'd simply been in the wrong place at the wrong time and she was a big girl—what she chose to do next was none of his business.

But he didn't feel she was going to get the wisest counsel from good old Reggie.

'You need me for anything else, Detective Sergeant?' he asked.

Ken shook his head. 'I have your details here if I need to contact you.'

Blake nodded. That was that, then. Duty discharged.

But before he could say goodbye her hand reached out and clutched at his forearm. 'Can you come with me?'

Blake looked at her, startled. *What the?*

Sure, he'd felt wrong about leaving her but he hadn't expected her to give him a second thought now she was surrounded by people to look out for her. And even though the same part of him—the honourable part—that had urged him to join the army all those years ago somehow felt obligated to see she was okay, the rest of him wanted nothing to do with Ava Kelly and her crazy celebrity life.

They were done and dusted. He was free.

He was on holiday, for crying out loud.

Not to mention he'd had enough of hospitals to last him a lifetime.

But her yellow-green eyes implored him and the doom he'd felt earlier today pounced. He sighed. 'Sure.'

Blake strode into the hospital half an hour later. He'd waited for the mass exodus of press chasing the blue lights of the ambulance at breakneck speed before he followed at a more sedate pace. Then he'd parked his car well away from the main entrance on one of the back streets. He wasn't sure why but when he spotted the bright lights of cameras flashing into the night as he got closer he was pleased he had.

Being photographed nearly every day on his arrival at Ava's and questioned *every freaking day* as to their relationship when clearly he was just the guy running the reno had been bad enough. He didn't need them spotting his car then adding two and two together and coming up with five.

He entered the hospital and enquired at the front desk and a security guard ushered him along the corridors to Ava. He clenched his hands by his side as he followed. Hospitals weren't exactly his favourite places and the antiseptic smell was bringing back a lot of unpleasant memories.

They stopped at a closed door where two other hospital security personnel stood, feet apart, alert, scanning the activity at both ends of the corridor. They opened the door for him and the first person he saw was Reggie speaking to a fresh-faced guy, clearly younger than his own thirty-three years, wearing a white coat and a harried expression. Reggie was insisting that a plastic surgeon be made available to suture his esteemed client's hand.

'That hand,' he said, pointing at the appendage in question, 'is worth a lot of money. I am not going to allow some *junior* doctor to butcher it any further than it already is.'

The doctor put up his hands in surrender. 'I'll page the on-call plastics team.'

'I need a *consultant*,' Reggie insisted. 'Someone who knows what they're doing.'

Blake caught a glimpse of the doctor's face as he backed out of the room. He looked as if he truly regretted coming to work today.

Blake knew exactly how he felt.

He was beginning to think Reggie was actually the bigger diva out of the two of them. He was surprised Ava put up with it. In three months he'd seen her fire an interior decorator, a PA and a personal trainer because they'd all tried to manage her. But she just lay docilely on the hospital trolley and let Reggie run the show.

He wasn't used to seeing her meek and mild.

But he supposed having your house shot at while you were inside it was probably enough to give anyone pause.

At least there was some colour in her cheeks now.

Ava looked up from her hand to discover Blake was in

the room. 'Oh, hi,' she said, levering herself up into a sitting position.

The last half an hour had passed in a blur and she'd been unaccountably anxious lying in the CT scanner. The doctor had assured her it was clear but it wasn't until right now she felt as if it was going to be okay. She hadn't been able to stop thinking about the way Blake had pushed her to the ground. It played over and over in her head.

He'd just reacted. In a split second. While she'd been confused about what was happening he was diving for her, pulling her down. She was on the ground before the noise had even registered as gunfire.

'I thought you'd skipped out on me.'

He returned her smile with a fleeting one of his own. It barely made a dent in the firm line of his mouth. Ava wondered how good he would look with a real smile. Would it go all the way to his dark blue eyes? Would it light up his rather austere features? Would it flatten out the lines on his forehead where he frowned a lot? Puff up the sparseness of his cheekbones? Would it break the harsh set of his very square jaw?

'I said I'd be here.'

Ava blinked at his defensive tone, his dialogue as sparse as his features. A man of few words.

'Everything check out okay?' he asked after a moment or two.

This time he sounded gruff and he glanced at Reggie, who was talking on his mobile, as if he was uncomfortable engaging in small talk in front of an audience. Ava was so used to Reggie being around, she barely noticed him any more.

'CT scan is fine,' she said. 'Just waiting for a plastic surgeon for the hand.'

He nodded and she waited for him to say something else but he looked as if he was done. Then Reggie finished his call and started talking anyway. 'I've booked you into your usual suite,' he said. 'We'll organise for a suitcase to be brought to you tomorrow.'

Ava watched the angle of Blake's jaw tighten at the announcement. 'I thought the point of lying low was to *not* go to any of her usual places?' Blake enquired.

The hardness in his tone made Ava shiver. *And not in a bad way.* Blake Walker was a good looking man. Not in the cut, ripped, metrosexual way she was used to. More in a rugged, capable, tool-belt-wearing kind of way. The fact that Blake Walker either didn't know it or didn't care about it only added to his allure.

The fact that Mr-Rugged-And-Capable was looking out for *her* was utterly seductive.

It had been a long time since someone had made her feel as if *she* mattered more than her brand. Her mother had cut and run when she'd been seventeen, leaving her to fend for herself in a very adult world, and Ava had never felt so alone or vulnerable.

Sure, she'd coped and it had made her strong and resilient—two things you had to be to survive in her world. But tonight, she didn't have to be any of those things because Blake was here.

'They have very strict security,' Reggie bristled. 'Ava will be perfectly safe there.'

Blake snorted in obvious disbelief. 'Have you cancelled her commitments yet?'

Reggie took his glasses off. 'I'm playing that by ear.'

'You know, in the army you learn that you don't secure an object by flaunting it in front of the enemy. I think you need to take the advice of the police and have her lie low.'

'If Ava put her career on hold for every whack job that ever wrote her a threatening letter she wouldn't have had much of a career.'

'Well, this whack job just signed his name in automatic gunfire all along the front of her house. I think her safety has to take precedence over her career for the moment.'

Ava had to agree. Frankly she'd been scared witless tonight. She took Reggie's advice on everything—he'd been with her a long time—but in this she needed to listen to the guy who had crash tackled her to the ground to keep her safe.

Who believed her safety was a priority.

Reggie hadn't been there. He couldn't understand how frightening it had been.

'I've known Ava a long time, Mr Walker,' Reggie said. 'A lot longer than you. And she's stronger than you'll ever know. She'll get through this just fine.'

'He's right, Reggie,' she said as the silence grew.

Just because she was strong, it didn't mean she was going to go down into the basement while she was home alone to investigate the thing that had gone bump in the middle of the night.

Because that was plain stupid.

And she hadn't had longevity in a career that wasn't known for it by being stupid. Strength also lay in knowing your limitations and accepting help.

After a solid sleep she might be able to think a little straighter, be a little braver, but tonight she just needed to feel safe.

'I'm pretty freaked out,' Ava continued. 'I think listening to the advice of the police is the best thing. At least for tonight anyway.'

'So where are you going to go, Ava?' Reggie demanded. 'You can't go back to your home and everyone else you know in London is as famous as you.'

Ava didn't even have to think to know the answer to that question. She just reacted—as Blake had done earlier tonight. 'I can go to Blake's.'

CHAPTER THREE

BLAKE GAPED AT Ava as her yellowy-green gaze settled on his face. '*What? No.*' He would rather amputate his other leg than have Ava Kelly as a house guest.

'Just for the night,' she said.

Blake shook his head. 'No.' She sounded so reasonable but he had to wonder if the bang to her head had sent her a little crazy.

He was on holiday, for crying out loud.

Reggie—bless him—looked at his client askance. 'Absolutely not!' he blustered. 'You don't know this man from a bar of soap.'

Blake watched as Ava pursed her perfect lips and shot her agent an impatient look. 'I have seen this man—' she pointed at Blake '—almost every day for the last three months. That's the longest relationship I've had with *any* man other than you, Reggie. This man—' she jabbed a finger in his direction again '—pulled me down to the ground and *shielded me with his body* while some nutcase fired bullets at my house.'

'And thanks to him you have a cut face, a gash in your

hand that requires stitching and an egg on the back of your head the size of a grapefruit.'

Blake bit off the bitter *you're welcome* that rose to his lips. He didn't expect thanks or praise for yanking her to the ground. His military training had taken over and he'd done what had to be done. What anyone with his background would have done. But he didn't expect to be accused of trying to maim her either.

Ava reached her hand out to Reggie and he took it. 'I was frightened, Reggie. Petrified. I couldn't…*breathe* I was so scared.' She'd been like that after her mother left—terrified for days. Then she'd hired Reggie. 'He makes me feel safe. And it's just for tonight.'

Reggie looked as if he was considering it and Blake began to wonder if he was invisible. 'Er, excuse me…' he interrupted. 'I don't know if either of you are interested but I said no.'

'You were the one who said she should lie low,' Reggie said, looking at him speculatively, clearly coming around to his client's way of thinking. 'You said the point was for her not to go to any of her usual places.'

Blake could not believe what he was hearing. They were both looking at him as if it were a done deal. As if his objections didn't matter in the face of the fabulous Ms Kelly's needs.

'I meant wear a wig, don some dark sunnies, throw on some baggy clothes and book herself into some low-rent hotel somewhere under a different name.'

'Please,' Ava said, the plea in her gaze finding its way directly to the part of him that was one hundred per cent soldier. 'I feel safe with you.'

'She feels safe with you,' Reggie reiterated, also looking at Blake, his hands in his pockets.

Blake shut his eyes and shook his head. 'No.' He opened his eyes again to find them both looking at him as if he'd just refused shelter to a pregnant woman on a donkey. 'For God's sake,' he said. 'I could live in a dive for all you know.'

Ava shrugged. 'I don't care.'

Blake snorted. 'Right. A world-famous supermodel who insisted on four thousand quid apiece tap fittings is happy to slum it?'

She shrugged again, looking down her nose at him this time, her famed haughtiness returning. 'I can slum it for a night.'

Blake's gaze was drawn to her mouth and the way it clearly enunciated each word. Her lips, like the words, were just…perfect. Like two little pillows, soft and pink with a perfectly defined bow shape. But somehow even they managed to look haughty—cool and mysterious. As if they'd never been touched. Never been kissed.

Not properly, anyway.

Kissed in a way that would get that mouth all bent out of shape.

If she really wanted to slum it—he could bend her perfect mouth well and truly out of shape.

A flicker of heat fizzed in his blood but he doused it instantly. Women like Ava Kelly didn't *really* want to slum it—no matter how much they thought they might. And he wasn't here for that. He'd entered into a contract with Ava to do the renos on her home. Nothing more.

Certainly not open up *his* home—*his* sanctuary—to her. And he'd held up his end of the bargain.

Duty discharged.

'I'm on holiday,' he said, his voice firm.

But Ava did not seem deterred. She just looked at him as if she was trying to figure out his price—and he didn't like it. Not one little bit.

'One million pounds,' she said.

Blake blinked, not quite computing what she'd just said. She actually *had* been figuring out his price? 'I'm sorry?'

'I'll give you that million pounds your sister needs.'

'Ava!' Reggie spluttered.

Blake gave an incredulous half-laugh, a half-snort. *'What?'*

Ava rolled her eyes. 'It's simple. I've had a very traumatic evening and I don't feel safe. I don't like not feeling safe.' It reminded her too much of when her mother left and she was supposed to be past that now. 'But you made me feel safe. And my gut tells me that means something. I've survived a long time in a cut-throat industry by going with my gut. So what's it going to be? You want the money or not?'

'Ava,' Reggie warned.

'Relax,' Ava told him. 'It's for a charity. It's all tax deductible.'

'Oh…well, that's okay, then.'

Blake shook his head as the heat that fizzed earlier flared again, morphing into white-hot fury. 'No,' he said through gritted teeth, 'it's not okay. You think you can just buy people? Just throw some cash around and get what you want?'

She shrugged that haughty little shrug again and he wanted to shake her. 'Everyone has a price, Blake. There's nothing wrong with that. This way we both get something we want.'

Blake ran a hand through his close-cropped hair. Joanna called it dirty blond and was forever trying to get him to grow it longer now he was out of the army. But old habits died hard.

Joanna.

Who he'd already failed once.

He'd told Charlie he'd think of a way to help their sister and the charity that meant so much to her—to all of them. And it was being presented to him on a platter.

By the devil himself. In the guise of a leggy supermodel.

A very bratty supermodel.

'You don't even know what the charity is,' Blake snapped, trying to hold onto his anger as his practical side urged him to take what was on offer.

'Yes, I do,' she said. 'I looked it up after we spoke earlier. A charity that supports our soldiers and their families. Very good for my profile, right, Reggie?'

Reggie nodded. 'Perfect.'

Blake had been in enough war zones to know when he was fighting a losing battle. He also knew he should do the honourable thing and offer her safe haven for free. But he resented how she'd manipulated him and if she could drop a cool mil without even raising a sweat then, clearly, she was good for it.

Still…it all sounded too good to be true.

'It's as simple as that?' he clarified. 'One night at my place and you'll give Joanna a million quid for her charity?'

Could he put up with a pain-in-the-butt prima donna for one night for a million quid?

'As simple as that.'

Blake regarded her. His practical side was screaming at him to take the cash but the other side of him, the one attuned to doom in all its forms, was wary as hell.

'You know there are thousands of men out there who would give anything to have me for a sleepover?'

She shot him a coy look from under her fringe and Blake glanced at her mouth. It had kicked up at one side as her voice had gone all light and teasy.

He didn't want that mouth *slumming* it at his place.

But one million quid was hard to turn down.

'Fine,' he sighed. 'But I leave in the morning for my holiday and you have to be gone.'

'Absolutely.' She grinned. 'I promise you won't even know I'm there.'

Blake grunted as his doom-o-meter hit a new high. *He sincerely doubted that.*

'*This* is where you live?'

Ava stared down at Blake's apparent abode floating in the crowded canal. They'd slipped out of a private exit at the back of the hospital into a waiting taxi after her hand had been sewn up with four neat little sutures and she'd been discharged. Blake had refused to tell even Reggie where he lived and she'd been too overwrought to care but even so *this* was a surprise. If someone had told her this morning she'd be spending the night on the Regent's Canal in Little Venice she'd have laughed them out of her house.

'You wanted to slum it.'

Ava took in the dark mysterious shape. 'People *actually* live on these things?'

'They do.'

Ava realised she couldn't have picked a better place to hide away—no one she knew would *ever* think to look for her here. But still…

She *was* used to five-star luxuries and, while she could

forgo four-thousand-pound taps, basic plumbing was an absolute must. 'Please tell me there's a flushing toilet and a shower with hot water?'

'Your fancy suite looking better and better?'

Ava was weary. It was past midnight. She'd been shot at, grilled by the police as if she were somehow at fault, then poked and prodded by every person wearing a white coat or a shiny buckle at the hospital.

She didn't need his taunts or his judgement.

Yes, she'd bribed him. Yes, she'd told him she could handle it. Yes, she was used to her luxuries. But, come on, she just needed to stand under a hot shower and wash away the fright and the shock of the day.

Why couldn't he be like any other salivating idiot who was tripping over himself to accommodate her? But, oh, no, her knight in shining armour had to be the only man on the planet who didn't seem to care that she was, according to one of the top celebrity magazines, one of the most beautiful women of the decade.

And she was just about done with his put-upon attitude. He was getting a million bucks and bragging rights at the pub to the story—embellished as much as he liked because she was beyond caring—of the night Ava Kelly slept over.

She felt as if she was about to crumple in a heap as the massive dose of adrenaline left her feeling strung out. All she wanted was a little safe harbour.

So, he didn't like her. She couldn't exactly say he was her favourite person at the moment either, despite his heroics.

Life was like that sometimes.

'Look, you're angry, I appreciate that. I railroaded you. But you have the distinct advantage of having being shot at before. I'm sure you're used to it. I'm sure it's *just another day to you.* Me, on the other hand…the only shooting I'm used to is from a camera lens. I promise I'll be out of your hair in the morning, but do you think in the interim you could just lose the attitude and point me in the direction of the hot shower?'

He didn't say anything for a moment but she could see the clenching and unclenching of his jaw as a streetlight slanted across his profile. 'You never get used to being shot at,' he said.

Ava blinked. His words slipped into the night around them with surprising ease considering the tautness behind them. It was a startling admission from a man who looked as if he could catch bullets with his teeth.

It struck her for the first time that he might have been more deeply affected by the incident than she'd realised. But his jaw was locked and serious. He didn't look as if he wanted to talk about it.

She did though—she really did. Suddenly she needed to talk about it as if her life depended on it.

Debrief—wasn't that what they called it in the army?

'Were you scared?' she asked tentatively, aware of her voice going all low and husky.

She was greeted with silence and she nodded slowly when he didn't answer, feeling foolish for even thinking that a brief burst of gunfire would rattle him. Charlie had told her Blake had been to war zones. He'd no doubt faced gunfire every day.

'Sorry, dumb question…'

The silence stretched and she was just about to say something else when he said, 'No, it's not.' Ava blinked at his quiet but emphatic denial.

'Any man who tells you that gunfire doesn't scare him is lying to you.'

Ava stared for a moment. If that had been Blake's impression of scared she had to wonder what level of danger would be required to actually make him look it.

Or maybe he just wasn't capable of strong emotion? *And wasn't that a big flashing neon warning sign?*

'But…you were so…' she cast around for an appropriate word '…calm.'

He gave a short laugh. She'd have to have been deaf not to hear the bitter edge. 'I'm sure my sergeant major, who chewed my arse off every day when I was a green recruit, would be more than pleased to hear that.'

He was being flippant now but she wasn't in the mood— she was deadly serious. 'I thought I was going to die,' she whispered.

His eyes were hooded as he stared at her and she wished she could see them, to connect with him. 'But you didn't,' he said.

His reminder was surprisingly gentle—not facetious like his last remark. 'Thanks to you,' she murmured.

Their gazes held for the longest time. It was quiet canal side and she realised they were standing close—close enough to feel as if they were the only two people in the world after what they'd been through together. To feel united. She waited for him to make some throwaway comment about the house saving her butt or the gunman being a lousy shot. He looked as if he was gearing up to say something.

But he seemed to think better of it, dragging his attention back to the longboat. She watched him step into the bow of the boat, then make a production of unlocking the door before he finally looked at her.

'You want that shower or not?'

The fridge was empty bar a six-pack of beer and Blake gratefully freed one of the bottles as the dull noise of shower spray floated towards him through the distant wall. He sat heavily on the nearby leather armchair, easing his leg out in front of him as he swivelled the chair from side to side. He was not going to think about Ava Kelly naked in his shower.

He was going to drink his beer, mentally plot his course for tomorrow, then crawl into bed.

Or the *couch* as the case might be.

Not his big comfortable king-sized sleigh bed he'd crafted with his own two hands—helping him forget the sand and the heat and the pain and the memories—specially custom-ised for the specs of the wide beam canal boat he'd restored. He could hardly make a guest—a female guest—sleep on the couch. Even if it was large and long and comfortable.

Especially considering Ava was shelling out one million pounds for the dubious *privilege*.

He could certainly hack it for one night. For one million quid he could hack just about anything.

Dear God—he was prostituting himself. A leggy blonde with killer eyes, money to burn and someone wanting her dead had made him an offer he couldn't refuse and he'd rolled over quicker than a puppy with a tummy scratch on offer.

He took a swig of his beer as he dialled his brother's number. 'It's after midnight.' Charlie yawned as he picked up after what seemed for ever. 'Someone better be dying.'

'Only me,' Blake snorted. Then he proceeded to fill his

brother in on the events of the evening including the details of the company car Charlie was going to need to pick up from the backstreets near the hospital.

Charlie seemed to come awake rapidly and found Blake's predicament hilarious after ascertaining everyone was okay. 'What is it about you that makes people want to shoot you? I swear to God, only you, brother dearest, could land yourself in such a situation.'

'Oh, it gets worse,' Blake informed his brother as he filled him in on the facts that had resulted in him cohabiting with one of the world's most beautiful women.

'Okay, let me get this straight. *She's* giving *you,* giving Joanna, a million quid to sleep at *yours* for the night.'

Blake shrugged. 'Essentially.' Charlie laughed and Blake frowned, suddenly angry with the world. 'What's so bloody funny?'

'Sounds like a movie an old girlfriend dragged me to once a lo-o-ong time ago. That one with Robert Redford and Demi Moore.'

Blake rolled his eyes. 'She's not asking for sexual favours, you depraved bastard. She's *scared.* She just needs to feel safe for the night. To hide away for a bit.'

'So you're not going to end up in bed together?'

The vehement denial was on Blake's lips before he was even conscious of it. 'I wouldn't sleep with her if we were the only two people left on earth.'

Blake could feel his brother's eyebrow rise without having to see it. 'Why not? I would and I've been happily married for a decade.'

Blake knew his brother would no sooner sleep with Ava Kelly than he would. He was as besotted with Trudy now as he had been ten years ago. 'Sure you would.'

'Okay,' his brother conceded. 'Hypothetically. You gotta admit, she looks pretty fine in a bikini.'

'She's a snooty, heinous prima donna who caused us endless trouble with all her first-world crap,' Blake said, lowering his voice. 'I don't care how good she looks in a bikini.'

'Maybe you should.' Suddenly Charlie's voice was dead serious. 'It's okay to let yourself go every now and then, Blake. Being beautiful and rich and opinionated isn't a crime. That's our demographic, don't forget.'

Blake shifted uncomfortably in his seat. He'd seen so much poverty and desperation in his ten years serving his country. It felt as if he was selling out to admit his attraction to a woman who represented everything frivolous and shiny in a society that didn't have a clue how the other half lived. But he was too tired to get into all of that now.

'She's here for one night and, in case you've forgotten, she's a client.'

His brother snorted. 'Not any more, she's not. Which makes it perfectly okay to…take one for the team, so to speak. How long has it been since you got laid?'

Blake shook his head, not even willing to go there. Just because he chose *not* to spend every night with a willing woman didn't mean he was about to die from massive sperm build-up as his brother predicted. He worked hard every day and came home every night to a place that he'd created that was far removed from the hell he'd known in foreign countries.

That meant something these days. More than some cheap sexual thrill.

Besides, Ava Kelly was so off-limits she might as well be sitting on the moon. If he wanted to get laid, he could get laid. He didn't need to do it with a woman who'd bugged him almost from the first day of their acquaintance.

No matter what vibe he suspected ran between them.

'Is Trudy awake?' Blake tisked. 'You know, your raging feminist wife who I happen to like much more than you? She'd be disgusted by your attitude.'

'She thinks you need to find a woman too. One who can tie you in knots and leave you panting for more.'

Blake didn't say anything for a long time. 'She's in *trouble*, Charlie,' he said as he contemplated the neck of his beer. 'She just needs to feel safe.'

Charlie was silent for long moments too. 'Then just as well she chose one of Her Majesty's best.'

'No,' Blake said. 'I'm just a builder, remember? *And* I'm on holiday. If she didn't come with a million-dollar price-tag attached I'd have walked away.'

Charlie laughed and Blake felt his irritation crank up another notch. 'Whatever helps you get through the night with Ava *freaking* Kelly in the next room.'

Blake snorted at the undiluted smugness in his brother's voice. 'I hate you.'

'Uh-huh. Ring me in the morning before you set out. I want details.'

Blake grimaced. 'Right, that's it, I'm telling Trudy, you grubby bastard.'

Charlie laughed. 'Are you kidding? She's going to want to know every minute detail. She has a huge girl crush on Ava Kelly.'

Blake sighed, briefly envying his brother's easy, loving relationship. 'Maybe she can come here for the night and they can play house together.'

Charlie laughed. 'Only if I can watch.'

Blake shook his head. 'Goodnight.'

'Night,' Charlie said and Blake could hear the laughter in his voice. 'Don't do anything I wouldn't do.'

Blake hung up the phone, not bothering to answer. There was no risk of that. He was tired. *And* annoyed. He wanted this night over and done with. He wanted her gone.

He did not want to *do* anything with Ava Kelly.

Blake lifted the bottle to his mouth and threw his head back, drinking the last mouthfuls in one guzzle. He contemplated getting another one but the shower spray cut out, spurring him into action.

He needed to change the sheets on the bed. And he needed to be out of his bedroom before she was done.

Five minutes later he'd just pulled the coverlet up over the fresh sheets and was reaching for a pillow to change the case when he sensed Ava watching him. He glanced behind him where she leaned heavily against the doorway as if it was the only thing keeping her up.

'You don't have to give me your bed,' she said, the world's weariest smile touching the corners of her mouth. 'Really. Any horizontal surface will be fine.'

He'd loaned her an old shirt and some loose cotton boxers and his clothes had never looked so good. The shirt slipped off one shoulder, outlined her small perky breasts and fell to just below her waist. The band of his obviously too big boxers was drawn by the string to its limits then turned over a couple of times, anchoring low on her hips. A strip of flat tanned belly was bare to his gaze.

And a lot of leg.

Not chicken legs like those he sometimes caught on the telly when shots of skinny models walking up and down catwalks came on the news. They were lithe and shapely. And a perfect golden brown—like the rest of her. He'd avoided looking at them the last three months but it was kind of difficult now they were standing inside his bedroom.

And he'd always been a leg man.

Oh, the irony.

He dragged his gaze up. Her hair was damp and looked as if it had been finger-combed back off her forehead, her face was scrubbed clean, her freckles standing out, her cheeks a little pink from the hot water, the tiny nick a stark reminder of why she was here.

She could have been the girl next door except somehow, even in a scruffy T-shirt, baggy boxers and her eyelids fluttering in long sleepy blinks, she managed to look haughty.

To exude a you-can't-touch-this air.

Should have had that second beer.

'How's the head?' he asked, ignoring her protest, returning his mind and his eyes to the job at hand, stripping the case off the pillow.

'Sore,' Ava said, pushing off the door frame to the opposite side of the bed, grabbing the other pillow and stripping it, managing it quite well despite the handicap of her bandaged hand.

Blake quelled the urge to tell her to leave it. He didn't want her here in his bedroom. Not while he was in it too. It all seemed too domesticated—*too normal*—especially after being shot at only a few hours ago. The bed was big and empty. Big enough for the two of them. And the night had been bizarre enough without him wondering how many times he could roll Ava Kelly over on it.

Or how good those legs would feel wrapped around his waist.

'Did you take those tablets the doc gave you?'

She nodded. 'Just now.' Then she yawned and the shirt rode up a little more. He kept his gaze firmly trained on her face. 'Sorry. I'm so tired I can barely keep my eyes open.'

Blake knew intimately how shock and the effects of adrenaline could leave you sapped to the bone. He threw the pillow on the bed, then peeled back the covers. 'Get in. Go to sleep.' *Soon it will be morning and you'll be gone.* 'You'll feel better tomorrow.'

She smiled at him again as she threw her pillow on the bed. 'I couldn't feel any worse,' she said, crawling onto the bed, making her way to the middle on her hands and knees. Blake did not check out how his shirt fell forward revealing a view right down to her navel.

He just pulled up the covers as Ava collapsed on her side, her sore hand tucked under her cheek, eyes closing on a blissful sigh, her bow mouth finally relaxing. 'Night,' he said.

She didn't answer and for a moment he was struck by how young she looked. For the first time she didn't look haughty and untouchable—she looked humble and exhausted.

Vulnerable.

And utterly touchable.

Who in the hell would want to kill her? Or had they just been trying to scare her? In which case it had worked brilliantly. Something stirred in his chest but he didn't stay long enough to analyse it.

Ava *freaking* Kelly was lying right smack in the middle of his bed—no way was he sticking around to fathom weird chest stirrings. Or give his traitorous body any ideas.

He stalked towards the door, an image of her long legs keeping him company.

Don't look back. Don't look back.

'Blake.'

Crap. He halted as her soft voice drifted towards him. *Don't look back. Don't look back.*

'Thank you,' she said, her voice low and drowsy.

Blake locked tight every muscle he owned to stop from turning around. He didn't need a vision of her looking at him with sleepy eyes from his bed. Instead he nodded and said, 'See you in the morning.'

Then continued on his way out of the room.

He did not look back.

CHAPTER FOUR

AVA'S PHONE WOKE her the next morning and for a moment she was utterly confused by her surroundings. What was the time? What day was it? Where the hell was she?

Where the hell was her phone, for that matter?

Her head felt fuzzy and her eyes felt as if they'd been rolled in shell grit. If this was a hangover then it was a doozy. The distant trilling of her musical ringtone didn't help. Inside her woolly head, her brain knew that it needed answering but her body didn't seem to be responding to the command to do something about it.

Then a shirtless Blake walked into the room and it all came crashing back to her. The gunshots, the police, the hospital.

Little Venice. Canal boat. Big, big bed.

His hair was damp as if he'd just had a shower, she noted absently as he strode towards her. And he had a hairy chest. Not gorilla hairy, just a fine dusting of light brown hair over meaty pecs and continuing down his middle covering a belly that wasn't ripped but was still, nonetheless, firm and solid. The kind of belly a man didn't get from the gym.

She stared at his chest as it came closer. The men in the circles she moved in were *all* ripped and smooth—every muscle defined, all hair plucked or waxed into submission. It took a lot of upkeep. Whereas Blake didn't look as if he'd ever seen the inside of a salon.

She'd bet her last penny Blake was the kind of guy who thought grooming belonged in the domain of people who owned horses.

'Yours, I believe,' he said, striding towards her and passing it over.

Ava took it with her good hand, ignoring its ringing for a moment. 'What time is it?' she asked.

'Time to go.' His voice was low and serious—brooking no argument. 'I'll make you a coffee.'

And then he turned on his heel and left her staring after him. *Obviously not a morning person.*

Ten minutes later, with Detective Sergeant Biddle's caution weighing on her mind, Ava followed her nose and her growling stomach in the direction of the wild earthy aroma of freshly ground coffee beans. With nothing as basic as a mirror in his room she'd pulled her messy bed-hair back into an equally messy ponytail and hoped Blake didn't have any wild expectations of what a supermodel should look like first thing in the morning.

She needn't have worried—he barely acknowledged her, instead enquiring how she drank her coffee, then handing her a mug. 'Thank you,' she said automatically, wrapping her bandaged hand around it even though the morning already held the hint of another warm day.

He didn't acknowledge that either so she wandered over to one of the two cosy-looking, dark-leather armchairs and sank into its glorious depths. She watched his back as he stared out of the large rectangular picture window above the sink in the kitchen area.

She could just make out the bustle of London traffic over his shoulder—could just hear it too. The sights and the sounds of the city gearing up for another work day. She soaked it in for a moment, preferring the low hum to the ever-expanding quiet inside the boat.

Her gaze fell to his broad shoulders.

She'd never really speculated about what lay beneath his clothes before—she'd been too busy wondering why he seemed completely immune to her. *Off the market? Playing hard to get? Gay?* But there'd been something about his naked, work-honed chest this morning that was more than a little fascinating.

With his back stubbornly turned, Ava had no choice but to look around her. She sat forward as she did, inspecting the luxurious interior. It was nothing like the old cheap and cheerful clunker she'd been on as a teenager with a friend's family—wider too if her memory served her correctly.

Everything about the interior screamed class. High quality.

Money.

The three stairs down which she'd trudged last night as she'd entered the boat opened into a very large, open-plan saloon dominated by two classy leather armchairs and gorgeous wide floorboards. It was the floors that drew her eye now—a gorgeous blonde wood polished to a honey sheen. In contrast the walls were dark-grain wood panelling until halfway up, then painted an elegant shade of champagne.

A massive flat-screen television sat in a narrow , built-in smoky glass and curved chrome cabinet on the wall opposite her along with a bunch of other expensive-looking gadgetry. On the other side of it, and sitting out from the wall slightly, was an old-fashioned pot-belly stove that no doubt heated the entire boat in winter.

The saloon flowed into a galley-style kitchen, all granite and chrome with no expense spared on the high-end appliances from the full-sized fridge to the expensive Italian coffee machine. They gleamed in all their pristine glamour.

Opposite the kitchen, on her side of the boat, was a booth-style table, with red leather bench seats.

Beyond the dining and kitchen area was a smaller saloon. A dark-leather sofa, looking well worn and comfy, dominated the space. A pillow and some bedding were folded at one end, reminding Ava that Blake had given up his bed for her last night.

Another coffee table with a massive laptop and piles of paper appeared to act as a work space. At right angles to the couch, on the wall that divided off the living area from the rest of the boat, stood a chunky wooden bar. The bottom boasted ten, mostly full, rows of wine and above that was a shelf crammed full of every alcoholic spirit known to man.

Beyond the wall she knew was the bathroom, and beyond that his bedroom. What was beyond that, she didn't know. The back of the boat, she guessed. What was that called? The stern?

Ava dragged her wandering mind back to the interior. All the dark leather, chrome and granite gave it such a masculine feel, like a den or a cave, yet the use of blonde wood and large windows gave it light and space. It was hard to believe that such a small area could feel so big.

Blake had done a fantastic job.

For she had absolutely no doubt that Blake had been responsible for the gorgeous interior—it had his signature all over it. She only had to look at the nearby coffee table to know that. It had been constructed out of a thick slab of dark timber complete with knots. It reminded her of the craftsmanship of her kitchen bench and she placed her coffee mug on it, then ran the flats of her palms across the polished surface.

It was absolutely stunning. She couldn't not touch it.

She glanced up at Blake—still contemplating the London traffic. Clearly he wasn't going to make conversation.

'I'm sorry I barely noticed the boat last night. It's...gorgeous.'

Blake should have known it was too much for her to just drink her coffee and let him call her a cab. He hadn't slept very well last night, which had done nothing for his mood. He took a calming breath and turned round to face her.

She was sitting in the lounge chair cross-legged. His shirt was still falling off one shoulder and acres of golden leg were on display.

She really needed to go.

Ignoring Ava's considerable charms when she'd been a picky, exacting client had been easy enough. Ignoring them when she was a damsel in distress and in the confines of his boat—not so easy.

'Thank you,' he said.

Ava waited for him to elaborate some more but nothing was forthcoming. 'I'm assuming it's all your own work?' she prodded.

Blake nodded. 'Yes.'

'Hobby, passion or business?'

Blake wondered if she'd shut up if he told her the truth. 'Therapy.'

Ava blinked. That she hadn't expected. She wanted to

know more but, as Blake checked his watch, she doubted he was a man who elaborated. 'Is it a narrow boat? I went on one when I was thirteen. It seems wider than what I remember?'

Blake stifled a sigh. 'It's a wide beam,' he said. 'It's twelve foot across. Most narrow boats are about half that.'

'Yes… I remember there wasn't a lot of space…a wide beam seems like a much more liveable option?'

He shrugged and her eyes tracked the movement of his very nice broad shoulders. He'd tucked her head right in under them last night and they'd felt so solid around her—as if they really could stop bullets. She could still remember how safe she'd felt under their protection.

'It depends what you want. Wide beams can restrict your travel options. Not all canals are made for wider boats.'

Ava was about to ask more but Blake drained the rest of his coffee, placed the mug on the sink, then turned to her and said, 'You done?'

Ava, whose mug was almost empty, understood the implied message. *Time to go.* Her night was up. She too drained the contents of her drink, then held the mug out towards him. 'That was delicious. Do you think I could possibly have another? I'm not really a morning person. Coffee helps.'

Blake contemplated telling her no. Something he doubted Ava Kelly had ever heard. But his innate manners won out. He strode towards her and took the mug, turning away from her and her temptingly bare shoulder instantly. He set about making her another cup, conscious of her gaze on his back the entire time.

It unsettled him. *Blake didn't like being unsettled.*

'That was Ken Biddle on the phone.'

Blake, who had been trying to tune her out, turned at the news. 'They got him?' he asked hopefully.

'No.' She shook her head and the ponytail swung perkily. Blake had a thing for ponytails.

'But they have some promising leads,' she said. 'They're confident they're closing in.'

'That's good, then,' Blake said, turning back to the coffee machine, away from ponytails.

'He thinks I'll only need to lie low for a few more days.'

A presentiment of doom settled around him at the casual note in her voice. 'What are your plans?' he asked, stirring in her three sugars.

Ava watched as Blake's shoulders straightened a little more. She took a calming breath. The second Ken had asked her to keep her head down for a little longer there'd only been one option for her. 'Well, actually… I was hoping I could…stay here.'

Blake dropped the teaspoon and it clattered against the stainless-steel sink. *No. Freaking. Way.* He turned slowly around, careful to couch his distaste at the idea in neutrality. 'But I'm going on holiday,' he said, determined to be firm but reasonable.

'Exactly,' Ava nodded. 'That's why it's perfect—don't you see? I could boat sit for you, at least until they find the person who shot up my home anyway. I can be anonymous here—certainly no one's going to be looking for me on the Regent's Canal and it'll look like someone's still home here, for a little while anyway. It's win-win.'

'The boat *is* my holiday,' he said, trying to stay calm in the face of her barefaced cheek. 'I'm going up the Kennet and Avon to Bath, giving the boat her first decent run since I finished the fit-out.'

Ava was only temporarily discouraged as the appeal of spending some time afloat, traversing the English countryside on Blake's gorgeous boat, took hold.

If she had to lie low, she might as well do it in style, right? 'Even more perfect. I can come with you.'

This time Blake didn't even bother to act as he stared at her as if she'd lost her mind. Had she seriously just invited herself along on his holiday? 'No.'

'Oh, come on, Blake, please?' Ava climbed out of the chair, feeling at a distinct disadvantage with him glowering down at her. 'It'll just be for a few days and you won't even know I'm here, I promise.'

Blake folded his arms as she neared. He hadn't believed that statement last night and, after a horrible sleep on his couch, he believed it even less this morning. 'No.'

'Look, I'll pull my weight. Seriously, I can help with locks and things. They're much easier with an extra set of hands. And I can... I can cook,' she said, desperately hoping that the way to this man's heart—or his empathy at least—was through his stomach. 'I am an *excellent* cook.' She marched over to his fridge. 'I can keep you well fed,' she said as she opened it, 'while you—'

Ava blinked. The fridge was bare save for a mauled six-pack of beer and a carton of milk.

'Good luck with that,' he said dryly.

Ava turned to face him as the door closed. 'You have no food?'

'I'm expecting a delivery in the next hour or so. It'll stock me up for the trip.'

'Yes, but...what do you normally eat?'

Blake shrugged. 'I have coffee. And there's plenty of places to eat on the riverside.'

Ava shook her head. Oh, man, he was going to want to marry her after a few days of her cooking. 'In that case,' she tisked, 'you definitely need me along for the ride.'

Blake could not believe what he was hearing. 'So, Ava Kelly supermodel, darling of the paparazzi, is going to be content to act like some anonymous little hausfrau-cum-first-mate, cooking and cleaning and being a general dogs-body?'

Blake refused to think what other services she might be able to render.

Ava folded her arms too. 'I think I could manage it for a few days.' She wasn't going to be swayed by his taunts. She'd been called worse things and had worked incredibly hard since she was fourteen. Getting away with him for a few days was the perfect solution.

'Reggie won't like it,' Blake warned.

She gave him one of her haughty, down-the-nose looks. 'You leave Reggie to me.'

Blake rubbed a hand through his hair at her persistence. Just his luck to be saddled with a woman who wasn't used to hearing no. 'Look,' he said, changing tack. 'You want to lie low on a canal boat for a few days? I think that's a great idea. Knock yourself out. There's plenty along here for hire.'

Ava was starting to get ticked off. People didn't usually argue with her so much. They were generally falling over themselves to agree with her. But not Blake. Oh, no.

And she didn't understand why. She knew, in the way that women did, that he found her attractive. And it hadn't been in the way he checked her out, rather in the way he'd *avoided* checking her out. Which was just as telling.

And, *when she hadn't been miffed by it*, she'd admired him for it.

He'd been the consummate professional and that had been a nice change. A man talking to her as if she had a brain and an opinion that mattered and who dealt with all her little niggles and foibles with patience and efficiency was a rare find. He hadn't been condescending. He hadn't humoured her. He'd been straight up. Yes or no or I'll get back to you.

But, sheesh, would it seriously be that repugnant to spend a few days in her company?

'Yes, but *you're* on *this* boat,' she said. Ava walked slowly towards him. She had to make him understand just how last night had shaken her. 'I feel safe with you, Blake.' She pulled up in front of him, standing close enough to reach out and touch him, far enough away not to freak him out. 'If this guy…this person…does happen to find me…if he tried to harm me…or snatch me…'

Ava shuddered just thinking about it. She didn't like knowing there was someone out there who wanted to hurt her. And she was more than happy to lie low until they were caught.

'Don't get me wrong, I wouldn't go down without a fight. I'd kick and scream like a madwoman. But a little extra protection never goes astray, right?'

Blake gaped at the fairy dust she was snorting. *The woman didn't have a clue.* 'Are you crazy? I only have *one* leg. If he *snatches* you, I'm going to be next to useless. My days of running fast are long gone.'

Ava blinked at him and looked at his legs. She'd noticed him limping occasionally but had just figured he'd injured himself somehow. 'You…do?'

'You didn't *know*?' He lifted the jeans on his left leg to reveal the titanium skeleton of his artificial limb. 'Why do you think I limp?' he demanded.

She looked at it askance, as if it were some unsightly blemish. He supposed someone who made a living out of defining physical beauty would be uncomfortable when confronted with physical imperfection. And then she looked at him with something akin to pity in her eyes and ice froze in his veins.

'Not so pretty, huh?' he taunted as he let the fabric drop back down.

Ava felt awful. She hadn't realised. Her cheeks pinked up—he must think her terribly self-involved. Not only had he pulled her to the ground last night, but he'd also given up his bed for her. Both actions completely without regard for his own safety or needs.

'How'd it happen?' she asked, searching his face.

'It doesn't matter,' he growled.

It *mattered* to her. 'Did it happen when you were deployed?'

Blake glared at her for a moment before answering. 'Yes.'

Ava didn't know what to say without sounding trite or macabre. She settled for, 'I'm sorry,' but even that sounded inadequate. 'I had no idea.'

Blake dismissed her apology with an annoyed wave of his hand. 'It's not your fault,' he said.

'That doesn't mean I can't be sorry it happened.'

Blake was taken aback by the quiet conviction in her voice. So many people said sorry as if it was the standard platitude expected of them. Ava sounded as if she really meant it. 'Thank you,' he said. 'But clearly, I'm not the type of protection you need.'

Ava frowned. 'Are you kidding? You're a war hero.'

He snorted. 'I'm not a hero.' He was so sick of the way

that was bandied around. 'I was just in the wrong place at the wrong time.'

'You get blown up and live to tell the tale? That's pretty heroic if you ask me.'

'Nah. That just makes me lucky.' *Unlike his brother-in-law.*

Ava didn't believe that for a moment. She couldn't even begin to imagine the resilience it must have taken to recover from something so life-altering. 'Well, it'll do me,' she said.

Blake was just about over her stubborn insistence. Time to stop being Mr Nice Guy. 'No,' he said, turning away from her to stare out of the window above the sink. *Case closed.*

Ava was even more convinced now that Blake Walker was her man. But how did she get through to him when his resistance seemed impenetrable? She stared at the set of his shoulders casting around for something…anything.

In desperation an idea came to her and she threw it down like the last card she knew it was. 'I noticed yesterday when I was researching your sister's charity that they don't have a high-profile patron?'

His back stiffened noticeably and Ava felt a moment of triumph. Ah, *that* got his attention. *Joanna.* He'd reacted the same way yesterday when she'd asked who Joanna was.

His *sister* was the chink in Blake's armour.

Blake turned around slowly and glared at her and she was even more convinced.

'So?' he said, his voice dropping dangerously low.

She shrugged. 'Every successful charity needs a patron. A big name. Take me with you until the police give me the all-clear and I'll do it. I'll become their patron. I'll attend every event and fund-raiser, I'll represent their interests, speak on their behalf, I'll work tirelessly.'

Blake was once again left speechless by Ava's impulsive offer. Joanna would be over the moon to have a woman of Ava's stature on board. 'Let me get this straight,' he clarified. 'For a few nights on *this* boat you're going to not only give a million pounds to my sister's charity but commit to being its patron?'

Ava nodded. 'Yes.'

Blake shook his head incredulously. 'Why? If you're really concerned about your safety, it'd be much cheaper and a lot less work for you to hire a professional bodyguard.'

'I'm not afraid of hard work, particularly in the name of a good cause,' she said, stepping in a little closer to him, to try and convey how strongly she felt. 'And I can afford it. As for the professional, I don't need one. I just need to lie low. But I also need to feel safe while I'm doing it and *you,* as we've already established, make me feel safe. I can't put a price on that.'

Blake still couldn't wrap his head around it all. 'I think you have more money than brains.'

Ava smiled at him then as she sensed him weakening. 'Please, Blake. If not for me, then do it for Joanna.'

Blake shook his head at her as soft lips curved up in perfect unison, nothing haughty about them now. Clearly she thought she had him all figured out. And certainly she'd found his soft underbelly. She'd made him an offer he couldn't refuse—and she knew it.

But if she thought she could just crook her finger at him and he'd come running, then she could think again. 'Does anyone ever say no to you, Ava?'

Ava let herself smile a little bigger. Was that resignation? 'I do believe you've said no to me several times this morning already.'

CHAPTER FIVE

BLAKE OPENED HIS mouth to tell her *no* one more time—Joanna or no Joanna—but her phone interrupted them and she turned away, heading back to the lounge chair where she'd left it.

'Crap,' she muttered as she recognised her mother's number on the screen. She did not want to have to deal with her now but, she knew from experience, her mother was best kept on a tight leash. 'I'm sorry, it's my mother,' she apologised to Blake.

Blake gestured with his hands for her to take it then turned back to the sink and his contemplation of London to give them some privacy. Except that was kind of hard in the confines of the boat with her standing just a couple of metres away.

To say Ava sounded strained was an understatement. Even with his back to her he could pick up the tension laced through her words. He hadn't realised how much he'd learned about the subtleties of her voice in three months, which was surprising considering Ava's mother seemed to be doing most of the talking.

He didn't hear Ava say once she was okay or retell the events of last night so from that he had to assume her mother hadn't asked. Ava seemed to be asking her not to do something, her request becoming less and less polite.

Then he heard, 'I'm with…a friend.' And, 'I can't say.' Then finally, 'I'll fill you in when I get back—just don't give any interviews in the meantime.'

Her mother was going to the press?

There didn't even seem to be a goodbye; he just heard Ava's phone clatter onto the dining table.

When he turned around she was staring out of the window currently flooding in sunlight, her back erect, her messy ponytail even now begging him to pull it out.

'You okay?' he asked.

She turned around slowly and the look on her face was in stark contrast to her self-assurance just prior to the phone call. She looked a lot like she had last night—vulnerable.

'I'm fine,' she dismissed, her voice weary. She lifted a hand and absently rubbed the muscles in her neck. The action caused all sorts of interesting movement inside her shirt. *His* shirt.

Blake kept his gaze firmly trained on her face—he was used to doing that. 'You know, you could have told your mother where you were.'

Ava gave a soft snort. 'Ah…no. She's the last person I would tell.'

Hmm. *Interesting.* 'I take it you two don't get along?'

'You could say that,' Ava said dryly.

'Doesn't she approve of you being a model?'

Ava gave a harsh laugh. 'Oh, no, she approves, all right. She's one of the original pageant queens. The same old story, never quite made it herself so lived out her glory through me. Put me in my first baby competition when I was a month old.'

Blake blinked at the bitterness in her tone. 'Let me guess—you won?'

Ava smiled despite the slight derision in his voice. 'I won every one I ever entered until I was two and my father put his foot down and insisted that I have a *normal* life.'

'But you got back into it later?'

'After Dad died, we were in a lot of debt. Mum worked really hard doing two jobs to keep the house payments going and then I won a nationwide search for the newest young model and...'

Blake nodded. 'You hit the big time.'

'Yes.'

He frowned. 'So...you two disagreed about the direction of your career?'

'No. Mum hired an agent for me. An old school friend of hers... Paul. He managed every aspect of my career, for those first three years. My jobs, my money, my image. I depended on him for everything—it was him, me and Mum against the world.'

Blake still wasn't sure what the issue was. 'That's...bad?'

'It is when he's embezzling your money behind your back and sleeping with your mother, screwing with her head so even when his treachery was discovered she stood by him, defending him in court, imploring me to give him a second chance, then leaving the country with him *and my money*, marrying him and leaving me, at seventeen, to fend for myself.'

A cold fist pushed up under Blake's diaphragm and he took two steps towards her. How could a mother abandon her teenage daughter like that? 'She chose him over you?'

Ava's lips twisted. It had been a long time since she'd let herself revisit how betrayed, how vulnerable, she'd felt. Dwelling on the past wasn't her thing. But it *had* been a most unusual twelve hours.

'Yes. She did. "You're going to be all right, darling," she said. "You're young and beautiful with contracts lined up out the door thanks to Paul," she said. "I need to be loved too," she said.'

Blake rocked his head from side to side as tension crept into his traps. He finally understood what Ava had meant last night when she'd said she'd learned early not to trust. She'd been betrayed by two people closest to her—no wonder she was a control freak.

'What happened?'

'They were divorced four years later. Mum came home trying to ingratiate herself but I'd already hired Reggie, who taught me three very important things—trust nobody, *always* control your own money and your agent is *not* your friend.'

Blake made a mental note to apologise to Reggie if they ever met again. He'd obviously armed Ava well in the years since her betrayal. *Maybe a little too well.*

It was a difficult concept for him to wrap his head around. Blake's family were big and loud and intrusive and totally in each other's business and that had been hard to take when all he'd wanted to do was hide away and lick his wounds.

But he'd *never* doubted for a minute that they had his back.

'Our relationship is…strained,' Ava said, her hand dropping from her neck.

'I'm sorry,' he said. 'You should be able to trust family.'

Ava couldn't agree more but sadly, for some people, that

wasn't possible. 'Don't be sorry,' she said. 'Just take me with you.'

She sounded so utterly defeated and Blake knew there was no way he could deny her when clearly, despite being surrounded by people, she was pretty much alone in the world. She didn't even have family to lean on, for crying out loud. Her father dead. Her mother abandoning her in favour of her agent.

Her *don't screw with me* act was just that—an act.

She needed someone she could trust and it looked as if it was going to be him.

A decision that would no doubt come back and bite him hard on the arse.

'Patron, huh?'

It took a second for the meaning of Blake's words to sink in. A spark of hope spluttered to life inside Ava's chest. 'Is that…a yes?'

Blake nodded, her caution so uncharacteristic it only added to his conviction. 'That's a yes.'

Ava felt a rush of relief flow through her veins so hot and hard it was dizzying. She smiled as tension leached from her muscles. Then suddenly, feeling light, feeling that every-thing was going to be all right, she laughed. Then she gave into temptation, crossing the short distance between them and throwing herself against his chest, her arms around his neck.

'Thank you, thank you,' she said, hugging him hard.

Blake sucked in a breath as the full length of her pressed into the full length of him and he liked how she fitted per-fectly. Her ponytail swung a little in his direct vision and he wasn't sure he could survive a few days with it scream-ing *pull me out, pull me out*.

He shut his eyes. *Safe haven, man.* You're her safe haven.

'Okay, okay. No touchy-feely stuff,' he said, prising her off him, setting her back, but then somewhere out on the street a loud bang cracked the air and she practically leapt back into his arms.

Blake's hands automatically slid onto her waist. 'Hey, it's okay,' he said after a moment or two, the frantic beat of her heart thudding against the wall of his chest as her hands clasped his T-shirt. 'It's just a car backfiring.'

Ava barely heard him over the whoosh of her pulse through her ears but she understood from his non-verbals—his calm, solid presence—that there was no imminent threat. 'Sorry.' She grimaced as she pulled away shakily. 'I'm going to be jumpy for a while.'

Her freckles were standing out again amidst the sudden pallor of her face, the tiny graze on her cheek looking more macabre as Blake's hands slid to her elbows. 'It's fine,' he said, squeezing her gently.

'Thank you,' she murmured, her voice thready.

Blake nodded, his gaze drifting to her mouth before pulling back again. *Not going there.* He took two steps away, putting some distance between them.

'I have conditions,' he said.

It took Ava a few seconds to shake the feeling that the boat had rocked beneath her. And as her mouth tingled she knew it wasn't just from the fright. She cleared her throat.

'Conditions?'

Blake nodded. 'Yes. Two.'

Ava regarded him steadily for a moment. 'Okay then, let's hear them.'

He held up one finger. 'No one knows our location. Not Reggie. Not your PA. Not any of your gal pals. You're supposed to be totally incognito and I'm supposed to be having a peaceful holiday. I don't want it turned into a three-ring circus when someone lets it leak to the paparazzi.'

Ava nodded. She was happy with that—she didn't want her location broadcast either, which was why she hadn't told her mother. 'Fine. I'll let Reggie know we're going away for a few days and—'

'No,' Blake interrupted. 'He knows how to get hold of you. He doesn't need to know you're leaving town.'

'I suppose not.' Ava frowned at him; his indigo eyes were shuttered. 'You don't like him much, do you?'

Blake gave a dismissive shrug of his shoulders. He liked him a lot better now he knew some more about the man. 'The question is do I trust him? And I don't.'

Anyone who was willing to put Ava's career ahead of her protection didn't have her best interests at heart as far as he was concerned. It might make him a great agent but it didn't say a lot for him as a human being.

Ava gave Blake a half-smile. She knew that Reggie came across as utterly money-grubbing but that was why she'd hired him. Her career was the most important thing to Reggie and he was *exactly* who she'd needed in her corner after sleazoid Paul.

Reggie was all about the business. 'He's the only person I *do* trust.'

In this industry where she trusted no one—she put her faith in Reggie's instincts and his ball-breaking rep. He wouldn't rat her out because he took his client confidentiality seriously—it was his calling card.

Blake thought it was sad that the only person Ava trusted had perpetuated her mistrust of others. 'Well, let's agree to differ on that one,' Blake said.

Ava allowed her smile to become full blown. 'I have a feeling that's going to happen a bit,' she murmured.

Blake grunted. *So did he.* Her smile reached out between them, making her mouth even more appealing, and for a moment he forgot that she'd bribed her way into his life—into his much coveted peaceful holiday. When she looked down her nose at him all haughty it was easy to remember that she was a spoiled prima donna who liked getting her way.

But when she smiled at him like a woman smiling at a man, things got a little hazy.

'Two,' he continued, dragging his mind off her mouth and taking another step back for good measure. 'You have to be in some kind of disguise. There's no point in you coming with me to lie low when you look like—'

Blake paused as his gaze skittered down her body and back up again. His boxers and T-shirt did nothing to disguise her body. Not with her bare shoulder, her hair swinging in a ponytail and legs that went on for ever.

He waved his hand in her general direction. 'That.'

A few months ago Ava would have been insulted at the brief survey of her body and his apparent dismissal. But she knew him well enough now to know that he was just too disciplined to give too much away.

She guessed that was the soldier in him.

She looked down at her body, smoothing her hands down the front to the exposed slice of her belly, which, thanks to a hundred crunches a day and regular visits to the tanning salon, she knew to be flat and toned and tanned and pretty irresistible to most people with a y chromosome and a pulse.

'Like what?' she enquired, looking at him innocently.

Blake gritted his teeth, not fooled by her little performance one iota. 'Like Ava *freaking* Kelly,' he said.

She quirked an eyebrow. 'Should I shave my head?'

Blake gave her a sardonic smile. 'I don't think we need to go quite that extreme. Would hate to incur the wrath of Reggie any more than I have. But maybe a wig? Or definitely hats, something to tuck your hair into. And big dark sunglasses.'

His gaze drifted to those legs again. 'And baggy clothes. No itty-bitty shorts and tiny little T-shirts. *No* red bikinis.' For his own sanity if nothing else. 'No make-up. Nothing that draws attention to you.'

Although he had the feeling she could be wearing a sack and men would still look.

'I don't want some yobo at a pub along the canal recognising you and deciding he can make a quid or two ratting you out to the media. Plain is what we're after,' he said. 'Baggy, too big, shapeless—they are your friends.'

Ava blinked. None of those things had *ever* been her friends. Camouflage wasn't what she did. She spent all her working hours flaunting and flattering her body. 'Well, *gee whiz*, that sounds like fun,' she said, her voice heavy with derision.

But still, she could see his point. People had made a lot of money out of her in the past by tipping off the press. And with the furore that was bound to have been whipped up by last night's incident and her going underground—she'd have a pretty price on her head.

And she couldn't help but wonder what it would be like to be utterly anonymous, even for a short while. *Not* famous for a few days? She'd been on magazine covers and in the public eye since she was fourteen years old and sometimes she was just so tired of the constant attention and scrutiny.

'They're my conditions.' Blake shrugged. 'Take it or leave it.'

'Take it.' She nodded. She could put up with any fashion sin for a few days. 'Not exactly clothes I have in my closet though.'

Blake shook his head. 'Too unsafe to go there, anyway.' He strode over to the dining table where his mobile was on charge, pleased to be out of range of her in his clothes. 'I'll ring Joanna,' he said. 'We can break the news to her about her windfall, then you can tell her what you need and she can buy it for you then bring it here.'

Ava blinked. 'I can't expect your sister to just drop everything and go clothes shopping for me.'

'Trust me—' he grimaced as the dialling tone sounded in his ear '—when she learns about your generosity, she's going to want to have your babies.'

Finally, almost three hours later, they were under way. The groceries had been delivered and put away. So had the second lot that Ava had ordered when she'd realised how basic the first lot were. And an excitable, starry-eyed Joanna had come and gone. The only people who knew that Ava Kelly was on the boat with Blake were Joanna and Charlie.

And Blake trusted them with his life.

God knew between the two of them they'd practically brought him back from the brink with sheer will power alone. All those days and nights when life hadn't seemed worth living, they'd been there getting him through. Loving him, fighting with him, crying with him, getting drunk with him. Whatever it had taken, they'd done it.

It was slow going through the busy London canal system as he headed west along the Paddington arm of the Grand

Union Canal. Tourists were out enjoying the narrow-boat lifestyle either through private hire or with the many companies that ran canal transport services. The weather was glorious—the sky blue and cloudless, the sun warm, a light breeze ruffling his shirt—and had it not been for his unwanted passenger, it would have been perfect.

Although, to be fair, Ava was exceedingly easy company—so far anyway. Dressed in a pair of baggy shorts that came past her knees and a loose T-shirt with her hair tucked into a cap and dark, saucer-like sunglasses completely obscuring her eyes, she looked like any other tourist standing at the helm. Watching the world go by as she soaked up some rays and intermittently answering half a dozen calls, all from Reggie.

Sure, if someone looked hard enough they'd be able to make out the slenderness of her legs, the erect, model-like way she held herself, the superb bone structure of her heart-shaped face. But at a quick glance she looked as far removed from a supermodel as was possible and no one gawked at her, nudged each other and whispered or pointed their fingers.

She was just another one of them.

Mission: Disguise Ava Kelly, accomplished.

But what surprised him was how much she didn't seem to care. Having braved a rabble of paparazzi most mornings for three months, who she kept sweet with the occasional gourmet snacks and frequent photo opportunities, he'd have thought she'd be missing the limelight already. But she seemed content to rub shoulders with him and make occasional conversation.

Not long after they'd cast off she'd disappeared for a while then reappeared twenty minutes later with two crunchy bread rolls stuffed with ham off the bone, crisp lettuce, a slice of sweet pineapple, seeded mustard and rich mayonnaise. Blake had been hungry but hadn't wanted to waste any more time getting away to stop and eat something, so the food had hit the spot.

'Thanks,' he'd said as he'd licked mayonnaise off his fingers and tried not to notice her doing the same.

'The least I can do is feed you,' she'd said.

And feed him she did. Popping down below every now and then, bringing back blueberry muffins warm from the oven one time and a bowl full of cut fresh strawberries another.

By the time they reached Bulls Bridge it was six in the evening, but with the days still staying light until nine they descended into Brentford via the Hanwell locks.

And Ava proved herself even handier with a windlass. Blake knew that the trip he'd planned out would be slow and physically demanding for one person and he'd been looking forward to the challenge. But having Ava operate the locks while he drove the boat did speed things up considerably.

He held his breath as she chatted with people from other boats at each lock, waiting for the moment of recognition. But it never came and they were mooring along a towpath in Brentford just before eight.

The smell of cooking meat hit Blake twenty minutes later as he stepped inside from making sure the boat was secure and helping the novice narrow-boaters who had pulled their boat up in front of them. His stomach growled at him.

But it was nothing to the growl his libido gave as his eyes fell on a scantily clad Ava shaking her very delectable booty to the music that was obviously filling her ear buds.

The baggy was gone.

She was in a short flimsy gown that fell to mid-thigh and seemed to cling to every line and curve of her body from the hem north—it certainly clung lovingly to every contour of her butt. It was tied firmly at the waist, which was just as well as she sang along, in a truly terrible falsetto, and stirred something in a bowl.

Ava Kelly might have excelled at a lot of things but singing was not one of them.

Her hair was wet and down. Her feet were bare.

The supermodel was back.

After standing gawping like an idiot for a moment or two he moved closer and cleared his throat to get her attention.

Ava looked up from the dressing she was mixing. 'Oh, sorry.' She grinned, pulling the ear buds out. 'This song always gets me going. Are you hungry? I'm cooking steak. Plus I think this is probably *the* most divine salad dressing—' she dipped her finger in and rolled her eyes in obvious pleasure '—I've ever made.'

A dark drop of the balsamic-looking liquid landed on her chest, just above the criss-cross of her gown at her cleavage and, God help him, Blake's gaze followed it down. She scooped it up quickly but not before he'd taken note of unfettered breasts. Not a line or a strap mark visible through the clinging fabric of the gown.

He looked back at her face. Hell yeh. He was hungry all right.

Freaking starving.

'I thought we'd eat at the pub up the tow path,' he said.

'Tomorrow,' she dismissed, waving her hand and turning back to the job at hand. 'If you want to have a shower, you have six minutes until these babies are ready.'

Blake shook his head. He was going to need much more

than six minutes to calm himself down—even in a cold shower. He'd settle for alcoholic fortification instead.

'Drink?' he asked as he opened the fridge and grabbed the long neck of a boutique beer, twisted the lid off and took a long deep pull.

Ava looked up, watching the movement of his throat as he swallowed. There was something very primal about a man guzzling beer. She wondered what he'd do if she sauntered over and slicked her tongue up the hard ridge of his trachea.

She looked back at the steaks cooking in the pan. 'I'll have one of those, thanks.'

Blake cocked an eyebrow. 'Beer. *You* drink beer?' he said as he pulled one out for her and cracked the lid.

Ava heard the surprise bordering on derision in his voice and looked at him. 'Yes. Why? What do you think I drink?'

'Wheatgrass smoothies,' he said, remembering how she often came home from somewhere in her shrink-wrapped gym gear slurping on something disgustingly green.

She took the beer from him. 'Not when I'm relaxing.'

Blake leaned against the fridge. 'Champagne? Fruity cocktails? Dirty cowboys…or whatever the hell those shots are called that women seem to like to knock back in bars these days.'

Ava laughed. He didn't sound as if he approved. 'I like champagne and fruity cocktails, sure. But underneath it all, I'm just a pint-of-beer girl.'

Blake snorted in disbelief.

But, just to prove him wrong, she tipped back her head and took three very long, somehow very erotic, swallows. His gaze drifted down her undulating neck, to her breasts again—not too big, not too small and extremely perky— then back up. She was smiling at him with that knowing little half-smile of hers, her eyelids shuttered, when his gaze returned to her face.

Ava's pulse skipped a beat as their gazes locked for long moments. Heat bloomed to her belly and breasts, making them feel heavy and tight. She toyed with the neck of the bottle, running her fingers up and down the frosty glass as their stare continued.

After three months of scrupulous politeness, he was finally looking at her. Really looking at her.

And there was a *very* definite vibe between them.

'You shouldn't judge a book by its cover, Blake,' she murmured.

Blake sucked in a breath as her voice broke the connection between them. Her cover had sure fallen away fast these last twenty-four hours since being shot at. And he wasn't sure he liked the unpredictable woman in front of him. At least he knew who the other Ava was.

'I'll set the table,' he said, turning away, grateful for something to occupy his mind and his hands.

Other than putting them all over her.

CHAPTER SIX

Ava was starving by the time they sat down to juicy steaks, a fresh green salad and warm rolls from the oven complete with garlic butter she'd whipped up.

'Where'd you learn to cook?' Blake asked as he bit into his steak. His groan of satisfaction caused a spike in her pulse and a pull in her belly that was entirely sexual.

She shrugged. 'My dad. He was a chef. My earliest memories were being in the kitchen cooking with him. It was our thing we did together. I think I learned through osmosis.'

Blake quirked an eyebrow. 'You said he died?'

Ava nodded. 'When I was twelve. Heart attack.'

Blake watched as the drying strands of her hair glided over each other, the caramel burnished to toffee beneath the expensive down lights. 'That must have been hard.'

Ava nodded. He didn't know the half of it. 'Emotionally and financially. He had his own restaurant, which was almost bankrupt. It was a tough time...'

Blake could tell she didn't want to elaborate on the subject of her father any more and he didn't push as he shifted the conversation to their route tomorrow. He understood.

He was a private person too, he wouldn't want a virtual stranger prying into his personal business either.

The army shrink had been bad enough.

But it wasn't what he'd expected from her. From what he'd witnessed these last few months she seemed to live so much of her life as an open book. In a goldfish bowl. It had been easy—and far preferable—to think of her as a *brand*, a *product*. As *Ava Kelly, Inc.* instead of a flesh and blood woman.

Except for the last twenty-four hours. Sleeping in his bed, cooking in his kitchen, dancing at his sink.

In her gown.

Her very short, very clingy gown.

Ava slid out of the booth and picked up their plates after they'd finished eating.

'Leave them,' Blake said, also standing. 'I'll do them.'

'I don't mind,' Ava said. She was very aware that she'd hijacked his holiday, completely disregarding his plans and inserting herself into the middle of them. The least she could do was make herself useful. She didn't want Blake to think that her jet-set lifestyle had made her too big for her boots—she didn't expect to be waited on.

He grabbed the plates. 'You cook, I clean. House rules.'

Ava resisted for a moment, holding onto the edges as he pulled them towards him, dragging her in close to him, just two dinner plates separating them. She became aware again of *the vibe*. It hummed between them, filling each breath with his essence, enervating each heartbeat with anticipation. What would he do if she just leaned in and kissed him? That was the beauty of being tall—she didn't even have to go up on tippy-toes. His mouth was right there, level with hers.

'*Boat* rules,' she murmured.

Blake swallowed as she looked down her nose to his mouth, lingering there for a moment before returning to his eyes. He had no doubt she was thinking about kissing him and he quelled a sudden urge to lick his lips for fear of what it might give away.

Or encourage.

She seemed to sway a little closer and he quelled his next urge—to do a little kissing himself—too. Instead he gave a brief smile and took a step back, the plates transferring easily to his hands. 'Boat rules,' he agreed briskly.

Ava blinked as he turned away from her and headed to the sink, gathering wits that had taken up residence somewhere south of her belly button. She'd been sure he'd been about to kiss her.

So why hadn't he?

Was he one of those guys who got a little stage fright when it came to kissing her? Intimidated by her being a *supermodel*? Performance anxiety? Funny, he hadn't struck her as the type. She'd have thought the whole good-with-his-hands thing would translate to the bedroom.

'Okay, fine,' she said, finally finding her voice. 'Your boat, your rules. Knock yourself out.' She looked around the saloon, for a distraction, her gaze falling on the television. 'Would you think me terribly vain if I turned the news on and see what they're saying about me?'

Blake shook his head—anything was preferable to her standing there, her gaze boring into the back of his head. 'Nope. Remote on top of the telly,' he said. 'I'll make us a coffee.'

Because staying awake all night on a caffeine high thinking about nearly kissing her in a gown that should have come with a highly flammable label was just what he needed.

Not.

Ava tucked her legs up underneath her as she flipped through the channels till she found some news. Apart from updates from Reggie concerning her situation, she'd been out of touch with the big wide world for twenty-four hours. And it was good to get engrossed in something other than Blake's big brooding presence.

By the time he joined her fifteen minutes later she was reasonably absorbed in the news. He passed her a mug and was just settling himself into the other chair when a segment on her was introduced. There was nothing new—no arrests, no suspects, just speculation as the events were recounted. And a little air of mystery as the anchor woman speculated as to Ava's whereabouts now that the famous model had *gone underground.*

There was footage of her house and brief glimpses of her last night in the back of an ambulance as well as loads of file footage of her strutting catwalks, shooting a commercial and her smiling at the gaggle of paparazzi as she left her house, patiently moving through them as they surrounded her.

Blake shook his head at the rabble, half of the photographers walking backwards—completely hazardous—to ring every last photo op out of her. 'I don't know how you do that every day,' he said.

Ava shrugged. 'You get used to it.'

Blake shuddered. 'I couldn't live like that, with every minute of my life on show, a camera in my face.'

'It's okay,' Ava said, swivelling the chair to face him as the segment finished and the anchor starting talking about a string of break and enters. 'I've had a camera in my face since I was fourteen so...' She took a sip of her coffee. 'You just make boundaries,' she said. 'Outside I'm public property, inside I'm off-limits.'

Blake thought that sounded like a fairly limited right to privacy. 'But aren't there days you just want to tell them to—?' He stopped himself short of the phrase he would have used had it been him and Charlie talking.

'Do something anatomically impossible to themselves?' she suggested.

Blake chuckled. 'Yes.'

Ava sighed. The sort of life she led was hard for every-day people to understand. 'I *have* to court them, Blake. I'm twenty-seven years old. That's bloody *ancient* in the circles I move in. *And* I'm getting older every day. The paparazzi, the press...they keep me current, keep me in the hearts and minds of people. Good press, good image equals strong in-terest. One day soon the interest, the jobs, will dry up but until then Reggie says the paps can make you or break you.'

Blake snorted. 'Your agent is a shark.'

'Yeh.' She grinned. 'That's why I hire him. Someone who's sole job it is in life to look after my career. He does it well. I wouldn't be where I am today without him.'

Blake rolled his eyes. 'Oh, please, you make him sound like he's some saint doing it out of the goodness of his heart. I'm sure he's being more than adequately compensated.'

'Absolutely,' she confirmed as she absently traced the hem of her gown where it draped against her thigh with her index finger. 'He's doing it for his fifteen per cent. But at least *that's* an honest business transaction. Telling the difference was a very hard-earned lesson for me.'

Blake heard the sudden steel in her voice and was reminded again that for all her privilege Ava hadn't exactly had it easy. His gaze dropped to where her finger was doodling patterns on her hemline. With her legs tucked up under her, the gown had ridden up some more until it was sitting high on her thighs. It covered what it needed with a little to spare but that still left a whole lot of long, golden leg on display.

Legs he'd managed not to look at or think about for three months. Legs that he was fast developing a fascination with.

She looked at him then and he dragged his gaze back to her face with difficulty. 'Have you thought about what you're going to do after?' It was the first thing that came into his head that didn't involve her legs. 'When the jobs dry up?'

She shook her head as her finger stroked and swirled.

'Not really. I won't *have* to do anything. I'm financially secure. I have the perfume line I'm launching and Reggie's always fielding offers from media and fashion to keep me busy. But I don't know,' she said, shaking her head. 'I've been modelling since I was fourteen... I *honestly* don't really know anything else.'

Her finger stopped tracing as she looked at him speculatively. 'What about you? Did you have some exit strategy for leaving the army?' Her gaze dropped to his leg then back to his face again. 'Were you...prepared?'

Blake grunted. 'No.' Certainly not prepared for the way he'd left. 'I was a career soldier. Never thought about getting out.'

Something shimmered in her eyes that looked a lot like

connection as she lazily swivelled the chair back and forth. He couldn't remember ever having a conversation with a woman like this—apart from his shrink. Ever really wanting to—*including his shrink*.

He hated those conversations.

But, for some reason, it felt as if Ava was in a unique position to truly understand—looking down the barrel of shortened career prospects.

'What *did* you do?' she asked.

Blake looked down at his left leg. 'Spent a load of time in hospitals of one description or another.' High-dependency wards, surgical wards, rehab wards. Surgeon's offices, prosthetic offices, shrink's offices.

He could feel the intensity of her gaze on his face as he stared at his leg. Feel it like an invisible bloom of heat swelling in his peripheral vision.

'I meant after that...?'

She said it so softly, Blake had to turn his head to catch it. *A mistake*. Her finger had stopped its hypnotic path but her gown clung, her hair was now dry, her mouth was soft and, for some inexplicable reason—maybe it was sharing last night's frightening episode—he felt he could talk to her. He'd spent three months avoiding it. Avoiding talking to her about anything other than the reno and her haughty demands.

But she seemed different now. Vulnerable, stripped back, human. Like a woman. Not a brand.

'Well, let me see... I spent the first six months with my head up my arse feeling sorry for myself, consuming large amounts of alcohol and pissing off just about everybody who knew and loved me.' He grimaced. 'I wouldn't recommend you do that.'

Ava smiled. 'Check.'

'Then I got a phone call—' He stopped himself before he went any further.

He'd only ever told the shrink this stuff. And while he felt some weird kind of kinship with her he just couldn't go there. Prior to last night he'd been hard put sharing with her something as basic as his relationship with Joanna. Now, twenty-four hours later he was ready to spill his guts?

It was confusing and he didn't like it.

He raked a hand through his hair. 'Let's just say I got some...news—' news that had shocked him to the core '—and I realised that there *were* worse things than having one leg and that it was time to stop acting like the only person in the world who'd ever had something bad happen to them and get on with it.'

'And that's when you and Charlie formed the company?'

'No.' Blake shook his head. 'That's when I bought this boat.' He looked around the interior. 'I spent a year fixing her up. Stripping her right back and rebuilding her from the hull up.'

He gave a self-deprecating smile. 'Manual work can be quite therapeutic.'

'I can imagine.' An image of Blake in a tool belt as he'd worked on her kitchen bench rose in her mind. Would he have taken his shirt off when he'd been working in the hull of the boat?

He nodded. 'Lots of things to tear down and rip out. Lots of pounding and hammering and loud noisy power tools.'

Ava laughed at the note of relish in his voice. 'Be still my beating heart.'

Blake found himself laughing too. 'It's a guy thing.'

'I'm guessing.' She grinned. 'So...your brother saw what

a great job you'd done here and you decided to start the company?'

'No. It evolved out of another company, that Charlie had started five years before that. I was doing some labouring for him in between doing up the boat.' He paused. 'Charlie and Joanna were determined to keep me busy…' He grimaced. 'And then, because I have an engineering background, I helped out with some design things and the company was really starting to take off, but it needed a cash injection to get across the line so he offered me a partnership.'

Ava let it all sink in. So not only was he a war hero but he was an engineer who could design stuff and was so good with his hands he could make his own designs too.

Clearly, he had plenty to fall back on.

'Wow.' She blinked. 'Somehow, despite what most would call an *exceedingly* successful life, you've just made me feel completely inadequate. All I know how to do is wear clothes.'

Blake chuckled at her blatant self-deprecation. 'Hey.' He smiled. 'People need clothes.'

She shot him a quelling look. They both knew people didn't need clothes a person had to earn six figures to afford. 'I'm going to be totally screwed when the next big thing pushes me off my pedestal.'

Blake laughed again. There was something very sexy about profanity coming from her posh mouth. 'Don't be discouraged. I hear they love ex-celebrities for those reality television shows the world can't seem to get enough of.'

Ava shuddered. 'No, thanks. I'm not going on any bug-infested island where I have to pee in a hole in the ground and build my own shelter.' She took in his big broad shoulders and those capable hands. 'Not without you anyway.' Although now the idea was out there it might be worth it to watch Blake in his natural element. Maybe with his shirt off?

A soft fizz warmed her belly as her gaze made it back to his face. 'Sorry.' She lifted and dropped a shoulder in a half-shrug. 'I just can't imagine me there, can you?'

Blake sobered as he followed the movement and the ripple effect it had across her chest. Her breasts jiggled slightly, the fabric clinging to them moulded the movement to perfection. He tore his gaze away, met her knowing eyes.

Crap.

'Before today, no,' he said, ploughing on, determined not to acknowledge either his perving or her awareness of it. 'But I've been impressed with how very unpretentious you've been today. There's been no hissy fit over the cut on your face or hand. No hysteria about career-ending scars. No sitting on your butt expecting to be waited on. You got in and helped *and*—' his gaze flicked briefly to her legs then back again '—current attire excepted, you disguised yourself just as I asked. I know bagging up couldn't have been easy for you, but you did *and* you were very generous about it.'

Pleasure at his praise flooded warmth through her system and heat to areas where pleasure meant an entirely different thing. She wasn't sure why *his* praise meant anything to her. She lived in a world that sung her praises daily—and she pretty much took that for granted. She certainly wasn't looking for more. Certainly not from him.

Maybe it was because he'd been so hard to engage during those three months he'd spent at her house? Ava was used to male attention, hell, she *loved* male attention and generally took it as her due. But there'd been a very definite line between them that *he'd* drawn in thick black marker.

Nothing personal had crossed between them.

He'd been polite and respectful, prompt with her queries and had kept his eyes firmly trained on her face. He'd been one hundred per cent professional, resisting slipping into an easier, more casual relationship she'd tried to establish.

Always holding himself back.

She hadn't been able to break through his reserve. And that had been frustrating, galling and intriguing all at once.

But these last twenty-four hours had seen that line disappear. And here he was actually praising her.

Even checking her out.

She wondered how much further she could take it. It could be fun to find out, to push him a little. Discover his buttons. They were both adults and the night was theirs. She smiled at him as she stroked her palm down her neck to her chest, three fingers finding their way under the lapel of the gown.

'It's a lot easier to be baggy on the outside when you're spoiling yourself underneath it all and there's nothing quite like sexy underwear to make you feel sexy all over no matter what you're wearing,' she said.

Blake frowned. Was she saying what he thought she was saying?

'Joanna agreed,' Ava added. 'She didn't think I should have to let myself go altogether.'

'I bet she did,' he said. His sister was always on some mission to set him up. *But Ava freaking Kelly was way out of his league.*

She ought to know he'd had enough drama in his life without inviting a diva in.

'And,' Ava continued, 'I have to say, she has a real eye for classy lingerie. Not that I have any of it on right now.'

Blake tried and failed not to follow the stroke of her fingers as they played with the lapel. Her fingers rubbed along the edge of the fabric, lifting it slightly, exposing a little more flesh to his view.

The air grew thick between them and Ava sensed that the time was ripe to make a move. It didn't faze her. She knew what she wanted and she had the confidence to go after it.

Some people called that bold. She called it decisive.

'I've been thinking,' she said, her gaze firmly trained on his face, 'about the sleeping arrangements tonight.'

She stopped. Waited. He wasn't objecting. Wasn't bolting. He was watching, intently, his eyes on her hand.

'I don't think it's fair that you should give up your bed for me again and so I thought…maybe we could…share…?'

Those words finally did the trick, dragging Blake's head back from the edge and his eyes back from her cleavage.

Was she…propositioning him?

'You mean…you lie on one side with your head at the top and I lie on the other with my head at the bottom and we both get a good night's sleep?'

Ava shook her head. 'Nope.'

The secret little smile playing at the edges of her mouth, the way she looked down her nose at him with blatant sexual interest, did strange things to Blake's equilibrium. It was just as well he was sitting down.

She *was* propositioning him.

There was nothing touch-me-not about this Ava. This Ava was very, very touchable.

Blake's heart rate slowed right down in his chest as blood rushed south. His brain might be saying no but other parts of him weren't listening. Ava Kelly was trouble with a capital T. And he'd had more than enough trouble to last him a lifetime. Being a supermodel's plaything for a night or two might be every man's wet dream but his doom receptors were working overtime.

'I…don't think that would be such a good idea,' he said.

Ava blinked. Not the response she was used to. *Frankly she thought it was the best idea she'd had in a long time.* But Blake *had* spent three months keeping his distance and she already knew he was the strong, serious, cautious type.

Well, she didn't get to the top of her game by taking no for an answer and she sure as hell wasn't going to tonight either.

'Okay.' She placed her coffee mug on the coffee table and stood. She walked the three paces that separated their chairs until the outside of her right thigh was brushing the outside of his. She looked down at him.

'I know this isn't what we planned. And I know this isn't the kind of relationship you and I have had to this point. But I'm just going to put this out there.'

Ava's pulse fluttered madly and her breathing sped up as she lifted her right leg to step over his thighs, placing them between her legs. He shifted in his chair and she shut her eyes briefly as the denim scraped erotically against the sensitive inner flesh of her bare thighs.

When she opened them again his indigo gaze was staring straight at the knot of her belt as if he was trying to undo it through mind power alone. Heat flared behind her belly button and tingled at the juncture of her thighs.

'I'm attracted to you, Blake,' she said. 'I think you're attracted to me. We have tonight…maybe a few nights on this boat together and we're both adults. I'm just saying…

we could have some fun. That wouldn't be such a bad thing, right?'

Right. Blake knew she was right. He had no problems with two consenting adults having a little fun together. He used to indulge in quite a lot of *fun* before the explosion. But since...

Sure, there'd been women but *fun* didn't really fit into his vocabulary these days. Sex was a lot of things—communication, connection, stress relief. An activity engaged in to relieve a build-up of testosterone.

Pleasurable. Enjoyable. Necessary. But not fun.

Because having fun felt wrong.

'Blake?'

He was still staring at that knot and she could tell he was teetering on the edge. She reached for it then, slowly worked at it with fingers that shook just a little until it slid loose and the belt fell to her sides. The two front edges of the gown slid over each other parting slightly.

She was still covered—barely.

Blake swallowed against a throat that felt as dry as the desert. His erection surged against his jeans and the urge to open her gown, to see more than a glimpse of cleavage, thrummed through his system like the steady backbeat of a tropical downpour. He glanced up at her to tell her to step away but her cat eyes looked back at him, her mouth parted.

He sucked in a breath and curled his fingers into the lounge beside him. 'Hell, Ava.'

Ava felt dizzy from the longing in his low husky growl and she squeezed her legs hard against his to stay grounded.

'I've shocked you, haven't I? I'm sorry. Not very lady-like I guess. I've always been a little too forthright for my own good.'

Blake snorted as her posh ladylike voice made excuses for her brazen proposal. In the grand scheme of shocking, it barely rated as a blip. 'I don't give a rat's arse for ladylike,' he growled.

He liked a *woman* between the sheets, not some snooty *lady* who was worried about getting her hair messed up.

Ava might talk a little on the posh side and have that haughty little look of hers well rehearsed but her frank proposition, the way she'd thrown her leg over him just now, the sureness of her fingers as she'd undone her belt, told him she was no *lady* in the bedroom.

'Well, okay then,' Ava said, smiling down at him. Their gazes locked and she waited for him to reach for her, to make the first move. *Or the next one, anyway.* But she could still see a glimmer of that famous reserve, that wariness in his eyes.

Surely he wasn't…intimidated? Blake didn't strike her as the kind of guy that needed his hand held, but if that was what was required…

CHAPTER SEVEN

AVA SMILED AT him encouragingly. 'It's okay, you know,' she said, 'to be a little...daunted. It's really quite common. Some guys are a little freaked out at first because of who I am... They don't want to screw it up and it makes them... nervous...reticent. But really, I'm just a woman.'

She leaned forward, conscious of her gown gaping a little more and the lowering of his gaze. She picked up his hand, and placed it halfway up her thigh.

'A flesh and blood woman,' she continued. 'Don't think of me as a...celebrity. I'm just Ava...a woman just like any other.'

Blake's gaze stayed fixed on where his hand met her flesh as Ava straightened. Her thigh was warm beneath his palm. And very, very female. Something his erection appreciated with gusto. So much that it almost made him forget her ridiculous statement.

Lord. Her ego sure as hell hadn't been scared into submission last night.

She didn't *intimidate* him.

But she definitely got under his skin.

He dropped his hand from her thigh before he did something completely contradictory like smoothing it up. All the way up. He looked up instead—a much safer alternative—as he mentally thrust the temptation aside.

'No, Ava.'

Ava heard the roughness of longing in his voice despite his denial. What *was* his problem? And then suddenly something else occurred to her and she felt both stupid and insensitive. Throwing herself at him—an *injured* war veteran.

'Oh, God, I'm so sorry,' she whispered. 'Your injuries...' She shook her head. 'I should have thought. I didn't realise you couldn't...that you can't...that you're...impotent... I'm so sorry...'

Blake almost choked at her wild assumption. Right at this second he'd never been more bloody potent in his life.

Or more goaded into proving it.

'Screw it,' he growled, forgetting all the reasons he shouldn't as he grabbed her hand and yanked.

Ava barely had a chance to catch her breath before she landed hard in his lap, looming over him, her thighs straddling his. Her gown had flown open and her bare breasts grazed the neckline of his shirt. Her hands clutched for purchase, finding the hard wall of muscle that constituted his chest.

But she didn't protest or stop to clarify. She just followed her instincts. And her instincts led her to his mouth. A mouth that was seeking hers, his fingers spearing into her hair, his hands dragging her head down to his.

Her mouth down to his.

And when his lips touched hers, full and firm and open, she opened to him too, parting instantly, her nostrils full of the intoxicating scent of him, her tongue savouring the hint of beer and the fuller, earthier taste of aroused man.

His hand slid over her hip to the small of her back, his palm pressing hard against her, and her belly contracted. He slid it up, following the furrow of her spine, and she shivered. He trekked it around to her front, filling his palm with the soft flesh of her breast, squeezing and rubbing his finger across the turgid peak of her nipple, and she arched her back and moaned, 'Blake,' against his mouth.

His other hand slid to her butt cheek and squeezed and she couldn't think for the bombardment of sensations. For the smell of him filling her head. The taste of him consuming her senses. She just needed more.

To be closer, nearer. To imprint herself. To feel him around her.

To feel him inside her.

She couldn't remember ever wanting a man as desperately as she wanted Blake. Men and sex came easy to her and Blake's resistance had been a challenge. But this wasn't triumph she was feeling. This was purely sexual. Blake gave and gave and gave—plundering, stroking, kneading, touching—and she wanted everything he had to offer.

She squirmed against him, signalling a need she was too far gone to ask for. And that was when she became aware of it. A hardness beneath her right thigh. A flatness. Not like his other thigh that had the flexibility of hot flesh over steely muscle. There was no give there. Just rigidity. And a very definite edge. *His prosthesis.*

But then he was yanking her hips forward, bringing her in contact with more flesh on steel. Something hard and long and very, very potent. Making her forget everything else. She tried to move, to obey the dictates of her body, to grind down on him, to feel every inch of his erection, but he held her there, both hands clamped on her butt now, kissing her deeper, wilder, wetter.

'*Blake,*' she muttered against his mouth as she tried to squirm, to rub herself shamelessly along the length of him.

Blake groaned as he held her fast. He'd only meant this as a demonstration of his capabilities but it was careening out of his control. Her mouth tasted like beer and sin and he wanted to taste her all over. He hadn't bargained for how perfect she'd feel in his hands. How she'd melt into him, all her can't-touch-this veneer evaporating.

Or how very much he'd been denying himself.

Ava Kelly was one hell of a woman and telling himself she was technically still a client and a pain-in-the-butt one to boot just wasn't going to cut it now his erection had taken control.

He wanted to get her naked, he wanted to get her horizontal; he wanted to get her under him. His head was full of her throaty whimpers, his hands were full of her flesh, his mouth was full of her taste but it still wasn't enough.

Her hand found his erection then and he moaned as she palmed it, pressing himself into her hand. His zip fell away beneath her questing fingers and then she was reaching inside his underwear, freeing him, her palm hot against him as she squeezed his girth.

Blake broke off the kiss on a guttural groan, his eyes practically rolling back in his head as he dragged in much-needed air. Her forehead pressed against his and he opened his eyes to the delectable sight of her breasts swaying hypnotically, the light pink nipples darker now as they formed two hard points.

With her hair falling around them in a curtain and the

only sound between them the thick rasp of their breath, it was as if they were the only two people in the world. Far away from the world of Ava Kelly and her entourage. Which was just as well with her hand getting so intimately acquainted with his freed erection.

He shut his eyes as she wrapped her hand around him and started to smooth it up and down the length of him.

'God, you're so *freaking* hard,' she whispered into the space between them. 'I knew there was a reason I'd put my trust in you.'

The words were like a bucket of cold water and Blake froze, his eyes snapping open.

Trust.

She had to use *that* word?

He looked down at himself, at her hand on him. *What the hell was he doing?*

God, how had this got so out of hand? He was only supposed to be proving he could get it up, not demonstrating its full working capabilities. Having sex with Ava was a bad idea and her being practically naked with a hand full of his erection didn't make it any less so.

Every instinct he owned—prior to five minutes ago—had told him to stay away, and he would do well to remember that.

She *trusted* him, for God's sake.

The woman had so few people in the world to put her faith in and he was taking advantage of her sucky situation.

'Stop…wait,' he said, shifting in the chair, covering her hand with his, grateful when she stopped the mindlessly good stroking.

Ava frowned, her hand stilling. Her head spun from the sexual buzz, her brain already someplace else where he felt good and hard inside her. 'Wha…?' she said, pulling away slightly.

'Just…no…hop up…' he said. 'Let me up.'

Blake struggled to get up, trying to displace her safely and stand himself without falling in a heap. Ava stood there looking confused, her gown open, her body flushed and lovely, and he turned away to dispel the image, to block it from his sight.

'Blake?'

He felt a hundred kinds of idiot at her plaintive query as he tucked his protesting erection in and zipped himself up. His breathing was still all bent out of shape and he raked a hand through his hair as he took a moment to gather himself.

When he turned back he was grateful she'd done up her gown. But she'd gone from looking confused and unsure to pretty pissed off.

Not that he could blame her. His erection knew exactly how she felt.

'I'm sorry,' he said. 'I shouldn't have started that… I was trying to prove that everything was in full working order. I just got a little…carried away.'

Ava glared at him. 'You think?'

'I'm sorry,' he repeated. Because what else could he say?

Ava tried to wrap her head around what had just transpired. 'I don't understand,' she said. 'What happened?'

Blake took a steadying breath. 'I don't want to do this.'

Ava snorted. 'You wanted it all right. You wanted it when you kissed me, you wanted it when you touched me and you sure as hell wanted it when I had my hand in your pants.'

Blake had to concede she made some very good points. 'Of course my *body* wants you,' he said. 'I'm a man and you're one of the most beautiful women on the planet and, as you pointed out before, we're attracted to each other. But I'm thirty-three years old, Ava, not some horny teenager who can't control himself. My brain's telling me this is a stupid thing to do.'

Ava gave another snort. 'That's not what your erection was telling me.'

'Yeh, well...' he raked a hand through his hair '...erections tend to be fairly unreliable indicators of what a man should and shouldn't do.'

'Well, at least they're honest,' she said vehemently. 'At least they tell it like it is. I know you wanted me right now, Blake, and I don't know why you're pretending you don't, why you're pretending it's a bad thing. We're just two human beings coming together, finding a little pleasure together. It's really not that complicated.'

Blake was struck suddenly by how spoiled she was sounding. He'd forgotten how irritating that was in the last twenty-four hours. Obviously she'd pegged him as a sure thing and she wasn't impressed with being knocked back. Clearly she was used to getting her way sexually too.

He half expected to see her stamp her foot.

'Is it *so* hard to believe that someone doesn't want to have sex with you?'

Ava heard the underlying disbelief in his question and it made her crankier. 'Frankly, yes.' Men wanted her—always had. And she'd taken her pick.

Blake almost laughed as her haughty look came back and, even barely dressed in a clingy gown, she managed to look imperious. 'Oh, my God, you've never been knocked back, have you?'

Ava gave a very definitive shake of her head. 'Nope.'

Blake did laugh this time. He'd always had a fairly high success rate with women, even since the explosion. But part of becoming a man, in his opinion, was realising that not every woman was going to think you were sex on a stick.

And it was how a guy took that news that separated the boys from the men.

'Well, welcome to the *real* world,' he said.

Ava *did not* think any of this was funny. She still felt jittery as her cells came down from their sexual high without the satisfaction they craved. 'Oh, I see,' she said, putting her hand on her hip. 'This is some kind of life lesson for me, is it?'

Blake should have been astounded by her egocentricity but nothing about her surprised him any more. 'You know, Ava, this may come as a surprise, but not everything is about you.'

Ava ignored his derisive put down in favour of getting to the bottom of a situation she'd never been in before. 'So... let me get this straight. You're attracted to me but you don't want to have sex with me?'

Blake smiled at her obvious confusion. 'Oh, I want to, all right. I'm just not going to.'

Ava stared at him. Well, now she was totally lost. Why not take what you wanted, especially when it was on offer? 'But...why not?'

Blake shook his head. She really had no clue about the real world. She was so used to getting her way and taking what she wanted from life, because she could, that she never stopped to think that some things were better off left alone.

'Because it's a whole lot of complicated for a few lousy nights, Ava.'

Ava folded her arms. 'There would be *nothing* lousy about them.'

Blake smiled at her snooty self-assurance. 'I'm sure you're right,' he conceded. If she did other things even half as well as she kissed he was doomed.

'So what's the problem?'

He sighed. Obviously she needed it spelled out. 'I'm supposed to be offering you safe harbour, Ava, not taking advantage of you.'

As a British soldier his uniform had been a symbol of security and he'd always taken that seriously. It just didn't feel right somehow to violate the trust she'd put in him. Just because he hadn't asked for it, didn't mean he was going to mess with it.

'And that would make perfect sense if I was here rocking in a corner and jumping at shadows like some little scared mouse. But *I'm* coming on to *you*. I think consent to take advantage of me is implied. So what else have you got?'

Blake pushed a hand through his hair at her casual dismissal of values he held dear.

God, she was irritating.

'How about, I don't like women who are spoiled and self-centred no matter how beautiful they are or how good they look naked. It's not an attractive quality and I'm not some guy who'll turn a blind eye to that just to get laid. I don't want to be your distraction of choice while you're *slumming it* on a canal boat. I'm not some plaything for a rich woman to amuse herself with.'

Ava blinked at his unflattering appraisal of her. Okay, she might be used to getting her own way but she wasn't a complete egomaniac either. She didn't regard him as a *plaything.* She just saw a situation they could both have a little fun with.

'I don't see you like that,' she said, dropping her arms until they wrapped around her waist. 'This isn't me being bored or spoiled either. I just don't see why we should deny ourselves when we both want this.'

'Well, I guess in your hedonistic world you wouldn't,' he said. 'But I learned a few years ago to stay away from things that can blow up in your face and, lady, you have highly explosive written all over you.'

Ava knew that he hadn't meant to flatter her but she was anyway. She was so used to being described as cool and snooty. The media had dubbed her *Keep-Away Kelly* when she'd really hit the big time because of the aloofness she'd worked so hard to cultivate.

It was her point of difference and she'd worked it.

To be told she was the opposite was strangely thrilling. 'Thank you.'

Blake rolled his eyes. 'It wasn't a compliment.'

Ava grinned at his terse exasperation. 'I know. Which strangely only makes me want you more.'

Blake shook his head. There wasn't much else that could be said here. He was determined to keep things between them strictly platonic. She seemed determined to do the opposite.

Ken Biddle had better catch his man quick. *Before Ava caught hers.*

'I'm going to bed,' he said.

Ava watched him turn away, admiring the back view of him as he veered to the left and headed down the corridor, presumably for the bathroom. His limp was barely discernible. 'You should know I don't give up so easily,' she called.

Blake felt her silky threat—or was that a promise?—land on target right between his shoulder blades. 'I'll consider myself warned,' he said, without turning around, then stepped gratefully into the bathroom and shut the door.

He leaned against it heavily, gripping the door handle hard, trying to get control of a groin that had leaped to life again at her sexy warning. His hand brushed something and he looked down to find a scrap of black lace in the shape of a bra.

He groaned as he pulled it off, and held it up in front of him, letting it dangle from his index finger. Pink ribbon weaved along the cup edges delineated them and a little pink bow at the cleavage, complete with diamanté, winked out at him. His groin went from aching to throbbing.

This was the sort of stuff she was going to be wearing under her clothes?

Fabulous.

He hung it back where he found it then pulled out his mobile from his pocket, scrolling to Joanna's number and hitting 'message'.

Thx heaps 4 the lingerie you meddler.

He hit send and waited where he was for the few seconds it took to get a reply. The phone vibrated in his hand and he read the screen. *Thought you might like.*

Blake tapped a reply. *I don't.*

A few more seconds. *OK. Sure. Keep forgetting you are the *only* man on earth not born with the lingerie gene.*

Blake shook his head. *Don't Joanna. Not going there.*

Joanna's *Uh-huh* reply rankled.

I'm not.

The reply came swiftly. *Uh-huh.*

He grimaced as his fingers flew across the touch pad.

God you're irritating. I should have let Charlie strap you to the front of his bike when you were 2.

Blake waited for the reply. And waited. He was about to give up and get into the shower when his phone vibrated in his hand again. Four words that hit like a sledgehammer.

What would Colin say???

Blake bumped his head back against the door. Low blow. His mate would think he'd lost his mind for just having turned down an invitation to heaven with one of the world's most nicely put-together women.

Another vibration. *He's dead. You're alive. So live.*

Blake hated it when Joanna played on his guilt over Colin. And she knew it. *I definitely should have let Charlie use u as a human bumper bar.*

A smiley face appeared on the screen. *Love you 2. Night xxx.*

Blake shoved his phone back in his pocket, pushing aside the unsettled feelings that both Ava and Joanna had roused. He shucked off his clothes and moved into the large glass shower recess. One of the beauties of a wide beam was all the extra space. It meant you could have more rooms. Or, as he had chosen, *bigger* rooms and he loved the decadence of his spacious bathroom.

On autopilot he went through the now almost second-nature process of taking off his prosthesis and placing it outside the glass area. Still on autopilot he reached for the gleaming metallic railing that was attached to the tiles at waist height the entire way. He barely registered the gritty, high-grip tiles beneath his foot.

He flicked the taps and the water rained down on him nice and hot within seconds. He shut his eyes, forcing himself to relax. To clear his head of his sister's unhelpful suggestions. And Ava's unhelpful seduction.

And the unhelpful build of sexual frustration.

Just because he was horny didn't mean he should act on it. *Not with her anyway.*

He turned, letting the water sluice over his neck, flopping his head first forward then back, enjoying the heat on traps he'd had no idea were so tense. His eyes fluttered open. And that was when he saw it.

A lacy black thong hanging over the shower screen.

Pink ribbon weaved along the waistband and a little pink bow sat dead centre, another diamanté winking down at him.

She'd been wearing that get up under her clothes all day? His traps tensed again.

Crap.

Blake woke the next morning after another fitful sleep to dreadful off-key singing and the smell of frying bacon. His stomach growled and his mouth watered despite the assault to his ears.

He hadn't been sure what to expect this morning after their...disagreement last night and he'd lain awake wondering what kind of a post-spat personality she was.

Was she a flouncer, a sulker, a brooder?

It certainly didn't sound as if she was any of the above if her peppy singing was anything to go by. He reached for his leg and put it on, then reached for his T-shirt and pulled it down over his head. He'd taken it off during the night as replays of Ava straddling him had made the warm night quite a few degrees hotter.

He rubbed a hand through his hair, taking a moment before standing and facing her. Ava's singing stopped momentarily and he could hear the lower murmur of a breakfast news programme on the television. Blake hoped that Ken had some *news* for them this morning. Like they'd found the person or persons responsible for shooting up Ava's house.

She started *singing* again and he made his way to the kitchen and just stood and watched her for a moment as she boogied in front of the cooktop. The gown from last night was on again but was floating loosely by her sides and he felt a sudden kick in his groin at the thought that she might just be naked under there and if she turned around then—

She turned around.

Everything leapt to attention for a brief second and not even the evidence of his own eyes—that she was indeed wearing something under that gown—could stop the rapid swelling of his erection. Because a spaghetti-strapped, clingy, not-quite-meeting-in-the-middle vest top and matching boy-leg undies on a tall, bronzed supermodel was something to behold.

Her face lit up. 'Ah.' She smiled at him. 'You're up. I'm making bacon butties.'

Blake swallowed. Up? *In more ways than one.* Was there anything more sexy than a woman in skimpy lingerie? Except maybe for a woman in skimpy lingerie cooking bacon?

Ava smiled as Blake's gaze roved all over her. *Yeh, buddy, this is what you're missing out on.* 'How'd you'd sleep last night?' she enquired sweetly.

Blake's eyes narrowed at the suspiciously smug question. So this was the kind of post-spat personality she was—a fighter.

Who liked to play dirty.

Well, he wasn't one of her entourage of men who fluttered around her and kissed her butt. 'Like a log,' he said.

Wrong choice of words as her gaze dropped to the area between his hips with its suspicious bulge.

Which *did not* help the suspicious bulge.

But then her smile slipped a little and a tiny frown knitted her brows together. He looked down at what she'd found so disagreeable and realised, unlike every other time she'd seen him, his prosthesis was on full display.

He supposed a woman as physically perfect as Ava would find his leg rather confronting. He felt absurdly like covering it up. And then he felt really freaking cranky.

Blake's teeth ached from clenching his jaw hard as he waited for her to say something. Something trite or clueless, something about how at least he still had one leg or how *marvellous* prosthetics were these days.

Instead she just dragged her gaze back up to look into his eyes. 'Take a seat. Eggs are just about done.'

CHAPTER EIGHT

THERE WAS NO news from Ken, although Ava Kelly was still the talk of the tabloids and breakfast shows. Speculation as to where she'd disappeared was rife and one talk-back radio station had even offered money to anyone who could produce pictorial evidence of her whereabouts.

Ken was far from impressed with that.

Blake was downright annoyed. He suggested Ava put Reggie to good use and sue their arses off for endangerment. She'd just shrugged, clearly so desensitised to press intrusion that the invasion of her human rights didn't even register.

They got under way again as soon as breakfast was done. They were travelling along a stretch of the tidal Thames and they had to fit into lock times that were mandated by the tide. His plan was to moor somewhere around Windsor overnight then on to Reading the next day where the Kennet and Avon canal began. Once they'd turned into it, they could putt along more lazily, but for now it was full steam ahead.

Or as full steam as possible when the speed limit was four miles per hour!

And Ava Kelly was your very distracting travelling companion.

Blake didn't think she was being deliberately distracting. She was fully bagged up again. Baggy shorts and shirt, her hair all tucked up in a cap, sunglasses firmly in place. She looked as anonymous as the next woman riding the canals.

But he knew what she had on under all those layers.

And that was pretty much all he could think about—every time she moved or talked or offered him something to eat. *Like freaking Eve with the apple.* In fact, even when she wasn't anywhere near him, he was thinking about her and what she might be wearing against her skin.

Did she have on the same spaghetti-strapped vest and matching boy-legs that had been under her gown this morning—the ones that displayed the most perfect belly-button probably ever created? Or had she changed into some other frothy, lacy, silky, maybe be-ribboned scraps of fabric when she'd changed into her outside clothes?

It was annoying how much brain space the speculation was taking up. He should be enjoying the gorgeous sunshine on his face, the breeze in his hair, the spectacular beauty of the English countryside. And while Ava had raved over the magnificence of Hampton Court, he'd barely registered it.

It wasn't good for his mood or his sanity, and it was the last straw when he caught himself trying to look down her top from his vantage point standing at the helm as she asked him a question from the bottom of the three stairs that led to the back of the boat.

'What?' he asked, when he realised he hadn't heard a

word she'd said because he swore he caught a glimpse of red satin.

Ava, who'd deliberately leaned forward a little, gave him an innocent smile. 'I said are you ready for some lunch now?'

'Yep. But not here.'

Blake knew he had to get off the boat. Get away from the lure of her and red satin. Put himself amongst people, where he had to behave rationally. *And not tear her clothes off with his teeth.*

'There's a pub just up ahead,' he said. 'About five minutes away. We'll moor and eat there.'

'Fab,' she said and smiled up at him.

Blake pushed the boat a little harder.

Ava was enjoying watching the array of boats go by and the sun on her face as they sat in the reasonably full beer garden that fronted the river. They were sitting at one end of a bench—the other end a family group were chatting away oblivious to who was sharing their table with them.

By tacit agreement, Blake had gone inside and ordered for them while Ava stayed out. Being incognito worked best when she exposed herself to scrutiny as little as possible. Sitting in a riverside beer garden just like any ordinary girl was clearly possible, but the more people she spoke to, the more she risked exposure.

She was pleased when Blake came back with two pints of cold beer. It was warm in the sunshine and she felt hot in her baggy attire. What she wouldn't give to be in her bikini now, or at least in clothes that didn't cover her from neck to knee.

'You remembered,' she said, smiling at him as she lifted

her glass and tapped it against the rim of his larger one. 'Cheers.'

Blake watched her guzzle it like a pro then lick the froth from her mouth. *Sexiest thing he'd ever seen.*

'Mmm,' she murmured after taking several deep swallows, quenching the thirst the hot sun had roused. 'That hit the spot. It's warm, isn't it?'

Ava put the beer down and pulled on the neckline of her shirt, fanning it back and forth rapidly to try and cool the sweat she could feel forming between her breasts. She hadn't done it to provoke Blake but it was pleasing when his eyes narrowed and followed the movement.

She was glad his sunglasses didn't obscure his eyes as hers did. She liked knowing exactly where he was looking.

He looked kind of hot and bothered himself and she smiled. 'Aren't you roasting in those jeans?' she asked.

Blake shrugged. 'I'm okay.'

Ava regarded him. Did he always cover up his prosthesis? She'd been surprised when she'd seen it this morning. Not because she thought it was grotesque but because Blake always seemed so sure of himself, so confident, so...able. Seeing his leg had been a reminder that he wasn't, or at least that it wasn't so effortless for him.

'Do you never wear shorts?' she asked.

He dropped his gaze to his beer and took another sip and she could tell he was uncomfortable with the subject.

'Perfect weather for them,' she pushed as he turned his head to take in the activity on the busy river. 'You don't like people knowing?' Ava guessed tentatively.

Blake sighed as he turned back to face her, putting his beer down. 'I don't care who knows or doesn't know. Jeans...avoid conversations I *don't* want to have.'

Ava got the message loud and clear. But she wanted to have the conversation anyway. 'Like how it happened?'

'Yes.'

'What a hero you must be?' she guessed again.

Blake rolled his eyes. 'Yes.'

'How brave you are?'

He nodded. 'Yes.'

The level of chatter around them was sufficiently high that they could talk without fear of being overheard and Ava really wanted to know more about the circumstances of his amputation. The man had pushed her to the ground as someone shot up her house, purely out of instincts that had obviously been honed during his time in war zones.

As far as she was concerned he *was* a hero.

'How *did* it happen?'

Blake didn't really fancy talking about it with her, but at least talking was keeping his mind off her red bra. In fact maybe he could use it to his advantage. 'If I tell you, will you promise to not hang your underwear in my shower?'

Ava was momentarily surprised by his blatant blackmail. But it was satisfying to know that her *under*wear was getting *under* his skin. 'Deal.'

Blake took another sip of his beer. 'It happened the usual way,' he said dismissively. 'On patrol in the middle of nowhere. A roadside bomb. An IED. All over red rover.'

Ava should have expected the abridged version. 'Did anyone die?'

Blake steeled himself not to flinch at the question. 'Yes. One.'

Ava nodded slowly at another abridged version that told her nothing of the emotional carnage he must have borne. 'And the leg? Did you lose it straight away or after?'

'It was pretty mangled. They amputated it as soon as I hit the hospital.'

His words were flat, his answers matter-of-fact but Ava could see the tension in his muscle, the tightness of his jaw.

'That must have been...incredibly painful,' she murmured.

Blake gripped his glass as the sounds of his screams flashbacked to fill his head all over again. He wondered if people—if Ava—would think him so heroic if they knew how loudly he'd screamed. Lying in agony in the dirt, his eardrums blown out, the warm ooze of his own blood welling over the hand he'd reached down to try and stop the pain.

If they knew his brother-in-law lay dead beside him and Blake hadn't even given him a single thought.

'It was.'

Ava was about to say more. To push more. To ask more. But the waiter arrived, placing their ploughman's lunches in front of them and an extra bowl of hot chips for Ava, and Blake's white-knuckled grip on his glass eased as he picked up his knife and fork.

'Let's eat,' he said.

Ava sighed. *Conversation over.*

They didn't talk much over lunch, for which Blake was grateful. Ava seemed happy enough to drop her line of questioning and just eat and enjoy the sunshine, with occasional questions about their route for the afternoon.

He didn't really talk about what had happened to him—not with civilians anyway. His family knew the most of it. The army shrink knew more. Joanna at one stage had wanted to know every detail and had wanted to go over and over it ad nauseam and, even though it had been horrible and he'd dreaded seeing her number flash on his phone screen or hearing her wobbly, strung-out voice in his ear, he'd done it because he'd owed her.

The only people he could really talk to about it with any level of comfort were the guys he'd served with because they were the only ones who could *truly* understand any of it. But he rarely saw any of them and when he did, contrary to popular perception, none of them were particularly keen to rehash old war stories.

Talking about it with Ava wasn't his definition of fun but at least he'd won a concession from her so maybe it had been worth it.

He watched her as she laid her cutlery on her empty plate then reached for the tomato sauce bottle and squirted great dollops all over her hot chips, then sprinkled a heart-attack quota of salt over the top. She picked one up in her fingers, and ate with gusto, sighing a little sigh. She added two more to her mouth, then, before they were fully swallowed, another two.

A dollop of sauce smeared at the corner of her mouth and Blake's gaze was drawn to it—he couldn't help himself.

'What?' she asked around her mouthful of hot chips. Then she picked up the remnant of her beer and washed them down, licking her lips free of sauce and beer residue.

The woman made the simple act of eating into a sexual enterprise.

'Isn't your body supposed to be a temple or something?' he asked. 'Aren't supermodels supposed to always be on some kind of diet that involves no carbs and lots of egg-white omelettes and running on a treadmill for six hours a day?'

'Ugh, no thanks.' Ava shuddered as she picked up another chip and popped it in her mouth. 'My mother used to be strict about that stuff as I was growing up and—'

Ava stopped. She didn't want to think about her pageant-queen mother. It was a long time ago and it always put her in a bad mood and the sunshine and company were just too good.

'Anyway... I do exercise...mostly...but...' She sighed. 'I have to admit, I'm not a fan and it's hard to see the point when I'm one of those people who have good genetics with a great metabolism and can pretty much eat whatever without putting on weight. I've been really blessed like that.' She grimaced. 'I'm one of those women other women hate.'

Blake could see that. Most women he knew had some kind of body hang-up or other trying to keep up with impossible images in women's magazines. Images that she perpetrated.

'The thing is,' she said as she chomped on another chip, 'I just freaking love food. I don't know if that's because of Dad's influence or not but it's just... I don't know, like... air to me. I *need* it.'

'And,' she said, picking up another two chips and dipping them in a puddle of sauce on the bottom of the bowl, 'I'm starving all the time, which is why I cook a lot at home and wanted an amazing kitchen, which you—' she jabbed another chip in his general direction before popping it in her mouth '—gave me in spades. No pics of me at restaurants stuffing a three-course meal down then asking for seconds of dessert. I eat like a supermodel when I'm in public and then come home and cook up something amazing in my beautiful kitchen because by then I'm so freaking hungry I'm almost faint with it.'

Blake knew it shouldn't, but her appreciation of both his kitchen and for food in general turned him on. Just talking about how much she loved food had clearly got her all enthused and excited. She was using the chips to emphasise her points and her cheeks were all flushed and her freckles were standing out. He wanted to whisk her glasses off and see if the yellow highlights in her eyes were glittering fit to match the sun on the Thames.

There was nothing haughty or spoiled about *this* Ava, who was chowing down on hot chips and cold beer.

Ava chose another chip, realising there were only five left and she hadn't offered him any. 'Oh, God, sorry,' she said, picking up the bowl and pushing it towards him. 'Do you want any? They were so good I got carried away.'

Blake chuckled at her half-hearted offer. He couldn't see her eyes but he'd have been deaf not to have heard the reluctance in her voice. 'They're all yours,' he said, waving them back.

'Good answer.' She grinned as she dived for the remaining chips.

Blake's breath caught in his lungs. If *this* Ava straddled him right now his powers of resistance would be totally useless.

By six o'clock that evening they'd moored just upstream from Windsor Castle. The unparalleled views of the extensive grounds surrounding the castle as they had floated past had been amazing and Ava, who had apparently *met* the queen, had been excited to see the royal standard flying high from the round tower indicating Her Majesty was in residence.

After last night, Blake hadn't expected to enjoy the day

as much as he had. He'd expected Ava to be petulant and difficult—like a spoiled child who hadn't got her way—but she'd been perfectly well behaved and he was smiling to himself as he came in from outside, pulling a beer bottle from the fridge and cracking the lid.

If Ava could keep up her ordinary-girl act and give the sex-kitten/prima-donna a rest, it could be an enjoyable time, while it lasted. Of course, it could be even more enjoyable if he allowed himself to be seduced. But he was determined to show her he was one of the good guys. That she *could* trust him.

A cutting board with chopped tomatoes and onions sat waiting on the kitchen bench and fresh basil spiced the air. Ava wasn't dancing around his kitchen and, as he'd heard the pump kick in while he'd been checking the ropes, he assumed she was showering.

His brain wandered to that delightful prospect before he pulled himself back from the image. *Do not think about her showering.* What he needed to do was go and grab some supplies out of his room while she wasn't in it. Some clothes and toiletries etc.

Except when he stepped into his bedroom he discovered she wasn't in the shower. He pulled up short just inside the doorway as his gaze fell on bare golden shoulders.

Ava looked up as Blake entered the room. Their eyes met and there was a world of surprise in those few seconds. But there were other things as well, especially when his gaze dropped and lingered at the point where her damp hair brushed her collarbones.

There was a hell of a lot of want in that lingering contact.

They'd had a good time today. Blake had seemed to relax more as the day had worn on and she was even left with the impression that he might actually *like* her. Certainly not how she'd felt after last night's debacle.

And there'd been something so sexy about the way he handled the boat. Maybe it was the whole *Captain Capable* thing he had going on or maybe it was just the way his T-shirt had fitted snugly across solid biceps.

Either way, his attraction had cranked up several notches since last night and her belly tightened at the thought of just how capable he might be on the big beautiful bed right in front of her.

'Hi,' she said, breaking the silence that stretched between them.

'Oh, sorry,' Blake said, dragging his eyes back to hers—no easy feat considering she was dressed in nothing but a towel. 'I thought you were still in the shower.'

Ava shrugged and watched as his gaze followed the motion. She raised her hand to where the towel was firmly tucked into itself between her breasts and was satisfied when his gaze took the trip with her.

'Nope. Not any more,' she murmured. 'All fresh and clean.'

Blake took an absent sip of his beer that he'd forgotten he was even carrying. 'Yes.'

A small smile played on Ava's lips at his obvious distraction. Blake could deny himself as much as he liked in the name of honour but it was pretty obvious what he really wanted. 'Did you want something?' she asked. 'Or were you secretly hoping to catch me getting dressed?'

Blake frowned as the words yanked him out of his stupor. He really hoped she didn't seriously think he'd come into the room to cop a perve. He wasn't some horny bloke who let the content of his underpants dictate his actions.

He'd proved himself to be pretty honourable under circumstances where most men would have cracked and she could take a flying leap into the canal if she thought otherwise.

But then he noticed that predatory gleam from last night in her eyes again, which suited all her languid feline grace, and he knew what this was.

Goodbye, ordinary girl. Hello, sex kitten.

Ava watched Blake transition from annoyed to wary but she wasn't about to let it stop her. 'It's okay, you know, to admit there's something between us, Blake,' she said, gliding forward. 'To want to do something about it. I know that you feel you're in a position of trust but I'm not going to think any less of you.'

Even in a towel, with acres of tanned, toned flesh on display, she still pulled off a superior look better than anyone he knew. Maybe he should have let her off at the castle for the night with the Queen.

At least she wouldn't be here, naked but for a towel, tempting him to forget what was right, forget that every instinct he possessed warned him to stay way away from her.

Her shoulders were, oh, so bare, oh, so lovely as she pulled up in front of him. Right in front of him. He doubted he'd even have to extend his arm its full length to brush fingers along her collarbones. To yank her body flush with his.

Blake pulled his gaze up, meeting her frank, knowing eyes. A whole world of temptation stared back at him. 'Yes, but *I'll* think less of me,' he said.

She looked at him through half-closed lashes like some silver-screen goddess, one of her snooty little half-smiles playing on her mouth. 'I promise you won't have to *think* at all.'

She seemed to have shifted tack from last night—from

brash self-assurance to coquettish flirtation and Blake decided he liked this Ava better. Almost as much as he liked the possibility of a little mindless sex despite the faint echo of warning bells clanging somewhere. He'd spent a lot of the last few years inside his head, thinking. Just like now. Letting that all go while he lost himself in Ava for a while was an attractive proposition.

He looked at her mouth, which was dead ahead. Right there, ready to claim, her lips two perfect arcs aside from the tiny dip in the middle of the top one that was incredibly fascinating. He'd really like to lick her just there.

And along those lovely collarbones.

It would be so easy. He leaned his shoulder into the door frame. 'Just leave my brain on the table by the bed, huh?'

Ava, encouraged by the way he appeared to be considering her words instead of rejecting them outright, broadened her smile. 'Well not entirely. Don't forget what they say about the body's largest sexual organ being the brain.'

Blake gave a soft snort. 'Only men with small penises say that.'

Ava was momentarily surprised by his quick, disdainful comeback and then she laughed. He was so serious and yet the quip had been fast and witty. If he'd just put a smile on that marvellous mouth it could even be classed as banter.

It definitely made him seem more approachable and her hopes soared. 'Well, that...' she let her gaze travel down to the area between his hips, then back up again '...counts you out.'

Blake's groin leapt to life at her blatant reminder. He could still feel the warm clamp of her hand around him. How right it had felt when she'd stroked him last night good and firm, *just the way he liked it.*

His fingers itched to touch her. To stroke along her shoulders, up her throat, along her mouth. But being dressed in only a towel was a double-edged sword. Sure, she might look sexy and gorgeous and utterly accessible, but it also reminded him of how vulnerable she was and he was reminded of her pallor and fright straight after the shooting.

He was reminded that she was under his protection. 'I was never in,' he said and hoped it sounded definite.

Ava sensed he was wavering. She smiled at him, not convinced that *he* was convinced. Still *convinced s*he could talk him round if she trod carefully. God knew, her abdominals were scrunched so tight in anticipation she'd never need do another sit-up again.

She sighed as she took a half-step closer. 'You're hard on a girl's ego, Blake Walker.'

Blake didn't trust her easy-going reply, not when she was somehow closer than she'd been a moment ago. Somehow more enticing.

Okay, this was getting dangerous. *Time to step away from the sex kitten.*

He took a mental pace backwards. 'I'm sure your ego can take it,' he said dryly.

Ava sensed his withdrawal but tried not to panic. She could still reel him in; she was sure of it. 'You know us supermodels.' She shrugged again for good effect, satisfied when his gaze locked on her shoulders. 'Always needing someone around assuring us we're beautiful.'

Blake battled the urge to assure Ava with his tongue down her throat, or in her ear or licking all the way down her body. Instead, he straightened in the doorway. 'Oh, you're beautiful, Ava Kelly,' he said. 'But I'm going to take a shower.'

A cold one.

Ava raised an eyebrow. 'Is that an invitation?'

Blake's groin roused further as a bunch of possibilities played through his head. *A very cold one.* 'No. It is not,' he said, then turned away.

No, no, no. Ava knew she'd lost him. Stubborn man. But she refused to give up. 'Blake.' She slipped a hand on his retreating shoulder.

Blake tensed. He wished she wouldn't touch him. He didn't want her to touch him. It made him want to touch her right back. And a bunch of other things too. He turned.

'What?' he asked impatiently. 'Time to offer me some more money?'

Ava gasped as if he had slapped her. It stung that he was throwing her bribery back in her face. But most of all it stung because he made it sound so cheap.

'Go to hell,' she snapped. 'You think you're such a goody bloody two shoes? You think self-denial is so freaking honourable? Go right on ahead, you believe it, whatever helps you get through the night, *buddy.* But you and I *both* know how badly you want this, how much you want to succumb and how it's only a matter of time before you give into temptation.'

Blake was taken aback by the ferocious yellow glitter in her eyes as all Ava's fierce feline juju leapt out at him. She was pretty angry at him and yes, he conceded, maybe that *had* been a low blow.

But she was hitting pretty low too and her accuracy was startling. Still, no way was he going to let her know that. 'Ava, I wouldn't succumb to temptation if you were lying naked on my bed,' he said, jabbing a finger towards it, 'with beer poured all over you.'

Ava knew there were only two possible comebacks to that. One was to slam the door in his face. Choosing the other, she reached over and plucked the beer out of his hands. 'Wanna bet?'

CHAPTER NINE

ANY ISSUES AVA might have once had with taking her clothes off in front of strangers had died very quickly when she'd hit the big time. Over a decade in front of one camera or another she could very definitely look at her body with objectivity—the way the people who paid her did. For them she was just a canvas for an artist aka fashion designer to decorate in whatever way he/she wanted.

Years on catwalks where quick crowded changes were paramount and modesty something that nobody worried about had taught her that nudity was passé and certainly nothing to be ashamed of or worried about. Parading around in clothes that often left little to the imagination—be it on the catwalk, or for a magazine shoot or a television commercial—had compounded this view.

So lying on her back on Blake's bed, wriggling to the very centre, then peeling her towel away was no biggie for her. Even if he'd never seen her in a single magazine, he'd been given a pretty good preview last night.

Except, at the last moment, as the towel fell away, she raised the leg closest to him, bending it at the knee and placing the foot flat on the bedspread, shielding the full view of her lower half from his eyes, providing a modicum of decency. She wasn't sure why she did it but she felt suddenly reluctant to strip off all the way.

Aware Blake was watching every single move, she raised herself up on one elbow and, facing the ceiling, she tipped her head back, her hair brushing the coverlet, and took a long deep swallow of his beer. Then she held it just above the hollow at the base of her throat.

Blake could *not* tear his eyes away from a butt-naked Ava sprawled in the middle of his bed. An erection big enough to cause cerebral infarction from lack of blood flow to his brain pressed painfully against the zip of his jeans.

Her breasts were firm, the slight side swell utterly tempting, her nipples enticingly lickable. Her belly dipped down from her ribs and the play of muscles there as she held her torso semi-upright was fascinating, drawing his attention to the inward swirl of her perfect belly button.

He swallowed. 'Ava.'

She looked at him for long moments, her gaze knowing, and he wished he could turn away from the delectable sight of her, but he was powerless to resist. She gave him a slow sexy smile as if she knew he was waiting for the show, then she slowly tipped the bottle up.

Blake felt her gasp hit him square in the groin as cold beer spilled down her naked skin. He watched as it flowed down her sternum, branching out as it ran down her body, sending rivulets across the swell of her breasts, her nipples ruching at the contact of the cold liquid. It dipped into the valleys of her ribs and washed down the centre of her abs, spilling down her sides and pooling in her belly button.

Her leg hid how much lower it might have flowed, which

was just as well. He did not want to think about *that* combination of beer and woman.

It wasn't conducive to clear thinking.

He shut his eyes, thinking about all the reasons why this was a bad idea. Damsel in distress. Knight in shining armour. Protector. Defender.

Honour.

Trust.

He opened his eyes in time to see her collapsing back against the bed. She held her hand out to him and said, 'Please,' like freaking Eve lying down on a bed of apples.

Really red, really juicy apples.

And something snapped inside him then. There was only so much provocation he could stand and what the hell he was holding out for when she was a grown woman who clearly knew her own mind was a mystery not even he could fathom any more.

He strode into the room until he was standing beside the bed, looking directly down at her. *At all of her.* Every last inch. A beautiful contradiction in femininity. Smooth and firm. Soft and supple—interesting curves and sculpted muscles.

And very, very sticky.

His gaze tracked the path of the beer from her throat to where it had pooled in her belly button and then lower. Yes, it had run lower, drenching the trimmed strip of hair at the apex of her thighs.

And he was suddenly very, very thirsty!

Her foot dangling over the edge of the mattress rubbed against his leg and streaked heat up his thigh, urging him on. And he wanted to. A part of him wanted to join her on the bed immediately and lick every last trace of sticky, beery residue off her until she was begging him to stop.

And then do it all again.

She lay looking up at him with lust in her eyes and a knowing little smile, as if she'd ghost-written the Kama Sutra, but part of him could see past her brash outer confidence now to the vulnerable woman beneath, and that was who he wanted to touch.

Ava suppressed the growing need to squirm under his scrutiny. Her nipples got harder. Her breath grew shorter as his gaze lowered and lingered between her legs, streaking heat *everywhere*. She could feel the trickle of moisture where he stared and she wasn't entirely sure it was all beer.

His gaze pulled away again and fanned up and over her. He was looking at her as if he wanted to eat her up but wasn't sure where to start. Other men looked at her as if she had a staple through her navel. As if she were some prize they'd won.

As if they'd scored with a supermodel and they were looking at her to perform like one.

Blake was looking as if he was trying to map her entire body. Locate all her hotspots. Work out what he was going to do to them. And how long he was going to spend doing it.

Like a recon mission.

Like a soldier.

Either that or he was committing her to memory before he did a bolt. Something she doubted she'd survive now he'd brought her right to the brink of arousal. *Without so much as touching her!* Because she was very, very aroused.

'Blake?'

Her voice was husky and she dragged in some quick

breaths to dispel the annoying weakness. But she was pleased when it seemed to bring him out of his intense study.

Not that he answered her or even said a word. He just locked gazes, put a knee on the bed beside her leg, leaned onto his hands and lowered himself slowly down, his head level with her belly. When he was a whisper away from the puddle of beer in her belly button, he broke eye contact and touched his mouth to her abdomen, his tongue swiping at the now warm liquid.

Ava gasped, her back arching, her hand reaching down, ploughing through Blake's dirty-blond hair. She held him against her, afraid he was going to stop or that she was going to float right off the bed.

Don't stop, she wanted to say, but there was no need as the hot flat of his tongue swiped and swiped in ever-widening circles around and around her belly until she was whimpering and calling his name.

'Blake.'

Blake looked up from his ministrations—all the way up. Over her belly and up her ribs, skimming her breasts, fanning up her throat to her mouth, opening and shutting, silently begging him for more. 'Yes?'

She raised her head and looked at him with eyes that weren't quite focused. 'I… I…'

I…what? *What?* Ava couldn't speak. All the man had done was lick her belly—after making her wait for two days *and several minutes*—and she was putty in his hands. But it didn't matter because he was lifting his head, travelling up, up, up and before she could protest the lack of him down there he was up top, his mouth on hers, his hands in her hair, his body pressing her into the mattress.

And he felt so good all she could do was hold onto him and follow where he led.

And he led with spectacular commitment. His mouth opening wide, demanding hers do the same, kissing and licking and sucking, dragging every morsel of lust and need and want from her lips. Groaning against her mouth, absorbing the husky timbre of her noises that alternated from strong and strident to weak and whimpery and desperate. Joining the shuddery husk of his breath with hers.

And all the time his hands stroked and caressed, from her neck down, flowing everywhere, whispering heat and seduction wherever they touched. Promising lust and good times and secrets she never knew existed.

Eventually, the drugging lash of his mouth left hers and she protested. 'No, no,' she moaned, grabbing for him, reaching for his head, for his face, to bring him back where she needed him, to her mouth, where he'd poured all the lust and desire she'd never have known was even there but for this bubble of time.

But then he was kissing her again, saying, 'Shh, shh,' against her mouth, hushing her with his kisses and the magic of his hands as they stroked over her belly. And then, pushing her arms up above her head, restraining her there saying, 'I want to lick beer off you,' as he licked lower, down her jaw, her neck, her chest.

And it might have been weak of her but Ava, under the influence of his very clever tongue, let him.

Blake knew the moment she let go. The moment she stopped wanting it to be about them and let him make it all about her. It was the second his mouth opened over her nipple and, even though every muscle in her body tensed, her back arching up, pushing more of the gloriously hard tip against his palate, she clearly surrendered to him.

Her hands stopped questing, stopped pushing against the bond of his, trying to move, trying to reach for him. Her body melted into the mattress. Her head fell back, her mouth open wide as if breathing was all she could manage.

He liked that.

He liked that he'd made her incapable of anything but the very basics of life.

It allowed him free rein and he took it mercilessly, tasting her everywhere. Ravaging her nipples to hard peaks over and over until she begged him for release. Leaving there to head south, laving her belly with his tongue again, skating around the juncture of her thighs despite the desperate lifting of her hips, using his tongue to devastating effect on the sensitive skin of her inner thigh, her legs wide open, the intoxicating mix of beer and woman ratcheting up his heart rate, making his mouth water.

Making him want to bury his head there and taunt her with his tongue until she came long and hard. But he was determined to have all of her as he licked down to her bikini-red toenails.

Ava was lost in a world where she floated somewhere off the ground in a place full of sensations that swirled and skipped in a kaleidoscope of pleasure, drenching her in sweet, sticky rain. And she surrendered to it—lolled in it. Twirling and sliding, getting absolutely soaking wet.

There was something missing; she knew that. It nagged at the back of her mind but she couldn't quite pinpoint it. Then his fingers brushed up her thighs then teased against the core of her and she cried out at the intensity of it, wanting it to end, urging him to get her there.

But knowing somewhere inside her she *never* wanted it to end.

His fingers stroked and swirled, round and round, going hard, then backing off, going hard again until she was begging him to end it. But he didn't. Instead the hard probe of one finger slipping inside her had her crying out, then another as his wicked tongue laved the flesh of her inner thighs.

And just when she thought she couldn't take any more his mouth was on her, tasting her, his tongue circling hard around the sensitive bud, and she bucked against him, crying out.

That was what was missing. She wanted to taste him too. Wanted to put him in her mouth and know the contours of him.

The velvet and the steel, the sweet and the salt of him.

She didn't want to just lie here and be serviced.

'Blake...' she panted trying to sit up, trying to reach him. 'Blake...please...let me taste you too...'

'No,' came the muffled reply, his hand clamping down hard on her abdomen, the vibrations of his voice exquisite torture against her ravaged flesh. 'You. Just you.'

Ava fell back against the bed. She should have said no. *No, no no.* Insisted they be equal partners in this. She should have been worried that his honourable streak was going to see her fulfilled while leaving him wanting but she'd just used up her one last rational thought.

So she surrendered to him and this time he didn't back off with fingers or tongue, he just drove her higher and higher until Ava could feel herself drawing tight, so tight she didn't think she'd be able to breathe, and for a moment as everything coalesced into one powerful pinpoint of time her lungs seized and she swore for a second or two she did actually stop breathing altogether.

Then air came rushing into her lungs and she grabbed it, sucking in and out as ecstasy slammed into her. She grabbed Blake's head, holding him where he was as it undulated through her body, bowing her back off the bed, forcing a primal cry from the deepest part of her soul.

And she rode it all the way to the end.

Blake's heart rate was still unsteady as he lazily kissed and sucked his way back up Ava's body. She was still away in the land of sexual limbo and he was taking full advantage of her inebriated state to touch her some more, to make sure he'd lapped up every last trace of beer from her very delectable body.

He hadn't known what to expect from this—sex with Ava. Frankly he'd spent most of his time trying *not* to think about it. But he'd never thought it would be so fulfilling just to get her off. For someone as sexually confident as Ava she'd given him control so easily—as if her control freak was a mask she wore but was only too happy to lose. And her complete immersion in what was happening to her body had been heady stuff.

He swirled a nipple in his mouth and she moaned long and low as he felt it grow hard against his tongue.

He released his mouthful to look up at her. 'You're back,' he murmured.

Ava smiled at him. She twined her fingers in his hair, as best as she was able amidst the short strands 'Barely. I think I died for a short while.'

Blake chuckled, stroking his fingers up her arm. 'It's okay. I would have given you the kiss of life.'

Ava rolled her eyes. 'That's what got me into this mess.'

Blake raised an eyebrow as he stroked lazy fingers over the rise of her right breast. 'Would we call this a mess?' Of course the situation had mess written all over it but enjoying Ava's body had been divine.

Ava shut her eyes as the caress hummed right through her still-buzzing middle. 'No,' she said, opening her eyes. 'We would not.'

Blake dropped a kiss on her shoulder and nuzzled her there. 'Good.'

Ava stroked his hair, her mouth brushing against the ends, absently noticing the way it just brushed his nape, falling far short of the neckline of his shirt.

'You still have all your clothes on,' she said.

Blake lifted his head. 'What can I say? You were insatiable.'

'I think we need to do something about that, don't you?' she asked, reaching down to the small of his back, and grabbing a handful of his shirt.

Blake considered her for a moment. He wanted to get naked and do the wild thing with her. God knew his erection was still a living, breathing mammoth inside his underwear and he wanted to feel it buried deep inside her. But it wasn't simply a matter of just taking his clothes off.

'Duck,' she said to him as she ruched his shirt up his back, pulling it up to his shoulders. 'I want to even the playing field.'

Blake looked down at her body, his gaze lingering in all the places he'd been. 'I like uneven playing fields.'

Ava rolled her eyes. 'I bet you do.' She tugged on his shirt again but he resisted. 'Blake?'

Blake sighed. 'There's not exactly a sexy way to remove a prosthetic leg,' he said.

Ava blinked. She'd forgotten about his leg. Hadn't thought about the...logistics of sex with a prosthesis. Or how it made Blake feel. 'Does it...embarrass you...to take it off in front of someone...in front of a woman?'

'No,' he said. Not that he'd ever taken it off in front of a woman who personified human beauty. 'But it's a bit like stopping to put a condom on...it's a big dose of reality, which can be a bit of a passion killer.'

Ava regarded him for a moment or two. 'Well, we can't have that, can we?' she murmured.

Then she pushed against his shoulders and, as he fell back on the bed, she followed him over, rolling up until she was straddling his hips. The juncture of her thighs aligned perfectly with the bulge in his jeans and she pressed herself against him, revelling in the hard ridge. It was satisfying to hear the suck of his breath and watch his eyes shut as his big hands came up to bracket her hips.

'Feels like the passion's very much alive to me,' she murmured.

Blake opened his eyes. She was a sight to behold. Her drying caramel hair fell in fluffy waves against lovely shoulders thrust proudly back. It emphasised the firmness of her high breasts boasting erect, perfectly centred nipples. Her stomach muscles undulated and her belly button winked as her hips rocked back and forth along the length of him.

Each pass rippled urgent pleasure through the deep muscle fibres of his belly. It also caused a fascinating little jiggle through her breasts and Blake couldn't drag his eyes off them.

'I don't know,' he muttered. 'I think I've died and gone to heaven.' Then he curled up and claimed a nipple.

Ava gasped as Blake's hot mouth sucked her deep inside. She raked her fingers into his hair, capturing his head to her chest, and holding him fast. His teeth grazed the tip and her head dropped back. He switched sides, grazing the other nipple as he sucked it hard and deep, and when his fingers toyed with the other one her lips parted on a moan as she dragged in much-needed air.

Blake revelled in the moan. But he wanted more. He wanted to taste her. To swallow her moan as it vibrated against his tongue. He broke away, sought her mouth, found it as she protested his absence.

'Shh,' he said against her mouth, his hands stroking down her naked back. 'I've got you.' And when she moaned again and opened wide to the invasion of his tongue he kissed her deep and wet.

Released from the intimate torture of her nipples, Ava was able to think a little clearer—even though all he'd done was switch from one form of havoc to another. The man could kiss for England! But she needed more than that now. He was thick and hard between her thighs and *that* was what she needed.

Ava grabbed for his shirt and pulled it up his back. Then she broke off the kiss and hauled it the rest of the way off, tossing it behind her. And then her hands were on his smooth, naked shoulders and she sighed and pressed a kiss to them, they felt so good.

His hands slid to her breasts and she shut her eyes for a moment as his thumbs stroked across her nipples and he started kissing her neck.

Then she shoved his chest hard and watched him fall

back against the mattress. 'Hey,' he protested, reaching out for her.

But she just shook her head and said, 'My turn.'

And if Blake thought she looked amazing before it was nothing to how she was looking now, astride him buck naked staring down at him as if he were the main course and she were *starving*.

Ava gazed down at all his broad magnificence. The dusting of hair over his meaty pecs, the solid firmness of his abdominals. A work-honed chest. A *real* man's chest. She stroked a finger right down the centre, from the hollow at the base of his throat to where the waistband of his jeans stopped her journey. Muscles contracted beneath her finger and his breathing became more ragged.

And then she just had to taste him.

Blake groaned as her mouth tentatively touched the spot where her finger had started its journey. Her hair fell forward, brushing his chest, and he slid his hand to her shoulder and stroked down her back, revelling in the feel of her skin beneath his palm as he revelled in the feel of his skin beneath her tongue.

By the time she got to his nipples there was nothing tentative about her touch. They circled and circled as he had done to her. Sucking and licking. Flicking her tongue back and forth over them and he shut his eyes and let the sensations wash over him.

Then she headed lower. Exploring his ribs, his stomach, his belly button.

And then lower.

His zip came down, his underwear was peeled back and at the first touch of her tongue to his screamingly taut erection he bucked and cried out. And then she was relentless.

Swiping her tongue up and down the length of him, filling her hot, hot mouth with him, sucking him in deep and hard, feeling so good, so right.

He buried one hand in her hair and the other one in the coverlet, gripping the sheets as she drove him out of his mind.

It wasn't long before the tug of an orgasm made its presence known. Under her ministrations it was inevitable that he would build quickly but he didn't want it to be like this.

Not the first time.

'Ava,' he said on an outward breath. 'Stop.' She didn't stop. If anything she sucked harder. 'Ava,' he said again, curling half up, pulling at her shoulder, pulling her up.

'Wha…?' she asked, looking at him, a frown on her face.

Blake almost gave in. Her mouth was moist and swollen and she had a glazed look in her eyes that almost undid him.

'If you don't stop that now it's going to be all over and I want to be inside you when I come,' he said.

Ava's brain took a second to power up again but quickly got up to speed. She smiled at him. She'd been wondering what it would feel like to have him hot and hard inside her for the last few months. 'Condoms?'

Blake smiled back and nodded towards the bedside table. 'In the drawer.'

She was off the bed and back at his side again in fifteen seconds, tearing at the condom with shaking fingers. And then she was sheathing him, and then straddling him and leaning over him, easing herself into position, kissing him as she slowly aligned herself.

He gripped her hips hard as she slid home and her gasp and his groan mingled as they both just stilled for a moment and enjoyed the feel of their joining. And then she was pushing up and away from him, sitting proudly, her breasts bouncing as her hips undulated, finding a perfect rhythm.

Her hair was wild, and her yellow-green eyes were even wilder, all feline and primal. And she didn't look haughty now, riding atop him. Actually, no, she did. She looked like a madam on her steed and he bucked hard into her as she picked up the pace.

'God, you're magnificent,' he groaned, holding out his hands to her.

'You're pretty magnificent yourself,' she gasped as she intertwined her fingers with his.

And then neither of them talked. They just moved. Up and down. In and out. Harder. Faster. Building, building, building. Using their joined hands to lever their actions, pushing hard against each other's palms, finding every inch and every bit of depth they could.

And then she was gasping, her eyes opening wide, and she was crying out, 'Blake! Blake!' and the urgency of it all slammed into his belly and he felt himself coming apart too, joining her, calling out her name too, 'Ava!' as he came and came and came, his heart rate off the scale, bucking and thrusting like a machine, determined to give her every last bit of him, their hips slamming together as he drove and drove and drove up into her.

And he didn't stop, not even after they were both spent, not until she collapsed on top of him.

CHAPTER TEN

IT WAS AFTER eight the next morning when Blake finally stirred. He'd always been an early riser but, given that he and Ava had spent a lot of the night burning up the sheets, it was hardly surprising that he'd slept in.

She felt good spooned against his chest. As did his erection, cushioned against the cheeks of her bottom, and the handful of her hip beneath his palm. He stroked his hand down her thigh and was rewarded with an enticing little wiggle.

'Morning,' he murmured as he nuzzled her neck.

Ava smiled sleepily as the prickles of Blake's whiskers beaded her nipples. She deliberately pressed her bottom back into him as she stretched. 'What time is it?'

Blake shut his eyes as her moving weakened his resolve to get going. 'Time to get up.' They should have been under way by now.

'Really?' she asked, slipping her hand behind her and between their bodies, finding him big and hard and ready. And not for a day on the water. 'I think,' she said, giving him a squeeze and smiling when he sucked in a breath, 'you're already there.'

Blake kept his eyes shut as her hand moved up and down the length of him. 'I am,' he said, his own hand dipping down her belly and disappearing between her legs.

Ava gasped as his fingers brushed against the thoroughly abused nub, already begging for more. She let him go, slipping her arm up behind his neck, anchoring herself as she angled her hips to accommodate the slide of his erection between her thighs and the glide and rub of it along the seam of her sex.

'Man-oh-man,' she moaned. 'That feels so good.'

Blake, getting under way completely forgotten, whispered, 'You ain't seen nothing yet,' in her ear and proceeded to rub and glide from one side while his fingers worked her from the other and it wasn't until she was begging him for completion that he whispered, 'Condom.'

And Ava didn't need to be told twice.

A couple of hours later they stirred again. Blake dropped a kiss on her neck. 'We really do have to get going at some stage today,' he murmured.

Ava's eyes fluttered open. 'Why?' she asked as she turned in his arms, one arm sliding over his waist, her head resting against the soft pillow of a pectoral muscle.

Blake propped his chin on top of her head. 'Because I'm on a schedule, here. I can't stay on holiday for ever.'

Ava smiled. 'You're a schedule kind of a guy, aren't you?'

He nodded. 'And proud of it. That's what over a decade in the military does for you. That's what got you your reno on time,' Blake reminded her. He looked down at her head.

'I've seen those behind-the-scenes-at-a-fashion-show docos on the telly—those things run to tight schedules too.'

'They do,' Ava conceded. 'And I can run to a schedule as professionally as the next model. But when I'm on *holiday...*' she glanced up at him '...schedules go out the window. That's *the point* of a holiday. It's all about being flexible.'

Blake smiled down at her. 'Oh, you're *very* flexible.'

Ava rolled her eyes. 'Why can men never resist an opening?' But she kissed him anyway because he was right there and he looked even more tempting this morning than he had last night.

'My point is,' she said, pulling back from the kiss, 'you're on holiday. You don't really have to *do* anything or *be* anywhere. For instance, we could stay here in bed all day together. We could kiss and cuddle, have lots more sex, doze off, wake up, watch some telly, eat gourmet snacks I can prepare. You know...just have some fun?'

Blake felt the usual clench of his gut at the word *fun*. He knew it shouldn't affect him, that he had as much right to a full happy life, *to fun*, as the next person, but it still felt wrong to be enjoying himself when so many guys he knew couldn't.

'We can do whatever we want,' Ava continued, oblivious to Blake's consternation, 'because *we're on holiday.*'

Blake forced himself to smile and push the downer thoughts away. *He was allowed to have fun.* His shrink had told him that over and over.

'Ah, but *you're* not on holiday,' he reminded her, injecting a deliberately teasing tone into his voice. 'You've just hijacked mine. *Bribed* your way in if my memory serves me correctly.'

The thought was sobering but Ava refused to let it get her down. 'Well, it feels like it. I haven't had a lot of idle days since turning fourteen.'

Blake heard the pensive note in her voice and stroked his finger down her face. The last thing he wanted was to drag her down too. 'Okay, then, you win. A rest day.'

Ava laughed. 'In that case I better get us something to eat. Cos I don't think either of us are going to be getting much rest.'

Blake smiled. 'No,' he said. 'Allow me.'

Ava quirked an eyebrow. 'You? You can cook? You who only had a six-pack of beer in the fridge two days ago?'

'I can manage coffee, toast and fruit,' he said indignantly as he rolled onto his back, then swung into a sitting position and flicked the wall-mounted telly on with the remote, handing it to her. 'See what the media is saying about your situation and then check in with Ken.' He reached for his leg propped against the wall. 'I'll get us some breakfast or brunch or lunch...or whatever it is.'

He went through the motions of getting into his prosthesis as Ava flicked through the news channels. He could have had crutches just to get around the boat, a lot of amputees used them for domestic purposes, but he hadn't wanted to become reliant on them, preferring to always use his leg.

Blake looked around for his clothes but as he had no idea where they'd ended up last night he figured he might as well just throw on some new ones.

Ava's gaze was drawn to him as he skirted around the bed, briefly interrupting her view of the telly as he strode to his wardrobe. His brawny masculinity wasn't diminished by the prosthesis, if anything it emphasised it—a silent testament to his heroism. But there was just something kind of surreal about it and she couldn't help but laugh.

He turned and quirked an eyebrow at her and she clamped a hand over her mouth. *Way to be sensitive, Ava.* 'I'm sorry,' she said, embarrassed by her behaviour. 'I'm not... I don't—'

'What's the matter?' he interrupted and she could see the teasing light in his indigo eyes. 'Never seen a naked man with a fake leg?'

'You look like Bionic Man,' she blurted out, still clearly suffering from foot in mouth. But he did. His broad chest and shoulders and his narrow hips were perfectly proportioned. The hard, powerful quads and calves of his good leg balanced out the hard moulded plastic and titanium lines of the prosthetic. He looked half man, half machine.

Strong. Super strong.

Ava kicked the sheets off and swung her legs over the side of the bed. 'It's kind of a turn-on actually.'

He watched her walk towards, him, one hundred per cent naked, one hundred per cent up to no good, staring at his body as if she wanted to eat him. His groin fired to life.

'You're not going to be one of those chicks who has a thing for amputees, are you? Hangs out on all the forums and dating sites?'

Ava shook her head as she sank to her haunches in front of him. 'No,' she said, looking up at him, past the rapid thickening happening before her eyes. 'Just for you.'

Blake's heartbeat pounded through his ears as her gaze feasted on the jut of his now fully fledged erection. 'Ava,' he warned as the muscle fibres in his belly and his buttocks turned to liquid. 'Food... Ken...'

'Later,' she dismissed as she raised herself up, her hands

gliding up his legs and anchoring at the backs of his thighs, her mouth opening around him.

Blake's groan came from somewhere primitive inside him as hot, wet, delicious suction scrambled his brain of any rational thought. He reached for the cupboard and held on for dear life.

Later that afternoon, Blake was sitting propped against the headboard of his sleigh bed, idly flicking through channels as Ava dozed by his side. It was another warm day and they'd kicked off the sheets a long time ago so she was lying on her back stark naked, completely comfortable with her nudity.

His phone vibrated on the bedside table and he checked it. Charlie. *Still hanging with the supermodel?*

Blake smiled. *Yes.*

The reply was fast. *Slept with her yet?*

Blake's gaze wandered to her naked body, his chest filling with something akin to contentment. His fingers slid across the touchpad. *You are a pervert.*

Another fast reply. *So that's a yes?*

Blake gave a soft snort as he typed his reply. *Goodbye.*

A little yellow face with a dripping tongue hanging out its mouth appeared on the screen and Blake shook his head at his brother's juvenile wit as he returned the phone to the bedside table.

He flicked his gaze back to the telly just as an ad break came on. He was about to change the channel when Ava came on the screen. 'Hey,' he said, giving her a gentle nudge. 'Wake up, you're on the telly.'

He couldn't believe he was in bed with a woman whose face was on the telly. Her celebrity had been easier to wrap his head around when he'd just been the guy renovating her house.

Ava stirred, opening her eyes to see the cologne commercial she'd shot last year. 'Oh, yeah.' She smiled, half sitting, wriggling back, insinuating herself between Blake's thighs, snuggling her bottom in and draping her back to his stomach, her head under his chin. His arms encircled her waist and they watched it together.

Ava was proud of the commercial and had had a lot of fun filming it with one of England's most dashing young actors. It was moody, edgy, very dark and sexy, suiting the bouquet of the cologne.

Blake wasn't so enamoured as Ava, showing almost as much flesh as she was now beneath a transparent white hooded gown, was chased and then caught, her dress ripped open down the front and her neck *and parts distinctly lower* thoroughly ravaged by a dark, brooding, shirtless man.

The voice-over said, 'Beast. For the animal in us all.'

Okay, no actual prohibited-for-PG-viewing bits could be seen, but it was a very fine line and the subliminal messages were heavily sexual.

'What do you think?' she asked, turning her neck to look at him as the commercial ended.

Blake cast around for something to say that wouldn't annoy her when clearly she was pleased with the results. 'I think if I owned these,' he said, his hands sliding up her belly to her breasts, 'I wouldn't want anyone else touching them.'

Ava smiled. She wasn't surprised by his reaction. People outside the industry didn't understand how it worked. She glanced back at the telly. '*I* own these,' she said, sliding her hands up under his, cupping her own breasts, his hands falling away.

She looked down at herself, at her hands, aware he was looking too before letting go.

'Anyway...it's all just make-believe. We did that shot about a hundred times, there's a full set of people watching you, a director telling you a bit to the right, a bit to the left, hot lights, make-up people, a ticking clock. It's not as sexy as it looks.'

'So how do your boyfriends cope with that? Because, frankly, I'd want to punch that guy in the head.'

Ava laughed. 'Well, that's very Neanderthal of you.' She knew she shouldn't find that attractive but somehow it fitted with his whole ex-soldier, Bionic Man persona and she was secretly thrilled.

Blake guessed he should apologise for his prehistoric possessive streak but he didn't. 'I just don't get how it works.'

'Which is precisely why I don't have *boyfriends*. Lovers, yes, boyfriends, no. Lovers are disposable, boyfriends tend to get jealous. And only from within the circles I move in because you have to be in the biz to understand how very little all that—' she waved her hands at the screen '—means. Models, actors...they know how it works.'

'Wow,' he said derisively. 'You really are slumming it with me.'

She glanced up at him but he was smiling down at her and didn't seem to be too insulted. She ran her hand down his thigh. 'I'm making a special exception for you.'

'So, you don't have...relationships?' Didn't all women crave relationships? Connections?

Hell, didn't all human beings?

Ava looked down, following her hand as it absently caressed his thigh. 'No. Best not to. Relationships require trust. I've had some major disappointments in that sector earlier in my career, a couple of guys talking to the press and with Mum and Paul…let's just say I wised up pretty quickly.'

'That sounds kind of lonely though…'

Okay, he wasn't exactly King of relationships either, but not because he didn't believe in them. He just wasn't sure if damaged goods made very good partners.

Ava traced the outline of Blake's quad with her index finger as she shrugged. 'I don't have time for men who want to hold me down…hold me back. I don't have time for their petty jealousies. I have a finite amount of years I can do what I do and I'll worry about relationships after. For now dating and the occasional spot of casual sex with a guy in a similar situation to me suits just fine.'

Blake absently rubbed his chin against the fineness of her hair as he absorbed her very definitive views.

Ava turned her neck to face him, unnerved by his silence. She'd come to her relationship conclusions a long time ago the hard way and it had never mattered to her before what anyone thought.

But somehow it did right now.

'You think that makes me cold and unfeeling?'

'No,' Blake said and meant it.

Ava had to be the least cold and unfeeling person he knew. Sure, her snooty *touch-me-not* public image was meant to convey that, but if he'd learned anything about her at all these past three days it was that she was a strange mix of hot and cold. Strong and vulnerable. Public and private.

And he felt privileged to know the real woman beneath the distant haughty smile.

'I think you've taken control of your life and you know what you want. A lot of people never do that.'

'Damn right,' she said as she looked back at her hand on his thigh, his chuckle vibrating against her back. 'What about you and relationships?' she asked. 'You're still single.'

Ava stopped tracing the quad on his good leg and drew a line with her finger down the thigh of his amputated leg, which seemed almost the same length as its opposite number. The quad almost as meaty. 'Has this stopped you?'

Blake looked down at her hand. 'No. But there's a lot of…baggage attached to me…and I'm not much of a talker. So…that makes it hard to see past the outside to what's underneath.'

Except Ava had. Ava had known him for three months before she'd even been aware he *had* a prosthesis. She hadn't treated him differently—no pity for the cripple or reverence for the returned war hero. She'd been demanding and snooty and utterly self-absorbed. As testy with him as everyone else around her.

And despite what a pain in the butt she'd been, he suddenly realised how refreshing it had been. How deep down he'd looked forward to going to her place for a slice of equity in a world where everyone in his orbit treated him just a little bit differently than they had before he'd lost his leg. He knew they didn't mean to or even realise that they were, but he was sensitive to the subtleties.

Would Ava have been so demanding and critical if she'd known he was an amputee? Or would she have *made allowances*?

'Yep,' Ava said. 'I hear ya.' She totally understood where he was coming from with that—people never looked past her outside package.

Her palm skated to the end of his thigh and tentatively cupped his stump. His quad tensed and for a moment she thought he was going to pull it away. But he slowly relaxed into her hand and she became aware of its rounded contours.

It felt so…smooth. So…healed. So…innocuous.

Nothing liked the jagged, shredded mess it must have been to have lost it. She shut her eyes against a hundred television images she'd seen over the last decade. She couldn't even begin to imagine what he'd been through. The trauma. The pain. The loss.

'Does it hurt?' she asked after a moment.

Her hand felt cool against the stump and so pretty against the blunt ugliness of it, it took all Blake's will power not to pull away. 'No.'

'Did it?' she asked. 'Sorry, of course it did… It's just that I saw this documentary once, interviewing returned soldiers, and there was this one guy who'd lost a leg and he said he was in so much shock at the time he didn't feel anything, no pain…nothing. He didn't even realise his leg had been blown off until he woke up in hospital. He doesn't have any memory of losing it at all.'

Blake's screams, never far away, echoed in his head. Unfortunately for him, his memory had perfect recall. 'It hurt,' he said grimly. 'A lot. I screamed like a baby.'

Ava turned at the blatant contempt in his voice. 'Your leg was blown off,' she said, frowning at him. 'That must have been *incredibly* painful… I can't even begin to imagine…did you think you didn't have the right to express that pain?' She lifted her hand off his leg to his face. 'Do you think *anyone's* going to judge you for that?'

Blake saw compassion and pity in her eyes. Just as he'd seen in countless people over the last three years. And, thanks to his shrink, he'd learned that it was a natural human reaction to a sad and shocking situation. But he still had problems accepting it at face value because the truth was he judged himself more harshly than anyone else could have.

'There were other men injured in the blast, Ava. Men who were *my* responsibility.'

Ava didn't need to be a psychiatrist to tell Blake was judging himself plenty. 'Blake…are you telling me you still have to be a leader when you're bleeding in the dirt somewhere with a severed leg?'

He stared at her. 'They were my men. They looked to me.'

Ava's skin broke out in goose bumps at the utter desolation in his voice and the bleakness in his eyes. 'Even when you're injured?' she asked gently. 'Wasn't there some kind of second in command?'

Blake nodded. 'Yes. He was dead.' Colin, dead in the dirt beside him.

Ava shut her eyes. *Not helping, Ava.* 'I'm sorry,' she said, twisting in his arms, moving, straddling him, settling her butt on the tops of his thighs until they were face to face. 'I'm so sorry,' she repeated.

Then she lowered her head and kissed him—slow and sweet. 'So sorry,' she whispered against his mouth as she pulled away, hugging him close.

It felt good to have his arms circle her body, bringing her in closer until they were flush, his head nestled against her neck, her chin on top of his head.

'What was his name? Was he married?'

Blake shut his eyes, dragging in big lungfuls of her sweet-smelling skin, trying to block out the image. 'Colin,' he said. 'And yes, he was married.'

Ava could hear the roughness in his voice and she held him closer for long moments. 'Do you blame yourself?' She pulled back to look at him. 'For him dying?'

Blake looked up into her earnest gaze. That wasn't an easy question to answer. There was the logical answer. And the emotional one. And they both blurred into each other.

Ava didn't wait for him to reply. 'Would *he* blame you? This… Colin?'

Blake shook his head. It was a complicated situation but he didn't have to think about it to know the answer to that one. 'No.'

'Well, isn't that your answer?' she asked.

Blake shook his head. *If only it were that simple.* 'I was supposed to look out for him,' he said.

'Because he was one of your men?'

Blake shook his head. 'No. Well…yes, but…' Blake paused, the desire for her to understand pushing hard at his chest. 'Because he was one of my closest friends and… my brother-in-law.' He placed his forehead against her collarbone, his lips brushing her chest. 'Colin was Joanna's husband.'

Ava shut her eyes as his heavy words felt oppressive against her chest. The guilt in his voice was undeniable. Oh, *dear God*—how had Blake survived that? She tightened her arms around him.

'I'm *so* sorry,' she said.

Having to face his amputated leg every day must be a constant physical reminder of what he'd lost. Having to face Joanna, *his sister,* must be a constant *emotional* reminder. She was surprised he'd ever got his life together again.

That must have taken real strength.

Her breath stirred the hair at his temple and Blake held

her tighter too. He was used to superficial sympathy from people but with Ava wrapped around him like this it felt real.

'Have you talked to anybody about any of this?' she asked after a few moments.

Blake gave a soft snort, pulling back from her neck. 'Ad nauseam,' he said. 'The army supplies a shrink.'

'So they should,' she muttered. 'Has he helped?'

'*She,*' Blake supplied and smiled to try and soften the topic and erase the anguish from her gaze. 'And yes, actually. I was kind of resistant but, yeh… I'm in a much better place after talking to her than I had been.'

'Well, that's…good,' Ava said, feeling slightly mollified.

Blake smiled and made a concerted effort to drag himself out of the funk they'd descended into. Even he knew this was a far cry from the *fun* she'd prescribed earlier.

'It is,' he murmured, dropping a kiss on the fluttering pulse at the base of her throat. 'Although I prefer other forms of therapy.'

Ava shut her eyes as his tongue traced wet circles up the hard ridge of her throat, sinking into the heat and the thrill of it. 'Like what?'

Blake smiled as her reply buzzed against his lips and she dropped her head back to give him better access.

She might not be able to do anything about the demons in his head or erase all the bad stuff that had happened to him, but she could definitely give him her body. Maybe that was wrong, maybe she should be trying to get him to talk and open up, but she couldn't help but think that a man who'd been through what Blake had been through deserved to choose his own path to wellness.

And right now, in this moment, there was something she *could* do to help him forget for a little while.

She was definitely up for a little sexual healing.

CHAPTER ELEVEN

THE NEXT THREE days drifted by in a perfect little bubble. A bubble where she wasn't a supermodel and he wasn't a one-legged pleb totally out of her league. No lady and the carpenter thing. Just good company and great food and amazing weather.

Laughter and sunshine.

Long days of lazily navigating the waterways of southern England. Waving to fellow boaters. Operating locks. Eating at pubs.

And the nights? Long, hot, sweaty nights of a more frantic persuasion. Eager to be naked and explore. Being bold and forthright. Pushing each other to the limits of their sexuality.

Never quite getting enough.

It was as if they both knew deep down it could never last and therefore the everyday masks they wore to face the world were stripped away. Pretence was shed and there was only room for the real and the raw.

The investigation was progressing according to Ken. They were tracking down leads, leaving no stone unturned.

But no arrests had been made and his advice to keep lying low remained the same.

Ava should have been getting antsy. Ordinarily she would have been going out of her mind, not doing anything, worrying about her time out of the limelight and how that might impact her career. Reggie certainly was. Fretting about it day and night with his increasingly desperate calls and texts. Pleading with her to allow him to feed the press something…anything…any morsel to keep them fed and watered and interested.

But after a decade of unfettered availability, anonymity was seductive. A simple life on the water with a simple man was even more seductive.

And while the British press and the paparazzi were in a feeding frenzy over *Ava Watch,* obsessing over her whereabouts, reporting any faux sighting as if she were Elvis, Ava was revelling in her new-found freedom to just…be.

To not put on make-up.

To not go to the gym every day.

To stuff her face with banoffee pie at a pub and not have to watch for a telephoto lens.

To kiss Blake publicly and not worry that she was going to read about her engagement or possible pregnancy in some tabloid the next day.

But the bubble burst late on day six with a very sombre intrusion. And it was the beginning of the end.

Blake's phone rang while they were having dinner at a pub in Devizes. They were talking about the Caen Hill staircase lock they were going to tackle the next day. A good six hours of lock after lock, twenty-nine in total.

Ava watched him frown at his screen and push the answer button. He didn't say much, just, 'Right…right,' and

'When?' and 'Where?' but his face got grimmer and grimmer and she could feel a cold hand slowly closing around her heart.

'What's wrong?' she asked as he pushed the end button.

'Change of plans. I have to go to a funeral tomorrow.'

Ava blinked. No more information appeared to be forthcoming. 'Oh. Okay...who?'

'A guy I served with.'

His reply was clipped and his face, which had been animated about the adventure ahead just a few minutes ago, was suddenly as bleak and forbidding as a thunderclap. 'Where?'

'A little village outside Salisbury. I'll hire a car in the morning. I can be back by nightfall.'

Ava nodded. She wasn't sure what she should do, or say. Should she push him for more—did he want that? Or should she take him back to the boat and distract him? She looked down at their half-eaten meal, suddenly not remotely hungry. She looked around at the cheery pub crowd enjoying the late evening warmth in the beer garden.

'You want to go back to the boat?'

Blake nodded. 'Yup.'

They walked along the towpath in silence. Blake was tight-lipped and she didn't even attempt to hold his hand as she had on their way to the pub. Once they were inside the boat and Blake had locked the door behind them she turned to him and said, 'Do you want to talk about it?'

Blake shook his head, grabbing her arm and yanking her flush with his body. 'No,' he said and slammed his mouth down onto hers as he swept her off her feet and carried her into the bedroom.

Distraction it was.

* * *

The next morning dawned cool and miserable. They woke to rain patting lightly on the roof and a grey light barely making it through the curtains.

The symbolism was not lost on Ava.

'I can come with you,' she said, snuggling her back into his front, her bottom into his groin, reaching for the bone-deep warmth that seemed to have evaporated in the cold grey light.

She felt him tense and hastened to assure him. 'Not to the funeral,' she clarified. 'But for the trip. For…company.'

She expected him to say no. And for a long time he didn't say anything at all, his warm hand firm and unmoving on her belly. 'Sure,' he said. 'Company would be…good.'

And then he was kissing her neck and his hand was slid-ing between her legs and Ava opened to him, welcoming another session of feverish sex, knowing instinctively that Blake needed a physical outlet for the grief he couldn't express any other way.

A few hours later they'd been driving for an hour in virtual silence when Ava couldn't bear it any more. The landscape was as bleak as the mood in the car and her indecision was driving her nuts.

Say something, don't say something.

But in the end, she couldn't pretend they were just going for a Sunday drive in the countryside.

'What's his name?' she asked.

Blake's knuckles tightened on the steering wheel. 'Isaac Wipani.'

Ava frowned. 'That's an unusual surname.'

'He's a Kiwi. His father was a Maori. Died when he was a boy.'

'Didn't you say you served with him?'

Blake nodded. 'He joined us from the New Zealand Defence Force after he met and married an English girl.'

'How old was he?'

'Twenty-nine.'

Ava almost asked him how it happened. But really, did it matter? A man was dead. A young man. A soldier. 'Did they have children?'

'Two.'

If anything, Blake's face got grimmer and any other questions died on her lips. She wished they had the kind of relationship where she could slip her hand onto his thigh, to loan him some comfort. She knew they'd shared something special the last few days but what were four days and nights of sex compared to a lost comrade?

And he looked so incredibly unreachable in his dark suit and even darker mood she was too paralysed to try.

They made it just in time for the funeral. Blake deposited her in a pub opposite the churchyard where the service was taking place and she sat at a cosy booth cradling a coffee, looking out of the rain-spattered window at the bleak day.

Lucky for her, Joanna had thought to include clothes for when the Indian summer came to an abrupt end, which it was always bound to. The black jeans and duffel coat were baggy but the tie at the waist helped and a slouchy knitted beanie even looked quite funky and fashionable when she tucked her hair up inside it and let it pouch to one side like a beret.

It was too dark inside to wear her sunglasses but Ava still felt utterly incognito.

Half an hour later and on to her second coffee, Ava noticed movement across the road and watched as six uniformed soldiers hefted a coffin draped with the Union Jack high on their shoulders through the churchyard towards the headstones. A woman in black and two little children holding her hand came next. Then other people, silent mourners, followed at a respectable distance. A lot in uniform. A lot of civilians too.

Ava could see what was happening very clearly from her seat as the procession stopped at a clearing on the outer edge of the headstones, fresh earth piled nearby. She knew she shouldn't watch. That it was a private affair, not some spectacle to gawk at. But the sight of those two little kids broke her heart. Her breath was heavy in her lungs and she couldn't seem to look away.

Her eyes sought Blake through the crowd. Needing to find him, to see him, to know he was okay. She started to panic when she couldn't locate him, her eyes darting around more desperately. And suddenly he was there— one grim-faced man amongst a group of grim-faced men, mainly uniformed standing to one side—and she breathed again.

A loud cry cracked the laden air like a whip and Ava startled at the unexpectedness. It had come from the direction of the gravesite and her eyes scanned for the source.

It was a man's cry. A warrior's cry. A call to arms. It had easily penetrated the four-hundred-year-old stone walls of the pub and no doubt was even now echoing right down the high street if the heads poking out of windows were any indication.

She looked back towards the church in time to see movement down the far end of the gathering, about a dozen khaki-uniformed men, in two lines, one behind the other.

The men were bouncing on the balls of their feet, their knees slightly bent, their arms folded out in front of them. They advanced towards the coffin sitting at the end of the waiting hole in the ground, calling out and grunting, their faces fierce. Then it became more organised, with the men all chanting in unison, stamping their feet in time as they slowly closed in on the coffin, slapping their hands against their chests.

Ava recognised it as the special dance she'd seen the New Zealand rugby team do at the World Cup a few years back. As the men surrounded the coffin, their forceful rhythmic chants echoing through the entire village, she felt tears well in her eyes and goose bumps prick at her skin.

It was raw and primitive and so achingly mournful she couldn't remember ever seeing anything so...savage be so utterly beautiful.

As suddenly as it started, it stopped, the angry chants falling silent, and there were long moments where nothing but the light patter of rain could be heard. Then, one by one the group of soldiers straightened, tall and strong, and slowly walked backwards from where they'd come, their solemn gazes locked on the coffin, their moving tribute to a brother-in-arms complete.

'Such a shame, isn't it?'

Ava dragged her gaze away from the window at the sudden intrusion. She looked up to find the woman from behind the bar, who collected her empty coffee mug. She held out a box of tissues and Ava realised her face was wet.

'Thanks,' she said, taking a couple and dabbing at the tears.

'Such a lovely family. Jenny, the widow, she grew up just outside here, went to school just down the road,' the older woman continued as she wiped Ava's table down. 'They got married in that church.' She shook her head, tucking her dishcloth in her front apron pocket. 'Offered him a full military funeral, you know, but he never wanted that. He was coming home in three weeks...'

Ava nodded even though she didn't know. Didn't understand. Probably never would. All she could think about was Blake and what had happened to him. What if he'd died? What if she'd never known him?

The thought was so awful she could barely breathe.

'Another coffee, luv?'

She nodded. 'Yes, please.'

Ava had almost finished the third cup when the pub door opened, letting in a blast of cold, miserable air and a rowdy bunch of uniformed men and a smiling Blake. She waved at him as he looked around for her and he headed towards her.

'Hi,' Blake said as he reached the booth. He smiled at her and then frowned as she barely managed one in return. She looked as if she'd been crying. 'Are you okay?'

Ava shrugged. 'I saw that...dance.'

'Ah.' He nodded. 'The haka.'

'Yes, that's it.'

'It was a funeral haka,' he said. 'Some of the guys Isaac served with in New Zealand were over here.'

'It was...' Ava rubbed her hands up and down her arms. Even though the duffel coat was thick she still felt chilled.

'Blake, you dirty dog!'

Ava was kind of pleased for the booming interruption. She wasn't ready to articulate how deeply the funeral haka had affected her.

'You never told us you had a bird waiting for you,' a strapping great blond guy said, slapping Blake on the back. 'And a very nice-looking one at that. How are you, darlin'?' he said, holding out his hand, which Ava duly shook. 'I'm James but they just call me Jimbo.'

'Ava,' she said after a slight hesitation and a quick glance at Blake. It might not have been a common name but it was hardly unusual.

Jimbo certainly didn't bat an eyelid over it. 'Hey, guys,' he called over his shoulder. 'Come check out Blake's bird. Bring those beers over here and a champagne for the lady.'

'Sorry.' Blake grimaced. 'I hope you don't mind?'

Mind? Blake was actually smiling, which, considering his recent grimness, was a miracle. It was the most comfortable she'd seen him apart from when he was sanding wood or steering the boat.

Ava quirked an eyebrow at the man who had interrupted them. 'Make it a beer, Jimbo.'

'Oh, mate.' Jimbo laughed. 'You're on a winner there.'

Blake smiled down at her and said, 'Yeh. I think you're right,' and Ava smiled back, suddenly warm all over.

The next several hours, squashed into a booth with five strapping men, were the most educational of Ava's life. She'd have thought the mood would be sombre, and certainly there was talk about Isaac and toasts drunk to him, but mainly they just talked guy stuff and joked around with each other.

Ava was good at talking to men and fitted into the easy banter as if she'd been born to it. Jimbo, who was drinking steadily, would look at her every now and then with narrowed eyes then look at Blake and say, 'She looks really familiar.'

But she'd just shrug and tell him she had one of those faces and change the subject, getting him to tell her another story about what Blake was like during basic training, which Blake weathered like a trouper.

In fact all four of the guys who'd joined them seemed to have great stories about Blake and she encouraged them outrageously. Clearly he was well liked and respected and she was enjoying hearing about that part of his life—before he'd become so serious.

She also listened to Jimbo's female woes. The only single man at the table besides Blake, clearly he found women puzzling. She dished out some sensible advice about what women wanted and explained why infidelity was generally a deal breaker for women.

'You're lucky to have her.' Blake rolled his eyes as Jimbo repeated the decree for the tenth time.

'I don't know,' Ava said. 'Maybe I'm lucky to have him.'

'Oh, you are, you are,' Jimbo agreed. 'Good. Honourable. And brave. The man was awarded the second highest decoration for bravery you can get for what he did.'

Ava stilled. This from a man who had rejected the term hero over and over? 'What did you do?' she asked, turning to Blake.

Blake shook his head. 'It was nothing,' he dismissed. 'I was just in the right place at the right time.'

'Pulled a wounded soldier and four kids from a house fire while some bastards shot at him,' Jimbo supplied.

Ava stared at him as silence descended around the table. 'You did?'

Blake sighed. She was looking at him differently. He hated that. 'Anyone would have done it,' he said.

Jimbo burped loudly. 'Nah,' he said belligerently. 'I don't think I would have.'

A murmur of *me neither* rattled around the table and Ava quirked an eyebrow at him. 'They're lying,' Blake said. He knew these guys inside out and back to front. 'Every one of them would have.'

'Yeh, but it was you,' Ava persisted. 'You who ran into a burning building, *under fire*, and pulled a wounded man and a bunch of kids out.'

'Because I was *there,*' Blake said, exasperation straining his voice. 'It's not like you think about it—you just react. I went in to get Pete and there were a bunch of kids in there too. What was I going to do, leave them?'

Ava shook her head. 'Of course not.' Blake would no sooner turn his back on them than he had on her in her hour of need. 'Sounds like hero material to me,' she said.

'Cheers to that,' Jimbo said, raising his glass, oblivious to the undercurrent between Blake and Ava. 'Captain Blake Walker, my hero.'

Blake opened his mouth to object. He wasn't going to have a bunch of guys still serving their country while he *sanded wood* toasting him as a hero.

'And Ava, his good looking bird. Never was there a man with such great taste in women.'

Blake didn't have a comeback for that. Neither did his good-looking bird. So they laughed along with the rest of the table until someone changed the subject.

'Stop looking at me like that.'

It was after five and they'd been driving for ten minutes.

Blake could feel Ava's sideways glances like prickles beneath his ribs. He didn't want to have a conversation with her about the revelations of the day. It was bad enough she knew—he could do without the analysis.

Seeing the guys he'd served with again was always a bittersweet experience. But today had been a sombre day, a day where they'd laid a mate to rest. It wasn't the time or place to be talking about an event that happened eight years ago during his first tour of duty. Some ancient history *glory* that the brass had deemed worthy of recognition.

'So…you don't think you deserve the medal, is that it?'

Blake sighed. 'I don't think they should give out bravery medals for an act of common human decency. Servicemen do stuff like that every day in war zones,' he dismissed. 'I was just doing my job.'

Ava couldn't believe how blasé Blake was being. 'You saved the life of four kids and a soldier.'

'No, Ava, I didn't,' he said wearily. 'Pete died.'

A cold hand squeezed Ava's gut. 'He didn't make it?'

'No. He did not. Between the bullet to his gut and his burns, he passed away en route to hospital.'

Some of his bleakness leached across the space between them and settled over her like a heavy skin. How had that made Blake feel?

'I'm so sorry,' she murmured. 'That's…awful.'

'Yeh, well…that's war for you.'

Ava didn't know what to say to that. How could she even begin to imagine the things he must have seen? She looked out of the window at the grey day, misty rain forming streaky rivulets of water as it hit the glass. She'd been given a unique insight into him today, seeing him through the eyes of a group of men who clearly liked and respected him.

Ava wished she knew that man. Or had known him, anyway. She had a feeling he didn't exist any more.

Blake brooded for the next hour as they drove in silence. He hadn't meant to be so harsh with her, but he'd been to one too many funerals over the last decade and they had a tendency to mess with his head. Their closeness of the last few days seemed a distant memory now and he was sorry he'd been the one to destroy it, especially when all he really wanted was to get lost in her for a while and forget about the world and how insane it could be.

Her phone rang, the sound of rock music shattering the oppressive silence. She pulled it out of her pocket and looked down at the screen before looking at him.

'It's Ken,' she said as she quickly answered it.

Blake assumed from the one-sided conversation and Ava's palpable relief that the police had finally caught the culprit, a fact she confirmed when she hung up a few minutes later.

'They made an arrest,' Ava said, smiling at him.

A heaviness descended upon Blake's chest. 'Who?'

'Grady Hamm.'

Blake frowned at the cartoonesque name. 'There's somebody in this world called Grady Hamm?'

Ava laughed. 'Yes. There is. He's an agent. Isobella Wentworth's agent.'

'Okay…and she is?'

Ava rolled her eyes at him. Hadn't everybody in the world heard about the seventeen-year-old catwalk débutante? 'An up-and-coming model. Britain's next big thing? And up for the same advertising campaign I am.'

'Ah.' The penny dropped. 'And he shot up your house to keep you out of the picture for a bit?'

She nodded. 'Well, he didn't shoot it up. He paid someone else to do it but, yes…it was just a scare tactic, apparently.'

A surge of anger jettisoned into Blake's system and he gripped the steering wheel as he remembered how frightened Ava had been. There was nothing *just* about it. 'A scare tactic that worked.'

'Yes. Until Isobella found out and dobbed him in.'

Blake whistled. 'That must have taken some balls for a teenage wannabe to turn in her agent.'

Ava nodded in agreement. It did. She knew the kind of fortitude that took intimately. 'I owe her, definitely.'

Blake contemplated the road for a few seconds as the full implications of the arrest sank in. 'So, you're free to go back home,' he said, injecting a cheeriness that felt one hundred per cent false after such a sombre day.

'Yes.' That should have been exciting but Ava felt as if they had unfinished business between them.

'It's time for your stitches to come out anyway,' he said, trying to be practical.

Ava looked down at the sticking plaster on her palm. 'Yes,' she said again.

'You should take the car as soon as we get back to the boat. You could be in London by nine.'

Ava knew that not only sounded feasible but sensible. But there was no way she was leaving Blake tonight.

Not after today.

'I'll go in the morning,' she said.

Blake opened his mouth to protest. There was no reason for her to stick around—their arrangement had only ever been temporary. But her phone rang again. 'Reggie.' She grimaced as she answered.

'Ava, darling, you have to get back here pronto!'

Reggie's voice was shouting in her ear as he spoke over what could only be a huge gaggle of press all yelling at him in the background. She could picture him now standing on the top of his steps leading into his Notting Hill office.

'Listen to them,' he said over the din. 'Come back, get a picture with Isobella. They're going nutso down here.'

Ava shook her head as she pulled the phone slightly away from her ear. She couldn't. And she couldn't explain why either. She just couldn't. 'I'll be back in the morning.'

'Ava…' Reggie spluttered. 'Don't be ridiculous. This is the kind of publicity you just can't buy.'

Ava was sure it was but that wasn't the point as she glanced at Blake. 'I'll see you tomorrow,' she said and hung up on his continuing protests.

'He's right, Ava.' Blake had heard every shouted word in the whisper-quiet confines of the hire car.

Ava shook her head. 'I'm not leaving tonight.'

'Ava.'

'I'm. Not. Leaving.'

CHAPTER TWELVE

AVA WASN'T SURE how long she'd been asleep when a loud cry woke her from her deep post-coital slumber. Her eyes flicked open and for a few seconds in the dark, her heartbeat thundering in her chest, she grappled to orientate herself. Then the cry came again—anguished, full of pain—and there was movement beside her and she realised Blake had vaulted upright in bed.

She groped through a groggy brain and leadened muscles to make sense of what was happening as he rocked back and forth.

'Blake?' She reached over and flicked on the lamp, her eyes shutting as the light hit them. 'What's wrong?' she asked, her hand sliding up his bare back as her eyes slowly adjusted to the light.

Blake sucked in a breath, biting back the expletive and another bellow of pain. 'It's my leg,' he seethed at the all too familiar sensation of hot jagged metal jabbing into his stump. Like the blast pain all over again. He raised his thigh and slammed it down against the mattress over and over trying to ease the crippling burn.

Ava shook her head as the mattress reverberated with the pounding. His leg? What did he mean? 'What's wrong with it?' she asked over his guttural groaning, looking down at it for signs of redness or bleeding or anything that could be causing him so much pain.

But it looked exactly the same as it always had.

He didn't answer her, just groaned louder as his movement grew more frantic and he became increasingly distressed. He kneaded his fisted hand so hard into his quad all the way down to his stump she winced and then he started pounding it, lifting his fist up then bringing it down hard.

'Don't, stop it,' she said, tears threatening in the face of his inconsolable pain and the brutality of his actions. She felt utterly useless. 'Please,' she said, pulling at his arm. 'Stop…you'll hurt yourself.'

He ignored her, shaking her hand off, his seething breath sucking noisily through clenched teeth as he pounded at his leg.

Ava didn't understand what was happening. Was he having a nightmare? Some kind of a flashback. Was he awake? 'Why are you doing that?' she asked, grabbing for his arm again.

'Because it helps with the phantom pains,' he yelled trying to shrug her restraining hands off.

Ava vaguely recalled having read an article on phantom limb pain a few years back. Something about residual nervous involvement in the amputated limb. Not that she remembered a single skerrick of anything that could be useful right now.

'That helps?' It was hard to believe anything so brutal could be used to treat pain—it seemed counter-intuitive.

'Yes.' Blake could already feel it starting to ease its grip. 'Pressure on the stump helps.'

Ava blinked. *There was pressure and there was pressure*. Surely it was going to be bruised tomorrow? Before she could think about it, she was shifting, moving, kneeling on her haunches between his legs. The fact that they were both naked hadn't even registered.

'Let me try,' she said, placing her hand over his fist, pushing it away, quickly replacing it with her hands, wrapping them around his stump and applying firm even pressure, squeezing rhythmically.

Blake felt himself slowly relax as Ava's hands worked their magic. He doubted they would have had any effect had it not already started to ease up—but they felt cool and heavenly now as the pain proper started to fade.

Ava concentrated on the job at hand, determined to at least try and help him, satisfied as he seemed to be slowly relaxing, his breathing settling, his death grip on the sheet with his other hand easing. 'Does this happen often?' she asked.

Blake shut his eyes and tried to focus on his breath and not the pain as the shrink had counselled. 'In the beginning quite a lot but I was one of the lucky ones able to get on top of it with medication…and time.'

Ava looked up at him. He had his eyes shut and despite his body slowly relaxing he looked haggard and tense in the lamplight. 'But it's obviously not cured.' She couldn't bear the thought of him, here alone, going through this with no one around to comfort him.

'I usually wear a sock-thing to bed over the stump, which is a good maintenance strategy that seems to keep them at bay. But…'

Blake opened his eyes to find her looking at him.

Ava didn't need him to finish. 'I've been here and you haven't been wearing anything to bed.' Guilt washed over her and tears pricked her eyes again—had *she* been responsible for this relapse?

He shrugged. 'It's okay. I doubt the funeral helped, either. I'm sure my shrink would say there's some psychological component as to why this is happening tonight.'

He sighed and rubbed a hand along the back of his neck, shutting his eyes again. 'It's been a hell of a day.'

Ava ducked her head as the tears threatened to become a reality. A hell of a day? It had been a hell of a *life* for him.

Serving his country. Earning a medal for bravery and just brushing it off as if it were nothing because he truly believed he'd only done what any decent human being would have done. Paying bodily for that belief. Still paying. Still going to funerals. Still waking in the night to excruciating pain from a leg that was no longer there.

The stump was smooth beneath her hand now but the pain… She couldn't bear the thought of the pain he must have endured. If what she'd seen tonight was just a tiny indication of how it must have been in those moments straight after the explosion, she didn't know how he'd got through it.

The haka chants drummed through her head with each knead of her hands—the anger and the anguish washing over her, swelling in her chest, building and building, pressure in her throat and her lungs and pricking at her eyes and nose.

Blake felt something warm and wet on his thigh and looked down to find a single drop of moisture. He glanced up at Ava's downcast head. 'Hey,' he said, trying to look under her curtain of caramel hair.

He slid his hand to her jaw and gently lifted her chin to find tears dampening her cheeks. 'Why are you crying?'

Ava shook her head. She couldn't answer. She knew if she said one thing everything would come tumbling out and that would not be pretty because it churned in a big ugly mass inside her with no real cohesion.

'Ava. It's okay,' he murmured, smearing a newly fallen tear across her cheek with a thumb. 'I'm fine now. The pain's gone. You helped,' he assured her. 'You helped a lot.'

He dragged her closer and she shifted until she was straddling him, her arms around his neck. He looked up at her, kissing her nose and eyelids and her cheeks. Kissing the tears away. 'Shh,' he said. 'Shh.'

The lump in Ava's throat became bigger. She'd never met a man so…good. He reminded her of her father and she clung even harder to his neck

'Talk to me, Ava,' he murmured quietly as he dropped butterfly kisses all over her face. 'Talk to me.'

She shook her head. 'I can't… I can't bear the thought of the…pain you must have been through,' she said, trying to talk past the constriction in her throat. 'You've been through so…much and here's me with my own pathetic little troubles. For crying out loud, you have no leg, you have all this guilt about Colin and get…terrible pain and you have to keep going to funerals all the time and I…and I…'

'Oh, Ava, no…shh,' Blake said, pushing his hands into her hair, cupping her face so she was looking right at him. 'Someone shot at your house—'

Ava could feel more tears clogging in her throat and squeezing out of her eyes. 'But it was just to scare me. It wasn't for real…not like what you've faced.'

'Hey,' he said, pushing her hair back off her face. 'I was there. It was pretty real if you asked me.'

Ava nodded even as her brain dismissed the sentiment. There was real and there was *real*. 'Were you scared...over there?' she asked.

Blake nodded. 'Sometimes...yeh.'

A sob rose in Ava's throat. Blake who was strong and brave had felt fear and pain and been exposed to so much loss because his country had asked it of him. 'Why do we fight each other?' she whispered.

Blake felt helpless in the face of a question he had no clue how to answer. Her yellow-green eyes were two huge pools of compassion and anguish. 'I don't know,' he said.

And then he kissed her because that he did know. He did know how he could make it better. For tonight anyway.

The parting the next morning was a lot harder than Ava ever imagined it would be. They weren't *just* two people who had shared a boat for a week. He'd been more than the safe haven she'd asked of him. They'd shared a bed. Intimacies. They'd opened up their bodies and shared themselves.

More than either of them had ever shared before with someone other than their nearest and dearest.

It was another rainy day and Ava snuggled into her coat as they stood by the hire car saying their goodbyes. 'Maybe we could see each other...when you get back to London,' Ava suggested.

She'd never been with anyone like Blake—for good reason. But maybe it was time to revisit that?

Blake shook his head, remembering the constant presence of media in her life, the way the paps had bayed for a comment at the roped-off area the night of the shooting.

And that commercial they'd watched together with the guy ripping off her gown and ravaging her.

He really didn't think he'd be very good with stuff like that.

'I think you and I live in very different worlds,' he said. 'I don't think I could live in yours and—' he glanced over at the boat '—I'm pretty sure you don't want to live in mine. Best to quit while we're ahead.'

Ava nodded. He was right, of course, but there was part of her that didn't want to let go.

'I'll see you around no doubt at the charity functions,' Blake added. 'The Christmas Eve fund-raiser is going to be huge. They've booked out the London Eye and I have a feeling Joanna's going to be working her new patron like a dog.'

Ava smiled. 'I look forward to it.'

Blake opened the door for her. 'Goodbye, Ava,' he said.

He could easily have leaned in and kissed her but, in his experience with Ava Kelly to date, he had trouble stopping at just one.

Ava nodded. 'Thank you for everything,' she murmured.

Blake grinned because the weather and the mood of the last twenty-four hours had been sombre enough without continuing it. 'It was my pleasure.'

She grinned back. 'And mine.'

And then she ducked into the car and he shut the door after her and she started it up and within a minute she was watching him grow smaller and smaller in the rear-view mirror.

The bubble had well and truly burst.

And for two long months she didn't see him. The frenzy and the endless speculation about Ava and Isobella had died down thanks to an A-list celebrity cheating on his wife, and the whole tawdry affair blew over. Ava went to America for ten days, and scored the new commerical. She did the talk show circuit—now more in demand than ever—and she and Reggie made inroads on her calendar for the next year while cultivating new contacts.

She flew to Milan and then on to Paris. All the designers wanted her because of her rekindled buzz and Reggie made sure they paid. But when she strutted onto the catwalk and caused a mini-sensation thanks to her recent notoriety the cameras popped and people noticed what she was wearing.

September became October back in the UK and all trace of that blissful bubble of sunshine on the English canals had vanished. The weather was bleak and dreary. Cold with endless drizzle that seeped damp into everything including the marrow.

Ava thought about Blake constantly. Wondered what he was doing. Wondered how his holiday had gone. If he was back at work yet. She picked up the phone to call or text him a dozen times a day. But never followed through.

Which was just as well—she was too busy anyway. There weren't too many nights she wasn't out and about on some dashing escort's arm—openings, galas, red-carpet events. If it was on and it was *big*, thanks to Reggie and Grady Hamm, she was there.

Not that she spent the night with any of her escorts. Her intentions were always open but as the night progressed she'd spend more and more time comparing them to Blake and it didn't seem to matter that they'd just been named in the top one hundred beautiful people or had landed a lead role in a Hollywood blockbuster.

None of them measured up.

She knew Blake was just an anomaly and had he been around he'd tell her she was just obsessing about him purely because she couldn't have him.

But that didn't make him, or the lack of him, any less distracting.

And then Remembrance Sunday dawned, another fittingly bleak day, and Ava lay in bed with the covers pulled up to her chin, not even bothering to get up. She wondered if Blake was attending a service somewhere. Maybe hanging out in a pub with some of his army mates?

Maybe getting quietly drunk on his boat?

It was only a knock at her door around ten a.m. that roused her from her lethargy. For a moment she even contemplated not answering it, but hauled herself out of bed, throwing on a polar fleece gown, welcoming any distraction.

Or at least she'd thought so until she opened her door to find her mother, conspicuous by her absence these last couple of months, flirting with the press with all her brash blonde falseness. She'd been on Ibiza when Ava's house had been shot up and, apart from that one phone call, this was the first Ava had seen or heard of her for six months.

Sheila Kelly air-kissed Ava's face for the sake of the cameras and swept inside requesting a tour of the renovations. Ava shut the door on the 'give your mum a kiss, Ava' calls coming from the little clutch of paps and girded her loins.

She complied to her mother's request but was mentally preparing herself for the catch. For the ulterior motive.

Sheila cooed appreciatively at all the big-ticket items—at the roof and the pool and the acres of glass and steel—but sniffed dismissively at the homey wooden kitchen.

'You could pay a personal chef on what you earn,' she tutted.

And there it was, the entrée her mother was clearly looking for. Ava waited patiently for her mother to come out with it. 'Paul rang offering me another book deal,' she announced casually.

Ava barely supressed a snort at the mention of her ex-agent's name, now doing shonky off-shore deals in the literary field. She didn't understand how her mother could still associate with him. Ava reached for her handbag that was on the kitchen bench. 'How much this time?' she asked, pulling out her cheque book.

'A quarter of a million,' Sheila said. 'Since your little… scandal with Isobella, the price for a tell-all memoir has gone up considerably.'

Ava gritted her teeth. She paid her mother a generous allowance every month that kept her in houses and holidays, but she stopped by at least a couple of times a year for a top-up.

'I should just write it, darling,' Sheila said. 'Paul said it could be very lucrative for me. I wouldn't need to depend on you then.'

Ava snorted—she bet he had. 'No,' she said, signing the cheque. 'No tell-all. You write a single word and I will cut you off.' She tore it out of the book as noisily as she could.

Ava didn't care what her mother wrote about her—her twisted version of the truth. Ava knew the real story. But she didn't trust her mother not to tell lies about her father and that she couldn't tolerate. She wouldn't let her father's memory be besmirched.

'There's no need for that,' her mother replied waspishly as she took the cheque.

Ava folded her arms. 'Good.'

They stared at each other for a moment, then Sheila said, 'I'll be off, then.'

Ava nodded. Of course. Her mother had got what she'd come for. There was no hug or air kisses this time—no cameras inside the house.

She watched as Sheila headed to the door and let herself out, surprised to find her hands were shaking as she put the cheque book back in her bag. A sense of being alone in the world assailed Ava, which, given how many people she had around her, was absurd in the extreme.

But she cursed her mother anyway, stupid tears in her eyes.

And before she knew what she was doing she was tracking back to her bedroom, picking up her phone off the bedside table and scrolling through her contacts.

Blake answered on the second ring. 'Hello?'

Ava shut her eyes, feeling foolish for having even rung him now, but his voice sounded so good.

'Hello?'

'Blake...'

There was a very definite pause at the other end before he said, 'Ava,' in a voice so wary she could practically cut the trepidation with a knife.

The tears built more insistently behind her eyes and she was glad she had them closed.

'Are you okay?'

Ava shook her head. 'No. Can you come over?'

Blake knew it was a bad idea when he left his boat the second her husky request was out. He knew it was a bad idea as he pulled up in front of Ava's house and four different cameras took pictures of him and one of the paps said, 'Hey, aren't you that builder guy?' He knew it was a bad idea when she answered the door in nothing but her dressing gown and a haughty look.

But it didn't stop him stepping inside when she pulled the door open. And it didn't stop him wanting to kiss her. It sure as hell didn't stop him *actually* kissing her when she shut the door, the haughtiness evaporating as she reached for him, and put her mouth to his.

Later he would come to know it as the FFK—the first fatal kiss—but in that moment nothing mattered. Not the two months of separation, not endless footage of her with other guys, not the giant divide in their lives so aptly demonstrated by the cameras on the other side of the door.

He just sucked her in, his senses filling with the smell and the taste of her as he pushed her hard against the nearby wall and devoured her mouth as if it were his last meal.

He groaned as she opened to him, kissed him back with equal vigour. He'd missed her—the feel and the smell and the taste of her. He'd missed her snooty little smile and the way she ate her food and her sexy, frilly lingerie hanging everywhere.

He missed her complete lack of inhibitions.

He missed the way she kissed—wide open and full throttle. The way he didn't have to duck and she didn't have to rise up on tippy-toe to align their mouths. The way her mouth was always just right there level with his and, God help him, always one hundred per cent willing.

Ava clung to Blake as the kiss went on and on. She hadn't realised how much she'd been starving for his mouth until it was on hers again.

And now it was time to feast.

'God, I missed you,' she said, pulling back slightly, their gazes meshing as she tried to catch her heavy breath, each oxygen molecule drowned in lashings of Blake.

Which was true—but not the full truth. She'd *more* than missed him. *She loved him.* As soon as she'd opened the door to him—no, before that—as soon as he'd knocked, she'd known.

Because he'd come.

She'd asked and he'd dropped everything to be here. No questions. Just action.

There'd only been two men in her life who'd done that for her and she loved both of them too. One was her father. The other was Reggie.

And now there was Blake. Her big, brave, wounded warrior who had come without hesitation when she'd called. Who was looking at her with desire and lust but also with a healthy dose of wariness, his barriers fully up, clearly *not* loving her back.

So there was no way she could tell him—she'd learned a long time ago not to give *any* man that kind of power over you.

But she *could* show him.

She *could* love him with her body. And whisper it in her mind.

Blake sucked in a breath as the noise of his zip coming down sounded loud enough to be heard outside. He bit back a groan as her hand brushed his erection, reaching down to stop her, shutting his eyes as he dragged himself back from the lure of what could be.

His head spun with the effort and the sweet intoxication of her. He hadn't come for this.

No matter how much he wanted it.

Nothing had changed between them. If anything it had reverted to what it had always been. Ava crooking her finger and expecting him to come running.

Which he had.

He'd told her once he wasn't going to be her plaything and he meant it.

He captured her hand and pulled it up, trapping it against his chest as he leaned his forehead on hers and drew in some unsteady breaths. They both did.

When he felt under control again he eased back a little and said, 'What's this about, Ava?'

Ava felt all the desperation leach out of her at his calm enquiry. She let her head flop back against the wall. 'Sorry,' she said, her voice annoyingly husky. 'My mother was here. She always makes me a little crazy.'

'What did she want?'

Ava's gaze met his. 'The same thing she always wants. *Money.* Paul, who's now in publishing, keeps waving a tell-all book deal under her nose and I keep matching his offers.'

Blake's jaw clenched against a wave of disgust. What pieces of work they both were. 'Did you give it to her?'

Ava shrugged, hugging herself against how tawdry it all sounded. 'I've got the money.'

Blake shook his head at her wretchedness, his need to smash things duelling with her need to be comforted. He'd tried to forget in their two months apart how truly alone she was in the world but here it was in full Technicolor.

Sure, she might not have been short for an escort to a film premiere but she had no real family to look out for her.

Except Reggie.

And now him.

He took two calming breaths, then closed the short distance between them, his hands sliding to her hips. He could be outraged later. For now she really did need him.

He stroked a hand down her face. 'I'm sorry,' he said. 'What can I do?'

Ava gave him a half-smile as she slid her hand onto his arm. 'Right now? You can help me forget about my mother.'

Blake dropped his gaze to her mouth then flicked it up again, his resistance completely shot. 'Just once.'

Ava's smile broadened. 'Absolutely. But she's a *very* hard woman to forget. Might take you all day.'

Blake grinned.

CHAPTER THIRTEEN

TWO WEEKS LATER Blake was up late working on a kitchen design for a client when he heard dainty footsteps on the bow and then a familiar little knock and his pulse kicked up in anticipation.

They shouldn't still be doing this.

But they were.

He was *still* helping Ava forget her mother—every single night. All night long. They didn't seem to be able to stop no matter how much they said they were going to as she left each morning.

It was that first fatal kiss that had done it.

He'd been fine resisting the *notion* of her for two months—finishing his holiday, going back to work, getting on with his life. Fine with her image seemingly everywhere. Fine with opening the paper and reading about her. Fine to be the *friend* Ava had referred to in her media statement on her return to London, which hadn't lessened the speculation as to how she'd managed to lay so low for a week.

But then she'd kissed him and a wellspring of craving had erupted inside him and he *could not get enough.*

He certainly couldn't stop.

He'd broken the seal on his resistance and there was no way he was getting that sucker back. It had flown the coop and there was no hope of recapturing it.

But the worst thing was, it was more than sexual—how much more he didn't want to think about. He just knew he actually looked forward to her company—something he'd have never thought possible a few months ago.

It was as if there were two different Avas—the public persona, *Keep-out Kelly*, who left them wanting more with her *touch-me-not* smile and her ball-breaking business sense. And then there was the private persona. The one who let her guard down. The one who tramped onto his boat every night fresh from some red-carpet event schmoozing with the A-list eager to be with *him*. The one who cooked gourmet snacks for him in her underwear, who burped after she skulled half a can of beer, who smiled at him with her t*ouch-me-everywhere* smile.

Who left the boat every morning looking a hot mess and didn't seem to care.

Maybe that was part of the allure, the continuing of what they'd had for that week out on the canals. Where she could be nobody and they could be lovers and no one was around to care. No paps taking her picture or fans asking for her autograph.

Just him and her and their bubble.

The knock came again just as he'd almost reached the door and a muffled, 'Open up, I want to do unspeakable things to your body,' had him quickening the pace.

'I beg your pardon.' He grinned as he pushed open the door to a freezing London night to find her standing huddled into a long black coat buckled at the waist and her collar up to keep her neck warm. 'I object to being so outrageously objectified.'

'Oh, really?' Ava said, raising an eyebrow, unbuckling her coat and opening the lapels to reveal her nudity.

Blake's eyes widened as he forgot all about the bracing cold pushing icy fingers inside the boat, his gaze fixed on the hard points of her nipples.

'*Now* can I do unspeakable things to you?' she demanded.

Blake grabbed her hand. 'I am all yours,' he said as he pulled her inside.

Half an hour later they were lying in the dark together. Blake was drifting his fingers up and down her arm enhancing Ava's post-coital drowse. The urge to blurt out her feelings was never far away but something always held her back. She thought Blake might feel the same way, or at least feel something more than sex, but things were so perfect—she didn't want to rock the boat.

Literally or figuratively.

'I love this boat,' she said instead, rolling onto her side and snuggling into him. 'It's like my secret hideaway.'

Blake smiled. *'Mi casa es su casa,'* he said and surprised himself by how much he meant it. She *was* welcome here any time.

'It was my hideaway for a long time. It was like a…lifeline or something…somewhere to lick my wounds.'

Ava brushed her lips against his shoulder. If anyone had needed a place to lick his wounds it had been Blake. If she'd gone through what he'd endured, she'd still be holed up in a drunken stupor.

'You mentioned once that you'd received some news that

made you realise there were worse things than having one leg. Do you mind me asking what it was?'

Blake stared at the ceiling for long moments.

'One of the guys in my unit…he had the same thing happen to him about six months after me, lost a leg. But…'

Blake hesitated. He'd never told anyone about this. But it felt right unburdening himself to Ava, especially in their private little bubble.

'He also had his genitals blown off.'

Ava gasped, rising up on her elbow to look down at him. 'That's…terrible.'

She felt absurd tears prick the backs of her eyes as she tried to grapple with what that must mean to a person. How would she like to go through her life never being able to be physically intimate?

Blake saw the shine in her eyes as he reached out to tuck a stray strand of caramel hair that had fallen forward behind Ava's ear and he gave her a gentle smile.

His Ava was surprisingly mushy on the inside.

His Ava. The thought was equal parts terrifying and tantalising.

'It made me rethink my attitude, that's for sure. I mean, there I was, essentially fully functional, while some guys… they're never going to be fully functional. At least I could still have sex. Still…' he looked into Ava's yellow-green eyes shining with compassion '…make love to a woman.'

Ava's heart felt like a boulder in her chest. She shifted, moved over him until she was lying on top of him, her forehead pressed into his neck, his heartbeat loud in her ear. His arms wrapped around her body and a tear slid out of her eye.

After a few moments she raised her head to look down at him. 'Make love to me,' she whispered.

Blake lifted his head and kissed her. He should say no. They weren't supposed to be dragging this impossible thing out. But he couldn't. He wanted to do exactly as she'd asked.

So he rolled her over and made love like there was no tomorrow.

Ava felt a lot more sombre the next morning as he saw her off the boat. The plight of the soldier he'd told her about last night had wormed its way under her skin and she held him a little longer, kissed him a little deeper. Usually Blake stayed inside the warmth of the boat as she exited but it was as if he could sense her sadness, and even though he was only in his boxer briefs and T-shirt he climbed out with her and held her for as long as she needed.

'You okay?' he asked as she finally pulled away.

She very nearly confessed then and there, but she felt absurdly close to tears again and she doubted she could get it out without being a big snotty mess and she had a magazine shoot to get to in just over an hour.

She gave him a small smile and a nod. And even though she knew she shouldn't ask she said, 'See you tonight?'

He kissed her. And even though he knew he shouldn't agree, that they should be ending this, he said, 'Tonight.'

But by two o'clock in the afternoon everything had changed.

Blake was at work when he got the first inkling of the storm that was about to take over his life. He was at his desk when he looked up to see Joanna and Charlie approaching and his keen sense of doom kicked into overdrive.

They pulled up in front of his desk looking like they did that day a few years ago they'd called by the boat together—a united front—ready for an intervention. 'What?' he asked warily.

Joanna fiddled with his stapler. 'I've just seen you on the telly.'

Blake frowned. *'What?'*

'On the news. Pictures of you,' she clarified. 'And Ava. On the boat.'

Blake's frown deepened. 'During my holiday?' he asked.

'Umm…no,' Joanna said, putting his stapler down and picking up a ruler, tapping it lightly on his desk. 'Apparently they were…taken this morning.'

Charlie folded his arms across his chest and eyeballed his brother. 'You *are* shagging her.'

Joanna dug Charlie hard in the ribs and he grabbed his side.

Blake stood as his mind went back to this morning. To kissing her goodbye out in the open. Not that he'd been looking, but he certainly hadn't noticed a clutch of paps. Maybe someone on a neighbouring boat recognised her and decided to make a quid or two?

'What kind of pictures?' he asked.

'I'm-shagging-Ava-Kelly pictures,' Charlie said. 'Or at least that's what your hand on her arse and your tongue down her throat says to me.'

'I mean do they look clear? Are they professional or amateur?'

'You can tell it's you and her *very* clearly,' Charlie said. 'But it looks like they were taken from a distance, like you see in all those magazines, with a telephoto lens or something.'

Blake plopped back onto his chair. Photographers had

been staking out his boat? Had they followed her or had someone tipped them off?

The very thought gave him the creeps.

'What did they say about the pictures?' he asked.

'They were wondering who you are and if you were Ava's latest,' Joanna said, still tapping the ruler. 'If you were the friend she'd hidden away with for that week she'd dropped out…stuff like that.'

Blake didn't know how to feel about the news except for the fact that it probably made it easier to make the break they should have made a fortnight ago.

Which should have made him relieved.

It didn't.

'Oh, well, I guess it pays to be nobody, huh?' he dismissed absently.

Joanne and Charlie looked at each other and Blake's skin prickled with unease. The tapping of the ruler got louder and Blake snatched it out of Joanna's hand. 'Just say it,' he said.

'They're already speculating about…your leg,' she said.

Blake frowned. *His leg?* Of course…his boxers this morning would have been no match for a telephoto lens. 'Must be a slow news day. I'm sure everyone will move on soon.'

He sure hoped so because the idea of a lens trained on his boat was a little too reminiscent of a rifle sight for his liking.

Joanna shook her head. 'The pictures are practically going viral online and on social media,' she said, her voice doubtful. 'The British press are still all dying to know where Ava went for that week… The whole thing with Grady Hamm has caused a huge stir, Blake. Combine that with the pretty intense interest her love life has always roused and I don't know that this is going to blow over so soon.'

Blake's phone rang. 'It's Ava,' he said as he answered the call.

'There's photos of us on the news.'

Blake almost laughed at her panicked opener. No preamble—just straight to the point. 'Yes. I know.'

'I'm *so, so* sorry. They must have followed me.'

Blake shrugged. 'Yeh, but I'm not anybody so... I'm sure it'll all blow over.'

Her groan was Blake's first indication that he might be underestimating the situation. 'Blake...they're going to know who you are within hours. Their editors are going to want to know every single thing about you and I wouldn't be surprised if it's in all the evening papers. There's probably someone going through your rubbish right now.'

Blake laughed. 'Why would they want to go through *my* rubbish?'

'*Because your hand is on my arse,*' she said testily. 'And they don't know who you are, which is driving them crazy. It's only going to be a matter of time before one of them realises you're the guy who was at my place for three months.'

Blake couldn't believe they'd be interested in a guy like him. 'And when they do they'll find there's nothing very exciting about me at all and they'll move on.'

'Oh, Blake. You don't know how intrusive this is... How could you?'

Her tone was hopeless and he started to worry. For her. 'I'm a big boy, Ava. I'm sure I'll cope.'

'I don't think you should go to the boat tonight.'

'*What?*'

'I think they'll be waiting for you. They're kind of persistent.'

And then it really dawned on him what she was saying. 'So...you're not coming tonight?'

'No.'

Blake tried to rein in his disappointment. A part of him could see it was a good thing—something they should have done a fortnight ago—but part of him didn't want to let go either.

'You know if you didn't want to come...if you wanted it over, you could just say.'

'Blake...no.' Her voice was instantly dismissive and he believed her. 'Trust me, you're not going to want me where they'll be. Maybe we can meet somewhere else. A hotel, maybe?'

'A hotel?' Blake couldn't believe what she was saying. 'You want a place that charges by the hour or do you prefer your *usual* suite?'

'Blake...please... I'm just trying to save you from this. It's probably going to get ugly.'

Blake snorted. *As if he cared about ugly.* It sounded like she was more interested in saving herself and her rep to him.

Fine by him.

He should never have let it get this far anyway. 'Well, you do what you've got to do,' he said tersely and hung up.

He looked at Joanna and Charlie, who had clearly been listening. 'What are *you* going to do?' Joanna asked.

Blake rolled his eyes. 'I'm going to finish up here for the day, then I'm going to go home.'

Charlie and Joanna exchanged looks and Blake resolutely ignored them.

By nightfall, Blake had changed his tune. The evening papers were full of his arse grope and when he was heading down the walkway to his boat's permanent mooring it was surrounded by paps. A few months back he wouldn't have known a paparazzo if he'd fallen over one—now he was all too familiar with them.

He'd backed away and ended up at Charlie's place with Joanna flicking between news stations.

Ava rang and texted several times but Blake, feeling grimmer and grimmer as the night progressed, did not feel like talking. By the time he'd bunked down on the couch the press knew his name, rank and serial number. By the time he woke in the morning they knew a lot more than that.

Charlie had got up early to buy all the tabloids and it was clear no part of Blake's life had been considered sacred.

Ava had been right—he'd had *no* idea how voracious the press could be. His army record was there for anyone, anywhere to read. His tours, the units he'd served with, the explosion and his subsequent amputation with a close-up of his prosthesis.

One paper exploited his military record with the headline—*Ava's Crippled War Hero.* Another took a different tack with—*The Carpenter and the Lady.* They'd got comments from his neighbours, people he used to serve with and clients he'd worked with.

But the hardest thing of all was the big splash about his commendation. His *act of heroism* was recounted in all its trumped-up glory. Blake felt ill. The news was making him out to be some kind of Second Coming and all he could see was Pete dying in the back of a military ambulance. Colin, lying dead in the dirt while he cried out in pain.

So many men dead and permanently maimed and this… *crap* was all they cared about?

How would the men he'd served with, *men who were*

still serving, still putting themselves on the line, feel about all this?

He was so angry he wanted to smash things with his bare hands. Angry about frivolous 'news' and first-world privilege, but mostly about confirming something he'd always known deep down—he couldn't live like this. Under constant scrutiny.

Ava and he were worlds apart and they never should have crossed the divide.

This was his worst-case scenario and he was living it.

His life was under the magnifying glass along with the lives of everyone he'd ever touched. People who'd never asked for this.

These last two weeks had been some of the happiest of his life. But this…nightmare was the flipside.

'Blake?' Joanna squeezed his shoulder and handed him a coffee. He took it and scooted over so she could sit beside him. 'They're not lying, Blake. I know you find this hard to take, but what you did *does* make you a hero to a lot of people.'

'Do you think Colin would say that?' he demanded and hated that he'd made her flinch.

Joanna recovered quickly and looked him straight in the eye. 'Colin would say it most of all.' She squeezed his knee. 'You were always his hero. He looked up to you. He was proud to serve with you. But you know what, Blake? He would have done it anyway. With or without you. What happened to him could have happened at *any* time.'

Blake shut his eyes against the way out in words. It could have-but it didn't. It happened on *his* watch.

A knock interrupted them. 'That'll be Ava,' Joanna announced, pushing herself up.

Blake almost choked on his first sip of coffee. 'And how *does* Ava know I'm here?'

'I told her, *stooped*.' Joanna grinned. 'She's my new best friend, didn't you know? Besties tell each other everything.'

'Joanna.' His voice held a warning.

'You have to talk to her, Blake. She's worried about you.'

'It's not going to work out between us, Joanna, so you can just stop planning the hen night.'

Joanna shook her head. 'Well, then, you're an idiot. She's the best thing that ever happened to you, Blake.'

CHAPTER FOURTEEN

BLAKE OPENED HIS mouth to rebuff Joanna but she was already heading towards the door and before he knew it Ava was standing in front of him and he was standing too.

She was wearing what appeared to be a very expensive, very glittery tracksuit, her hair up in a ponytail.

And she looked as if she hadn't slept a wink either.

She took a step towards him but his, 'I hope no paps followed you because I do not want Charlie and Trudy embroiled in this circus,' stopped her in her tracks.

Ava sucked in a breath against the hostility in his tone. It was as if the last five and a half months hadn't happened at all and they were back at square one.

'I know a thing or two about shaking the press,' she said tersely.

Blake snorted. 'Apparently not enough.'

'Look, I'm sorry,' she sighed. 'I never wanted this to happen.'

'And yet here we are.'

Ava shoved her hands into her pockets. Her fingers were freezing and it didn't have much to do with the cold November morning. 'Reggie's working on it,' she said. 'We can fix it. We can salvage it. I'm going to put out a statement.'

'Saying what?' he demanded.

Ava took a deep breath. Time to lay her cards on the table. She hadn't wanted it to be like this but fate had forced her hand. 'Well, we could deny it. Say that we're just friends. Or...we could say that our relationship is new and we'd like privacy while we explore it.'

Blake blinked. *What the*? 'So I can be your bit of rough?' he snapped. 'The *carpenter* to your *lady?* Or some...pity-screw to make the *crippled* war hero feel better about himself?'

Ava shut her eyes against the ugliness of the headlines he'd just thrown in her face and the contempt in his voice. He had every right to be angry. Tears built behind her lids but she forced them back. His life had been turned upside down because of her—it wasn't the time for stupid girly tears.

'I'm sorry about what they're saying,' she said, opening her eyes. 'About what they've revealed. If I could turn back the clock, believe me, Blake, I would. But I'm *not* sorry you're being recognised for what you did. You deserve those accolades.'

Blake shook his head. She didn't get it. She really didn't get it. The men who'd died, who were still fighting—they were the ones who deserved the accolades.

'Pete *died*, Ava. I don't want his family reading all about the *hero* who didn't *quite* manage to save their loved one in the newspapers, dragging up all their grief again. Thinking I'm using his death as some cheap publicity stunt to pull a supermodel.'

Ava felt the cold from outside seep inside her at his suggestion. *Surely no one would think that?*

'Don't you think it's hard *enough* for them this time of year, with Christmas around the corner?'

Ava felt helpless. She was used to this level of intrusion from the press, immune to it in a lot of ways, but she still remembered how shocking it had been in the beginning.

'I'm sorry for them that it's being dragged up,' she murmured. 'But I for one think heroism should be celebrated. Too often we celebrate beauty and money and power and yet there are guys like you, defending the free world. I think we should recognise heroes more often.'

Blake ran a hand through his hair. 'You don't get it,' he said bitterly. 'I don't want to be a hero, Ava. Men are still over there. Others are *dead.*'

Sometimes, when he woke in the middle of night, the guilt over that was more than he could bear. He looked over her shoulder and caught Joanna's eye before returning his gaze to Ava.

'I'm *not* going to cash in on *their* accolades.'

Ava felt almost paralysed by the hard line of rejection running through his voice. He hadn't even been this harsh with her in the beginning and her pulse hammered a frantic beat against her wrist.

She didn't want to lose him. She couldn't.

'Fine. What about just being my hero, then?'

Ava moved in closer until there was just a coffee table separating them. She knew if she didn't say it now she never would. And maybe if she'd said it earlier they wouldn't be where they were. 'I love you.'

It took Blake a few seconds to compute the revelation. And even then it was too hard to wrap his head around. *'What?'* he spluttered. *Love?* That was the most ridiculous thing he'd ever heard. 'I thought this was just…a fling, a… casual thing.'

Ava put her hand on her hip, her fingers digging in hard at his rejection, at his trivialisation of her love. She'd never told any man she loved him before and it felt like a knife to the heart to be so summarily dismissed.

'Really? Is that what you thought?' she asked scathingly.

This was a lot more than a casual fling between them and they both knew it.

'*Really?*' she repeated. 'All those things we've been through, all those nights lying in bed talking and talking and talking? That was just casual?'

Blake didn't even try to pretend she wasn't right. Ava had been a bright spot in what had become a pretty beige life. A life he'd thought was fine. But never would be again.

He folded his arms as he cut right to the crux. 'I can't live in a goldfish bowl.'

Ava bit her lip. His words sounded so final and she swore she could hear her heart breaking over the silence in the room. 'I'm not *just* a girl on a boat, Blake. I *never* was. That goldfish bowl is my life for the conceivable future.'

Blake nodded. 'I know. But I don't want any part of it.'

She put her hand on one folded forearm feeling suddenly desperate, tears threatening again. 'So that's it?' she asked, her voice wobbling. 'You're not even going to fight for us? You can fight for this country but not for me?'

Blake hardened himself to the injury in her voice. Only Ava could be so dramatic. 'There isn't an us,' he said testily.

'Please,' Ava whispered, her hand tightening around his arm. There *was* something between them. She knew it. And she knew it could be good. 'We could make it work. We just have to want it bad enough.'

Her plea cut right to his heart but Blake shut it down. He'd had enough of complicated in his life. He'd sensed right from the beginning that she was going to be trouble and he'd been right.

Now his face was splashed all over the national newspapers. *Pete's* life and death splashed about too. Blake's grief and his guilt staring back at him in black and white for the entire nation to share.

All he'd wanted when he'd got things back on track was to have a quiet conflict-free life.

A life with Ava would be *neither* of those things.

Blake dropped his arms and her hand fell away. 'I don't want it bad enough,' he said and turned away.

And this time Ava did hear the crack as her heart split wide open.

The following wintery weeks were the perfect foil for Ava's mood. Christmas in London was always beautiful as decorative lights went up everywhere and the Christmas tree arrived in Trafalgar Square, but Ava didn't really notice. She didn't notice the roasting chestnuts vendors or the ice skaters at Hyde Park or the elaborately dressed windows in the department stores.

It was all too bright and sparkly for her when inside she identified more with the barren trees than the gay lights of Oxford Street.

She was merely going through the motions. Smiling and talking when she needed to and just trying to get through the rest. The media, as always, nipped at her heels but it was pleasing to note they'd stopped camping out regularly at Blake's boat since she'd denied their relationship in a press release, citing him as a friend only.

It didn't mean she stopped thinking about him. Stopped wishing in her darkest hours that she *were* that girl on the boat. It just made it easier to bear not to have to see his face next to hers on the news or in the papers every day.

But Christmas Eve came around quicker than she'd hoped and she knew she was going to have to face him again. The charity gala was the event of the year and, as the new patron, Ava was expected not only to attend but to shine.

And that was exactly what she told herself as she dressed to the nines. She had a certain image to project—glamour and sophistication—and she had every intention of wowing Joanna and all the others who had paid five thousand quid a head to ride the London Eye with her for a couple of hours.

Including Blake.

She wore a plush crimson, long-sleeved velvet gown that clung to her body and swept to the floor in a short train. A fur-trimmed hoodie attached to the back set it off and loaned her a touch of the regal when she smiled for the cameras with her famous haughty smile in front of an il-luminated Eye.

And she spent the next three hours in a glass bubble, sip-ping champagne, laughing and chatting with people, new ones with each revolution. Smiling until her face ached, forcing herself not to search the bubbles above and around her for the one person she wanted to see the most.

Maybe he hadn't come?

On her second-last revolution for the night, Joanna and her founding partners along with some of the charity work-ers joined her and Ava relaxed a little. They talked about the success of the night and the upcoming events for the New Year and where she could help out. They also talked about their husbands, about how much they'd loved Christmas and Ava listened as they laughed and smiled at fond memories.

About five minutes from the revolution ending Joanna

manoeuvred Ava to one side. She smiled at her and said, 'You know Blake's here, right.'

Ava nodded. 'I assumed he was.'

'You should talk with him.'

Ava gave a sad smile. 'I don't think your brother wants to talk to me.'

Joanna narrowed her eyes. 'You love him, right?'

Ava blinked and then laughed. Joanna was definitely a Walker—no subtlety. 'Yes.'

'So talk to him.'

Ava shook her head. 'He was pretty angry.'

Joanna regarded her for a moment or two and Ava felt as if she was being weighed up. 'Do you know the soldier that was killed the day Blake was injured was my husband?'

Ava's nodded. 'Yes. He told me when we were on the boat.'

Joanna looked taken aback. 'The last thing I said to Blake when they left for their tour was to look after Colin for me, to bring him home safe.' Joanna paused. 'He's not angry at you. He's angry at himself. That he's alive when so many aren't. That he *survived*. Every time he has fun or lets himself go, the guilt bites him hard.'

Ava's heart broke all over again for Blake. He shouldn't have to live his life eclipsed by guilt because he made it through when others didn't. 'I...didn't know that. I mean, I know he feels guilt about Colin...about the commendation...but not about surviving.'

Joanna grimaced. 'Well, he's not much of a talker. But I do know he was happy when he was with you and that he's never told *anyone* about Colin except for his shrink. I don't know if he'll ever be able to fully let go of the guilt and that's his *real* wound, not his leg. But I think if anyone can help him heal it's you.'

Ava couldn't agree more. But…'I can't if he won't let me in.'

The capsules were coming back down to the exit platform again and everyone was gathering at the door to clear the capsule in time for it moving on to the next platform where it would load again for the last revolution of the night.

'Well, they do say absence makes the heart grow fonder, right? And anyway, it's Christmas, it's the time for miracles.'

Joanna smiled and pointed to her brother standing rather grimly amongst the dozen people patiently waiting to get on.

Ava's gaze devoured him in all his tuxedoed glory. Who'd have thought a man who looked so good in a tool belt and a T-shirt could look just as good in a tux?

'Good luck,' Joanna whispered as she joined the exodus.

Ava sighed as Blake's gaze meshed with hers and he gave her a grim nod of his head.

She was going to need more than a miracle.

Blake had barely been able to take his eyes off her all night. Whatever capsule he'd been in, he'd tracked her movements, his sight starved of her for weeks now. And the second he entered the capsule and was offered a glass of champagne he took two and made a beeline for her.

He'd planned to patiently wait his turn and then make polite conversation with her, but as soon as the door had shut behind him the aura surrounding her grabbed him by the gut and yanked hard as a tumult of emotion flooded his chest.

What a fool he'd been.

He loved her.

And he didn't care how much anyone had paid for some time in her company, he was monopolising all of it.

'I've been an idiot,' he said as he elbowed someone else aside and handed her the glass of champagne.

Ava blinked as Blake's broad magnificence filled her vision. 'You…have?'

He nodded. It might have come totally out of the blue for Blake but he knew it as surely as he'd known he'd wanted to serve his country.

'Yes. I don't talk a lot and I'm not into staring at my navel and blabbing about my feelings. But I do believe in the truth and I've been lying to myself these past few weeks. Only I didn't realise it until right now. I thought I was doing so well and then I see you tonight and I realise that I'm in love with you and these last few weeks have been…*crap.*'

Ava looked around, pretty sure *everyone* was eavesdropping. 'You…love me?'

He nodded, wondering if she was going to stay monosyllabic for the rest of the night. 'Yes.'

'Oh.' Ava's heart tripped in her chest. *Well, that she hadn't expected.* Neither, she suspected, had Joanna.

It looked as if it was her night for miracles after all.

The temptation to let herself go and fling herself into his arms was enormous but there were still a lot of obstacles in their path and she needed to be sure. She needed *him* to be sure. 'What about the goldfish bowl?'

Blake sighed. 'I still can't live like that, Ava. But I was wrong a few weeks ago—*I do want it bad enough.* So I guess we're going to have to figure that one out. Compromise a little. Because I *want* this. I want you.'

Ava smiled at him for the first time, relief flushing through her veins making her almost dizzy. She reached out a hand and grasped his lapel, steadying herself. 'Well,

I guess we could find somewhere to live that's more secure and not so accessible to the media?'

Blake slid his hand onto hers and held it against his chest. 'And you could stop feeding them gourmet snacks,' he suggested with affectionate exasperation, slipping his other hand onto her hip. 'And getting Reggie to report your movements to them so they know where you are every moment of every day.'

Ava nodded. 'I could do that. I could also set limits with them over you and your information. I've not done it before but I know others do and… I think you're a pretty good trade-off.' She grinned.

Blake pulled her in closer. 'And I promise to *try* not to punch every man who touches you during a photo shoot or a commercial or whatever you're doing for work.'

Ava felt stupidly teary at this concession. She knew how hard that would be for his Neanderthal, Bionic-Man streak. 'Thank you,' she whispered.

Blake smiled at her, wanting desperately to kiss her, to push her up against the glass and show her how much he loved her, but knowing they needed to talk first. 'And clearly, you can't live on a boat so I could sell it.'

'No way,' Ava objected. 'Keep that. I have very…' she ran her fingers under his lapel, feeling the firmness of his chest beneath the superb cut '…fond memories there,' she said, her smile widening.

He leaned in and nuzzled her neck. 'You're right. We'll keep the boat.'

Ava's heart dared to sing as she sank in closer to him. 'But is it going to be enough for you?' she asked, pulling back slightly.

Blake looked down into her yellow-green eyes. The whole Thames was stretched out behind her, the Houses of Parliament and Big Ben illuminated in a soft orange glow, a truly magnificent sight. But he only had eyes for Ava.

For the woman he loved.

'It's a start. And we'll get better at it. We have to, because I'm miserable without you.'

'Me too,' Ava admitted. But still her mind wandered to her conversation with Joanna and Ava felt anxious all over again. 'Joanna told me you feel guilty about surviving the war when Colin, when others, didn't,' she said.

Blake felt the usual punch to his gut at the mention of Colin's name. 'Did she now?'

Ava looked into his eyes because she needed to be sure that he understood what she was saying. 'I don't pretend to know what you went through, Blake. And I don't pretend to think it can be fixed through love alone. I know you're not a talker but I don't want you to shut me out either. I want to know *all* of you. Even the bits you don't want me to know. I can't be part of a relationship where you hide away all the dark bits...all the sad bits. I can't promise to know how to handle them, but I *do* want to try. I need you to promise that you'll *talk* to me. That *nothing* will be off-limits.'

Blake took a moment or two to absorb what she was asking. Opening up had never been easy for him, but he'd never met someone who'd meant so much to him either. He knew this woman in his arms and she was warm and sexy and giving and nothing like the woman he'd first thought her to be. She'd taken the risk and opened up to him, put her trust in him, surely he could do the same?

Because she was definitely worth fighting for.

'I promise,' he said. 'I don't promise I'll be very articulate but I promise to talk to you.'

Ava's heart swelled in her chest. She knew that couldn't have been easy for him. 'That's all I want.'

And for long moments they just looked at each other, absorbing all the details of each other's faces, trying to imprint this memory on their retinas for ever.

'You know there's going to be a bit of a frenzy to start with, don't you?' Ava warned.

'That's fine,' Blake said, lifting his hand to push the hoodie back off her hair. 'Let's just not feed it, huh?'

Ava nodded. 'Deal.'

Blake smiled down into her face. 'You're so beautiful,' he said. 'I can't believe it took me all this time to figure out I loved you.'

'I can,' Ava murmured. 'It took you a million pounds to even pay me any attention.'

Blake chuckled. 'I love you,' he said.

Ava sighed at the healing power of three little words as her heart felt whole again. And she was going to spend the rest of her life with her wounded warrior, helping him to feel whole again also. 'I love you too,' she said.

Their lips met and Ava felt as if it were New Year's Eve instead of Christmas Eve as fireworks popped and sparkled behind her eyes.

The sound of a dozen mingled sighs and the burst of spontaneous applause in the capsule added to the celebration as did the pop and flare of paparazzi lenses far below.

Best. Christmas. Ever.

* * * * *

Keep reading for an excerpt of
SEDUCED BY THE BILLIONAIRE:
AT THE ARGENTINEAN BILLIONAIRE'S BIDDING
from India Grey and Harlequin

PROLOGUE

TAMSIN PAUSED IN front of the mirror, the lipstick held in one hand and the magazine article on 'How to seduce the man of your dreams' in the other.

Subtlety, the article said, *is just another word for failure.* But, even so, her stomach gave a nervous dip as she realised she hardly recognised the heavy-lidded, glittering eyes, the sharply defined cheekbones and sultry, pouting mouth as her own.

That was a good thing, right? Because three years of adoring Alejandro D'Arienzo from afar had taught her that there wasn't much chance of getting beyond 'hello' with the man of her dreams without some drastic action.

There was a quiet knock at the door, and then Serena's blonde head appeared. 'Tam, you've been ages, surely you must be ready by—' There was a pause. 'Oh my God. What in hell's name have you done to yourself?'

Tamsin waved the magazine at her sister. 'It says here I shouldn't leave anything to chance.'

Serena advanced slowly into the room. 'Does it specify you shouldn't leave much to the imagination, either?' she croaked. 'Where did you get that outrageous dress? It's completely see-through.'

'I altered my Leaver's Ball dress a bit, that's all,' said Tamsin defensively.

'That's your *ball dress*?' Serena gasped. 'Blimey, Tamsin, if Mama finds out she'll go mental—you haven't altered it, you've *butchered* it.'

Shrugging, Tamsin tossed back her dark-blonde hair and, holding out the thigh-skimming layers of black net, executed an insouciant twirl. 'So? I just took the silk overskirt off, that's all.'

'That's *all*?'

'Well, I shortened the net petticoat a bit, too. Looks much better, doesn't it?'

'It certainly looks *different*,' said Serena faintly. The strapless, laced bodice of the dress, which had looked reasonably demure when paired with a full, ankle-length skirt, suddenly took on an outrageous bondage vibe when combined with above-the-knee net, black stockings, and the cropped black cardigan her sister was now putting on over the top.

'Good,' said Tamsin firmly. 'Because tonight I do *not* want to be the coach's pathetic teenage daughter, fresh out of boarding school and never been kissed. Tonight I want to be...' She broke off to read from the magazine. '"Mysterious yet direct, sophisticated yet sexy".'

From downstairs they could hear the muffled din of laughter and loud voices, and distant music wound its way through Harcourt Manor's draughty stone passages. The party to announce the official England international team for the new rugby season was already underway, and Alejandro was there somewhere. Just knowing he was in the same building made Tamsin's stomach tighten and her heart pound.

'Be careful, Tam,' Serena warned quietly. 'Alejandro's gorgeous, but he's also…'

She faltered, glancing round at the pictures that covered Tamsin's walls, as if for inspiration. Mostly cut from the sports pages of newspapers and from old England rugby programmes, they showed Alejandro D'Arienzo's dark, brooding beauty from every angle. Serena shivered. Gorgeous certainly, but ruthless too.

'What, out of my league? You don't think this is going to work, do you?' said Tamsin with an edge of despair. 'You don't think he's going to fancy me at all.'

Serena looked down into her sister's face. Tamsin's green eyes glowed as if lit by some internal sunlight and her cheeks were flushed with nervous excitement.

'That's not it at all. Of course he'll fancy you.' She sighed. 'And that's exactly what's bothering me.'

Above the majestic carved fireplace in the entrance hall of Harcourt Manor was a portrait of some seventeenth-century Calthorpe, smiling smugly against a backdrop of galleons on a stormy sea. Across the top, in flamboyantly embellished script, was written: *God blew and they were scattered.*

Alejandro D'Arienzo felt his face set in an expression of sardonic amusement as he looked into the cold, hooded eyes of Henry Calthorpe's forebear. There was no discernible resemblance between the two men, although they obviously shared a mutual hatred of the Spanish. Alejandro could just remember his father's stories, as a child in Argentina, of how their distant ancestors had been amongst the original *conquistadors* who had sailed from Spain to the New World. Those stories were one of the few tiny fragments of family identity that he had.

Moving restlessly away from the portrait, he ran a finger inside the stiff collar of his shirt and looked around at the impressive hallway, with its miles of intricate plasterwork ceiling and acres of polished wooden panelling. His teammates stood in groups, laughing and drinking with dignitaries from the Rugby Football Union and the few sports journalists lucky enough to make the guest list, while the same assortment of blonde, well-bred rugby groupies circulated amongst them, flirting and flattering.

Henry Calthorpe, the England rugby coach, had made a big deal about holding the party to announce the new squad at his stunning ancestral home, claiming it showed that they were a team, a unit, a *family*. Remembering this now, Alejandro couldn't stop his lips curling into a sneer of savage, cynical amusement.

Everything about Harcourt Manor could have been specifically designed to emphasise exactly how much of an outsider Alejandro was. And he was damned sure that Henry Calthorpe had reckoned on that very thing.

At first Alejandro had thought he was being overly sensitive, that years in the English public school system had made him too quick to be on the defensive against bullying and victimization—but lately the coach's animosity had become too obvious to ignore. Alejandro was playing better than he'd ever done, too well to be dropped from the team without reason, but the fact was that Calthorpe wanted him out. He was just waiting for Alejandro to slip up.

Alejandro hoped Calthorpe was a patient man, because he had no intention of obliging. He was at the top of his game and he planned to stay there.

Draining the champagne in one go, he put the glass

down on a particularly expensive-looking carved chest and glanced disdainfully around the room. There was not a single person he wanted to talk to, he thought wearily. The girls were identikit blondes with cut-glass accents and Riviera suntans, whose conversation ranged from clothes to the hilarious exploits of people they'd gone to school with, and whom they assumed Alejandro would know. Several times at parties like these he'd ended up sleeping with one just to shut her up.

But tonight it all seemed too much effort. The England tie felt like a noose around his neck, and suddenly he needed to be outside in the cool air, out of this suffocating atmosphere of complacency and privilege. Adrenalin pounded through him as he pushed his way impatiently through the groups of people towards the door.

And that was when he saw her.

She was standing in the doorway, her head lowered slightly, one hand gripping the doorframe for support, giving her an air of shyness and uncertainty that was totally at odds with her short black dress and very high heels. But he didn't notice the details of what she was wearing. It was her eyes that held him.

They were beautiful—green perhaps, almond shaped, slanting—but that was almost incidental. What made the breath catch in his throat was the laser-beam intensity of her gaze, which he could feel even from this distance.

His footsteps slowed as he got closer to her, but her gaze didn't waver. She straightened slightly, as if she had been waiting for him, and her hand fell from the doorframe and smoothed down her short skirt.

'You're not leaving?'

Her voice was so low and hesitant, and her words halfway between a question and a statement. He gave a twisted smile.

'I think it would be best if I did.'

He made to push past her. Close up, he could see that behind the smoky eye make up and the shiny inviting lip gloss she was younger than he'd at first thought. Her skin was clear and golden, and he noticed the frantic jump of the pulse in her throat. She was trembling slightly.

'No,' she said fiercely. 'Please. Don't leave.'

Interest flared up inside him, sudden and hot. He stopped, looking down at her sexy, rebellious dress, and then let his gaze move slowly back up to her face. Her cheeks were lightly stained with pink, and the eyes that looked up at him from under a fan of long, black lashes were dark and glittering. Seductive, but pleading.

'Why not?'

Lowering her chin, she kept them fixed on his, while she took his hand and stepped backwards, pulling him with her. Her hand felt small in his, and her touch sent a small shower of shooting stars up his arm.

'Because I want you.' She smiled shyly, dropping her gaze. 'I want you to stay.'

* * * * *

MILLS & BOON®

Find out more about our
latest releases, authors
and competitions.

 Like us on facebook.com/millsandboonaustralia

 Follow us on twitter.com/millsandboonaus

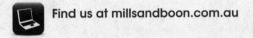 Find us at millsandboon.com.au